# AN UNCERTAIN REFUGE

Carolyn J. Rose

# AN UNCERTAIN REFUGE

## Carolyn J. Rose

2011

An Uncertain Refuge
Copyright © 2011 Carolyn J. Rose

www.deadlyduomysteries.com

ISBN: 978-0-9837359-0-8

Cover design by Allen Chiu
Digital editions produced by Booknook.biz

For Nancy, who found a safe haven.

And for all those who aid the wounded creatures of this world.

# CHAPTER 1

Later, Kate Dalton often wondered how things might have turned out if she had been a little stronger or a lot weaker, if she had refused a mother's plea, or if she had spoken the truth while it was still hers to tell. But on that February morning when a scream shattered both the fretful calm of the shelter and the constricted structure of her life, Kate did exactly what she'd trained for—and exactly what she'd been warned against.

In two steps she crossed her narrow office and punched the internal alarm button. Electronic blasts ripped the air, muffling the second scream. Feet pounded from the kitchen and playroom. Women called to children, shepherded them to the upper floors, and bolted doors behind them as they'd been taught. As Kate crossed the hallway to the front door, she saw pinched faces, heard whispers tight with fear. Daily drills had restored some of the confidence husbands and boyfriends had battered from these women, but drills would never restore innocence or a sense of safety. Kate had never suffered physical abuse, but she knew about dominance in the name of love, knew about limited options and the desire to escape.

"It's okay," she told a slender redhead with waxen skin, a listless baby on one arm and a cast on the other. "Just another drill. But hurry."

The woman darted up the stairs as the third scream pierced the air. Probably kids playing in the street. Kate clawed at the peephole's metal cover and squinted through a fish-eye lens at a compressed, flattened view of the yard. Her gut clenched. Amanda Blake knelt on the cracked concrete walk, head bowed, arms stretched toward the man who loomed over her, his right fist raised, his arm corded with muscle. Kate flinched. Amanda brought her hands together as if praying.

Praying in vain. Kate gripped the red metal handle of the panic alarm and swung her weight against it. She'd never done that before, hoped she'd never need to. Occasionally, acting on a request from the police, she triggered a signal to test emergency services. Firefighters and paramedics normally responded within six minutes, police sometimes sooner. A lifetime.

As Kate watched, the man smiled with all the compassion of a shark and hammered his fist against Amanda's ear. She crumpled to the gray slab and curled into a fetal position, arms cradling her head, blood smearing the sleeves of her pink gingham blouse.

Kate shuddered and turned away, taking quick, harsh breaths. Shelter policy shackled her on this side of the door, responsible for those inside. The rules were sound, made for the greater good. But they aided and abetted this assault.

Clenching her teeth, she peered through the peephole again. She would witness Amanda's beating with as impartial a mind as she could and memorize details so her testimony couldn't be shaken by an attorney hired to defend this monster. Shaking with rage, she made a mental list: clean white T-shirt, stiff dark jeans with no signs of wear, high-topped brown leather work boots with yellow rawhide laces.

The man kicked Amanda's shoulder. Even through the two-inch door, Kate heard the sickening crunch. She yanked the handle of the panic alarm a second time and amended her mental list: steel-toed boots. "Come on. Come on." How much time had passed? Fifteen seconds? A glacial age?

The man brushed tobacco-colored hair from his forehead and nodded toward the peephole. Kate gasped, nearly ducked. He seemed to see her, sense her frustration. He licked his lips as if that was seasoning for the meat of his task, and drew his boot back.

"Damn you!" Kate flipped the bolt, gripped the knob, and opened the dull green metal door. "Get away from her!"

The man shook his head and launched the kick. It connected with Amanda's hip. Wailing, she flopped from the concrete pathway onto grass slick with the night's rain. The man's lips pulled back into a grin that revealed white, even teeth. No, Kate thought. His teeth should be brown and broken. Evil should be ugly. "I've called the police," she yelled. "They're on the way."

He laughed. Two discordant notes. "I'll take her out and be gone."

"Please, Wayne," Amanda mewled. She crawled toward the porch, fingers clawing at the greening grass. "Think of our son."

"*My* son!" he roared. "He's *my* son." His feet dug at the sodden ground like a bull signaling its charge. "Where is he? I want him."

"Get away from her!" Kate planted one foot on the spongy rubber weather stripping of the threshold. No farther!

A boot connected with Amanda's knee. "You sent me to prison," Wayne bellowed. She rolled into a tighter ball, her screams merging into one prolonged wail. "You divorced me. This is your fault. You deserve this." He kicked with each accusation, grinding grass and mud into Amanda's faded jeans, checked blouse, and milky skin.

With fingers curled around the doorknob as if it were a lifeline, Kate inched one foot onto the first plank of the meager porch. How had Wayne Jessop tracked Amanda to Arkansas? How had he found the shelter? The address was known only to staff and board members, police, firefighters, and women who sought sanctuary.

"Please, Wayne," Amanda moaned. "I'm sorry."

*Sorry?* A flash of white anger seared Kate's brain. That was the most destructive word in a victim's vocabulary. It shouldered undeserved blame. It corrupted justice.

Wayne threw his head back and laughed. "I'll show you sorry." He yanked a knife from the pocket of his jeans, flicked it open. "I'm gonna cut you so bad a freak show wouldn't take you. I'm gonna slice you once for every day I was inside."

Pale sunlight flashed on the blade. Amanda sobbed. Fingers tearing at tender sprouting blades, she struggled to her hands and knees and crawled, head hanging low.

Twenty feet. Then six shallow steps. And five feet across the porch. It might as well be the distance to the moon. Kate strained her ears for the pulsing wail of a siren. Nothing. Her gaze swept the houses across the way. Blank windows. Closed doors.

Wayne strolled after Amanda, whistling between his teeth, tossing the knife from hand to hand. "Hey, I'll bet you thought I forgot today is Valentine's Day. Maybe I'll carve a heart on your chest. Put our initials inside it." He winked at Kate and laughed once more.

*She'll die while I stand by, following the rules.*

Kate released the door, bolted down the steps, and anchored herself with one hand on the railing. The door snicked closed. Locked.

No choice now. "Leave her alone, Wayne!"

Wayne slanted his eyes across Kate, sized her up and shrugged. She felt a flash of anger followed by smug satisfaction. Good. Count me out. Give me power.

"Wait your turn," he sneered. "I'll get to you in a minute."

Like a striking snake, he threw himself on Amanda and plunged the knife into her hip. Amanda shrieked. Wayne jerked the knife free, kicked her onto her back, and slashed at her breasts, slicing her hands as she tried to defend herself. Bright blood spattered the yellow-green grass.

The rank scent of her own fear prickled Kate's nostrils. Years of self-defense training prepared her body to act and react, but those skills came with a rule: "Don't fight until you have to." Waiting for that point of no return, however, let the mind create terror that annihilated confidence and paralyzed muscles.

Wayne slashed at Amanda's face. Kate pushed off against the bottom step and charged. She leaped onto his back, clawing at his eyes and ears, yelling "No! No! No!"

He bucked and rammed an elbow into her ribs. Air exploded between her teeth. She flung herself away, skidded, fell, rolled, and scrambled up again, knees bent, arms out, hands cupped toward him. Calm fatalism replaced fear.

"Damn you!" Wayne staggered to his feet, pawing at the oozing scratches on his face. Amanda held herself, wailing softly.

Kate flexed her fingers, pointing her bloody nails toward him. *How long will I have to hold him off?* "Come on, Wayne. Or are you afraid of a woman who fights back?"

"I ain't afraid of nobody." He raised the knife and advanced, hazel eyes narrowed and muddied, lips twitched into a salivating smile.

A siren throbbed in the distance. Wayne's head jerked toward the sound and Kate surveyed the terrain. Her back was now to the gate in the chain-link fence that enclosed the front yard. If she turned and ran he'd catch her as she opened it. A six-foot cinder block wall, topped with metal spikes, surrounded the back and side yards.

No options. No choice.

The siren keened again. Wayne's eyes shifted to Amanda.

*No you don't.* Kate edged to her left. "You can't finish her until you finish me."

She planted her left foot, her pivot foot. He was at least eighty pounds heavier and six inches taller. With his short, thick neck and bulky shoulders, he resembled a football player in full gear. She'd thrown larger men in practice sessions. Her legs trembled. Practice sessions. She sucked in a quavering breath. He had mass and weight. She had speed and agility.

Wayne crouched, raising the fist that clutched the knife. His biceps bulged, tweaking the edges of the crude tattoo of a naked woman. Her legs spread as the muscles swelled.

"Come on, Wayne," Kate taunted. "Fight me or run like a chicken."

With a roar, he sprang.

Kate flinched, but stood her ground. *Wait. Wait. Wait. Now!*

She swiveled and whipped out her right leg to hook his. He crashed face first into the fence. It gave a few inches with a metallic clatter. Wayne thudded to the ground. The siren, still distant, echoed his howls of rage.

He lurched to his feet. "I'm gonna kill you." He wiped blood from his lips and one eye and raised the knife again. "But first I'm going to hurt you so bad you beg me to finish it."

Kate swallowed bile and licked chill sweat from her upper lip. *Make him mad. Make him rush.* "You only feel like a real man when a woman begs?"

"Save your breath for the begging."

*It's all about sex and control. Use that.* Kate forced a thin laugh from the back of her throat. "You can't get off unless a woman begs, can you?"

His dropped a hand to finger his belt, gaze slewing toward Amanda who lay motionless, whimpering softly. "She tell you that?"

"She didn't have to. I can tell by looking at you."

"Liar!" He edged around her. Kate turned with him, keeping her left foot planted, watching his eyes, waiting for them to betray him.

*There!*

He surged toward her, knife arm raised. She wheeled to her left. He veered. She spun back, came in under his arm, seized his wrist, and twisted. Momentum bore him to the ground. He roared, rolled onto his back, and tore loose the knife embedded in his groin. A scarlet fountain spurted. He squealed again and clamped his hands over it. Blood bubbled between his fingers and flowed into a glistening puddle on the grass. His eyes flared.

"Help me," he shouted. "I'm cut bad."

The house and sky seemed to whirl around Kate. Shock. She struggled to keep her balance, her heart thudding in her throat.

The siren whooped. Only a few streets away. Kate closed her eyes for a second, then kicked the knife to the gate and bent over Wayne. The coppery smell of fresh blood burned like acid at the back of her throat.

"Don't let me die," he moaned. "I didn't mean to hurt her. I'm sorry."

Sorry. That word again. Destructive. Dangerous. And, this time, a lie.

Wayne's lips blanched; sweat glistened on his forehead. "Don't let me die." Each word encased in a shallow puff of air. His eyes laced with pain. "Help me. Please."

*Put pressure on the wound. Slow the bleeding.* Kate yanked her blouse from the waistband of her slacks and fumbled at it with icy fingers. A lavender button popped loose, jittered along the walk, and rolled into the grass.

Gory hands gripped Kate's wrists. "No."

Amanda shoved Kate backwards. "Don't listen." Rusty blood crusted her face and neck and clotted in her hair. Her blouse was sodden. "Don't help him."

Kate dropped her elbows, but Amanda's fingers tightened and her voice rasped like a file. "He'll hurt us if you help him. He'll come back and hurt us bad. That's all he knows how to do."

She shoved Kate away, staggered to him, and kicked at his head. "Are you begging, Wayne?" she screamed. "Are you begging now?"

Wayne wormed away from her. "Please don't let me die." His lips were like parchment, his skin sallow.

"Stop! Amanda, stop." Kate flung her arms around her.

"Let me go!" Amanda arched her back and kicked at Kate's legs.

"Help me," Wayne whimpered.

"Die!" Amanda spat at him. "Die now."

Tires screeched on pavement. A police cruiser rocked around the corner. Wayne's legs jerked. His mouth worked like that of a fish tossed high on a bank.

"Die!" Amanda shrieked. "Die now!" Her words gave way to a primal wail and she slid from Kate's grasp, crumpling to the bloody lawn.

Kate knelt beside her. So much blood. How could she be alive? "Lie still."

The cruiser screeched to a halt beside the open gate. An officer vaulted out, gun drawn, using the door for cover.

Kate stood and thrust out her hands, palms forward. "I'm the shelter director," she called. "My name is Kate Dalton. We need an ambulance." She nodded toward Wayne. "This man attacked us with a knife. He fell on it. It's in the street."

The officer held his position, speaking into a radio clipped to his shirt.

"My son," Amanda gasped. She rocked to her knees. "Way-Ray. My son."

A second police cruiser roared up. Another cop leaped out, crouched with gun drawn, and advanced into the yard. "We need an ambulance," Kate called. "We need help now."

The cop holstered his gun and barked into his radio.

"No," Amanda clutched at Kate's slacks. "Don't help him. Way-Ray thinks his father is dead."

Wayne's fingers twitched and his hands slid to his sides. Blood welled from his wound. His eyes widened and then emptied.

Kate bent and took Amanda's hands in hers. "He is."

# CHAPTER 2

Kate warmed her hands on her coffee mug and studied Emory McCoy, who tapped the stack of laminated newspaper clippings squared up to the corner of a mahogany desk the length of a vintage luxury car. McCoy's college quarterback glory days were thirty years and fifty pounds behind him. A banker now, he called financial plays from a twentieth-floor corner office with acres of sculpted moss-green carpeting and a panoramic view of the Arkansas River.

Flanking him were Mickey Whipple and Jessica Corley. Mickey, the vice chair of the shelter board, had met Kate in the outer office, offering the mug instead of his usual two-handed shake and generous grin. When she asked the purpose of the meeting, he ducked his head and showed her through the door saying McCoy, the chairman, had the agenda. Jessica, writing in a tiny notebook, looked up only long enough to nod when Kate took the straight-backed chair centered before the desk.

McCoy cleared his throat. "The Wayne Jessop incident got us a lot of attention."

His voice was more bleat than baritone, a signature of speech like his lengthy pauses. Those encouraged mental rambling, and Kate suspected were designed to trap those who rambled too far.

9

She cast a glance at her watch. 8:03. There was paperwork waiting at the shelter. Last night a police officer brought in a pregnant woman with cigarette burns on her face and breasts.

McCoy adjusted the lapels of his gray pin-striped suit and tapped the stack again, the college ring on his right hand flashing in the light from a green-shaded lamp. "Donations are up nearly three-hundred percent since February."

Ah, so this was about money. And Mickey hadn't wanted to steal McCoy's thunder. Kate nodded. She forfeited two raises because of budget constraints: now came a reward for her sacrifice. Not that she needed money—she had enough to get by—but a salary set value and raises indicated respect and appreciation for skills. She slid her gaze toward Jessica, the secretary/treasurer of the board and the one member who volunteered at the shelter. Jessica kept her gaze locked on McCoy while her fingers smoothed the pleated skirt of a lilac linen suit.

"That publicity raised awareness and created public debate on the issue of domestic violence." McCoy fanned the clippings, spreading them like oversized playing cards.

They made an impressive array. Both local and national papers devoted gallons of ink to the final moments of Wayne Jessop's life. One tabloid had referred to her as "Karate Kate," and another had headlined the story, "Safe House Heroine Slays Homicidal Husband." TV and radio coverage was intense. Prodded before the cameras, she'd made a point of honesty, stating that she broke shelter safety rules. She also took complete responsibility for admitting Amanda.

McCoy's meaty fingers herded the clippings together. "We certainly can't argue about the extent of that initial publicity."

Other than the headlines, Kate saw none of it. She turned her radio and TV off and tossed unread newspapers into the recycling bin. Since then, she wrestled daily with doubt, guilt, and self-blame. Had there been another way? And, putting aside the question of what he might have done had he survived, could she have fought harder to try to save Wayne's life? Would he be alive if she'd slowed the bleeding until an ambulance arrived? On most days, she doubted that, but she would never know.

She sipped. Coffee burned like acid on her lips and she leaned forward to set the mug on the edge of the desk. McCoy scowled.

Jessica stood. "I'll take that so it doesn't tip over."

"Later," McCoy grunted. "When we're done."

Jessica dropped back into her chair, hands bunched in her skirt, eyes on the offending mug. Mickey patted her shoulder. Kate checked her watch. 8:06.

McCoy riffled the clippings, plastic sliding against plastic. "Of course, critics have said that such extensive and impassioned media coverage is also detrimental to the mission of a domestic violence shelter—protecting residents and shielding their identities."

Ah. McCoy had found a cloud to wrap around the silver lining. But, as he often pointed out, getting to the bottom line was his function. He proudly claimed he balanced other board members because he didn't possess a bleeding heart, didn't have knee-jerk sympathy for a hard-luck story, and didn't reach for his checkbook without careful deliberation.

Kate studied Jessica again, searching for a sign. A well-groomed, well-meaning career wife, Jessica longed for children but couldn't conceive. She cuddled shelter babies and bought tiny shoes and suits. As Kate studied her, Jessica compressed her glossy lips and slid a tissue from her purse, all without shifting her focus from McCoy.

Kate swung her gaze to Mickey, an ad man always ready with a smile that displayed flawless teeth against inky skin. His jaw dropped and his gaze shifted to his cufflinks.

Were they about to tell her she'd get only a few percent, and not until the end of the year? Kate sighed. Well, she took this job to make a difference, not get rich. She checked her watch once more. 8:09.

McCoy tented stubby fingers and leaned back in his gray leather swivel chair. Its springs didn't squeak. The leather didn't creak. If a chair defied him, she imagined that McCoy would toss it out. Correction: he'd have someone else toss it. Probably the same minion who unearthed the inquisition model in which she sat. "Now, I say having a shelter director who's a lightning rod for national publicity and public debate is a good thing."

"Excellent way to express it," Mickey agreed, straightening the broad knot in a tie the colors of ketchup and scrambled eggs. He echoed McCoy, his voice deepening as if he were speaking into a microphone, recording the words for a used-car-lot commercial. "A lightning rod."

Kate conjured a mental vision of herself clinging to a steep roof, lashed by a storm, her clothing in tatters, her screams lost in the wind. She swallowed and realized her throat felt as raw as if she'd been screaming since the minute Wayne Jessop died. She declined counseling because she knew that drill. And because she believed, by long family tradition, in finding her own harmony with a prime mover, she didn't cart her concerns to those her father had labeled "middle managers of faith." The legal system had ruled her justified. Still, she often yearned to confess her complicity in Wayne's death, to hand over responsibility for her soul, be punished or absolved, and then move on. Now she wondered what became of a lightning rod that took a strike. Were its particles realigned, its core melted and reformed? Could it channel the next strike? And the one after that? Or would it shatter?

McCoy leaned forward in his mute chair and levered himself to his feet. "But my concern is that you're letting opportunities pass us by." He hitched at his belt, and came around the desk. "We need to make the most of the . . . incident. You're not getting with the program, Kate."

Kate blinked. "The program?" She heard wariness in her voice and not a little sarcasm. McCoy loomed inches from her left shoulder. "Which specific program are you referring to?"

"It's not exactly a specific—" Jessica began.

"It's just that we ought to take full advantage." Mickey adjusted the creases in his tan slacks.

12

Kate suppressed a groan. This was what she hated about meetings, about the process of getting everyone involved in the process. They all had to have input—meaningful or not—and they all had to feel included, part of the team.

She didn't have time for process. She had work to do. "Advantage?"

"Exactly." McCoy draped a hand across her shoulder. It felt limp but hefty, like a slab of sirloin.

Kate clenched her jaw and willed herself not to signal her annoyance. His touch was a sign of possession: not man-to-woman, but employer-to-employee, master-to-slave. The least movement and the hand would clamp tighter, demonstrating his power. He had much in common with abusive men whose women ran to the shelter. "Could we get back to the program I need to get with?"

McCoy released his flaccid grip. "All right. Yesterday I got a call from a movie producer." He returned to his desk, drew a sheet of paper from his top drawer, and consulted it. "Howard Dean Seidellman."

The creep who referred to the shelter residents as "battered babes."

"He tells me," McCoy continued, "that he offered you a substantial sum to serve as the advisor for the movie he's working on—offered a large donation to the shelter, too—but you turned him down. Flat." McCoy smacked his palms on the desk. "He says you were rude."

Kate felt bile rise in her throat. Rude was all he seemed to understand.

McCoy shoved his hands toward her and spread the fingers. "My main concern is that you didn't bring this issue to the board. We set policy, not you."

Policy? This wasn't about policy. It was about decency, dignity. And failing to acknowledge McCoy's authority. She looked to Jessica and Mickey. Neither met her gaze.

13

"This movie presents a tremendous opportunity." McCoy ambled to the window, turned his back. "Yet you didn't consider the additional publicity and donations."

Money again. Kate stifled a sigh. In his two years as chairman, McCoy had campaigned to cut corners, costs, and compensation, to run the place like the kind of business his bank would approve for a loan. "The movie is exploitive. He used the word 'sexy.' Is that how you want the shelter represented?"

Jessica shook her head a fraction of an inch. Mickey frowned. McCoy simply shrugged. "My opinion doesn't matter. We can't afford to get up on a moral high horse, Kate. It takes an enormous amount of money to run that shelter. And we have to go begging for the majority of it."

Begging. Kate saw Wayne Jessop's eyes, life leaching from them. She blinked the image away as she had a thousand times.

McCoy stalked to his desk, seized the note, and rattled it. "When I see a sure-fire opportunity to meet our payroll for the next few years, I put aside petty concerns and get on board before that train leaves the station."

Petty concerns? Kate squared her shoulders. "This movie is—"

"Enough," McCoy snapped. "You're with us or you're not." He glanced from Mickey to Jessica. They nodded like marionettes. "It's that simple."

It was light years from that simple.

McCoy rattled the note once more. "I'm waiting, Miss Dalton."

Emphasis on the title that labeled her female, weak. Kate shrugged. "If it's that simple, Emory, then I'm not with you."

Mickey winced. Probably less because of Kate's refusal than at her use of McCoy's first name. Employees shouldn't entertain radical thoughts about equality or, worse, camaraderie.

McCoy, however, didn't glower as she expected. "I'm sorry to hear that, Kate," he said in a tone she imagined he cultivated for funerals and foreclosures. And there was that destructive word again—sorry. Clearly a lie. "Since you won't cooperate, I must tell you—"

"I'm fired." Kate shot to her feet, feeling as if she'd risen to the surface of dark water and gulped sweet air.

Jessica gasped, rooted through her bag, and snatched out a tissue to press to her offending lips.

McCoy blinked slowly. "I would prefer we didn't use that word."

"Emory, I no longer care what you prefer." Her father's voice echoed in Kate's ear: *Don't burn your bridges, Katherine.*

But the trestle was in flames. "I quit. Effective immediately."

"All right. But it will go on the record that since your contract expires at the end of the month, and since we have concerns about your effectiveness, the board voted, last night, to terminate your services." He inclined his head toward Mickey and Jessica.

Neither met Kate's gaze. Puppets. Cowards.

"We've provided a liberal severance check," McCoy continued, "and we'll continue your health insurance through the end of the year." He opened the top drawer of his desk and, using the tips of his thumb and forefinger, removed a plain white envelope and flipped it toward her. It landed on the edge of the desk, teetered for a second, and fell.

Kate steeled herself not to glance at it, not to bend to grasp it. She wouldn't humble herself before this toad of a man. "I hope you won't have to go *begging* for the funds to cover all that, Emory."

McCoy's nostrils flared. "Should a prospective employer inquire, we will, on the advice of our attorney, be limited to acknowledging only that you worked for us, nothing more."

Kate fought to conceal a jolt of panic. As the penalty for her rash behavior, Emory McCoy would use the good-old-boy network to poison the employment well. Rage incinerated fear. "Judging by the stains on your tie and the fact that you can't button your jacket, the only recommendations you're fit to provide are for places that serve all-you-can-eat grits and gravy."

McCoy's eyes shifted to his tie. A purple flush spread across his nose and cheeks.

Kate felt a warm explosion in her gut, as if she'd chugged a shot of brandy. Gotcha. *You thought I'd knuckle under, like I always have, for the greater good.* "Emory, I'd sell my car, hock my watch, and eat my shoes before I work for anyone who would base my employment on *your* recommendation."

Before McCoy blustered up a reply, Kate kicked over her inquisition chair. Her only regrets were that the carpet muffled her footsteps and the hydraulic device on the door prevented a wall-shaking slam. She passed a prim executive assistant with a polka dot blouse and plunged along a hallway that widened into a marble-tiled lobby presided over by an aging cool blonde with the look of a woman who'd seen it all—twice.

Kate jabbed the elevator button. Something buzzed on the receptionist's console. Kate jabbed the button again. The receptionist spoke into a tiny microphone jutting from her earpiece. She tilted her head, peered at Kate, and beckoned with her index finger. "Yes, sir," she said to the microphone.

*No, sir!* Kate bolted for the stairwell, yanked the door open and hurtled down, grateful she'd left her purse in the car and had both hands free.

The landings slipped past to the echo of her pounding feet. *"You stayed here too long. It's time to move on."*

"Move on." The words bounced back to her from the walls of the empty stairwell. "Move on," she repeated, "move on." Muscles cramping, she descended the final flights and opened the door to the main lobby.

Jessica Corley, torturing the remnants of her tissue, blocked her path.

16

# CHAPTER 3

Kate had nothing to say to this woman and no intention of listening. "Step aside, Jessica."

Jessica blanched and dropped the tissue. It fluttered to the black marble floor like a tattered flag of surrender. A gust of chilled air sent it skimming toward gray glass doors. Chewing at her lower lip, Jessica reached into the beige leather bag that matched her low-heeled shoes and withdrew a white envelope. "He would have mailed this," she whispered, chin quivering, "but that seemed so, so . . ." She thrust the envelope toward Kate. "I feel awful. I'm so sorry."

*That deceptive and dangerous word.* Kate plucked the envelope from Jessica's fingers, folded it, and stuffed it in the pocket of her slacks.

"I'm truly sorry, Kate—" Jessica touched the sleeve of Kate's green cotton jacket with the tip of her index finger. "I always admired you. You did so much for the shelter." Her eyes glistened and she dug in her purse for another tissue.

Kate shifted from foot to foot and reminded herself that Jessica, despite her expensive clothing and carefully coifed hair, was also a victim, hostage to her husband's aspirations. She'd traded her freedom and self-respect for the trappings of a designer lifestyle.

A few moments ago Jessica realized how far she'd been sucked under. Now she wanted Kate to forgive her, save her. Pointless. Kate shook her head.

Jessica plucked at Kate's sleeve. "What will we do without you?"

Kate laughed, the sound spattering like hail against the marble walls. "Emory will find someone."

"But you're so competent. So strong. He won't find anyone like you."

Kate stepped to one side. "Emory doesn't want someone like me. He'd prefer someone like you."

Jessica's brow furrowed. "Like me? But I'm not—"

"Exactly. Thanks for the check. I've got to go."

"Go?" Jessica seemed startled. She gripped Kate's sleeve. "Where?"

Somewhere undefined, unconfined. A single word leaped into her mind. "West."

Jessica's brow furrowed. Her gaze focused above Kate's head. "You could go to the papers, the TV stations. You could get a lawyer and take the board to court."

*Stand up to Emory McCoy as your proxy?*

"I could make a copy of the minutes," she breathed, words barely audible. "Some of us felt . . . coerced."

"Of course you did. He holds your husband's loan. And without the bank's advertising account, Mickey would have to trade in his sports car."

Jessica averted her eyes. "The vote was close. If you went to court, you might win."

Win what? Reinstatement? Money that belonged to women who had no one else to trust, nowhere else to go? Kate had no moral strength for a battle of principle that she would lose even if she won. Besides, she wanted a new life, not more of the same.

An elevator pinged. Jessica released Kate's jacket, stumbled backward, and spun toward the sound, tensing like a rabbit beneath the shadow of a hawk. Two gray-suited men stepped out, immersed in a debate about the merits of the bond market. Neither looked at the women as they passed. Their shoes struck the gleaming floor with self-appointed authority. Their dark reflections preceded them to the doors, passed through, and became blunted shadows on the shallow granite steps outside.

"Goodbye, Jessica." Kate stepped into the slowly folding fan of sunlight on the lobby floor.

"Kate."

Kate didn't look back.

"What will you do now?"

Gripping the brass handle, Kate felt the closing door pull against her fingers. She drew the handle to her, stood for a second in glaring sunlight, and then strode down the steps to the sidewalk, conscious of the muscles rippling in her legs. She had no husband with whom to confer and compromise, no dog, no cat. From now on she would define her life not by what she would do, but by what she wouldn't. She straightened her shoulders and lengthened her stride.

* * * * *

A gray ribbon of road unfurled between green hills rolling like slope-shouldered waves. Kate crested a hill, wind sluicing through the open windows, carrying the scents of hay and heat and the exhaust of eighteen-wheelers that swept past her on the downslope, buffeting the SUV as if it was a tumbleweed. The dirty gray ribbon flattened beneath her wheels and spooled out in the rearview mirror.

She felt free, eager, awakened, and anxious. For the first time in her life, she had no destination, no specific plan.

"Life is defined by work and purpose, Kate," her father had often said. "Work with a purpose," her mother would add, "beyond the paycheck. Life is about duty, not desire." Even the few family vacations centered on educational opportunities.

She slid her fingers into the box of crackers open on the passenger seat, captured one of the buttery disks, placed it on

19

her tongue, and let it dissolve against the roof of her mouth. She tasted sweet beneath the salt and had a vague memory of a fourth-grade teacher, balding and intent, passing out similar crackers, urging Kate and her classmates to chew slowly, to experience the way saliva turned starch into sugar. She imagined the way her face must have looked, eyes closed, all thought centered on the taste spreading through her mouth. If only all of life's lessons were as simple, as pleasant to recall.

She swallowed cracker mush and punched the scan button on the radio, searching for something that wasn't Country, wasn't Western, wasn't right-wing talk. Nothing. She clicked the radio off, guessing there would be more choices when she got within range of the next large city. She sipped cola and considered pulling over and rooting through her meager collection of CDs. But that would take time. Her goal was to blast through Oklahoma, cross into Texas, and reach New Mexico before dark, to speed past the exit for a place called Grassy Ridge, the town from which Amanda Blake had called the night before.

Kate had been packing the distillation of her life. The few cartons and suitcases held a dozen favorite books, her most serviceable clothing, four photo albums with cracked spines, sets of heirloom china and silver she hated but felt a guilty obligation to keep, a selection of pots, pans, utensils, blankets, and pillows. After a day-long yard sale, her furniture had been reduced to two lawn chairs, a floor lamp, an air mattress, a sleeping bag, and the phone. It squatted in a pale rectangle on the carpet as if reserving space should the bookcase decide to run from its new owners and return. Why hadn't she let the phone ring itself out? Because she'd been trained to answer. Always.

"I heard about what they did to you, Ms. Dalton, and I know it's my fault." Amanda's tone was one of determined penitence.

"No," Kate insisted, weariness clotting her voice. "It's not."

"It is. And I'm s—"

20

"No. Don't say that word, Amanda! I never want to hear that word again."

Amanda gasped but said nothing for a time. Kate longed to hang up but, shackled by a bond of blood with this woman, lowered herself to that pristine rectangle of carpet and leaned against the wall, running her fingers through hair lank with sweat and humidity. They had nothing to say to each other. And yet . . .

"I hear you're going west in the morning."

"Yes." Kate wondered how Amanda knew, but forced herself not to ask. It didn't matter.

"I'm living in Grassy Ridge right now," Amanda said. "Grassy Ridge, Oklahoma. It's not far off the highway. You could be here in time for lunch."

Kate struggled for a response that would be firm, clear, and yet within the boundaries of cool politeness she'd seen her mother draw with succinct words and a brisk delivery.

"It won't be much, just sandwiches and berry cobbler, and iced tea."

"Thank you for the offer, but I have—"

"I won't keep you long. I promise."

Kate abandoned etiquette. "No."

"I have to see you Ms. Dalton. I have to talk with you about something important. You owe me that."

*I owe you?* The bloody image of Wayne Jessop burst into her mind and Kate rubbed her forehead. *You came to me. You fought to keep me from helping Wayne. You owe me.*

"It's like a proverb," Amanda said. "From China maybe? You saved my life. Now you have a say in what I do with the rest of it."

Kate bit back frustration and anger. "No, I don't. No one can take that responsibility but you." She swallowed, felt the rasp of air in her throat.

"I'll be watching for you late in the morning," Amanda replied with calm certainty. "You can't miss Grassy Ridge. You go south on—"

"I don't need directions. I'm not coming."

"Okay," Amanda said. "You can find it for yourself. It's not hard. Mine's the second driveway off Prairie Pony Lane. I'll see you in the morning."

For a moment or two, Kate listened to the drone of the dial tone, and then she unplugged the phone, carried it to the car, and tossed it inside. It struck with a jangled complaint and, cord coiling, slithered into a crevice between two boxes. She'd left her cell phone—shelter property—on her desk. Perhaps she wouldn't have a phone when she reached her destination. After all, who would she call? Her parents were dead and she'd parted with her most recent lover before Christmas.

The dense June night seemed to clog her pores and stifle her breathing; she gulped saturated air. Moving on had always been inevitable. It was what she knew best—from college to Africa and the Peace Corps, to Chicago for a masters program, to Texas and a school for migrant workers, and then to the shelter. Change allowed her to lead an unexamined life, as confident, decisive, and emotionally cool as her parents intended when they emphasized intellect and competence, discouraging introspection and second-guessing.

So she chose friends too absorbed with their own concerns and motivations to consider hers. She chose work situations that guaranteed respect, and possibly admiration, but also provided social distance. Saint Kate the Uninvolved.

A mileage sign loomed before her. She blinked and focused on the mass of information printed on the rear doors of the big rig ahead. The truck was licensed in Texas, maybe heading home. If she drafted along behind, kept her eyes on the buxom silhouettes on the swaying mud flaps, she wouldn't see the exit for Grassy Ridge. Later, if conscience nagged, she'd tell herself she was preoccupied and hadn't noticed until she'd gone fifty, seventy-five, even one hundred miles too far.

Hadn't she done enough for Amanda? She'd ridden with her to the hospital, filled in the paperwork, and applied to the victims' reparation fund.

The highway surged up another hill and the truck slowed. Kate flexed her foot, letting up on the gas. The speedometer needle shuddered and plunged toward sixty. A second truck thundered up behind, crossed into the left lane, and passed with a clatter and rattle of rusty chains dangling from the undercarriage. The truck ahead faltered. She tapped the brake and the speedometer needle dove. Rear doors filled her field of vision and she saw that someone with a four-letter-word vocabulary had traced a finger through the grime. With a long growl and a clash of gears, the truck crested the hill, belched a blast of black smoke and lumbered onto the shoulder. Following in its wake, Kate's wheels slipped off the highway.

"Damn." She punched the gas and jerked the wheel to the left.

*Too fast! Too far!* The SUV rocked and lurched toward a solid wall of big rigs making up time on the downslope. She wrestled the wheel, foot hovering over the brake. Boxes shifted and rumbled and the phone jangled as if calling for help.

The SUV slewed across the right lane and onto the shoulder again, tires biting grit and debris. Kate heard the sharp crunch of breaking glass, the ping of metal on metal. She feathered the brake. A trucker blew a long blast on his air horn. Her right tires thumped over something that gave beneath them. Three cars blew by, passengers open-mouthed. She jammed in the clutch, stood on the brake.

With a final bump and shudder, the SUV stopped. Swirling dust overtook her and sifted through the windows. She sneezed, hiccupped, and sneezed again.

"Stupid, Kate. That was really stupid. You're lucky you didn't roll it."

A car slowed, the passenger pointing. Kate waved her on, slipped the shift into neutral, and yanked the emergency brake. She unhooked her belt, opened the door and on juddering legs stepped out to assess the damage.

Far back, the truck she'd been following idled, the driver crouched beside a wheel. Dust hung between them like a tattered sequin curtain, motes glittering in the sun. Broken glass crunched beneath her sandals. Tires intact, no fluid spewing from ruptured lines. A second car slowed and eased onto the shoulder, a man eyeing her bare legs from beneath a thicket of brow. *Creep.* Kate waved him on. He raised the brow and leered, but then accelerated. She released a sigh.

The cola, seated deep in its cupholder, hadn't spilled. She pressed the cool can against her forehead, then drained the dark liquid, feeling it collect in the tense grip of her stomach as she fished a tissue from the console and mopped prickling sweat from her hairline.

With infinite care, she angled into a long break in traffic. She shifted tentatively, as if she were just learning, and accelerated in ragged bursts, confidence shaken. She took the next exit, vowing to buy a fresh cola, splash cold water on her face, and be back on the road in ten minutes.

But, at the end of the ramp stood a sign for a real estate development in Grassy Ridge. The letters loomed over her, insinuating themselves between this and any other destination. She and Amanda had forged a bond of blood, like soldiers who hunkered together in a foxhole, surviving a firefight. They had, in therapy-speak, "unfinished business."

Amanda believed she was owed something.

And Kate had always paid her debts.

She turned south.

# CHAPTER 4

With a grimace of resignation, Kate jounced along a rutted driveway, aiming for a battered silver trailer listing on concrete blocks. Portrait of poverty and despair. Kate frowned, told herself trailers were mobile homes, real homes, reminded herself she'd lived in huts and shacks. By choice. Did Amanda have a choice?

She glanced at the dashboard clock. 11:30. "Back on the road by 1:00," she promised herself. The SUV wallowed in the ruts and she eased up beside a compact car with crumpled fenders and balding tires that had exhaled until only a few ounces of air remained between rubber and rims.

An object plummeted from the forlorn tree. "Yahoo!"

Kate flinched and stomped brake and clutch. The object somersaulted through the air and landed beside the driver's door. A barefooted boy wearing ragged cut-offs, a blue and red striped T-shirt, and a five-hundred-watt grin struggled to keep his balance while splaying his arms in Olympic dismount form.

"Ta da!" He stumbled and regained his footing, red dust as fine as talcum powder spurting up between his toes. "Are you Kate?"

Before she could answer, he smacked the side of his face with the palm of his hand. "Duh! You gotta be. Mom said you

25

were coming from Arkansas. And your license plate says Arkansas, so you gotta be Kate, right?"

The onslaught of words ceased. Kate nodded. "Right." She shut down the engine, unbuckled her belt, and opened the door.

"And you would be . . . ?" She winnowed her mind for the name Amanda had gasped as she lay bleeding on the lawn.

"Way-Ray," the boy crowed. "My name's really Wayland Raymond Blake, but nobody hardly ever says all that." He plowed a furrow through the dust with his big toe. "Well, except my grandma. We used to live with her. Before we moved here." He jerked a thumb toward the trailer. "She took me to a baseball game and everything. But she died. Last month. She was real, real, real sick. But she didn't tell anybody. Mom says she didn't want us to worry and there wasn't anything we coulda done anyway."

"I'm . . ." Struggling to find a way around the word "sorry," Kate slid out and closed the door.

"Mom says we don't hafta be sorry." His eyes were the burnished brown of autumn acorns and just a shade lighter than the straight hair swirling about the cowlick at the back of his head. "She's with the angels now. She don't hurt anymore."

Kate wondered how to respond. She was accustomed to talking with children about danger, pain, and loss, but she always felt awkward, unsure. So much depended on what a child already knew, acknowledged, or chose to believe. Had Amanda's discussion of the grandmother's death encompassed more than angels and lack of pain? Better to change the subject. "How old are you, Way-Ray?"

"Ten." He plowed a parallel furrow with his other foot, squinted toward the trailer, and chewed his bottom lip. "Well, almost. My birthday's in September."

"So is mine."

"Cool." He grinned. "What day? Mine's on the seventh."

"Mine's the seventeenth."

"I'll come to your party and bring a present. But not a big one, 'cause we don't have a lot of money." He took a breath. "How old are you gonna be?"

"A lot older than ten," Twenty-eight years older. She felt those years around her like boulders brought down by an avalanche. How had so much time slipped past? What had she done with it? She felt a biting urgency to get somewhere, to start again. "A whole lot older."

Way-Ray darted in front of her. "How much older?"

"Too much." Where was Amanda? Kate had heard no sound from the trailer.

"How much?"

A conversational vortex. "Didn't your mother tell you never to ask a woman her age?"

"Nope." He shrugged. "Why shouldn't I?"

The screen door opened on complaining hinges. "Because you don't want to put a lady in a position where she might be tempted to tell a white lie."

Amanda lowered herself to the top of the pyramid of concrete blocks that served as steps. She held one hand against her left breast and moved as if she feared that at any moment her flesh would sag from her bones like warm gelatin. She wore a long-sleeved, dark green T-shirt over white shorts and her legs seemed little more than spindly bones and stringy muscles, knotted at the knees. Even her hair seemed leached of color and life. It lay against her skull like old straw. Kate told herself not to let pity influence her vow to leave in ninety minutes. "You made good time," Amanda said.

"How can a lie be white?" Way-Ray asked. "Grandma said all lies are black and evil. And why would it be *my* fault if a lady lied about her age? You told me people aren't supposed to lie, no matter what. Remember?"

Amanda frowned, but then lifted the edges of her lips in a tight smile that lent no light to her eyes. "Yes, Way-Ray, I did tell you that." She lowered herself from the final step and released the door. It whapped against the frame, then slumped open a few inches.

"But it's different for ladies? As long as it's white lies?" He wiggled his nose. "How come they're called white lies? How come they're not pink or blue?"

Kate nearly smiled, then noticed Amanda's ashen eyes pleading like those of a whipped dog that sees the lash raised again. Amanda had told her son Wayne had been dead for years. What color was that lie?

"It's never okay to lie," Kate told the boy. At the back of her mind she heard her father's stern voice, "Lies corrupt trust and will not be tolerated." Her mother had amended that in a whisper as they'd folded sheets, "White lies are social custom. A white lie can prevent conflict, smooth things over." Could Way-Ray grasp the distinction? "White lies can keep you from hurting someone—or hurting their feelings, anyway. For some ladies, the truth about age hurts."

He tipped his head back, blinking. "Huh? Why?"

"Some ladies don't like to think they look as old as they are, so they subtract a few years and put on a lot of makeup to look younger."

Kate watched Way-Ray study her worn leather sandals, baggy khaki shorts, faded orange T-shirt, and cropped chestnut hair. "You're not a lady like that, are you?" His tone made it clear that was more statement than question.

Kate threw back her head and laughed. "You have the observational powers of Sherlock Holmes coupled with a politician's silver-tongued flattery."

"Huh?"

Amanda patted his cowlick. "Go in and wash up. It's time for lunch."

"All right." He leaped to the steps, snatched at the screen door, and flung it wide. High-voltage exuberance. He could both drain and sustain Amanda. He turned in the doorway. "Did you get potato chips? The kind I like? Did you beat up that cream and make it all sweet and puffy?"

28

"Yes, yes, and yes."

Way-Ray paused. "Lots and lots of cream?"

"The most we've ever had."

"Yay!" He hurtled through the door. It whapped against the frame once more, a sound that punctuated Amanda's days. Proof of place, proof of life.

"He loves whipped cream," Amanda said, her gaze on the torn screen.

"So I gather."

"He's a good boy. Truly he is. There wasn't much in Wayne that was kind and decent, but every bit of it came out in Way-Ray." She turned to face Kate, eyes the color of fog, stark against skin with the bluish translucency of reconstituted powdered milk. "He thinks I got hurt at the hardware store where I worked. He still doesn't know about his father, that he went to prison, the way he died."

Kate clenched her teeth. Amanda had built a house of lies on a foundation of quicksand. Kate's father would have snorted in disgust and walked away, her mother a pace behind. "What—?"

"Come on, Mom!" Way-Ray kicked the screen door open. "My hands are all washed."

"Both sides?"

He flipped his wrists and kicked the door again. "Yeah. And I'm starving!"

Amanda caught the door before it swung closed. "We have company, Way-Ray. You promised to be on your best behavior. Kate will think you have no manners."

"I have lots of manners," Way-Ray argued. "But it's hard to keep all those stupid rules straight when I'm so hungry I could eat a buzzard sandwich."

Amanda's hand tightened on the door, fingers bloodless. "Young man, I've—"

"Wait!" Kate stepped up on the blocks. A sense of humor should be nourished. "Are we having buzzard for lunch? I had that for breakfast."

Way-Ray cocked his head and squinted at her. "You did not."

"Did too. I stopped at the Buzzard Barn and had fried buzzard eggs, biscuits, a side order of buzzard toe hash, and a big cup of buzzard beak tea." She rubbed her stomach and faked a burp. "Excuse me. Best breakfast I ever had."

"Liar, liar, pants on fire." The boy danced aside, drawing her up the remaining steps into a cramped living room. It was populated by two slouching green velvet easy chairs, an orange and brown striped loveseat, and an assortment of low tables, edges scalloped by gouges and cigarette burns. No knickknacks, no pictures on the walls. Worn linoleum, its triangular pattern barely detectable, dragged itself through the living room and into a miniscule kitchen where it halted at a closed door, its duty done.

Way-Ray darted to a narrow table folded out from the wall between short benches. As Amanda washed her hands, he snatched a potato chip from a dented red metal bowl. "Your nose is gonna grow."

Kate clapped a hand to her face. "Good thing I brought my handy dandy nose clippers, otherwise I'd have to remove the windshield so I could drive."

Way-Ray crunched the chip, mouth open. "I bet you don't have nose clippers, either."

"You're right. You know, you're pretty clever for a short person."

He snorted, blowing slivers of chip onto the table. "And you're pretty short for a clever person."

Kate chuckled and scooped up chips. "Umm. My favorite—barbecue."

"My favorite, too. But only the kind without the bumpies."

"I don't like those either." Her awkwardness had vanished. She was enjoying this banter. "You're clearly a man on the cutting edge of potato-chip style and substance."

He gaped, showing a wad of half-chewed chips on his tongue. "Huh?"

30

"She means that you're an expert on chips." Amanda pointed to the bench. "Sit down, Kate. Make yourself comfortable as you can in this shoebox."

Kate ignored the social cue that called for her to offer false reassurance and wedged herself onto the wooden slab.

"You didn't wash your hands," Way-Ray informed her. "You hafta do that around here or you don't get any lunch."

"Use one of these." Amanda offered a plastic box of sanitary wipes.

"I never get to use those," Way-Ray said. "I hafta use real water because Mom says I'm a dirt magnet."

Amanda hauled a pitcher of iced tea, a bowl of tuna salad, and a jar of mayonnaise from a skinny refrigerator, set them on the table and pulled a loaf of whole wheat bread from a cabinet. "Do you want your bread toasted? Way-Ray always has his toasted."

"If Way-Ray says toast is in vogue, I'll never eat raw bread again."

"Raw bread? That's silly. The bread was cooked before we bought it at the store." Way-Ray popped off his bench and poked the loaf with a stubby index finger. "It's not raw, is it Mom?"

Amanda opened her mouth, raised her brows, and shrugged. "Maybe we'd better toast it twice."

Kate noted that her voice had a shade of color and spirit.

"Yeah. Toast it twice," Way-Ray insisted. I don't want no raw bread around my sandwich." He bounced back to his bench.

"I don't want *any* raw bread." Amanda slid the bread into a toaster oven.

"What you said." He crammed three chips into his mouth, chomped, and swallowed. "But I think she's lying about the raw bread."

"It's not lying when it makes you laugh." With a sharp sense of transgression, Kate added to her mother's amendment of her father's creed. "And when we both know it's not the truth. It's comic embellishment."

"Relish mints? Who wants mints that taste like relish?" Kate chuckled. Relish mints. That would make her smile for days.

Amanda sighed and transferred the toast to a plate that she set before her son. "Make your sandwich and fill your mouth, Way-Ray, you're driving me crazy. I'm sure you're driving Kate crazy, too. But she's too polite to tell you."

"No she's not." Way-Ray got to his knees on the bench, scooped a mound of tuna salad onto one piece of toast, and mashed the other side on top. Filling slurried from between the slices. "I bet Kate has less manners than I do."

"*Fewer* manners," Kate corrected. She sounded like a spinster schoolteacher, but Amanda nodded as she slid more bread into the toaster.

"What you said," Way-Ray mumbled. He lifted the sandwich, wedged a corner into his mouth, and took a huge bite. Tuna salad plopped onto his plate and spattered his shirt.

Amanda shot him a look that made him put his sandwich down, squirm to a sitting position, and unfold his napkin. "We seldom have guests," Amanda told Kate. "And as you can see, Way-Ray loves an audience. I've encouraged him to be an extrovert, but I continue to hope he'll master self-control as well."

Kate nodded, conscious of the language Amanda had used. She wondered about Amanda's background and education. How had she wound up here? Did it all come down to Wayne?

Amanda laid two slices of toast on Kate's plate. "Thank you." Kate shook out a napkin and reached for the bowl of tuna.

"I've got lettuce and tomatoes, and sweet pickles." Amanda wedged another plate onto the table. "Way-Ray likes his tuna without the frills."

But frills were there if he changed his mind. *If I had more choices as a child, would I be here now?*

Way-Ray snatched up a nubbly pickle. "If Kate keeps lying, this is what her nose is gonna look like when she's old."

Kate put aside her regrets and stifled a laugh.

"Don't encourage him," Amanda said. "He gets sillier if you do."

"Yeah, don't encourage me." Way-Ray pretended the pickle was a cigar. Holding it with his thumb and forefinger, he took an imaginary puff it and blew an equally imaginary smoke ring.

Kate choked back another chuckle, lowered her gaze, and concentrated on spreading mayonnaise and layering tuna, lettuce, and tomatoes onto her toast. Just past noon. Plenty of time to eat, prod Amanda to the point, and get back on the highway.

Amanda gestured for Way-Ray to move over and balanced herself at the edge of the bench. She took a single slice of bread, tore it in half, and folded a tablespoon of tuna salad into one section. Most of her tiny sandwich remained untouched when she got up to serve warm berry cobbler and whipped cream.

The crust was both sweet and salty, the thickened berry juice tasted of nutmeg, and the cream was flavored with vanilla. "Ummmm." Kate let it linger on her tongue, savoring its warmth and comfort, drawing out the experience as she watched Way-Ray encase his square of cobbler in cream. He smoothed the sides with a knife, building a white tower, a fortress. When he was finished he licked the knife, then lopped off the pointed top, and excavated to the berries inside. Kate had never considered such creative license. Food was nourishment, nothing more.

"My mom's the best cook in all of Oklahoma," he crowed. "The best in the whole world."

Amanda squeezed her eyes shut for a second, gasped in a breath before she smiled at her son. "Way-Ray thinks the status of a chef is determined by how liberally he or she uses whipped cream."

Kate scraped up the last smear of cobbler on her plate, yearning to prolong her pleasure with a second helping. But that would only postpone her departure. She tipped her wrist and glanced at her watch. Twenty after twelve. "That culinary theory has merit."

Way-Ray grinned from beneath a cream mustache. "What she said." He licked his spoon with an audible slurp and nudged his mother. "Can I go out?"

"*May* I go out."

He licked the other side of the spoon. "Okay. *May* I go out now?"

"Yes, you may." Amanda stood and he scooched across the bench, shot past her, and hit the door like a linebacker. Hinges wailed in dismay.

"You should be proud," Kate told her. "He's a terrific kid."

"Small for his age. I couldn't always provide all he needed." Amanda dropped to the bench. "And he has a lot of growing to do in other ways, too."

"He'll catch up," Kate said.

Amanda's eyes, filmed with tears, shone like stones in a shoaling stream. "I hoped you'd like him." She glanced out the narrow window, pressed her lips together, nodded once, and then faced Kate.

"I want you to take him."

# CHAPTER 5

Kate felt her chest compress. "Take him?" She swallowed viscous air.

"Yes," Amanda whispered. "Take him with you."

Kate coughed and took a long pull at watery iced tea. Surely she meant only that Way-Ray needed a ride, perhaps to a relative's house. The car in the driveway was a highway hazard and Amanda appeared too stressed to drive farther than the grocery store. Kate drew in breath and released it in five precise measures. "Um, you mean give him a lift to, uh, to a friend's house?"

"No." Amanda's eyes blazed. "Take him forever."

Kate gasped. Forever? The word had the weight of a granite monument.

Amanda half stood, ripped a paper towel from the roll beside the stove, and blotted her eyes as she dropped back. Her pain was palpable. It fluttered between them like a wounded bird. "Take him wherever it is you're going."

"I don't *know* where I'm going."

Amanda shrugged. "That doesn't matter."

Kate shook her head. Not only was this a huge imposition, but it could be dangerous. The trip might expose him to strange people and situations. Or they could have an accident. "You know next to nothing about me, Amanda. I might drink myself into a stupor every night. I might join a lover in a commune of pot-smoking nudists."

Amanda shook her head. "You don't. You won't."

Kate felt judged, found vapidly normal. "How do you know?"

"I just know."

Amanda's smug confidence detonated a burst of anger in Kate's brain. "Did you *know* that Wayne was an abuser? Did you *know* he'd try to kill you?"

Amanda's face crumpled, but Kate ignored a twinge of guilt. She swung her legs to the end of the bench and felt a splinter ram the soft skin at the back of her knee. "Ouch." Lurching to her feet, she plucked at it with her fingertips. "Damn it."

Amanda grasped her wrist. "You'll only make it worse. Let me get it."

Kate jerked away. "I can manage."

"I know you can." Amanda's voice was mild, factual, resigned. "You don't have to prove that to me." She scurried to the closed door, opened it only far enough to slide through, and closed it behind her.

Kate waited, seething. She heard sounds of desperate rummaging, a rattling of what might have been pill bottles. Had caring for Way-Ray deprived Amanda of the rest she needed to restore her health—mental as well as physical? Kate's irritation turned back on itself. She shouldn't have lashed out at Amanda. She was angry with Emory McCoy. And Wayne. Predators, both of them.

Amanda emerged with a pair of tweezers and a brown bottle of peroxide. Before she pulled the door closed, Kate spotted two narrow beds with a few inches of space between them, a stack of cardboard boxes, and a closet no bigger than a phone booth. Bleak. She felt herself flush with shame. "Isn't there a relative who can take Way-Ray for a while? So you can get some rest."

Amanda shook her head. "There's no one. My mother's dead. I heard Way-Ray telling you."

"Yes. I'm . . ." Kate caught herself. "You must miss her."

Amanda set the tweezers and peroxide on the table and brushed the condolence away with the back of her hand. "Cancer." She spoke the single word as if it provided complete explanation. Tears glimmered in her eyes but her mouth remained a tight line.

She tore a paper towel from the roll and slammed it to the table. "That leaves Wayne's family, and I wouldn't let them care for a dead cat. His half-brother's doing time for robbery and assault. I hoped his mother was dead, but she called the hospital. Told me I'd burn in hell for what I did to her sweet boy."

Amanda unscrewed the top of the peroxide bottle and released a bitter laugh. "Her sweet boy. There's no limit to how a drunk distorts the truth. If Justine loved them, she wouldn't have crawled into the bottle and stayed with men who beat her and took a strap to the boys." She seized the tweezers. "Turn around and let me get at that splinter."

Kate obeyed, gripping the table, telling herself she'd already stepped into Amanda's life once—and stepped too far. She heard Amanda's knees pop as she squatted, felt cool fingers on her skin, a pinch, and then the sting of peroxide. "Got it." Amanda's knees popped again.

"Thanks." Kate turned, found her face only inches from Amanda's, so close she could see deep creases bracketing her mouth, a spider webbing of red lines in her eyes. "Amanda, I can't do this. Perhaps there's a friend who—"

"Wayne drove off the few friends I had. By the time he went away, I was in the habit of not allowing anyone close."

A habit Kate knew well. "Maybe there's a day care serv—"

"No." Amanda clutched Kate's wrists. "You have to take him." Her eyes flashed and something dark and slick writhed in their depths. "You owe him."

Kate blinked. Did she? The bloody specter of Wayne Jessop rose between them. She staggered backward, blinked it away. Wayne claimed his own fate. And he was a father by biology only. She flexed her fingers, relaxed in Amanda's grip. Stress had pushed this woman to the edge of sanity.

"Be a mother to him, Kate. Raise him. God help me, I can't. Not since—" She released Kate's wrists, slumped to the other bench, and buried her face in her hands. Her shoulders heaved, the convulsions shaking the table, rattling the ice in Kate's glass.

Kate reached to stroke Amanda's hair. *No.* Contact would make this worse.

She steadied the glass instead and peered through the window at two rusty poles and the sagging clothesline strung between them. Weathered wooden pins staggered along that line like soldiers who had broken formation. When Amanda cried herself out, Kate would persuade her to get professional help. Straightening her shoulders, she checked her watch. Fifteen minutes to one.

Amanda clawed a paper towel from the roll and blew her nose. She raised her blotched face to Kate. "I know what you're thinking. I've been to counseling, Kate. I've listened to well-meaning experts who have no earthly idea how it feels to be inside my skin and skull." She rubbed the side of her head above her right ear. "I've read books. I've gone to three churches and to a faith healer in a ratty tent. I prayed for direction and I prayed for help."

She wadded the towel and set it aside. "And you came. From now on I will pray only for forgiveness."

Kate held her palms out as if she could push away this burden. "I can't take—"

"You have to." She brought her hands up to cover her breasts. "Every time I look at him I see his father standing over me. I feel that knife in my chest. I see myself fighting you and telling Wayne to die."

Kate shook off the image. "But Way-Ray doesn't look—"

"It's deeper than skin. Wayne's in that boy."

Kate couldn't argue against the power of the mind to alter the shape of reality or create its own. Wayne haunted her, too. "Way-Ray wasn't even two when Wayne went to prison. He beat me . . . . He beat me all the time." She hung her head for a second, then raised her chin and squared her narrow jaw. "I have no excuse for staying with him as long as I did, so I won't bore you by making one. I went into that marriage with brains and ability and I came out the other side as dumb as dirt."

"You're not—"

"I am." Amanda brushed it aside. "But I'm not a drunk like Justine." She blew her nose again and took a breath. "I was weak and scared—more scared of leaving than of staying. I took it until the day he raised his hand against Way-Ray, and then I fought him until I couldn't get up anymore. When he roared off in his truck like he always did, I called the police. I made sure they found his drugs and stolen credit cards. That's what they sent him away for, not for what he did to me."

Kate bit her lip. She'd seen it happen that way a hundred times and tried to convince herself that the important thing was to get the abuser out of the house, break the chain of beatings, and punish him—no matter what the charges. But she seethed when domestic violence charges were dropped or plea-bargained away. "You got out before Way-Ray got hurt. That's what matters most."

"But I almost didn't." Amanda shivered. "And then I couldn't think how to explain it. Way-Ray was in first grade before he asked why he didn't have a father. I told him Wayne had gotten sick and died. I hoped . . ."

Kate filled in the blanks. "You hoped that Wayne wouldn't come looking for you or, if he did, that he wouldn't find you."

"I divorced him, changed my name, and moved as soon as I could scrape up the money. I moved a lot." Amanda sniffed. "But I was a fool. I expect he had friends keep track of me. I remember a man at the hardware store who never bought anything but the quarter chocolates at the register."

Kate wondered if his friends were watching still. She felt a frisson of fear and gripped the edge of the table while she cast her mind back over the preceding months. Had she spotted sinister shadows, received strange phone calls? No. At least not that she could remember.

Amanda seemed to read her mind. "I moved here at night. I wasn't followed. The car's registered to my mother and I rented this place under a fake name—Betty Bishop. The same with the phone and my post office box." She rubbed the knob of her collarbone. "I've got a shotgun under my bed with a blanket over it. It worries me to have it there with Way-Ray around, but I'd be more scared if I didn't."

"It sounds like you're safe enough for now." Kate spread her hands on the pitted table and struggled to her feet, wary of the bench. "I can't take him. I don't know where I'm going. I don't know how long I'll be getting there." She dug in her pocket for the key. "Children need structure: mealtimes and bedtimes, playgrounds and familiar toys."

"None of that matters a bit to a child if he's not loved."

Kate winced. She'd had structure: exact times, precise limits, specific amounts. She'd survived the lack of love. "You love him, Amanda. I *know* you love him."

"Yes." Amanda lurched to her feet and blocked the door. "I love him more than anything in the world. But his father's between us. Please." She clutched at Kate's arm, chilled fingers clamping once again with surprising strength. "If you don't take him, I'll have to give him up."

Kate felt her jaw drop in disbelief. "Give him up? For adoption?"

Amanda's fingers tightened, grinding skin against bone. "Yes."

It was unconscionable to consider this and to use it as leverage. "Amanda, the odds against a boy his age being adopted are huge. And the alternatives—" She shuddered, imagining Way-Ray in a string of indifferent foster homes, victimized by older kids, beaten, abused, and abusing in turn.

Amanda dug her fingers into hollow cheeks, stretching slack skin, bending the corners of her mouth into an arc of lament. "But that might be better than learning I hate and fear the part of him that's his father." She stared at Kate from eyes as bleak as an Arctic landscape. "You're Way-Ray's only hope. Save him from Wayne. Save him from me."

The magnitude of the choice set off icy spasms in Kate's gut. Her knees wobbled. She stumbled to the bench and sat, jarring the table. The tea glass rocked, ice cubes chiming against the sides, brown liquid sloshing over the rim. Amanda grasped the glass, emptied it into the sink, plucked a rag from the counter, and went about mopping the table. Wayne's knife had sliced more than skin and muscle. Amanda looked as if she had gone without adequate food and sleep for weeks, as if she were torturing herself as penance. If Kate took Way-Ray, she might save two lives.

But what about her own?

While Amanda puttered at the sink, Kate stared at a shred of lettuce drying on the table, frayed and graying like an old dollar bill. She couldn't do it. She wouldn't do it.

The sound of whistling floated through the open window—breathy, off-key.

Sliding her hands over her ears, Kate shut out the sound. Yes, there were horror stories about foster homes. But there were success stories as well. Way-Ray appeared to be resilient, imaginative, sure of himself—that might carry him through. She uncovered her ears, but heard no more whistling. She prodded the lettuce with a fingernail, peeling it from the tabletop. A puff of air from the window sent it tumbling toward the edge. She corraled it with her other hand before it could drop.

Amanda wrung the rag out over the sink and stowed the remnants of their lunch.

A second puff of air lifted the dry lettuce above Kate's restraining hand. Before she could capture it, it fluttered to the floor. She turned away before it landed and studied the clothesline with its weary pins. Time! She needed time.

A crow of joy filtered through the window. Way-Ray was bright and funny, good company. He could turn flight into journey, escape into exploration. They'd hike in the Rockies, detour to the Grand Canyon and Monument Valley. She imagined a grin swelling his cheeks. Then she imagined him tired, peevish, petulant, asking for his mother.

"He won't go with me." She made no effort to hide her relief. "Not without you."

"He'll go if I tell him to," Amanda said without turning from the refrigerator. "He'll go because he's bored. He wants adventures."

Kate stood, blood pounding in her temples. "What will you tell him when he asks why you're not coming? Another white lie?"

"Yes, I'll lie to him." Amanda turned to face her, eyes fierce, lips drawn back. "And so will you. We killed his father."

Wayne Jessop seemed to rise between them again, bloody and begging. Kate pushed at the air. The vision shattered and was gone. Damn him! "No. That was self-defense. That wasn't our—"

"Fault doesn't matter," Amanda hissed. "Dead is dead. Take Way-Ray."

Kate gritted her teeth. "I can't. I won't."

Amanda's eyes hardened. "Then I'll give him up."

Kate closed her eyes. Damn the parents who'd brought her up to do the right thing no matter how difficult. And damn Amanda for seeing that. Amanda was overwrought and overtired. But her maternal instincts were strong. She broke the chain of abuse when Way-Ray was in danger and she'd change her mind now. She had to.

"Two weeks," Kate said. "I'll send him home in two weeks."

# CHAPTER 6

From the corner of her eye, Kate watched Way-Ray cram another handful of caramel corn into his mouth and crunch it into paste. "How many days before I go home, Kate?" His words sounded thick and sticky.

She answered without taking her eyes from the twisting highway that hugged the Oregon coast. "Three. Counting today." And today was half over. So, two and a half. And then she could get her life back on track. As soon as she discovered that track.

"And I ride on a plane when we get to Seattle, right?" She heard pride, excitement, and a trace of fear in his voice. He'd never flown before and had quizzed her about what he might expect, the interrogations punctuated by lengthy silences or spates of tuneless humming and whistling she interpreted as efforts to combat anxiety. He'd crafted a litany and he repeated it now. "And I get to take candy bars and snacks with me and walk through a tunnel thing and the people on the plane will give me all the sodas I want and I'll be way up in the clouds and houses will look like little tiny toys and they'll put my suitcase someplace way down under my seat and I'll get it back on a big spinning thing and my mom will be waiting for me, right?"

"Right." She threaded the SUV through a turn and a razor of sunlight slanted in the side window, stabbing the edge of her eye. The visor did no good, so she raised her left hand and

43

anchored it in the hollow of her cheek, using her fingers as a screen. The summer sun had a different character along the edge of the continent. Back in Arkansas it had been confined within an oppressive dome. Sealed in a sweltering sky, it seemed too near, an angry and relentless enemy she could elude, but not escape. But this sun was more playful. Its beams skipped off the waves, scattered into eddying air, slid behind the spires of a stand of Douglas fir, and flitted amid wisps of fog.

The road climbed into cool shade and she pinched the bow of her sunglasses, pulled them off, and tossed them onto the dashboard. In an hour or two they'd search for a place to stay. The highway was packed with minivans and motor homes, which in turn were packed with tourists. In the past hour she'd noticed a number of glowing red "No Vacancy" signs. If they waited too long, they'd be stuck with shabby furniture, worn sheets, and grungy bathrooms, or prices far higher than she'd budgeted.

The road straightened. She allowed herself a second to study the boy pressing against his seat belt to peer along the dim green furrow the road plowed between trees. Way-Ray had entertained her with a running commentary on places, faces, and food selections, but filling his need for adventure and answering an unceasing barrage of questions left her brain empty. By the time he dropped into sleep each evening, she had no inclination toward introspection. Worse, she had the sensation of suffocating under the needs of another personality, a sensation she hadn't experienced since high school.

With a sigh, she wondered what became of sweet, funny, clingy Jimmy Goodwin, who after only a few dates had shared in excruciating detail his plans for the rest of their lives. Gasping for breath, Kate blurted that her parents said she was too young to be serious about a boy, then stumbled from his car and bolted for the chafing security behind her front door.

"Are we going in the ocean again when we stop? Do you think it will be warmer than yesterday?" Way-Ray bounced in his seat, caught the sack of caramel corn just before it spilled, twisted the bag closed, and wedged it amid the clutter in the back seat. "Can we get some more of those crispy clammy thingies like we had last night?"

"Fritters," Kate said, shaking off her brooding thoughts. "Sure. If we can find a restaurant that serves them, we'll get a mountain of fritters."

Way-Ray bounced again. "Two mountains. And I get the biggest."

"And you get the biggest," Kate agreed, slowing for a tight corner that put the SUV so close to a stream of cascading water that drops splattered across the windshield. Way-Ray crowed with delight. She clicked on the wipers and peered past them as the road, clinging to the hillside, slipped between rows of stubby evergreens bowing eastward like penitents. The variety and size of the trees amazed her. Several times she pulled over to walk among them. She craned her neck to glimpse the fog-shrouded tops of old-growth fir and hemlock and ran her hands along the warped and twisted branches of pines and cedars bent by the force of a relentless wind sweeping across thousands of miles of open water. Cuffed by rain-laden gusts, they seemed to have turned the other cheek only to be assaulted again. Like abused women, unable to break away from their tormentors, they—

"And I'll get lots of tater sauce." Way-Ray interrupted her darkening thoughts.

"Tartar sauce," she corrected automatically, suspecting he misspoke in an attempt to force her to smile. He did that often. Perhaps it was an effort to feel more comfortable with her. Or perhaps he sensed her struggle to maintain both physical and emotional distance.

"What you said. Tar. Tar. Like sticky, stinky black tar two times. Or like the bad yellow stuff that grows on my teeth. That's why mom makes me brush twice a day. Sometimes even more." He drew back his lips and flipped down the passenger-side visor. "Hey, I can't see my teeth. You don't have a mirror over on this side. What a rip. You should get a new car."

"I like this one." Kate tapped the gray dashboard with her fingertips. "Besides, it's got a compass so we know where we're going." She flicked a nail against the round black plastic casing and returned her hand to the wheel to ease around another turn. The compass swung from northeast to east and then to northwest.

Way-Ray leaned to the full extent of his seat belt and put his nose up against the compass. "Where are you going?"

Kate checked the compass. "Northeast."

"Duh." Way-Ray blew air from between his lips. "I know that! I mean after I go home. Are you going home, too?"

Did he mean Arkansas? Had she ever thought of that as home? No. Since childhood, she hadn't thought of anyplace as home. She felt chilly, forlorn. "I'm going to find a new place to live."

"Why?"

"Well, I guess because I can."

"Because you don't have any kids, huh?"

"Right." Where would this lead? How much could a nine-year-old understand about biological clocks and committed relationships, human population growth, concerns about the future of the planet?

To her relief, he seemed to accept the answer as complete. They rode in silence for a mile or two as the road wound down from a headland and slipped into the narrow slot between the ocean and a low ridge. Shards of sunlight splintered off the water, and Kate reached for the sunglasses she'd set on the dash when they'd plunged into the trees. Way-Ray squirmed in his seat and shaded his eyes, searching the rolling surf.

During their first day, she'd noticed him crossing and uncrossing his legs and asked whether he needed to use the restroom. He'd blushed furiously, shook his head, and said in a belligerent tone, "No. Do you?" Kate seized the opening, said she did, and pulled off at the next service station. There gave him five dollars for snacks and, in a loud voice, asked the attendant if he could point out the restrooms. She'd lingered inside a rank and sweltering ladies room until she heard the flush of a toilet and the slap of sneakers on pavement. Since then she'd made other excuses to pull over. She couldn't remember if she had been as embarrassed by bodily functions but, with upright and uptight parents, how could she not have been? She got past that in the Peace Corps where personal privacy was often only a dim concept.

"There's a wayside up ahead." Kate pointed to the sign. "Want to stop and look for agates?"

"I've got lots of agates already," Way-Ray said. "I found a whole bunch yesterday, remember? My suitcase is getting real heavy."

"No more agates then."

"Unless we find a real special one. For my mom." He leaned forward, gazing at the compass as if it were a tiny crystal ball. "When you get where you want to live, is it gonna be hard to find a job?" He squirmed and faced her, chewing at his lower lip. "My mom says it is. That's why we move a lot."

Kate felt needle points of anxiety pricking her gut. She'd collected employment sections of newspapers in New Mexico, Colorado, Utah, Arizona, and California. She had a stack six inches thick crammed behind her seat. How would she recreate her career? She grimaced. Perhaps "resurrect" was a better term. Or "rehabilitate." In terms of money made and saved, it hadn't been much. In terms of making a difference to those she served, well, unless she hunted down all the huddled migrant families and mistreated women, how could she know whether she'd simply slapped a bandage on a problem or changed the course of a life? Had they forged kinder lives, or merely taken another step along a circle that led them back to despair?

She felt her chest tighten and wondered if the surge of emotion was for them, or for herself. Was she also a victim, locked in a tight circle? "Oh, I'll find something." She heard a quaver in her voice. "But don't worry. I saved up so I can buy all the clam fritters I want until I do."

He nodded and scratched his ear. "Maybe you could go back and get a job at that place with all the rides. And then I could come and visit and get in for free."

"I think I'm too old." At least she could rule out one career path. In fact, she could rule out the entire entertainment industry. She'd been called interesting, intelligent, and complicated, but never entertaining. Not even by Jimmy Goodwin.

"You're not too old," Way-Ray consoled her. "But I don't think you're smiley enough. I mean," he amended, "you're not smiley all the time like some people." He hooked his index fingers into the corners of his mouth, stretched out a broad grin, and then released it. "You only have an outside smile when you have an inside smile."

Kate blinked and considered his observation as the road veered away from the ocean and through a rolling meadow. True. She seldom exercised her facial muscles in an effort to flatter or fawn. Had she ever smiled at Emory McCoy before the moment she quit? Probably not.

Way-Ray dropped back into his seat and retrieved the sack of caramel corn. "Kate?"

What was coming next? Based on past interrogations, it could be anything from a question about why dinosaurs weren't around anymore to an observation about nose-picking techniques. "Ummm?"

He munched, chose a few kernels, and chomped them to bits. "How did you and my mom meet?"

She'd expected that one and had practiced her lie. "At the hardware store."

"But you came from Arkansas."

She was ready for that, too. "That's right. I was a supervisor for the company, and I met your mom when I came to Oklahoma to check on that store."

"And you liked her a lot, huh?"

"Yes."

"Do you think my mom will be home when we call tonight?" His voice was solemn and tentative.

Kate delayed her answer, attempting to quash her own growing anxiety. During the first six days of the road trip, Amanda snatched the phone up at the first ring and asked dozens of questions of both of them—questions for Way-Ray about what they'd seen and done, and questions for Kate about how he was eating and behaving. On the two nights after that, Way-Ray left a message and she called back. Their conversations were brief and she didn't ask to speak with Kate. The next two nights she was home, but on Friday and Saturday nights there was no answer and no return call.

Focusing on the center line, Kate tried to fill her voice with confidence. "Of course she'll be there. I'll bet she went away for the weekend and she's getting home right now and looking at the postcard you sent with the picture of that roller coaster."

"Yeah. That was so cool. And I didn't get scared at all, did I?"

"No. You were braver than I was."

Way-Ray chuckled. "*Everybody* was braver than you, Kate, even the little bitty kids. You screamed so loud I plugged my ears. You're a big scaredy-cat."

Kate pointed her nails at him. "Meow. Better watch out. Scaredy-cats have claws."

Way-Ray barked. "Dogs aren't afraid of scaredy-cats." He growled and barked again.

*Good, we're off on a tangent.* "You'd better turn back into a boy before tomorrow night. I don't think they let dogs into the ballpark in Seattle." That would be their last treat. He told Amanda about it and informed Kate that his mother was going to borrow a more reliable car to drive to the airport. Proof that Amanda changed her mind, couldn't give him up.

Way-Ray let out a rapid series of barks and yips, and then followed up by throwing his head back and unleashing a howl worthy of any young alpha wolf. Riding his energy, Kate stomped the gas pedal and swung out into the left lane to pass three trundling RVs. Way-Ray rolled his window down farther and howled at the drivers. One, an elderly man in a plaid snap-brim cap, jerked his hands from the wheel. His huge trailer slewed into Kate's lane. She punched the gas again and squeaked past.

"Cool it, cowboy, you're making the herd nervous."

"Cowboy!" Way-Ray laughed. "I'm not a cowboy. Cowboys have horses and saddles and ropes and stuff. And there are no cowboys at the ocean." He snorted in disgust. "Don't you know anything?"

"I guess not."

"Yeah." He rocked in his seat and Kate turned her attention to a crimped curve that appeared out of nowhere. She loved her SUV, but had to admit it cornered like an ocean liner. And got about the same gas mileage. Every fill-up was another forty dollars. Every day's meals another sixty or more. Kate hadn't asked for money when she agreed to take Way-Ray. She expected, given the appearance of the trailer, that there was little to spare, but Amanda had dug a handful of rumpled bills from a kitchen drawer. Two hundred dollars. Gone before they reached California.

"Kate?" Way-Ray's voice was tentative, with an undercurrent Kate hoped wasn't fear. "Where do you think my mom went?" He wadded up the caramel corn bag and shoved it into the back once more.

Kate tamped down her concern and made her voice bright. "I bet she went to the movies."

"Nuh-uh." He shook his head. "She only goes to movies with me."

"Maybe this time she went to some grown-up movies," Kate improvised. "And she went shopping." Where else did women go? What would he believe? "And then she got a haircut."

Way-Ray raised his feet and kicked the dashboard. Kate noted that both little and big toes had now emerged from the sides of black high-top sneakers faded grimy gray. She hadn't gone through his suitcase to check, but he wore them day after day. He'd need new ones before school started. New shirts and jeans, too. Denim gaped at his knees and his washed-out yellow T-shirt was frayed at the neck.

"Get real, Kate," Way-Ray scoffed, kicking the dash again. "Mom doesn't do any of that stuff. She does mom things."

"Mom things?"

"You know. She cleans the house and hangs up the laundry and makes stuff to eat and tells me not to jump out of the tree and makes me read every night before I go to sleep. Like that. Mom things."

Kate grimaced. Mom things sounded like maid things. Repetitive. Thankless. She shrugged. "I knew that. I was just testing you."

"Why?"

She suppressed a sigh. This was like working on assembly line; there was always something coming at her. "Uh . . . so you'll be ready when school starts and they make you take tests every week." She made a mark in the air with her index finger. "You passed my test with a big fat A."

The boy grinned. "That's all I ever get. A. A. A. In everything. Even math."

"Sounds pretty boring," Kate teased. "Maybe your teachers are too easy."

"Are not. They're tough. And mean, too." He folded his arms across his chest and stuck out his lower lip. "Why wasn't my mom home?"

Kate reviewed the excuses she'd tried out on herself. "Maybe she went to the doctor."

He kicked the dash hard enough to joggle the compass. "No way. She said she wasn't going to the doctor ever again because it just keeps hurting anyway, and nothing he gives her makes it feel any better."

Kate remembered Amanda's pale, pinched face and the way she splayed her hands across her chest. Was it pain that had made her see Wayne in this boy?

"And she said we didn't have to go to church anymore, either," Way-Ray said. "Because no one was listening and no one was helping. Not the preacher and not even . . ." He was silent for a few seconds and when Kate glanced over he cut his eyes toward the roof of the SUV. "Not even you know who."

How should she respond to a child who's been told a higher power was no longer on the job? Should she use the "mysterious ways" defense? Allow her beliefs to color the answer or—somehow—strive for neutrality?

Way-Ray pointed left. "There! Go there or we'll miss the lighthouse and the whales. There. Turn now. Hurry!"

Kate braked, slapped the turn signal, waved an apology to the truck riding her bumper, and wheeled onto the scenic route. It led to a lighthouse on a promontory where Way-Ray had been assured that he'd see whales. Kate smiled. Maybe. If the ocean was calm and the leviathans came in close and tap danced along the waves. So far their search for whales had a lot in common with belief in an invisible higher power. "You know that whales aren't like the creatures on those rides, don't you? They don't pop up when someone pushes a button."

"Of course I know that." Way-Ray dug around in the back seat and unearthed a pair of binoculars. "I'll be the lookout and I'll look as hard as I can and I'll find lots and lots of whales."

"And if you don't?"

He rubbed his nose with his palm. "Then . . . then I'll look again tomorrow. Deal?"

"Deal," Kate agreed, relieved that the search, futile as it might be, distracted him.

\* \* \* \* \*

Later, clutching a book about whales, Way-Ray fell asleep on the fold-out sofa in a lower-level unit of the Wade in the Waves Motel. The sofa sagged in the middle like an old mare, the end tables were battered, and the wallpaper was out of date by twenty years, but the room was clean, just across a grass-studded dune from the water, and the last one available in Castaway Beach. They were lucky to get it, and lucky to get twenty percent off for paying cash.

Way-Ray had thrilled to the tale etched on a historical marker, the story of the only sailor to survive a shipwreck and make it to shore on a wintry night. He imagined himself in that role and darted among the dunes, deciding where to build his fort, how to make a fire to signal passing ships, and how to fashion a raft. Later he chased receding waves and ran shrieking from incoming water. After reading posted warnings about sneaker waves and undertows, Kate hadn't allowed him to venture into the rough and unforgiving surf that tugged at rocks, shells, and driftwood, rolling them up the beach and dragging them back again.

To her amazement, they had indeed spotted a whale from the lighthouse. It slapped its tail—flukes Way-Ray had informed her after consulting the book—on the water about a hundred yards out. He clicked off every remaining shot on a disposable camera, although she doubted he'd see more than a distant blur when the film was developed. With all the excitement, he fell asleep without calling home.

Kate's concerns, however, hadn't diminished. She tucked the sheet around his shoulders, scooped up her purse, and tiptoed out into the twilight, locking the door behind her. On their way to dinner, she'd spotted a pay phone beside a tiny market and bait shop. Without Way-Ray listening in, she intended to make it clear that her promise had been for two weeks and that time was nearly up.

Trudging along the shoulder of the highway, Kate squinted against oncoming lights. The June evening had yet to release the heat of the day and scorching blasts of exhaust from eighteen-wheelers and RVs seared her face while grit and pebbles flung up by their wheels stung her legs. The shoulder narrowed and sloped into a ditch filled with knee-high grass and the castoffs of those who ignored the threat of fines for littering: beer cans, plastic bags—even a pink teddy bear and a cracked toilet seat.

A gap opened in the traffic. She jogged across the pavement and continued past the cluttered display windows of a hardware store, a real estate company, and a combination liquor and gift shop. Could she work there? Could Saint Kate the Judgmental sell liquor to those she suspected would abuse it?

She walked on to the phone booth and found its glass and metal walls etched and painted with the symbols of teenage identity, romance, angst, and boredom. Like partners in a bad marriage determined to sabotage each other, the door refused to close and the dome light therefore refused to shed any illumination. Kate pawed in her purse for a small flashlight, clicked on the beam, and clamped it in her teeth while she opened her address book to Amanda's number and propped her phone card on the shelf. "Be there," she muttered around the flashlight handle. "Be there."

She punched in the 800 sequence and her ten-digit code and then Amanda's number. She heard a faint hum and series of sharp clicks and then the phone rang with a metallic grinding. After three rings, Kate heard another series of clicks and then Amanda's voice, slow and solemn. "Amanda Blake is no longer here. There will be no forwarding number or address. Please direct all inquiries to her attorney, Philip Jacobson."

# CHAPTER 7

Kate's jaw dropped. The flashlight tumbled from between her teeth, slammed against the narrow metal shelf, flickered, and went out while Amanda's voice reeled off a ten-digit number. The answering machine beeped, hissed, and clicked off, but Kate stood in the gathering darkness, listening to the droning dial tone, concentrating on its mindless sound, trying to swallow rising fear. When she couldn't manage that, she set the phone in its cradle.

"Later," she whispered. "I'll get the number later." Amanda would return. She had to.

That hopeful fiction enabled her to take a full breath. But as she groped for the flashlight, fear strangled her once more. Was Amanda being followed again?

Kate shivered. She felt exposed, vulnerable—alone in a dark phone booth in a town in which she knew exactly no one. She swept her hand across the ridged metal floor of the booth. Something pricked her right hand. Jerking upright, she bolted into the cone of light beneath a streetlight. A slim shard of glass protruded from her ring finger. Blood oozed around it.

"Damn." She plucked the shard from her skin, releasing more blood, then squeezed her finger so blood would cleanse the wound. After breakfast she'd deal with Amanda's lawyer, Way-Ray's future, and her own. Right now she needed strong light, hot soapy water, and the first-aid kit buried somewhere in the back seat of the SUV. Then she wanted to pull the covers over her head and pretend that Amanda's line had been busy.

With her left hand clamped around the bloody finger, she made her way back to the motel beneath a violet sky darkening to murky obsidian with a sprinkle of stars above the eastern hills. The headlights of passing cars illuminated chuckholes, culverts, and a car parked within inches of the asphalt by someone who apparently believed other drivers would look out for his vehicle better than he did. Her ring finger throbbed and her head ached with the effort of trying not to think about Amanda.

Yet, that was all that her mind would allow. Long after she bandaged her finger and slid between sheets smelling faintly of bleach and lemon, the words on the answering machine played in her mind behind an image of Amanda, hands spread across her scarred chest.

\* \* \* \* \*

Kate?"

Way-Ray's voice. She opened one eye. Gray light sifted between the slats of plastic mini-blinds. Dawn. She opened the other eye and focused on the clock radio. 5:12. "Ssshhhh. Go back to bed." Without turning, she plumped her pillow and snuggled deeper into the polished feel of the sheets against her bare legs.

"Kate?"

"Sshhh," she repeated. "Close your eyes. If you're all slept out, turn the TV on. But real soft." She folded the pillow around her head, covering her ears to shut out the television as well as the yowling anxieties massing at the edges of her mind. *Don't think. Sleep.*

She felt a hand on her shoulder. "I'm tired, Way-Ray. Let me sleep a little more, okay?"

"But my stomach hurts."

"You ate too many clam strips last night. Drink a glass of water."

"I did. It still hurts." His voice was thin and wispy. "It hurt all night long."

Kate groaned. What had he eaten besides clam strips and fries, hamburgers and pancakes? Not any serious roughage. "Maybe you need to go to, uh . . ." She halted, recalling his embarrassment.

"I already did." She felt him poke her arm through the thin blanket. "It still hurts. A lot. Like somebody punched me."

Kate rolled over and turned on the bedside light. Way-Ray's skin was blotchy—pale around his mouth, pink across his cheeks. She stretched out a hand and touched his forehead: warm and damp. Flinging aside her sheet and blanket, she tugged down the oversized T-shirt she slept in, and peered into his eyes. "You didn't fall on your stomach, did you?"

"Duh!" He pointed to his knee-worn blue cotton pajamas patterned with faint images of stars and spaceships. "I was in bed."

"What about yesterday, when you were jumping around on the logs?"

He shook his head.

She touched his forehead again. Food poisoning? She inventoried their food intake from the day before. They'd eaten the same things except that she had a chicken sandwich instead of a burger at lunch, she had coleslaw with her clam strips, and they picked different flavors of ice cream at a roadside stand. Could his burger not have been cooked enough? Had he developed an allergy to shellfish? "Do you itch anywhere?"

He shook his head again.

"Are you having trouble breathing?"

He lifted his chin and puffed out a few experimental breaths. "Not unless I think about it and get messed up about whether the air goes in or out."

"Then don't think about it." Back to that bacteria-laden burger. "Do you feel like you have to throw up?"

"Sorta." He put a hand on his belly. "And sorta not."

"Okay, when you went to the bathroom, did you do . . ." she searched her mind for the correct code ". . . number two?"

The flush on his cheeks deepened. He nodded.

"Did you have diarrhea? Did it hurt?"

He rolled his eyes. "Ewww. What you said. Gross."

Kate stifled a sigh of exasperation. Boys. Way-Ray would probably describe the result of a bowel moment to a friend in graphic detail, but that information was off-limits to a female. "I know it's embarrassing, Way-Ray, but if I take you to a doctor, he'll ask the very same questions."

"I don't want to go to a doctor. Mom doesn't have money for doctors so we have to take good care of ourselves and eat all our vegetables."

"She's right. But you haven't eaten vegetables for days."

"Nuh-uh. I ate pickles. And potato chips. They're vegetables, right?"

"Not in my book. But we won't worry about that now, okay? Just tell me if it hurt."

"It kinda hurt." He slid his hand below his belly button and off to one side. "Down here."

Kate closed her eyes, trying to visualize the drawings in her college biology book. Which organs were there? "Was it a sharp pain? Or more like an ache?"

"It's both." He winced. "There. That was a sharp one."

Gas? No surprise after fried clams. She placed her hand on his forehead again. Did it feel warmer than it had a minute earlier? "Lie down and I'll take your temperature."

He trudged toward the living area. "I'll call Mom. She'll know what to do."

Kate froze. She couldn't let him hear the message. "Let's take your temperature first. We don't want to worry her if it's nothing."

"I guess not." He shuffled to the sofa, voice growing plaintive. "But I forgot to call her yesterday. And she doesn't know where I am."

"Well, I'll bet she got one of your postcards yesterday. That's as good as a call." Thinking that her tone was too fake, too fragile, Kate dug out the digital thermometer.

Way-Ray flopped across the sofa bed, opened his mouth, and stuck out his tongue. "Close your mouth gently. Don't bite. And don't talk." His lips twitched, but then he clamped them around the thermometer, squinted at it, and crossed his eyes.

Kate covered them with her hand. "Don't do that. It's bad for you. And you can't see the numbers anyway." But she could and, with a feeling of queasy horror, watched the digits to the right of the decimal place leapfrog each other, driving the readout past 99, past 100, and on to 103.5. Forcing a poker face, she plucked the thermometer from between his lips and mashed the button to clear it.

"I wanna see." Way-Ray stretched out a hand.

"Too late, I already zeroed it."

"Then do it again."

"I don't think it's working right." Kate slipped the thermometer into its case and stuffed that into her purse. Did he know that normal was 98.6? "Let's take it someplace and have it checked."

He touched his stomach with his fingertips. "Do we hafta?"

"Only if you want to see a baseball game." She gathered underwear, a pair of jeans, and a clean T-shirt from her suitcase and headed for the bathroom. "We can't leave here with a broken thermometer."

"I guess," he muttered. "But I'm not taking a bath."

"You don't have to," she allowed as she closed the door behind her.

A few minutes later they emerged into a cottony fog that deadened the sounds of surf and highway traffic. As she stowed their gear, Kate saw that the drapes were drawn on the managers' office and remembered that the surly young woman who took her money had informed her that it was open from nine until nine, no exceptions. "I need my rest," she said, her words slightly slurred, her breath reeking of beer, "so you'd better keep your son quiet." She went on to rattle off a string of rules against running on the deck and leaving dishes unwashed.

Kate shook her head. Waking that woman to ask directions to a hospital seemed foolhardy. She remembered seeing a sign as they wound back to the highway from the lighthouse. Yesterday. Twelve hours ago. Things had been far simpler then.

She studied Way-Ray as he levered himself into his seat with one hand tight across his belly. Kids ran fevers. Kids got stomachaches. This was a virus, a bug. It had to be.

She drove thirteen endless miles to the hospital, fighting to hold to the speed limit and chattering in a shrill voice about everything they passed: eagles, fishing boats, cows, coffee shops, tsunami warning notices with arrows pointing inland. "Duh," she said to that one. Way-Ray only grunted and leaned his forehead against the passenger window. He didn't look up, even when she stopped beside the emergency entrance with its red sign glowing like an ember in the mist.

When she opened his door his eyes were dull and his face strawberry red. She touched his forehead. Hotter than before. She unsnapped his seat belt and dug the thermometer from her purse. "How about you carry this, and I'll carry you?"

"Whatever." He sighed, gripped the thermometer, and wrapped his arms around her neck. His skin seemed to scorch hers as she slid one hand behind his back and the other under his knees and pulled him to her. Staggering, she lurched through the automatic doors into the lobby, the soles of her running shoes screeching on the waxed linoleum. Two women stood behind a high counter: a tall brunette with stained and wrinkled green scrubs, smudged mascara, and a wide yawn, and a shorter, older, plumper one with crisp fuchsia scrubs that set off ebony skin, graying hair fluffed around her head, and a smile that lit her brown eyes.

"We need help," Kate told them. "Way-Ray's had a stomachache all night and he's running a high fever."

"And the 'mometer's broken," Way-Ray mumbled.

The brunette squinted at them. "Excuse me?"

"You go on." the smiling woman patted her arm. "I've got it. My shift starts in five minutes anyway." She hustled around the end of the counter, took Kate's arm and steered her along a short corridor. "We'll get a doctor to take a look. I'm sure he'll be right as rain in just a few minutes."

\* \* \* \* \*

But an hour later, Kate and Way-Ray huddled in a white-curtained cubicle that smelled of bleach, alcohol, and fear. Way-Ray, wearing a blue and white striped hospital gown meant for an adult, kept casting his eyes toward the pile of clothes on a nearby chair as if he someone might steal them. Kate, her mind pinwheeling, held his hand with stiff fingers while a doctor with a receding hairline, bloodshot eyes, and a graying mustache explained what an appendix was and why Way-Ray's had to be removed. In a voice more bored than matter-of-fact, he described how a surgeon would snip it out, and sew up the hole.

Way-Ray craned his neck to see the spot the doctor prodded. "Can I watch?"

"No." The doctor laughed. It seemed hollow and forced, the sound of a man not comfortable relating to others. "We're going to give you a special kind of shot to make you go to sleep."

Way-Ray wrinkled his nose. Kate gave him a smile that felt as phony as the doctor's laugh. He stretched out his free hand and touched the doctor's stethoscope. "Can Kate watch?"

"No," the woman who'd escorted them in interrupted. Her name tag read "M. O'Bannion." Her voice sounded both cheerful and genuine. "The operating room is very small. There's only space for you, the doctor, and the nurses. There's no room for your mother."

Way-Ray's forehead creased into a frown. "Kate's not my mother."

"Oh." M. O'Bannion glanced at the form on a metal stand beside the bed and Kate cringed. She'd penciled in Way-Ray's name and age, but nothing more, hoping the problem would be minor and cash would make paperwork unnecessary. "I assumed you were."

"No. I'm . . ." What could she say in front of Way-Ray? How much would she say if he weren't listening? "I'm a friend."

M. O'Bannion crimped her lips. "Is his mother available?"

"No, she's—"

"She's back home in Grassy Ridge, Oklahoma," Way-Ray piped up.

M. O'Bannion and the doctor, whose nametag read "S. Weatherill," exchanged glances. "Well," the doctor plucked a ballpoint pen from the pocket of his coat and clicked the point in and out. "We'll need to get her permission before we proceed." Click. Click. Click.

M. O'Bannion nodded. "And we'll need her insurance information, of course."

"We don't have insurance," Way-Ray said, his voice tightening. "Mom says we can't afford it until she finds another job." He struggled to sit up. Kate put a hand on his shoulder as M. O'Bannion and the doctor exchanged another glance. "Does that mean I have to stay sick?"

"Of course not." Kate gently pushed him back, surprised at his strength as he resisted. "Don't you worry about insurance, or money, or anything except getting well." She shot an angry glance at M. O'Bannion, who dropped her gaze to the form. "I'll take care of everything,"

*How?* The voice in her mind screamed.

She stroked Way-Ray's forehead and struggled to tamp down her fear. "I'll call your mother right now, okay?"

"Okay," Way-Ray whispered.

Kate dug for her address book. She'd get the number for Amanda's attorney. Attorneys existed to navigate paperwork mazes created by other attorneys—like those who worked for hospitals.

Way-Ray plucked at her T-shirt. "Tell her I want her to come." He winced and rubbed his belly. "Right now, okay? Tell her to come on a plane. A really fast plane."

"The fastest there is." She patted his head. "Now you wait here and I'll take care of this silly paperwork." She scooped up the form, nodded at M. O'Bannion, and strode toward the lobby, thoughts churning. What would she do if the attorney happened to be on vacation or in a trial?

"I'm sorry. I didn't mean to upset the boy." Kate spun on one heel and saw M. O'Bannion hustling after her, a hand patting her springy hair. "I honestly thought you were the mother."

Kate longed to unleash her frustration, but couldn't afford to alienate this woman whose apology seemed heartfelt. "I understand the reason for nametags, but I can't connect with just an initial. What does the M. stand for?"

"Why . . ." the woman lowered her gaze to her plastic tag "Maureen." She laughed. "Not what you expected, huh? Well, my dad was what they call black Irish, from Boston. He got the wanderlust after the big war, met my mother in the Congo and," she spread her arms, "here I am, the darkest little angel they ever saw in the school Christmas pageant."

Kate forced a grin, thinking the truth about Amanda wouldn't fly, even with a woman as up-front as Maureen. She'd have to be creative. Another sanitized expression for lying. "Okay, Maureen. Here's the situation. Way-Ray's mother is . . . ill. Very ill." She touched her temple, allowing Maureen to draw her own conclusions. "She sent him along with me so that she could rest." She leaned on the last word, implying, she hoped, white-coated attendants and medication in paper cups. Maureen nodded. A co-conspirator. "I'm not sure I'll be able to reach her. Do you absolutely have to have her permission before you can operate?"

Maureen glanced at the form. "Well . . ."

Kate seized on her hesitation. This rule could be bent. "If he'd been in a car accident and was bleeding to death, would you need permission?"

"Well, no, but that would be an emergency situation."

"Acute appendicitis isn't an emergency?"

"Not at this point, no."

Kate felt anger surge, pound in her skull. "But the doctor said it could burst." She dug her nails into her palms. *Calm. Stay calm.*

Maureen put a hand on her arm, the fingers smooth and cool. "There's a phone over there." She pointed to six soft yellow chairs huddled around a low table strewn with mangled magazines and shredded bits of a foam cup. A beige phone, grimed with fingerprints, hung listlessly on the wall beside a nearly-empty water dispenser.

"I want to help you," she said in a low voice as she followed Kate. "I want to help that boy. But you have to understand that there are rules and regulations so—"

"So you don't get sued." Kate seized the phone and clamped it to her ear.

Maureen's plump shoulders rose and fell. "There are legal considerations, certainly. This is a litigious society. But there are other concerns, too."

Kate set her purse and the form on the table and punched in her long distance access code, resentment steaming from her pores. "Yeah, like how you'll get paid if there's no insurance."

Maureen backed away two steps, planted her fists on her hips, and jutted out her chin. "No, like whether I should call the police."

"The police?" Kate felt the phone slipping from her fingers. She clutched it against her chest. "Why?"

"Situations like this—behavior like yours—raise red flags. There's a possibility that you," she touched her forehead, "may be the one who's ill."

"Me?" Kate shook her head. "No. It's his mother."

Maureen held up her hands, fingers spread. "I'm sure that's true, but it would be wise to have the police determine whether she's aware that he's with you or . . ." Maureen glanced over her shoulder. ". . . whether he was abducted."

# CHAPTER 8

"Abducted?" The idea was ludicrous, outrageous. Kate put a hand to her throat. Her pulse fluttered beneath the skin. "If I abducted him, would I bring him to a hospital?"

Maureen's eyes seemed to ice over. "There have been cases where that happened."

*Do I look like someone who would steal a child?* Kate struggled to remain rational. "Does he *act* like he was kidnapped?"

Maureen's eyes didn't thaw.

Kate pointed toward Way-Ray's cubicle, noting that her hand shook. A sign of guilt, or an emblem of innocence? She dropped her arm and stuffed her hand into her pocket. "Go ask him." Her voice grew shrill, brittle. "Go ask."

Maureen raised her hands until she was peering through her splayed fingers, using them almost as a shield. "If children are afraid of being hurt or punished, they'll say almost anything to protect themselves—or their families."

"But he's not afra—" Kate's throat constricted. How could she prove that? Anything she or Way-Ray said would be viewed with suspicion.

She snatched the dangling phone and slammed the receiver onto the hook, bit her lip, and slumped into the nearest chair. Venting emotion was a luxury she couldn't afford. Maureen was correct. Kate had seen it at the shelter: children insisting their fathers never hurt them or their mothers, children bargaining to escape pain, to stay alive. "I understand your concerns and obligations." She rubbed her eyes and peered up at Maureen. "Go ahead and call the police. Let's resolve this so they can operate."

Maureen nodded, lowered her hands, and glanced toward the desk.

One corner of Kate's brain crafted a version of how she and Amanda met that edited out Wayne Jessop and hid the truth from Way-Ray. She smoothed her rumpled T-shirt and ran her fingers through unwashed hair stiff with salt spray. As she dug through her purse for a comb, she realized that Maureen hadn't moved. Kate offered her a weak smile. "I apologize for acting like a raving lunatic. I'm just so worried about Way-Ray— about his mother, too. I didn't mean to take it out on you."

Maureen shrugged. "It doesn't spell that out in my job description, but it seems that's what I'm here for." She chewed at her lower lip, and then rubbed her chin with the knuckle of her right thumb. "Listen, why don't you get his mom to call me at the number posted on the wall by the phone."

Kate felt her breath quicken. "And if I can't reach her? If she's not home?"

"Keep trying." Maureen pointed to the form. "Fill that out. We'll see where we are when you're finished."

Kate clutched the form as if it were a life preserver, paper wrinkling in her fingers. "And if Way-Ray's right and there's no insurance?"

Maureen made a backhand gesture. "Keep your cart behind your horse. We'll find a way. We always do." She glanced toward the parking lot. "We haven't tossed anyone out into the street in a hospital gown yet. Although there have been a few who've tempted us." She grinned and slid the paper from Kate's fingers. "Let me get you a fresh one."

"Thank you." Kate closed her eyes, tipped her head back against the wall, and tried to force air to the bottom of her lungs. "It will work out. It will work out," she chanted in a whisper.

"Here you go."

Kate opened her eyes, accepted the form, and squared it on the table. Acutely aware of Maureen's gaze, she scrabbled through her purse for a pen. It slipped from her fumbling fingers and skidded across the floor. She gritted her teeth against a curse of annoyance. The old Kate Dalton didn't drop pens. The old Kate's hands didn't tremble.

Maureen bent with a slight grunt and retrieved the pen. "I don't think there's any need for me to call the police," she said in a low voice as she handed it to Kate. "I saw the way that boy looked at you. I could be wrong, but I believe there are some things you can't convince me about, no matter how good an actor you are: one is a genuine preference for black velvet paintings, shag carpeting, or stewed okra, and the other is real love."

Kate smiled, feeling the knot in her chest loosen.

"Now I've got things that should have been done twenty minutes ago, and a fresh pot of coffee to make," Maureen said with a wink. "You get on that phone. And then get back in there with that little boy. He needs you." Before Kate could thank her again, she bustled behind the tall counter and got busy at a computer terminal.

Kate levered herself to her feet, got the attorney's number from Amanda's recording, and called him. "Philip Jacobson's office," a woman with a sharp twang answered after the fourth ring.

"Hello. My name is Kate Dalton and—"

"We've been hoping we'd hear from you, hon," the woman interrupted. "Mr. Jacobson is available. I'll put you right through." She clicked off. The line hummed, then crackled.

"Miss Dalton. I've been expecting your call." Jacobson's deep voice had just a trace of a New York accent and a hint of aggressiveness held in check. "There are a number of issues we need to dis—"

"Later." She cut him off, her voice sharp, whetted. "Way-Ray has appendicitis. We're at a hospital in Oregon. I need a medical release so they can operate. I need it now."

"Certainly. I have the form you need all signed and notarized." His tone didn't change. He didn't falter or search for words. "Give me the number. I'll have my secretary get it to the hospital immediately."

Immediately. The word had the sound of "Christmas" or "chocolate" or "free." Kate felt her shoulders straighten as she rattled off the number. "Tell her to ask for Maureen O'Bannion."

"Hold on a moment," he instructed.

She held, listening to the empty hum of the line and bouncing on the balls of her feet. Was Way-Ray worrying because she'd been gone so long? Was someone with him, or had the doctor left him alone in that sterile cubicle? "Come on," she muttered, stretching the phone cord, attempting to peer down the hallway and through narrow windows on swinging doors. She heard a phone ring and saw Maureen clamp a receiver to her ear and give her a thumbs-up.

Jacobson's voice replaced the hum. "The document is on the way. Now, there are a few things we need to—"

"Insurance," Kate blurted. "Does Way-Ray have health insurance?" She slanted her gaze toward the form and its still-blank lines.

"Insurance? Let me see what I can find." Kate heard the shuffle of papers and what sounded like a pen tapping against a desktop. She tried not to get her hopes up. Way-Ray had insisted his mother had none. But Amanda and Jacobson had foreseen the need for the medical document, so perhaps . . . Kate crossed her fingers.

Jacobson cleared his throat. "I can't find any specific notations. It's possible he may qualify for a government-subsidized program." He cleared his throat again. "But she didn't mention applying."

Kate's fingers curled into a fist. "Well, she needs to apply now. How can I reach her?"

"I have no idea."

"But you're her attorney!"

Jacobson cleared his throat once more. "Miss Dalton, I recognize that you're in a difficult position and you're under a great deal of stress, but—"

"Stress." Kate hissed through her teeth. "Stress doesn't cover it. I'm out here at the edge of the continent with a sick little boy who wants his mother." Kate felt her frustration shift from Jacobson to Amanda. What kind of a mother would put her child through this? What kind of a mother wouldn't be available when her child needed her the most? Kate thought of his pinched face, his quavering voice. "Way-Ray's very sick. She needs to know that."

Jacobson sighed. "Yes she does." Matter-of-fact. Maddening.

Kate glanced over her shoulder, saw Maureen squinting over a long sheet of paper and lowered her voice. "Mr. Jacobson, I don't panic easily, but ten minutes ago I was practically accused of being a kidnapper."

Kate heard the tapping sound again, faster this time. "All right. The situation is this: Amanda Blake retained me, in essence, to make her will and to execute the disposition of her estate for the benefit of her son. She felt that you, as the boy's guardian—"

Kate gasped. "Guardian?"

"Yes. I have the form right here. Her intention is that you adopt him as quickly as possible. Once this medical crisis is resolved, you'll need to contact an attorney up there and I'll—"

"Adopt him? No. I agreed to take him for two weeks." Her voice fractured. Maureen must be staring. And why not? Kate Dalton was undoubtedly the most interesting show in town. "Two weeks! That's all I promised!"

"I wasn't aware of that," Jacobson said. The tapping picked up its pace and then slowed again. "She led me to believe that you had agreed to the guardianship and the future adoption."

Another of Amanda Blake's white lies. Lies that weren't supposed to hurt anyone. "I didn't."

"I see."

Kate was certain he didn't. "I'll be glad to take care of Way-Ray until he's well enough to return to Oklahoma, but I can't adopt him. If Amanda knew he was this sick, I'm sure she'd forget this . . ." Stupidity? Selfishness? Short-sightedness? "There has to be some way to reach her."

Jacobson sighed heavily. "There isn't."

Was he shielding her! Was he abetting her insane plan to give up Way-Ray. "Let's cut through the bullshit," she hissed. "I won't adopt her son. You call and tell her that. Now!"

"I'd like to do that," Jacobson said, his voice sincere, no longer flat. "But she's vanished."

# CHAPTER 9

"Vanished?" Kate clutched the phone, resentment simmering behind her eyes. Amanda had decided what she wanted for her son and disappeared to make it happen. And Kate, meanwhile, had been naïve enough to imagine Amanda was in jeopardy, worry she was being stalked by Wayne's friends. "When?"

Jacobson spoke as if weighing each word before he released it. "She was . . . she appeared to be quite ill when she came to see me Friday afternoon. She wanted the documents prepared immediately and Pearline—my secretary—got them together over the weekend." He said that with a trace of both awe and gratitude and Kate decided that he, unlike Emory McCoy, recognized the value of his staff. "We executed the papers yesterday morning," he continued, "and somehow she left without taking her copies. When Pearline called to tell her we'd put them in the mail, she heard the recording."

Kate's empty hand clenched. Amanda had recorded the message before she signed the papers. She never planned to return to Grassy Ridge. "We have to find her. Maybe the police can track her car."

"Her car is on the street near my office." Jacobson's flat voice offered no encouragement. "Pearline spotted it this morning. The doors are unlocked. Someone went through the glove box."

Or Amanda rifled it herself to make it look as if she was running from someone. "They could trace her credit cards, couldn't they? Or watch her checking account?"

"No cards. No account. She paid me with a diamond ring she said belonged to her mother."

Kate shook her head in disbelief. Amanda bartered her dead mother's ring to hire an attorney to give her son away. It reminded her of an O. Henry story she'd read in grade school. With a jolt, she recalled the words Jacobson used earlier: Will. Estate. Had guilt and obsession pushed Amanda to take her own life as an act of atonement? Was her body even now floating in a river or lying in a weed-choked ditch?

Kate felt the sting of remorse. "Do you think she killed herself?"

"I wish I knew," Jacobson answered. "And not simply because it would clarify my course of action." He sighed and his voice grew softer and less controlled. "For the sake of argument, and my position as her attorney, I intend to proceed as if she is alive. But, I will also attempt to gather information that will enable me to determine whether I need to reassess that assumption." Legalese for waiting for Amanda to surface, but being mentally set to learn of her death.

Kate imagined Amanda's waxen body stretched out on a steel table. The image morphed into Way-Ray, feverish, tossing on the narrow bed down the hall. She had to get back to him. But there was that damn form to fill out. "What about the hospital costs?" She cast another glance toward Maureen, busy at her computer, head cocked, listening without an attempt to pretend otherwise. "Will they expect me to pay?"

"They'll want payment, of course, but I'm sure you'll be able to work something out. Amanda told me you're a bright and resourceful woman."

The compliment rankled. Amanda had pushed his buttons too.

"And if Amanda is deceased, at some point you may receive the victims' reparations settlement to use for Way-Ray's care."

Blood money. But money was the least of it. What she wanted was someone else to take responsibility. Never, since the day she tossed that fistful of sodden earth on her father's coffin, had she felt so alone. She rested her throbbing head against the wall and caught a movement from the corner of her eye—Maureen, waving. Way-Ray's image flashed across her brain. He was alone, too. "I've got to go," she told Jacobson. "I'll call back."

She hung up without waiting for a response and trotted toward the desk. "They're prepping him." Maureen scurried out from behind the counter. "I'll take you." She gripped Kate' arm above the elbow and towed her down a hallway behind the reception desk. Kate wondered what Maureen's job entailed—she seemed to know everything, to be allowed everywhere.

"You didn't get that form filled out, did you? Well, don't worry, you'll have time." Maureen straight-armed a set of swinging doors. "The surgery won't take all that long, but it will be a while before he wakes up." She turned a corner and pushed through another set of doors. "Here we are."

Way-Ray lay on a bed in a room with stark white walls, stainless steel counters, and a tile floor the color of nausea. A young woman with tight red curls and flowered scrubs was showing him a length of clear plastic tubing. He whipped his head toward Kate. His eyes were enormous, his skin glistened with sweat, his teeth gnawed at a bottom lip flecked with blood. "Did you call my mom?" His voice was a wisp of sound. "Is she coming?"

Kate's stomach lurched. Amanda predicted she would lie to him, and now she was faced with it.

She hesitated, stumbled, felt Maureen's grip tighten. "Of course she is," Maureen told Way-Ray. "Just as soon as she can."

Kate gawked at her. "I—"

Maureen's fingers clamped into the soft flesh above Kate's elbow.

"I don't want to have an operation," Way-Ray whimpered. "It's gonna hurt."

"I know, sweetie." Maureen steered Kate to the bed. "But if you don't have the operation now, it will hurt a whole lot more and a whole lot longer."

He worried his torn lip. "I don't care. I want to go home." He clawed at Kate's wrist. "Can't we go back to Grassy Ridge?"

Maureen shook her head. "It's a long, long way, sweetie, and you're too sick to travel. Besides, your mom said you're going to come through this just fine because you're such a big boy and because you're so tough." Releasing Kate's arm with a final forceful squeeze, Maureen moved to the head of the bed, and brushed damp hair from Way-Ray's forehead. "And she wants Kate to have your favorite ice cream ready. Is that chocolate? Vanilla? Cookie dough?"

"No."

Kate noted that his anxious eyes hadn't moved from her face. His fingers burned like sizzling wires against her skin. If Amanda never returned, could she complete an emotional circuit with him, or had she insulated herself too well? She remembered visiting her dying mother, hating the hiss of oxygen, the screens with green blips, the periods of denial and hope and, worse yet, the moments of acknowledgement and acceptance. Was that normal?

"Peanut butter?" Maureen guessed. "Rocky Road? Pistachio?"

Kate had intended to share those feelings of failure with her father, but while she waited for an opportunity, he committed himself to the grave. He hadn't pined, hadn't wasted. He simply laid down one night and quit living, as if it had been a tedious task finally completed to his satisfaction.

"Chocolate mint?" Maureen guessed. "Fudge ripple? Strawberry? Cherry? Blueberry?"

Kate forced herself to stop floundering in the past and smile into Way-Ray's yearning eyes. "I know what your favorite flavor is."

"Do not," he whispered.

"Do so. It's buzzard."

"Buzzard?" Maureen opened her eyes and mouth wide in a parody of disbelief. "Go on. There's no such thing as buzzard ice cream."

"Not out here in Oregon there isn't." Kate stroked his fingers. The skin felt icy now and the bones far too fragile. "But there is in Grassy Ridge, Oklahoma."

He grinned and laced his fingers through hers. "Yeah. What you said."

"He likes caramel cream buzzard best," Kate said in the lightest voice she could manage, "but they only make it in the summer. It's hard to cream a buzzard in the winter when they're almost frozen."

Way-Ray giggled and Maureen gave Kate a broad wink. "I hope you're making all this up." The red-headed nurse frowned. "I'm going to Oklahoma at Christmas to meet my boyfriend's parents."

"Well, then you'll have to try a peppermint buzzard blitz shake."

The nurse shuddered.

"That's my mom's favorite," Way-Ray chimed in. "It has big chunks of buzzard in it."

The nurse shuddered again. "Ugh."

"Too bad she won't be able to bring you any when she comes," Maureen told him. "It would melt. I guess you'll have to settle for the ice cream we have out here."

"We had some yesterday," he informed her. "I got two scoops in a big cone: chocolate chip with chocolate and peanut butter on top of it." He used his hands to demonstrate the height. "Kate had something with nuts in it."

"Butter pecan," Kate said.

76

"All this talk is making me hungry." Maureen licked her lips and patted her stomach. "Let's get you into the operating room so we can have ice cream."

"We could have some now," Way-Ray suggested, eyes pleading. "Before the doctor cuts me."

Maureen shook her head. "You can't have anything to eat until after. The doctor doesn't want to hunt through chocolate chips to find your appendix."

"But you could have some."

"Didn't you know? Nobody in the hospital is allowed to eat while an operation is going on."

"Nobody?" His eyes narrowed.

"Nobody," Maureen confirmed in a voice that implied no arguments would be considered. "It's a hospital rule." She pointed her chin at the nurse who nodded assent.

"Well," Kate said, struggling to infuse credibility into her tone. "We wouldn't want to break a hospital rule, would we?"

"No." Way-Ray's skeptical eyes shifted from face to face. "But Kate didn't have any breakfast. Because of me."

Kate felt tears well in her eyes. "It's okay, Way-Ray." She patted her hip. "I need to lose a few pounds. I've been eating too many crispy clams and too much tartar sauce lately."

Way-Ray fingered the sheet and then tugged at the nurse's sleeve. "Can you get the doctor now? Can you tell him to take my appendix out real fast?"

The nurse smiled. "As soon as you tell Kate and Maureen to get out so we can get you ready."

Way-Ray released Kate's hand. "Get out," he ordered. Tears glittered in his eyes.

"Yes, sir." Maureen saluted. "Come on, Kate."

"In a second." Kate bent and kissed Way-Ray's forehead. His skin tasted of sweat and fear, salty and acidic. "See you in a bit."

"What you said." His voice quavered and he blinked. "No eating or you'll be in big trouble."

"I'll remember." She turned before he could see her tears and bolted through the swinging doors.

"Here." Maureen pressed a tissue into her hand. "Let's get some coffee."

Kate wiped her eyes and blew her nose. "I didn't want to lie about his mother."

"I know." Maureen shrugged and laid a hand on Kate's shoulder. "But I didn't see that you had a choice." Her voice was placid. "When my kids were young, I thought of white lies as a way to protect and guide them until they could understand the complexities of reality."

Kate tried to remember if her parents ever lied to her. Probably not. They took evasive action—changed the subject or closed the discussion—but if they were pressed, they never masked the truth. She once overheard a neighbor describe her mother as tactless and her father as honest to the point of pain. She brushed Maureen's hand aside. "That wasn't a white lie."

"Then call it an expedient lie."

"It's still not right. No matter what you call it."

Maureen turned to face her at the second set of doors. "Dumping the truth on him might make you feel virtuous," she hissed, "but it won't help him recover."

"I don't want to hurt him," she protested. "It just . . . feels like I'm playing god."

"Listen!" Maureen gripped Kate's wrists. "You're between a philosophical rock and an ethical hard place. If it feels better, call it story-telling. You did fine with that tall tale about buzzard ice cream."

"That was different." Kate remembered when they started the buzzard joke in Grassy Ridge, when they decided that if it made you laugh, it wasn't a lie. "He knew that was a joke. He was in on it."

"He may be in on this, too. Children know a lot more than we give them credit for. I'll bet he doesn't believe that no one can eat until he's out of surgery. And he may suspect that you couldn't reach his mother." She pushed through the doors. "Let's get that coffee. Then I've got work to do."

Behind the tall counter, Maureen filled two cups. Kate accepted one and added powdered creamer while Maureen poured three sugar packets into the second and stirred with what looked like a tongue depressor. "You'll know when he's ready for the truth." She sipped and added more sugar. "In the meantime, you better find a place to stay for a few days."

Kate remembered all the No Vacancy signs lit up in red neon, the carloads of tourists she'd seen turned away after she and Way-Ray checked into their room. Had that been just yesterday?

"He's going to need a place to rest—a place with a TV and DVD player for sure. He'll get bored and whiny. And when he gets his energy back, I expect he'll be a real trial." She chuckled, then grew serious. "I overheard that phone call. If you need help, let me know and I'll see what I can do."

"Thank you." Kate touched the soft, cool skin above her elbow.

"No sweat." A phone rang and Maureen spun away. "Go get that form filled in as best you can."

Kate turned and trudged toward the paper with its demanding questions and the spaces as devoid of certainty as her future.

# CHAPTER 10

Kate shifted in the flimsy metal chair beside the hospital bed, watching through the rails as Way-Ray's narrow chest rose and fell beneath the sheet tucked tight across it. His hands lay limp at his sides, his fingers furled like the fern fronds growing in the shadows beneath the looming trees on the trail to the lighthouse. A bubble of spit formed between his slack lips, expanded, then broke with a soft "pwopf."

He should be awake by now. Really awake, not dream-talking with unfocused eyes—telling her about riding horses in the waves and making a roller coaster run backwards by saying magic words.

She uncrossed her legs, searching for a comfortable spot on lumpy padding that seemed to slide beneath its plastic cover like a pat of butter on warm toast. Way-Ray's chest rose and fell. The sluggish rhythm was torturous. Her breathing fell into sync and she felt lightheaded.

She stood, pushing the chair aside with a soft squealing protest—rusted casters grinding on aging linoleum—and inched around the bed to the paltry window overlooking a carpet business. She watched a bandy-legged man wrestle a thick roll into his pickup and rope it down. Another job she wouldn't want. She paced back past the door to the stark bathroom and into the corridor where a stooped woman with a hairnet pushed a rolling set of shelves stacked with covered trays. Kate smelled coffee, roasted chicken, and the scorched odor of gravy too long in the pan. Lunch. But not for Way-Ray. He had a needle in the crook of his arm and a tube that delivered clear liquid. When Kate asked how long it would be until he could eat real food the nurse said, "That all depends."

Maureen used the same words about insurance, citing programs, plans, and policies, rules and exceptions, black, white, and enormous gray areas. She promised to look into things, saying she knew the ropes and it would take her far less time than it would for "a virgin."

She muttered out of the side of her mouth as she dug out more forms. "It's shameful. Rich country like this." Then she cautioned Kate against being too eager to take financial responsibility. "The mother disappeared without a word to you or her lawyer? Only a sadistic bureaucrat would expect you to foot the bill." She cut her eyes left and right as if some of those very bureaucrats were lurking beside her desk. "Don't volunteer. Pay only if they hunt you down, tie you up, and pound toothpicks under your fingernails."

Kate winced and linked her hands behind her back. Taking responsibility before it was thrust upon her had been the way of her life. Saint Kate the Trustworthy. She didn't want to be accused of milking the system. Daltons paid their own way. Even if it broke them.

Shoving her fingers deep into her hair, she tugged it into tufts. What she needed most was time out. Time when she didn't feel pulled in a dozen directions by stampeding buffalo. Time for herself.

"Kate?"

The whisper was so soft she dismissed it as hopeful imagination. But when she turned, Way-Ray's eyes were open. He reached toward the bandage that held the needle in place.

She nearly screamed "don't touch that," but bit back the words. Too negative. Too much like the messages of her childhood. Stepping to the bedside, she intercepted his hand with a modified high-five and held it. "Hey, sleepyhead. How are you feeling? Had any more amazing dreams?"

"Uh-huh." His eyes crossed, and then seemed to drift in their sockets, working independently of each other. "I was driving a great big boat out in the ocean and I could see whales and fish and everything." He blinked and tried to untangle his fingers from hers. "What's this thing in my arm?"

She squeezed his squirming fingers, so small, so pale. "That's how you'll eat for a little while."

He squinted at the tube and the plastic sack from which it emerged. "It looks like water."

"Well, it's not. It's special hospital stuff. It's got germ killer and vitamins."

"Oh." He peered at the slow drip of solution. "What does it taste like?"

Kate shrugged. "I don't know." Did anyone? "But I guess it's kind of salty and sweet. You can't taste it though, because you taste with your mouth and your tongue, and this goes right into your blood and then to your arms and legs and head."

He nodded and his eyes drifted again. "It goes in awfully slow."

"Well, they can't put in too much at once."

He chewed his lower lip. "Will my arm explode if they do?"

She laughed, then saw the hurt in his eyes. He was serious. "No. Of course not."

He nodded. "I think my stomach wants real food. Can I have some pizza?"

Kate thought of the nurse's answer to that question. Way-Ray wouldn't settle for "that all depends." She felt ignorant, foolish, and certain he could see through her. "The doctor will check you in the morning," she improvised. "And if he's sure that the hole he made got all closed up so stuff won't fall out, he'll let you have soup and juice. And if that doesn't leak out, and if you don't barf it up, then he'll let you have ice cream and pudding."

He gnawed at his lower lip. "And if that doesn't leak, then I can have pizza?"

"Exactly. But the doctor decides. Okay?"

"I guess." He picked at the sheet where it was folded back across his chest. "Kate? Is my mom almost here?"

Kate's mouth went dry. She glanced toward the window, caught herself, and met his gaze. She knew he'd ask—he *had* to ask—but with each minute he slept, she allowed herself to sink deeper into denial. "I'm not sure." Her tongue felt chalky as it scraped against the roof of her mouth.

"Oh." Way-Ray closed his eyes and rubbed his fingers against the sheet. They made a dusty sound and released a faint scent of disinfectant. "I dreamed about her."

Blinking, Kate bent to smooth an imaginary wrinkle in the sheet. If, as Maureen hinted, he suspected a problem, seeing her cry would create cold certainty. She cleared her throat. "That must have been a nice dream."

Way-Ray kept his eyes closed but gave her a ghost of a smile. "She brought me ice cream." He opened his eyes and turned his head, peering through the railing. "I want to call her."

Kate ducked her head and faked a sneeze to hide another surge of tears.

He pointed to the chipped metal bedside stand cluttered with a water pitcher, plastic cup, box of tissue, and a metal basin shaped like a kidney bean. "Where's the phone?"

"It's broken." Stashed in the closet out of sight. "But your mom's on the way, remember? We have to wait for her to call us."

To her surprise, the lies didn't stick in her throat.

Way-Ray frowned. "Planes go real fast, don't they? Even all the way from Oklahoma, huh?" His voice quavered and his lips quivered.

Had Maureen told Way-Ray that Amanda was flying out? Kate couldn't remember. But he seemed convinced of it, and when Amanda failed to appear tomorrow, he'd be frantic. The moral issue aside, lies led on to more lies, like roads branching off each other and winding into unmapped terrain, crisscrossing until you weren't sure where you'd been, where you were, or if you'd ever get back. "That's right. Planes go faster than the speed of sound. But your mom isn't coming on a plane."

He frowned again. "She's not?"

Kate's mind churned. *Not lying. Storytelling.* "She . . . she couldn't get a ticket because lots of people travel in the summertime. So she's driving, just like we did."

"But driving will take a long time. What about . . . what about me?" He sniffled, shrugged one shoulder up, and wiped his nose on the sheet.

"Well, since you're such a big, brave boy, she knew you'd be fine." Kate laid a hand on his forehead. The skin felt hot, dry, papery. "I know it's not the same, Way-Ray, but I'm here."

He swallowed and wiped his nose against the opposite shoulder. "I know," he whispered.

"And you know I'll take good care of you, don't you? I have so far, right?"

He nodded without looking into her eyes.

"And because you're sick, I'll take extra special care. As soon as you're able to eat ice cream, I'll get a whole bunch."

He chewed at his lip. "With chocolate sauce?"

"You bet. Whipped cream, too. And those bright red cherries to put on the top."

His lips curled into a faint smile, but in a few seconds they quivered again and he tugged the sheet loose. "I don't like this hospital. It smells like stuff my mom uses when she washes the windows. Do I have to stay here for a long time?"

"No. Just until tomorrow morning. Then we'll go someplace where you can rest and get better."

"Where?"

Kate clenched her teeth. Another question she couldn't answer. "I'm going to find a place with a nice soft bed and a big comfortable chair and a TV and a DVD so you can watch movies, and a freezer where we can keep all the ice cream."

A spark flashed across his eyes. "By the ocean?"

Would he understand about vacancies and reservations and tourist season? "Well, I—"

"Where we stayed before, okay? I want to look for another whale. Did you tell my mom I saw a whale? And that I went up by the light in the lighthouse and everything?" Way-Ray's voice trailed off. His eyes drooped, but after a moment he opened them wide. "Kate?"

She squeezed his chilly fingers. "What?"

"Will my mom be able to find me when she gets here?"

Kate felt heartsick, enraged, powerless. "Sure she will."

He pulled his hand from hers and picked at the sheet again. "But what if she doesn't come until after I get out of the hospital?"

"She'll find you."

His eyelids drifted closed and for a long moment he was silent. "How?" His lips barely moved.

How did mothers cope with such constant questioning? "I'll leave a note here at the hospital."

He bunched the sheet in his fists. "What if somebody loses the note?"

"Oh, sweetie." Kate brushed his hair back from his forehead. His skin, dry a moment earlier, now felt spongy, clammy. Should she call a nurse? "Nobody will lose the note. And even if a big wind comes and blows it away, she'll find you."

"How?"

"I don't know how." She bent and kissed his forehead, tasting rubbing alcohol, uneasy sleep, and anxious fear. This was the bitter skin of an old man, not of a boy sweet from buttery sunlight, salty sweat, and warm wind. "I just know that a mother has a way of finding her children, no matter what."

Unless that mother didn't intend to look.

# CHAPTER 11

By the time she reached Castaway Beach, Kate felt, as the plumber who'd made repairs at the shelter used to say, "lower than day-old whale shit." It was only two and every motel she'd passed had its "No Vacancy" sign lit. The Wade in the Waves Motel was no exception, but Kate turned down the narrow street and bumped across the railroad tracks. Perhaps the motel would have an empty room tomorrow. Crossing her fingers, she traversed a constricted, pot-holed alley, eased along the side of the motel, and parked in one of two empty spaces on the broad gravel lot between the L-shaped motel and the grass-covered dune.

As she opened the door, a police car shot into the space beside her and an officer vaulted out. He appeared barely old enough for a legal drink, with a buzz cut, freckles, bulky shoulders, and biceps that threatened to split his sleeves. He hitched at a wide belt and strode toward the office. Had someone presented a stolen credit card or a bounced check? Could that create space for her? Feeling a guilty optimism, Kate trailed him to the corner of the L where a second-floor deck linked the two buildings.

"You can't prove anything," a woman yelled.

Kate recognized the voice—the surly manager who'd recited the litany of rules. Stepping into the deep shadow of the deck beside the laundry room, Kate watched the manager level her index finger like a revolver at two men and a prim woman with short, highlighted hair and a beige pantsuit. "You can't prove I didn't sign guests in right. You can't prove I stole money." She aimed the finger at the cop. "They're trying to ruin my reputation. I'll sue them for the deed to this dump."

The two men glanced at each other. One shook his head slightly and both inched backward, using their companion as a shield. She remained toe-to-toe with the seething manager. "You just do that. We have the right to hire and fire managers, and we won't be blackmailed."

"Blackmail?" the manager screeched. She spun toward the cop. "Did you hear that? Did you hear what she accused me of?"

The cop held up his hands and said something Kate couldn't hear. A stringy man with a cap pulled low across a jutting ridge of brow emerged from the office carrying a cardboard box overflowing with limp T-shirts. He stowed it in the back of a rust-riddled green van, glared at the owners, and patted the manager's butt as he passed.

"Everything she told you is bullshit," the manager protested to the cop. "She's a frickin' liar."

Kate knew she should walk away, but the minidrama held her, distracted her.

The cop patted the air. "Calm down, Belinda," he said. "Be civilized."

"I'll show you civilized!" The manager flung another string of invectives. The stringy man shuttled another box into the van and, before slouching back into the office, spat at the owners' feet. The larger of the men side-stepped. The woman didn't flinch.

Kate heard light footsteps behind her and turned to see a lanky woman emerge from the laundry room. She had thick black hair pinned into a loose knot on top of her head. Her face was tanned, weathered, and completely without makeup. She wore a yellow T-shirt and frayed jeans covered by a blue smock with enormous pockets. A plastic nametag pinned to the shoulder of the smock read Rhea Whitaker, Head Housekeeper.

Rhea leaned against one of the deck supports, drew a crumpled pack from one capacious pocket, and fished out a cigarette. Kate took a step back. Rhea flicked a match, fired up, and exhaled a cloud of smoke. "Of course she shorted the till." She nodded to Kate. "I saw her do that with the room you rented."

Kate remembered the deep discount for paying cash. "Did *you* report her to the police?"

"Me?" Rhea puffed in another lungful of smoke, turned her head and blew twin streams of vapor out through her nose. "No. The owners must have figured it out somehow." She pointed her chin toward the three people confronting Belinda. "They sent her a registered letter last week. Told her to be out by noon today. Too bad she won't go to jail like she deserves."

Kate felt a bud of anger behind her eyes. "Why won't she?"

"There's knowing." Rhea blew smoke. "And then there's proving."

"But you said you saw her take my money." Kate nodded toward the owners. "Tell them!"

Rhea put a hand on her arm. "Think a minute. That's one mean woman and one nasty excuse for a man."

Kate studied him as he loaded another carton into the van. He seemed to sense her scrutiny and, dumping the carton, shoved his hat back on his forehead and stared at her with icy blue, unblinking eyes, stared as if memorizing every pore in her skin. Kate dropped her gaze.

"See what I mean? Evil-nasty. Best not to get too close." Rhea snorted smoke. "You back here looking for another room?"

"Yes. My . . ." Kate paused, wondering how to explain her relationship to Way-Ray, deciding to skim past that. "Way-Ray had to have his appendix out. He's in the hospital." Sleeping, she hoped. Before she left he tried to prove that he was well

88

enough to get to the bathroom by himself. A nurse had activated the bed alarm. "We need a place to stay while he recovers."

"Doubt we have any vacancies." Rhea blew a smoke ring. "But who knows? Belinda may have been holding rooms empty to pad her paycheck. As soon as she and Stan take off, I'll check the reservation book." She nodded toward the owners standing up to Belinda. "Nadine's the president of the condo association. The big guy's the vice president. The shrimp's the treasurer. Nadine and the relief manager—that would be me—will be running the place until they find a new manager. Not easy to do this time of year."

She bent, stubbed out her cigarette where concrete walk met gravel, and tossed the butt into a nearby trash container. "Or any other time. Job doesn't pay a whole lot, but they expect you to be on-site 24/7, so you get an apartment and utilities." She fiddled with the hairpins securing the knot of hair on top of her head. "Maybe you should apply."

"Me?" Kate laughed. "I don't know anything about managing a motel. Why don't you do it?"

"Because I've got two boys, a husband with a full-time business, and a sickly mother-in-law at home." Rhea counted off on her fingers, studied her thumb and added, "And a dog with a deviant personality. Eats underwear if you leave it on the floor. Which of course the boys do almost every flippin' day." She sighed. "I work here just to have some time to myself and a place I can smoke in peace. If I tried to get out more than thirty hours a week they'd hunt me down and drag me back by my hair."

Kate smiled at the image of four people and a deviant dog hauling Rhea home.

"I'm gonna get a lawyer," Belinda screeched. "Don't think I won't." She threw herself into the van beside Stan, slammed the door, and shrieked out the open window. "You'll be sorry. I'm gonna sue you for more than this shithouse is worth."

Stan fired up the engine. The van's wheels whined, spun, caught. Belinda flipped the bird and the van roared into the alley, its churning wheels pelting the owners and the cop with sand and small stones.

"She does know how to make an exit," Rhea observed. "So, you want the job or not?"

"I don't—"

"You'd be good at it."

Kate analyzed her voice for sarcasm, studied her face for any trace of a smile. "How do you know that? You don't even know my name."

"Kate Dalton."

Kate blinked.

Rhea shrugged. "It was in a book you left. I checked the registration card—thought I might send it to you—but you didn't give an address." She lifted a hand to the cop as he passed on his way to his cruiser. "Hey Curtis, how're you doing?"

He jerked a thumb over his shoulder, and grimaced. "Yeah, good riddance," Rhea agreed. She turned back to Kate. "Do you want the job or not? $1500 a month, plus a gas allowance."

A place right on the beach, Kate thought. An income—not much, but enough to buy groceries and clothes for Way-Ray.

Rhea cocked her head. "I'll tell them you're interested in taking it until they find someone." She rolled her eyes toward the owners. "Listen, they've only got ten units here, but they have the deluded idea they need a couple to run the place, even though they got me and Jackson. Jackson Scovell. He's the handyman. Only some days he's not too handy. He's bad to drink."

She sighed and fiddled with her topknot again. "Can't really blame him, though, considering what he's been through. Anyway, I'll tell them you're a working fool. A perfectionist." She tucked in a few rogue strands. "The kid would be a deal-breaker, though. Don't mention him."

Kate's squared her shoulders. "I can't lie about—"

"Don't lie. Just finesse it."

Finesse it? Before Kate could protest, Rhea strode toward the owners, who had brushed off their clothing and were milling by the office door as if reluctant to enter. Rhea herded them inside and Kate felt her stomach tighten. Allowing Rhea to pitch her for this job was irresponsible.

She strode across the parking lot and through the sea grass to the top of the dune. The wind was calm, the tide at a low ebb, the ocean almost placid. Waves built, toppled, and curled gently, then lapped at the sand like cats before slinking away. A pair of huge rocks offshore wore ballerina skirts of mist. A boat balanced on the thin line of horizon. She balanced on the edge of—

The old Kate Dalton wouldn't spontaneously apply for a job like this. When she stepped outside the shelter, had another Kate emerged from the cocoon of the past, a Kate who was far less rigid, far more adaptable, and if not ready, then at least willing to attempt to go with the flow? She'd set off without knowing where she was going, acquired a nine-year-old boy before she went five hundred miles, and saw him through an appendectomy. Why couldn't she run a motel? Why shouldn't she?

A shred of sound fluttered on the breeze. "Hey! Kate! Kate!" She turned to see Rhea in the center of the parking lot, waving her arms.

Kate took a long breath to calm the fluttering in her stomach and trudged toward her future, ignoring stiff blades of grass that sawed at her ankles and sand that sucked at her shoes as if trying to hold her back. She glanced at her grubby running shoes, jeans, and T-shirt. She'd packed two suits in a box wedged behind the passenger seat. She could shake out the wrinkles, unearth the heels that might be in the large suitcase beside the spare tire, and—

"Get a move on," Rhea called. "I've got three rooms to clean before the next crop of inconsiderate tourists arrives."

Kate grinned and broke into a jog, skidding on the slope, shoes filling with sand. The new Kate didn't dress for interviews. The new Kate was all about "what you see is what you get" and taking chances. She leaped a shallow drainage ditch, landed in deep gravel, and went to one knee.

"Watch it," Rhea cautioned. "The owners hate it when they have to dust off their liability insurance policy." She took Kate's arm and marched her to the office. Kate felt as if she'd been swept up by a tsunami. "You don't happen to have a resume, do you?"

"Yes."

"Good." Rhea made a left turn to the SUV. "Nadine loves resumes. She checks them for spelling errors. Hope you don't have any."

"I don't." The resume was the work of the old Kate.

"Then you're practically hired. Hey, I forgot to ask you what you did BC."

"BC?"

"Before you came to the coast. BC." Rhea sighed as if Kate disappointed her. "It's a different world here. Anyway I told Nadine you were a friend of a friend and made up some vague stuff about management and organizational skills."

A friend of a friend? Was she the only person in this different world committed to the truth?

"Don't get your undies in a bunch." Rhea turned at the sound of wheels on gravel and waved to the two male owners as they drove off in an ancient, sun-bleached Volvo. "I don't think she was listening, anyway. Nadine's like that. Don't take it personally."

Kate excavated a leather briefcase from a slim space beside the spare tire. She opened it and drew out three pages in a clear plastic binder. "Look, maybe this isn't such a good—"

"There you are," a woman's voice said. Kate turned, clutching the resume to her chest. Nadine patted her hair with a thick-knuckled hand; crimson faux nails winked in the sunlight. "Rhea's told me wonderful things about you."

Rhea smirked at Kate and plucked the resume from her fingers. "Here's her resume. I'm going to get those rooms ready." She smirked again and hustled off, smock flapping.

"Thank you, Rhea." Nadine lifted the rhinestone-studded reading glasses swinging from a gold chain around her neck and anchored them on her nose. "Hmmm. Managed a domestic violence shelter, applied for grants, and assisted the board in budgeting." She flipped to the second page. "Impressive. Hmmm. Very impressive." She removed the reading glasses and fixed a pair of intense brown eyes on Kate. "Why would you want a job like this?"

Kate blinked. *This is the interview.* She cleared her throat. "As you can see, I've lived and worked in a number of regions of the country, and in Africa—I guess you could call that my way of sightseeing." She paused to allow Nadine to smile or comment, but the woman's lips didn't twitch. "I've been traveling for the past two weeks, trying to decide where I'd like to live next. I need a change of scenery and this place has plenty." She flipped a hand at the dune and the ocean booming beyond it. Casual. Collected.

"Hmmm." Nadine snapped the reading glasses to her nose again and studied the resume. "Why did you leave your position at the shelter?"

An image of Emory McCoy flashed before Kate's eyes. He wore a self-satisfied smile and seemed to be mouthing the word "gotcha." She clenched her fists. "I felt that I accomplished all of the goals I set for myself and, to be frank, I needed a break from the stress and responsibility."

Nadine furrowed her brow and pursed her lips.

*Wrong answer. Salvage time.* "Don't get me wrong. I don't think this job would be a cakewalk. I'm sure there are budgetary concerns and deadlines, and I know your guests have needs and demands. But they aren't running from abusive relationships and don't need a range of social services."

Nadine nodded and viewed Kate over the top of her reading glasses. "There's a tremendous amount of responsibility

93

involved in this job. You'd be taking reservations, handling cash and credit card receipts, making bank deposits, accounting for room occupancy, and sending weekly reports to me as well as to our bookkeeper. You'd be supervising the housekeepers and the man who does the maintenance and yard work. You'd be responsible for washing all the linens and sweeping the decks and patios." She shook her head. "Our policy has always been to hire a couple. I simply don't think that one person could handle it." She shook her head again and thrust the resume at Kate. "We've always hired couples."

Kate kept her hands at her sides, refusing to accept both the papers and the negative response. She wasn't sure whether she wanted this job, but she knew she wanted the choice to be hers. "Your policy makes sense. But there are ways to work it out so that everything gets done to your satisfaction—without spending more money."

Nadine narrowed her eyes. "For example?"

"Well, I don't know how long it takes to do the laundry, but if I couldn't manage, then perhaps you could pay me a little less and put the difference into extra hours for the housekeepers."

Nadine considered. Her lips pushed in and out and her fingers twisted the chain that held her glasses. "We paid the last couple $1500 a month. Would you work for $1350 if you didn't do laundry?"

Kate did the math. $16,200 a year. A financial joke. But with an apartment and utilities provided.

"There's a gas allowance," Nadine added. "And you don't have to worry about paper towels and toilet paper—we buy that in bulk and you use what you need. And there's cable in your unit."

The balance of power had shifted. Nadine was wooing her. Kate tried not to let the knowledge show on her face.

"We don't mind if you use the motel phone some—as long as your charges are reasonable. And of course you may use the motel washers and dryers and our sheets and towels, unless you prefer your own." Nadine turned and marched toward the office.

"Why don't your take a look at the apartment? It's furnished with the essentials."

Furnished! Even if the furniture was beat up—and having seen Stan and Belinda, she was sure it would be—that would save hundreds of dollars.

Nadine opened the office door and led Kate through a gate beside the desk, past a computer, printer and fax, and into a large room that appeared to be part kitchen, part den, and part storage area. The countertops were covered with dirty dishes, crusted pots, and greasy pans. A few flies lifted off, smacked against the window, buzzed, circled, and settled back. The carpet was littered with scraps of paper, beer cans, and crushed potato chips. The linoleum was dark with grime. "The downstairs isn't much," Nadine said, "and the former managers left it a wreck. I'll ask Rhea to have one of the housekeepers get to work in here. You can call the carpet-cleaning service." She nodded over her shoulder toward the office. "The number's in the file. We run an account with them."

She took a few steps toward a half-open door through which Kate spotted a cramped bathroom, the corners packed with discarded towels, the sink gray with soap scum, the toilet speckled with substances Kate didn't want to dwell on. The odors of mildew and urine were palpable.

Nadine waved her hand in front of her face and backed away. "There's a three-quarter bath down here. Rhea will see that it gets cleaned. It needs painting if you're interested in making a little extra money. And there are two bedrooms and a full bath upstairs." She gestured to a narrow staircase that divided the living area from ranks of storage shelves. "The larger bedroom has a private deck. It's small, but it faces south. Go on up and take a look. I apologize in advance for the mess I'm sure they left."

She waved her hand in front of her face again and fixed her eyes on Kate. "There are a lot of things a resume won't reveal, and no one brings up their faults during a job interview."

Kate fought a chill, nodded with what she hoped was an expression of sympathy, and climbed the stairs. Just look. Don't let yourself want this.

But when she reached the top of the stairs, her good intentions vanished. She saw past the filthy carpet, the discarded shoes and stained underwear, the rumpled bed and gouged, cigarette-scorched nightstand. She saw the view framed in the smudged glass of the sliding door: looming rocks, white-crested waves, honey-colored sand, and a tribe of children in red and blue bathing suits rushing in and out of the surf. She hurried to the door, opened it, and walked onto the deck. She'd put plants out here and a wind chime. Way-Ray would line the railings with the rocks and shells he collected.

"I'll have Rhea get these rooms cleaned," Nadine said.

Kate turned and saw her lift her upper lip in disgust. "You'll want to toss out those blankets and pillows and get fresh ones. Mattress pads, too. There are spares in the laundry room." She tapped Kate's resume. "I think I can persuade the other owners to give you a try. Would you be able to start today?"

"Today?" Kate echoed.

"Tomorrow then." Nadine tapped the resume once more. "Unless there's something else we should know."

# CHAPTER 12

Kate's palms grew clammy. Rhea had warned her not to mention Way-Ray, but if she said nothing, how would she explain if Nadine learned the truth later? She wiped her hands on her jeans.

"All right, then. Let's go fill out the paperwork so I can beat the traffic getting back." Nadine snorted and rolled her eyes. "Not that there's any way to avoid that snarl short of chartering a plane."

Kate felt a sizzle of hope deep in her chest. Nadine was in a hurry. She might bend policy once more. After all, Way-Ray wouldn't need constant supervision. Kate turned from the window, dry swallowed, and sucked in a breath. "I have—"

Nadine waved her off. "Questions. Of course. I'd worry if you didn't." She started down the stairs, talking over her shoulder. "I'm sure Rhea can answer them. She knows more about how this place is run—how it *should* be run—than I do. She'll work alongside you until you get the hang of it."

Kate opened her mouth again, thought about Way-Ray in his hospital bed, gazed once more at the view, and then followed Nadine. She'd do what must be done today, and think about the rest tomorrow. Right now she had to get her hands on a vacuum, a mop, and about a dozen giant-sized trash bags.

\* \* \* \* \*

Kate glanced at a moon-shaped clock as she plumped fat pillows and smoothed a royal blue bedspread with gold stars and silver comets. "We made it with time to spare." She stepped back to admire the effect. "What do you think?"

"I think I'm exhausted." Rhea leaned against the wall, jammed one hand into her smock pocket, and then drew it back as if she'd been stung by a scorpion. The Wade in the Waves Motel had a strict no smoking policy and Rhea adhered to it, but her definition of "outside" often put her just inches from doors and windows. Did guests ever complain? Had former managers? "I'm too old for this late-night, early-morning, nonstop cleaning," she sighed. "But I have to say that you worked a hundred-dollar miracle."

More than a hundred. Kate glanced at the games, magazines and books stacked in the bookcase she'd managed to assemble, despite a sheet of instructions meant only for consumers in Japan. Her eyes shifted to the dresser drawers where she'd stacked fresh underwear, socks, T-shirts, and shorts. When Way-Ray felt stronger, they'd get shoes and jeans.

Rhea seemed to read her mind. "More like five hundred. That spaceship lamp there runs thirty-nine bucks, at least. And all that matching stuff in the bathroom doesn't come cheap."

Kate grinned. Never in her life had she allowed herself such a shopping spree. She always purchased what she needed—not what she wanted. She bought good quality, but never anything showy or fancy, and she'd never been interested in decorating themes and coordinating patterns. That was the legacy of parents who had stocked their home with sturdy wooden furniture, long-wearing carpets, and dark curtains with obscure patterns that wouldn't show dirt.

Kate tweaked the bedspread tighter across the pillows. Her bedroom was furnished with odds and ends Rhea had unearthed from a storeroom. The bed was made up with standard motel sheets and a frayed comforter. Utilitarian, practical, boring. This room was none of the above. In a few days, when they both settled into a routine, she'd paint the walls—maybe in stripes and swirls—and attach plastic stars and planets that glowed in the dark.

Her hands clenched on the spread. None of that could make up for being abandoned. How would Way-Ray react as the days stretched on and he realized he might never see Amanda again?

Rhea laid a hand on her arm. "He's lucky to have you."

Kate nodded, knowing that would be no consolation.

"You ever thought of having kids of your own?"

"Uh . . ." Kate ducked her head, avoiding Rhea's probing brown eyes. In the past, she had often answered this unwelcome question with one of her own: "You ever thought of minding your own business?" Now she bit her tongue. She had to work with Rhea, needed her guidance.

"You've got good instincts," Rhea continued as if there'd been no gap in the conversation. "You're willing to put the kid first."

But maternal instinct could be derailed. Kate had heard women at the shelter confess to horrible transgressions against their children. Sucking in a breath, she tried to keep sarcasm out of her voice, but didn't succeed. "Are you basing that character analysis on my decision to give him the large bedroom?"

"While you sleep in a closet?" Rhea shrugged and raised her palms. "Lots of women wouldn't do that for their own kids, let alone for a nephew."

Kate started at the last word and reminded herself that she'd claimed to be caring for him while her sister got her life back together. Yet another lie. She'd soon need a cross-reference system.

"Maybe it's good you're not married." Rhea patted her smock pocket as if reassuring herself that tobacco and nicotine were within her grasp. "Husbands have a way of wanting to come first. My granny said men are just tall children."

Kate smiled. What would a husband have said about her working at the shelter? About stepping out to confront Wayne

Jessop? She imagined endless argument, insistence, and recrimination. If she ever had a child of her own—and the possibility grew more remote every day—it would be by a man who was strong enough to give up power and control, who would do the right thing naturally and spontaneously. Were there such creatures?

"Hey." Rhea pinched her arm. "You've got to get to the hospital. And I've got rooms to clean. Six guests going out this morning and six coming in this afternoon." She patted the cordless phone clipped to her smock. "Plus the damn phone will ring all day with fools who waited until the last minute to book a full week and have the nerve to ask me, 'Is it always this full in the summer?' She rolled her eyes. "No, summer's our slow season. Arghh!"

"I'll be back as fast as I can."

Rhea waved that off. "The extra hours I'll claim will be my revenge. I warned Nadine that Belinda was a grade A skank." She chuckled. "But, hey, it's your ass she'll chew when she gets my bill."

Kate blinked. "Mine?"

"It's your job to keep a lid on expenses." Rhea yanked the cigarette pack from her pocket. "Better buy yourself a set of cast iron shorts while you're in town."

Kate tried to laugh and got only a nervous explosion of air. What had she gotten into?

\* \* \* \* \*

When Kate peered into his room, she spotted Way-Ray perched on the edge of the bed, dressed in another outfit she'd purchased yesterday: a white T-shirt with a picture of a leaping orca, a pair of khaki shorts with enormous pockets, and dark blue flip-flops. He'd rolled the shirt up at the waist and shoved the elastic waistband of the shorts down. As she watched, he anchored the shirt under his chin and picked at the edge of the bandage.

"Did the doctor say you were allowed to peek under there?"

He flushed, yanked his shirt down, and peered up at her from beneath tangled hair in need of a trim. "You're late, Kate."

She checked her watch. "No I'm not. I'm right on time."

"Let me see." She held out her arm and he studied the watch. "Well, okay, but it feels like late to me. I'm tired of this stupid hospital. I want to go to the place by the ocean."

"Me, too." She sat beside him, thinking that he seemed smaller, thinner, and as pale as the inside of a marshmallow. She'd get him out into the sun and make a batch of oatmeal cookies with nuts and chocolate chips. She laid a tentative hand on his shoulder, feeling the rounded bone close beneath the skin. "Just as soon as they bring the wheelchair up, we'll make like a tree and leave."

"What you said." He giggled, raised his arm to give her a high-five, winced, and lowered it again.

Kate ached for him, longed to take on the pain.

"How come we have to wait for a wheelchair?"

"Hospital rules. They don't want you to fall and end up back in the operating room."

"That's stupid. I'm not a baby. I won't fall down." He splayed a hand across his stomach. Kate got a flash of Amanda clutching her chest, winced.

She squeezed his shoulder. "I know you won't."

"Then let's not wait. Let's go now." He squirmed from beneath her hand and slumped over onto his side, legs stretched toward the floor, tongue clamped between his teeth in concentration.

Kate gripped the back of his shirt, bunching it in her fingers. "No, Way-Ray." She drew him against her side. "We have to follow the rules."

"Why? They're stupid." He slapped at the bed with both hands. "Like when they said you couldn't eat until they were done operating." He glared at her accusingly. "You don't like stupid rules, either. You argued with the woman at that sandwich shop who said you couldn't have tuna fish on that curvy roll thing with the funny name because that was only for breakfast and tuna fish was for lunch."

Trapped. And for wanting tuna on a croissant at a chain sandwich shop with Draconian regulations governing a marriage of bread and fish. She allowed herself a limited sigh. If she was going to function as a guardian and not simply a friend, she'd have to lead by example and, obviously, be more careful about expressing opinions. An ironic glitch in the karmic justice system. Hadn't she been due more freedom of speech when she walked out on Emory McCoy?

"You argued," Way-Ray insisted. "I heard you."

"You're right, I did. I guess . . . um . . . sometimes it seems like people make rules just because they can. But most of the time, they make rules for good reasons." Kate paused, remembering the one she broke at the shelter, dreading the day he'd learn about that. "Rules can keep us from getting hurt. And we ought to—"

"Someone in here need a wheelchair?"

Kate looked up to see a man with a grizzled beard and mustache and a gray ponytail tied with a piece of red yarn. The shirt of his purple scrubs stretched tight across his belly and the pants bagged over dirty-white rubber-soled shoes, frayed hems dragging on the linoleum. "Someone getting out?"

"Me!" Way-Ray shouted. "Me! Me!"

The orderly grinned, his blue eyes twinkling. "Not too anxious to leave us, are you?" He rolled the chair beside the bed.

"I hate this place," Way-Ray told him. "All they do is stick me with needles and all I got to eat was soupy stuff." He wiggled from beneath Kate's arm and flopped to his side again.

"I got him." The orderly winked at Kate. "Soupy stuff, huh?" He grasped Way-Ray's arms and helped him slide from the bed. "I kind of like soupy stuff myself, but only with crackers. I'll bet you didn't get any crackers, did you?"

"Not even one." Way-Ray settled into the chair, fingering the wheels.

"Hands off the wheels or we're staying here." The orderly nodded at Kate as Way-Ray obeyed. "No crackers. What a rip-off."

"What you said," Way-Ray crowed. He patted the padded arms of the chair. "How fast can we go?"

"Only as fast as this old Deadhead can ramble." The orderly chuckled and took off in a pigeon-toed trot, his ponytail bouncing between his shoulder blades.

Kate glanced around, saw there was nothing she needed to take and nothing she wanted to remember, and then jogged after them. She caught up just as the chrome elevator door slid open. Maureen, in brilliant turquoise scrubs, grinned at them. "Going down?"

"Hey," Way-Ray said, "I know you."

"And I know you, too." Maureen patted his cheek as the orderly rolled him into the elevator and spun him to face the front. "Only the last time I saw you, you had a bad appendix and a high fever."

"*Now* I've got a scar." He pointed at his stomach with obvious pride. Kate stepped in beside him and the door slid closed. "But you can't see it and neither can I 'cause I'm not allowed to take the bandage off and look at it yet. That's one of the rules that isn't stupid," he added with a solemn nod. "Kate says we have to follow those 'cause they keep us safe."

Maureen nodded in return. "I see."

"What about all the other rules?" the Deadhead asked in a voice that grated with sarcasm. "Do we have to follow them?"

Maureen raised an eyebrow. Kate sucked in a sigh.

"Um . . ." Way-Ray rolled his head from shoulder to shoulder. "I guess we have to think about them real hard and decide if they're stupid or not."

"Good plan. But personally, I think—"

"Most rules are there for a good reason." Maureen gave him a frown that would freeze the Mississippi in July. "At least the intention—the idea behind them—is usually good." She patted Way-Ray's cheek again. "But I'm glad you're going to think carefully about *each and every* rule. A lot of people don't think—carefully or otherwise." She cast another glacial glance at the Deadhead. "That's how they get in big trouble."

The Deadhead sucked at his mustache and dropped his chin. Message received. "For you, big trouble means being grounded until you're old enough to vote," he told Way-Ray.

The elevator emitted a sound like a strangling hedgehog and stuttered to a stop. "Nuh-uh," Way-Ray said. "I'm not gonna vote. My mom says voting just encourages the idiots who mess everything up. Whatever that means."

The Deadhead hooted and slapped his thigh. "Good one." He pushed Way-Ray out the door and across a lobby filled with weary plants, overstuffed racks of pamphlets, and swaybacked sofas.

"You're going to have your hands full." Maureen chuckled, then took Kate's arm and lowered her voice. "Hang in there, kiddo. I'll keep my fingers crossed that his mother turns up. And I'll be in touch about the paperwork."

"Come on, Kate," Way-Ray called from outside the front door. "You have to open the door so I can get in."

"I'm coming." Kate offered her hand to Maureen. "Thanks for everything."

"You're welcome. Do the best you can and don't be worrying about whether that's enough." Maureen stepped past the outstretched hand and folded Kate into her arms. She smelled of apple-scented shampoo and rubbing alcohol.

Kate stiffened. She'd never hugged people she barely knew—another trait passed on by her parents. But that was BC. She took a deep breath, threw her arms around Maureen's waist, and returned the hug with force, feeling the solid core of muscle beneath Maureen's extra pounds. "Thanks again."

"Kate! Stop hugging the lady and come on."

"Mr. Impatient demands your attention." Maureen broke the hug. "Who put you in charge?"

"I put myself in charge," Way-Ray responded, pointing at his chest. "Come on, Kate. We gotta go get ice cream and look for whales and . . ." His eyes scrunched up and his voice quavered. "Did you leave a note for my mom? So she can find me?"

Kate glanced at Maureen, got a nod of encouragement. Storytelling. White lies. "I left her a great big note. And a map, too. She'll find you."

# CHAPTER 13

"Want to peel up the bandage and see my scar again?" Way-Ray squirmed among the pillows and tugged at his T-shirt.

"Not right now." Kat set a glass of orange juice on the nightstand. "I've got a pile of laundry to do. Lots of guests are checking out today." Until she got to the point where she could handle office chores without leaning on Rhea, she felt obligated to wrestle with the laundry.

Way-Ray lifted the T-shirt and tucked it beneath his chin. "But it might look different than it did when I woke up. It might be enough better so I can go down to the ocean all by myself."

Kate sat beside him, massaging a mild cramp in her right calf. Two weeks on the road without regular exercise had eroded muscle tone and it felt good to get off her feet after hauling sheets and towels down from the upper rooms. Once she got into the groove, she'd make time to jog, practice her self-defense moves, and get a set of hand weights, too.

Loosening his grip on the T-shirt, she eased it over his bandage. "You know you promised not to go on the beach alone until you learned all the rules about waves," she cautioned, hoping this sounded more like reminding than nagging. "And you can repeat them without stopping to think." *And until I'm convinced you won't blow them off.* "But right now you need to drink some juice and take a nap or you won't be awake to watch a movie after dinner."

"No!" He drummed his heels against the mattress, winced, and kicked again. "I'm not a baby. And besides, naps are boring."

Kate sighed and counted silently to ten. Rebellion was normal. For two days, limited by pain, he'd been cooperative, almost docile. But now he was anxious to resume life at full speed. He'd waged a war of petty demands and arguments since he woke up, complaining that she hadn't bought the correct cereal, the milk tasted funny, the bowl was too small, the chair in the living room felt way too soft and lumpy.

She gave him a toothy smile and hoped he wouldn't detect frustration in her voice, realize he'd driven her to the edge and decide, as kids often did, to push her over. "Naps are when your body heals." She flipped the sheet over him. "I'll bet if you watch for whales," she pointed through the glass doors, "you'll go to sleep without trying. And when you wake up you can have more pizza and ice cream."

He kicked his heels again. "I'm tired of pizza and ice cream."

Kate gritted her teeth. "Then we'll have burgers and fries."

"I'm tired of those, too."

A sigh leaked between her teeth. "Then we'll have crispy clams and peanut butter pie."

His eyes lit up and he started to smile, but then snapped his lips into a taut line. "I still don't want to take a nap. I bet my mom wouldn't make me."

The trump card. "I bet she would." Kate stood, took the remote control from the nightstand, and set it on top of the TV. "I bet she'd make you take twice as many naps as I do."

He shook his head. "Nuh-uh."

She nodded. "Uh-huh."

He shook his head harder and faster. "Nuh-uh-uh." His fine hair whirled like a young tornado, his eyeballs seemed to jiggle, his nose became a blur.

"You're going to get whiplash if you keep doing that."

"What's whiplash?"

"A pain in the neck."

He grinned. "Like me, huh?"

Kate laughed, wondering at what age children developed the ability to step outside themselves and see their behavior as others did. She knew so little and instinct would hardly be enough. Anger flickered at the base of her skull. Damn Amanda. She plucked the binoculars from the dresser and placed them in his hands. "I'll expect a full report on whale activity when I come back. Okay?"

Way-Ray wrinkled his nose, glancing from the window to the TV. "Okay." He jerked the sheet higher and clamped the binoculars to his eyes. Kate scooped up a dirty plate and glass and started for the stairs. "Kate?" His voice was low, nearly a whisper. "Shouldn't my mother be here by now?"

Kate paused, chewing at her lip, grateful that her back was to him. She needed a few more days—time to get organized, to master her job, to . . . find what didn't exist—an easy and painless way to tell him the truth. She turned by inches and kept her voice toneless. "Remember how we looked at the map and decided that when she gets here will depend on which way she's coming?"

He nodded, binoculars bobbing. "But I want her here now."

Kate set the plate and glass on the dresser and dropped to the bed beside him. "I know you do." She riffled his hair; they'd washed it that morning and it was as soft as down.

"I want her to call me." He batted her hand aside.

Kate knitted her fingers together so she wouldn't reach for him again. "Maybe she'll call tonight, just as you finish eating your crispy clams." Anything was possible.

Way-Ray smiled for a few seconds, but then tears glistened in his eyes. He yanked the sheet over his head. "I'm tired." His voice was thick, clotted. "Go wash the towels and stuff and leave me alone."

Wishing she could inoculate him against some of the torment to come, Kate rose, retrieved the dirty plate and glass, and trudged down the stairs.

* * * * *

Fifteen minutes later she'd stuffed all four washers with dirty linens and added bleach, soap, and steaming water. The tiny laundry room echoed with sloshing gasps, groans, and grunts, counterpoint to penetrating metallic scrapings. Each machine had a unique sound, a version of a death rattle. A spray of shrapnel, she imagined, would accompany their ultimate demise. The three massive dryers were no better. Rhea said they were on their last legs. "And those legs are about to break," Kate muttered.

And then what? In the past two days, she learned motel revenues had declined substantially over the winter and the owners had been forced to dip into a contingency fund they'd siphoned from before and never replenished. If there was no money for repairs, would Kate have to lug sheets and towels to the pay machines behind the market, or beat them on the rocks beside the nearest river?

Smiling at that image, she got a clipboard and yellow pad and set to work making an inventory of cleaning supplies stored on listing, lint-crusted shelves above the dryers. There wasn't much. Another sign of belt-tightening? Or had the departed managers sold the supplies to pad their salaries?

"I need money."

The voice was solemn and so low Kate barely heard it over the complaining washers.

"Money for gas."

She spun to see a dark and rangy mutt of a man slouching in the doorway. His hands were shoved deep into the pockets of greasy jeans, his faded plaid flannel shirt was rumpled and stained, and his gray eyes were half closed. Despite that, Kate could almost feel them piercing her skin. She clutched the clipboard to her chest. "Excuse me."

"Gas," he repeated in a near whisper. Only his lips moved. He stepped into the room and slouched again, this time against shelves jammed haphazardly with stacks of clean sheets and towels, extra pillows, paper towels, and toilet paper.

One part of Kate's mind cataloged that disorder as she stared at him. Was he homeless, a passing tramp? Should she give him a few dollars or turn him away? Which choice involved less danger?

"Gas money." He slid his right hand from his pocket and thrust it toward her. A jagged scar the color of raw liver cut across his palm from the base of his thumb to the stub of little finger.

Kate recoiled, clipboard clutched tighter, heart pounding. Hemmed in by washers and dryers. No way out.

Rhea appeared in the doorway, wadded sheets under one arm, a glowing cigarette in her hand. She glared at the man. "I told you not to bug her." She took a drag, ground the butt out on the sidewalk, and tossed the sheets into a mangled pile at Kate's feet. "You never listen, do you, Jackson?"

Kate felt her shoulders sag with relief. Jackson. The handyman. He didn't acknowledge Rhea, but slid his hand back into his pocket.

"Those scorpions cleaned out the petty cash drawer," Rhea explained. "The lawnmower's running on fumes."

Kate allowed herself a deep breath and studied Jackson, remembering Rhea saying that he was bad to drink. She patted the pocket of her jeans where she'd stuffed change after an early morning run for a quart of milk. "I've got three dollars here. Will that do?"

Rhea held up a hand. "Don't be too hasty to ante up your funds."

"Bad habit." Jackson's lips barely moved.

"Sometimes you don't get paid back for a month or more," Rhea added. "The bookkeeper's a hundred miles away and when it comes to money going out, Nadine's in no hurry to sign checks."

Kate shrugged. Although her parents had referred to it as being thrifty, she felt quibbling about small change was mean-spirited. "Can't we charge the gas?"

Rhea shook her head. "No credit card."

Jackson grunted again. "No credit."

"Bills didn't get paid anywhere near on time over the winter," Rhea said.

"Well, if I don't pay for it, how do we get gas? Siphon it from a guest's car?"

Jackson cocked his head, apparently considering. Rhea reached for her cigarettes but snatched her hand back as if she'd been scorched. "I guess you'll have to—"

"I'll get it," Jackson said.

"With what?" Rhea anchored her fists on her hips. "You've been on a binge for two weeks. How the hell are you going to buy gas?"

A flush darkened Jackson's bronze skin. "Don't need much," he muttered, eyes on the floor. He nodded to Kate without raising his eyes. "Sorry to bother you. Good luck with the job." Pushing past Rhea, he set off across the parking lot, his left leg swinging in a wide arc with each step. Kate was reminded of a geometry-class compass and of a poem she'd read using that image to describe a pair of lovers. She almost laughed at the idea of a drunk like Jackson having a lover.

Rhea reached for her cigarettes, tore one from the pack, jammed it between her lips, and felt her pockets for her lighter as she backed through the doorway. Six inches beyond the threshold she lit up, standing firmly on the letter of the no smoking rule. "He gets spells where he crawls up inside a bottle and stays there until he runs out of money."

That explained the length of the grass and the state of the shrubbery. "Why doesn't—?"

"Jackson doesn't do much of a job." Rhea breathed out a wreath of smoke. "But he's been here for years and he's about the only game in town." She sucked at her cigarette like a woman who found water in the desert. "You'll get used to him."

Kate shook her head. Her job would be tough enough without dragging dead weight. There had to be others who knew basic plumbing and carpentry. Maybe a high school student could mow and trim.

Rhea blew a series of rings. "Look all you want, but you won't find anyone. At least not anyone reliable."

Kate felt a harsh laugh rip from her throat. "Jackson's reliable?"

Rhea shrugged. "When he's sober. And he'll be that way for a few weeks now. He'll work hard."

Kate shook her head. "Until he starts to drink again." Her words were edged with disgust and contempt. Saint Kate the Disciplined.

"Nobody's perfect." Rhea's tone was matter-of-fact. "Guess I might do the same if I hurt inside and out the way he does."

Kate recalled that left leg, swinging as if it had been fused at the knee and ankle. "What happened to him?" She cringed inwardly, could almost hear her mother lecturing about prying.

If Rhea had gotten similar lectures, she'd apparently disregarded them. "Logging accident broke his leg in as many places as there are places. Before that, a whole lot of top secret military stuff messed up his head. If he talked about it, he might get past the drinking, but he can't—or won't."

Checkmate. Kate sighed. What kind of a heartless woman would fire a man with that in his backstory? And, she thought selfishly, if Jackson had worked here for years, the owners were aware of his problems. They wouldn't blame her for his shortcomings.

Rhea took a last drag and ground out her cigarette. "He likes you."

"You're joking."

"Or he's gone round the bend." Rhea used a finger to make circles by her head. "He never offered to spend his own money before. Think I'll go mark this day on the calendar." She went off, whistling "Strangers In The Night."

Kate groaned. One of the washers echoed her sentiment and another lurched into its spin cycle, thumping its companions as it coughed water out through a pipe that, in turn, clattered against the concrete wall. She threw open the lid and wrestled sheets into balance—no easy task, they'd tangled themselves like mating snakes. "Come on." She tugged and twisted and, even above the rumble of the other washers, heard a damp ripping sound. "Damn."

"You're not my friend anymore!"

She spun toward the door and saw Way-Ray, one hand tight against his stomach, tears on his cheeks, eyes hot and bright.

"You're not!"

She stepped toward him, one hand stretched toward his forehead. Did he have an infection? "Does your stomach hurt?"

"No!" He swatted at her hand. "I want my mother!" He raised his chin and balled his hands into fists. "Where is she?"

"She's on her way." The lie was automatic.

"I don't believe you." His voice rose to a crackling shout. "You're lying!"

Kate's mouth went dry and her tongue thickened. She clung to the threadbare lie. "She's . . . she's coming to take you back to Grassy Ridge."

"No she's not." He stamped one foot, winced at the pain, and glared at her. "Her phone says she doesn't live in Grassy Ridge anymore."

# CHAPTER 14

Kate sagged against the dryer. She should have known he'd grow impatient and call. Now what? Could she convince him such messages were common when people intended to be gone from home for several weeks? She stretched her hands toward him, fingers trembling. "Sweetie, I—"

He backed away, his eyes dark with pain. "Don't call me that! And don't tell me any more lies, Kate. It's not funny." He stabbed his index finger at her chest. "When it's not funny, then it's a real lie. A bad lie." Tears caught among his eyelashes for a few seconds and then trickled down his cheeks. "You told me that."

Kate nodded, longing to hug him, press him against her chest, inhale the warm scent of his hair and skin. "I remember."

"Where's my mother?" His whisper was barely audible over the washers' mechanical grievances.

Kate knelt before him and hung her head. "I wish I knew."

"You have to know." His voice soared, fractured. "Where is she?"

Did he believe—with the perfect confidence of young children—that adults knew everything? A memory flitted across her mind: walking in a forest with her father, pointing to trees, and asking him to name them. Had he? Or had he changed the subject, perhaps asked her to recite the times table or quizzed her about state capitals?

She shook her head and the memory splintered, vanished. Forcing a factual tone, she addressed the floor. "Nobody knows where she is."

"Not even the guy the phone said to call?"

"Not even him," Kate confirmed, raising her head and meeting his eyes, tearless now, clouded and bewildered. She sucked in a breath, relieved to tell a portion of the truth. "I called him. He doesn't know where she went."

He scowled. "Who is he?"

Kate felt a cool wave of relief. Way-Ray hadn't asked her when she'd called, when she'd first known Amanda was missing. "He's a lawyer."

He chewed his lower lip, tears glazing his eyes again. "But lawyers are for people who get arrested. Did Mom—?"

"No. Of course not."

"Then why does she have a lawyer?"

Dodge one bullet, step in front of another. Kate's mind churned, latched onto one of Amanda's lies, rationalized that it wasn't the same as creating a new one. "Remember how your mom got hurt?"

He nodded. "At the store where she worked."

"Right. Well, the store has to give her some money because it was their fault, and she hired a lawyer to make to sure she gets all she should."

"Oh." His eyes narrowed. "Are you lying again?"

Kate longed to confess. But if Amanda had dodged the repercussions of revealing the truth, why should she take the fall? She shook her head, more at the torturous situation than as an answer.

Way-Ray wiped his nose on the sleeve of his T-shirt. "I'm not supposed to cry," he said, his voice prickling with anger. "My grandma told me I'm too old to cry and I have to be a man and be strong 'cause my mom needs me. Except maybe now she doesn't." He drew in a long and shuddering breath and held it for a few seconds before his face crumpled. "Why did my mom go away? Why doesn't she want anyone to know where she is?"

The cold sickness of uncertainly coiled in the pit of Kate's stomach. "I don't know."

His voice rose to a wail. "Why did she go without me? Why did she leave me all alone?"

"I'm here, Way-Ray. You're not alone."

He stamped his foot again. "Yes I am."

Kate tamped down her frustration. In his world, she didn't count right now. "Way-Ray, even if you don't think much of me, I'm still your friend. I care about you." *More than I ever thought I would.* "I don't know why your Mom disappeared. But I know she loves you. You believe that, don't you?"

His eyes slid to the left, then shifted back. "I guess."

Frustration withered. Kate forced her lips to turn up—not a joyful smile, not a happy smile, but a make-the-best-of-things smile. When she had it set, she opened her arms, realizing how much she yearned for him to step into them, how much she needed him to validate her tiny outpost at the edge of his life.

He blinked, took two foot-dragging steps, and fell against her shoulder, his body shaking with sobs. She patted his back tentatively and breathed in the salty odor of his damp skin. "It's okay to cry, Way-Ray. Lots of men cry when they hurt—lots of big, strong men cry."

Her mind raced, trying to think of one in case he asked. Someone from a movie? A TV show star? A cartoon character? The laundry room was hot and confining—a Petri dish breeding misery and confusion, guilt and inadequacy. The washer ground to a halt and she heard the snarl of a lawnmower in the distance. A door slammed above her and footsteps thudded down the stairs and crunched across the gravel. The small sounds of life going on.

Way-Ray snuffled against her neck, gasped and sobbed again. She arched her back and fought to hold them upright, knees aching, shoulders straining. "It's okay," she repeated. "I'll take care of you."

*Until when? Next week? Next year? Forever?*

She set the nagging questions aside. She couldn't abandon him. She wouldn't. "You'll stay with me until your mom comes back."

Way-Ray stiffened and pushed away. His face was blotched, the whites of his eyes shot with red streaks, his lips bloodless. "No." He turned and lurched toward the door. "We have to go back to Grassy Ridge. We have to find my mom."

Kate struggled to stand on feet so numb they seemed part of the floor. She stumbled and bumped against the tilted shelves, sending rolls of paper towels bouncing to the floor. *Damn.* She cleared the doorway and spotted Way-Ray plunging along the sidewalk, arms outstretched like a sleepwalker.

As he approached the office door, Rhea stepped through it. "Hey, Way-Ray, are you okay?"

"No," he told her. "I gotta get my stuff and we gotta go back to Grassy Ridge. Right now!"

"Oh." Rhea cocked her head and widened her eyes at Kate. Kate turned a thumb down. Rhea's eyes flickered. "Okay, but that's an awful long drive. And I'll bet it's pretty bumpy in that SUV, isn't it?"

"Real bumpy. So what?" Way-Ray tried to step around her.

Rhea blocked the doorway and gave Kate an okay sign. "Hmmm. Real bumpy, huh? That could knock all your stitches loose."

"I don't care about my darn stitches. Me and Kate are going."

Kate shook her head. Rhea nodded and squatted in the doorway, her eyes on a level with Way-Ray's. "Well, maybe you don't care, but your doctor will pitch a fit. He'll slap you back in the hospital and put the stitches in again and they'll hurt twice as much."

Way-Ray held his ground and stuck his lower lip out in a pout. "You don't know anything."

Rhea presented him with a pout of her own. "I do so. I know lots of stuff."

"No you don't. My stitches didn't bump loose when Kate drove me here from the hospital."

"That because she drove real slow. But she can't drive that slow all the way to Oklahoma."

"Why not?"

"Because people who drive too slow cause accidents. Other drivers smack right into people just poking along. So cops arrest them. Do you want to be arrested?"

Way-Ray bit down on his pouting lip. "No. But I want to go home." He spun toward Kate. "We could fly home. Couldn't we?"

"Uh . . ." Kate cursed silently. Always a step behind.

Rhea jumped in. "Not until you've healed a little more. All those changes in pressure when you take off and land are bad for your insides." She paused for a fraction of a second, and then nixed other forms of transportation. "And there aren't trains straight from Castaway Beach. Or buses, either."

Kate noted how the word "straight" mitigated the fabrication.

Way-Ray knuckled his eyes and slumped against the side of the building. "But my mom is lost. What if she's sick or hurt? What if her car went off the road and crashed?"

Kate wanted to tear at her hair. There was no way out of this stinking swamp of lies. She could only pick her way from one hummock of truth to another. "The lawyer had a man go out to Grassy Ridge and check on your house. And police patrol the roads all the time for crashed cars. That's what they're trained for. They're much better at looking than you or I would be."

"But she's my mom," he sniffed.

"And she'd be proud to know that you care so much about her," Rhea told him. "But for now the best thing you can do is take good care of yourself and get well as fast as you can."

"That's right," Kate agreed. "Your mom's lawyer knows where we are and how you had to go to the hospital. If . . . *when* she calls, he'll tell her everything and she'll call us the very next minute."

118

Way-Ray snuffled and kept his eyes on the ground. Kate held her breath. Rhea's hand patted her cigarette pocket. "But what if she's someplace the policemen don't look? What if she bumped her head and doesn't remember who she is, like happens in the movies?"

Rhea's hand slipped into the pocket, the outline of her clenching fingers and the oblong pack evident through the fabric. Kate's brain felt like a chunk of icy marble.

Way-Ray seized her hand and tugged at it. "Can't we get someone to go look for her? A detective?"

"Like in the movies?" Rhea's words were toneless, dry, rags she'd twisted to wring out all emphasis and emotion.

"Yeah," Way-Ray told her. "Like in the movies." He threw his arms around Kate's waist. "Please. Can we get a detective until I get all better and we can go and look?"

Rhea drew the cigarette pack from her pocket and gazed at it as a starving dog regards a steak. No delusion or self-deceit. Committed to her vice. Kate felt a surge of something akin to jealousy.

"Please," Way-Ray pleaded.

What could it hurt? But what would it cost? Guilt stabbed her heart. How could she measure money against this child's emotional well-being? "Okay. We'll get a detective."

"Just like in the movies," Way-Ray informed Rhea in a smug voice.

She nodded, slid a cigarette from the pack, stuffed it between her lips, and flicked her lighter. Through rising smoke she squinted at Kate.

"I'll explain later," Kate mouthed. She stroked Way-Ray's hair. "Just like in the movies," she agreed. "Let's go make some calls and then get you settled so I can finish the laundry."

"And I'll put on clean sheets so guests can dirty them up for you to wash." Rhea strode off trailing a ribbon of smoke.

"She shouldn't smoke," Way-Ray observed. "My mom says it's bad for people."

"It's very bad," Kate agreed. "Maybe when we get to know her better we can help her quit." She opened the office door and guided him around behind the desk. In the top drawer, beneath the notes she'd taken as Rhea had showed her how to run the motel, was Philip Jacobson's number. She dug it out and picked up the receiver.

"Kate," Way-Ray muttered without looking at her. "I . . . I got a question."

Kate set the receiver in its cradle. The skin at the back of her neck prickled, but she tried to keep her tone light. "I hope it's not a math question. I'm not very good at math. Especially division."

He kept his head down. "What happens if my mom never comes back?"

Kate yearned to say "of course she'll come back." She longed to believe in that lie as she had never believed in anything before.

"If she doesn't, do I . . . ?" Way-Ray dug at the carpet with his heel and spoke in a choked whisper. "My grandma's with the angels and so is my dad. If we don't find my mom, do I have to go to the orphan place?"

"Of course not." Kate lifted his chin. His eyes were glossy with tears. "Why would you think that?"

He shrugged, hunched his shoulders and looked away. "Alex had to go to the orphan place. He was in my grade last year. His mom and dad died and nobody wanted him."

"I want you." Kate wrapped her arms around his meager chest, knowing that she meant it, that it was one true thing she could hold fast to. "I'll take care of you."

Way-Ray's muscles grew rigid and he seemed to draw into himself. His eyes took on the distant and vacant gaze of a wooden soldier. "For how long?"

There was only one answer. "For as long as you need me."

# CHAPTER 15

Way-Ray, arms out like airplane wings, circled the tiny living area as Kate dialed Philip Jacobson's number. The phone rang seven times. "Philip Jacobson's office. Please hold," a woman's voice twanged.

Way-Ray reversed direction, circumnavigating a scarred wooden rocker, a coffee table with a splinted leg, and a slouching gray love seat with threadbare arms. Would a slipcover help, or would that be like putting lipstick on a pig? "The lawyer's secretary answered," she told Way-Ray. Pearline. That was her name. A fanciful name that spoke of the South. "I'm on hold."

He nodded and changed his course for the kitchen, running one hand along the curved tops of the only two chairs that had been able to stand without assistance once she'd scrubbed off thick layers of grime. "Watch for splinters," she urged. When she had time, she'd check thrift stores for replacements and consign these to the dump.

"Sorry about that," Pearline said. "How may I help you?"

"This is Kate Dalton and—"

"I'm sorry, Miz Dalton. Mr. Jacobson's in court and the phone is ringing itself silly. Always happens that way." She paused and Kate heard a series of moist sneezes. "And my hay

fever is flaring up. My nose is about to run right off my face."
She sneezed again. "Hold on. Let me get my inhaler."

"The lawyer's in court today," Kate told Way-Ray. "But maybe his secretary knows a detective."

"A detective? Sure thing, hon," Pearline said. "Ted Dyson. He's no spring chicken, but old TD's the best around. You want him to find Miz Blake?"

"Yes, I, uh—" Kate raised her voice a little. "*Way-Ray* wants to hire a detective to find his mother." The boy abandoned his aimless circling and hustled to Kate's side.

"Well, bless his little heart. How's he doing after that operation?"

"He's healing." Physically.

"That's good, hon. Well, let me give you TD's number before I start sneezing up another storm." Pearline rattled off a string of numbers that Kate jotted on a sheet of Wade in the Waves Motel stationery. "He's already been out to Miz Blake's trailer." She sniffled and swallowed. "TD works fast and he works alone. He doesn't have a secretary. And his reports show it. They're chock full of spelling errors." She chuckled, and Kate felt that she was fond of the man, in spite of—or because of—his faults. "He's real good about checking his messages, though. Tell him I told you to call."

"Thank you." Kate wrote Dyson's initials beside the number.

"TD," Way-Ray crowed. "That means touchdown. He must be a real good detective." He tugged at Kate's sleeve. "Let's get him."

"He'll do a good job," Pearline assured Kate. "Oh—I almost forgot—we got a letter for you."

A letter? Kate's heart hammered. Who but Amanda would write in care of Philip Jacobson?

"No return address, but it could be from Miz Blake," Pearline speculated. "The handwriting looks a bit like her signature. I'll forward it out this afternoon if you give me an address."

Kate hesitated. Forwarding could take days. She'd call back later, while Way-Ray was napping, and have Pearline fax it. "The detective needs our address," she told Way-Ray. He nodded gravely. As she read the street number from the letterhead, he lip-synched every word and then punched his index finger at the phone number. Kate nodded, remembering she had yet to call the phone company and arrange for her own service. "Here's the number for the Wade in the Waves Motel where we're staying." She read that off, too. "There's a message machine."

"Got it. We'll only give that number to TD or Miz Blake, not to that old drunk, so don't worry about her bothering you."

Way-Ray's surviving grandmother? Kate's stomach lurched. "Oh?" She tried to sound cool and disinterested, but the word came out with a squeak. Way-Ray didn't seem to notice. He'd opened the desk drawer and was making a chain of paperclips.

"Said she was kin and had her rights, demanded we have Miz Blake call her. Mr. Jacobson told me if she called back I wasn't to give her the time of day. That's fine with me. Drunks shouldn't have any rights where children are concerned."

She flung that sentence down and paused as if giving Kate a chance to argue if she dared. "You're right," Kate said, meaning it.

"And the less I know, the better," Pearline said. "I've been told I have a tendency to run off at the mouth. In fact, there are some folks say I gossip." She made a noise that seemed part snort and part sneeze. "Not that I'd tell a soul about you and the boy. Or Miz Blake. Wherever she is."

"I understand." Kate abandoned the plan to call back later and have Pearline open the letter and fax it.

Way-Ray laid aside the paperclip chain, seized her pen, and drew a circle around the detective's number. Kate nodded. "Thanks for the information."

"You bet. I'll have Mr. Jacobson call you when— Oh, there's that dang phone again. Gotta run."

Kate's mind thrashed as the dial tone hummed in her ear. What rights would a grandmother have? Would it matter that she was an alcoholic or would a judge simply hand Way-Ray over to next of kin?

"Are you gonna talk all day?" Way-Ray tugged at her sleeve. "Can we call the detective now?"

"Sure. Let's do that." Kate broke the connection.

"Me! I want to do it."

"Okay." Kate handed him the phone. "Dial a one before you start the number."

"I know." He jabbed at the numbers with a rigid index finger.

"He might not answer," Kate warned. "The secretary told me he's out of his office a lot."

"That's because there aren't any clues in his office," Way-Ray informed her. "Detectives have to go places to find clues. And bad guys chase them and they get beat up a lot."

A concept of reality assembled from life as Hollywood saw it.

"It's ringing," he said. "Now it's ringing again."

"You might get his machine."

"Then I'll leave a message." His voice was nearly a shout, his words clipped. "I know how to do that. I'm not a baby."

"I know you're not." Kate took two steps away, giving him space. Was she, in an effort to make up for past tragedies and shield him from an uncertain future, sheltering him too much? She rubbed her temples. Being a parent must feel like walking blindfolded through a minefield.

"Hi Mr. TD," Way-Ray said. "My name is Wayland Raymond Blake and I want to hire you to find my mother 'cause no one knows where she went and I'm afraid she might be hurt and scared. She lives in Grassy Ridge, Oklahoma. I'm in Oregon. That's by the ocean. Call me, okay?" He rattled off the number, then repeated it more slowly. "It's real important. And I'm hanging up now. 'bye."

"Nice job." Kate kept her voice neutral. Praise, but not false praise.

"I know. My mom taught me how to leave messages. How long before he'll call?"

Kate glanced at her watch. "It's two o'clock here, so it's four in Oklahoma. Maybe he'll check his messages before dinner."

Way-Ray nodded. "Unless he's on a real important case." His face seemed to crumple and the veneer of self-reliance and bravery shattered. "What if he thinks I'm just a little kid playing a joke?"

Kate ached for him. "Then he's not a very good detective, is he?"

Way-Ray studied the carpet. "I guess."

"If he doesn't call us by tomorrow, I'll get the name of another detective." She forced the most chipper voice she could manage. "I'll bet there are lots around."

Way-Ray dragged a toe along the carpet and said nothing.

"But you'll see," Kate assured him. "TD will call."

\* \* \* \* \*

And he did. Kate was at work on a tuna noodle casserole with Way-Ray supervising to make sure it turned out exactly as his mother's had. The likelihood of that was uncertain, however, because he couldn't remember which ingredients, besides tuna and something green, the recipe called for. He objected to noodles until she pointed out they were in the name of the casserole, but he was positive about the topping: "lots and lots and lots of potato chips."

"This is Ted Dyson," a deep voice rumbled when she keyed the cordless phone. "I had a message to call Wayland Raymond Blake."

"Yes. Just a moment." Kate glanced at Way-Ray who was kneeling on a chair absorbing every word of text on the label of a can of cream of mushroom soup. She turned down the heat under the pot of noodles and moved toward the office, sliding her hand over the transmitter. "Watch that pot, Way-Ray, okay? Turn the burner all the way off if it starts to boil over."

He nodded and she carried the phone into the office, to the corner by the door. "This is Kate Dalton. I'm Wayland's . . . guardian. He's nine. Almost ten," she added, knowing that was important to Way-Ray. "He . . . *we* want to hire you to look for his mother. I'll pay, of course."

"It's likely to be money wasted," Dyson said. "Looks to me like she disappeared on purpose."

"That what I think, too. But she's Way-Ray's only family." Pruning the drunk and the jailbird from the family tree. "He needs to know that we're doing all we can to find her."

"Might as well set a match to your cash, lady," Dyson grumbled.

Kate bristled. "Lady" was sexist and demeaning. This gruff man made it sound hostile, too. "It's *my money*, Mr. Dyson. I worked hard for every cent. If you don't want it, I'll find someone who does."

There was a brief silence on the line, and then Dyson laughed, a sound like gravel cascading from the tilted bed of a dump truck. "I guess you told me. My fee is thirty an hour, plus expenses."

"Fine. I'll contract for forty hours. When can you start?"

"Tomorrow. But you might better ask where. Like I said, she didn't leave any clues."

"Then find one," Kate snapped. "That's your job."

Dyson laughed again. "I do like a woman with grit."

Kate ignored that. "Call back in a minute. Way-Ray will answer the phone. Pretend you haven't talked to me or been out to the trailer. Let him hire you."

"But you . . . Okay. Whatever floats your boat, lady."

"And don't ever call me lady again."

"Aye, aye, ma'am." He chuckled and hung up.

For a moment, Kate considered calling back and telling him to forget it. No matter what Pearline said, his language and attitude didn't fill her with confidence. But she promised Way-Ray and she'd stick to that—unless it looked like TD intended to ride the clock and milk her bank account.

Decision made, she returned to the kitchen and set the cordless phone on the table. "Are those noodles done?"

Way-Ray shrugged. "You didn't tell me to test them, just to make sure they didn't boil over."

Kate smothered a laugh. "Well thanks for that." She prodded a noodle with a fork and lifted it from the water; it slithered from the tines and landed on the counter with a plop.

Way-Ray giggled. "That one tried to escape." He slurped it up. "Tastes done to me."

Laughing, Kate dug into a cabinet beneath the counter, and found a colander she'd purchased during her spending spree. She was draining noodles when the phone rang. "Could you get that?"

Way-Ray's hand hovered. "What do I say?"

"Say this is the Wade in the Waves Motel. If someone wants a room, I'll be with them in a minute."

"Okay." He picked up the phone and pressed the "talk" button. "Wade in the Waves Motel. Yes, this is Wayland Blake. Hi, Mr. TD." He held the phone away from his ear. "It's the detective. What do I say now?"

Feeling needed, and frightened by that, Kate cleared her throat and spoke in a voice she hoped would carry to Dyson. "Tell him what you want, Way-Ray. See if you think he'll do a good job."

"Okay." Way-Ray chewed at his lip and put the phone to his ear. "My mom's missing. Could you find her?"

Kate shook the colander, releasing a cloud of steam that hid her tears. As she listened to Way-Ray, she thought about hope. More than wish or desire, but not exactly trust or confidence, it was a fragile yet powerful thing. Hope could stretch and hold, like a bungee cord anchored above a chasm, or it could splinter like a frozen twig in a winter storm.

# CHAPTER 16

The next morning, Way-Ray woke her at 6:30 and informed her that he wanted chocolate milk and tuna casserole for breakfast. As he darted down the stairs, Kate noted that he no longer held his hand over his stomach. He grinned at the hisses and crackles from the microwave, laughed when a bit of tuna exploded, and dug in when she set the bowl before him.

Before she sat down to coffee and wheat toast with peanut butter, she fielded two calls from California tourists hunting for bargain prices. She offered one couple a two-bedroom unit for a night later in the week, but told the second there were no vacancies.

"Just as well," she muttered as she bit into the cold toast. The woman was a high-maintenance whiner, demanding discounts, and insisting she needed only a one-bedroom unit for five people and two dogs while a screaming argument and continuous barking raged in the background.

"How come your toast looks like rubber?"

Kate laughed and waved the soggy slice at Way-Ray like a small flag. "It lost all its toastiness while I was on the phone."

"Well, it's your own fault." He pointed his fork at her nose. "You should have told them to call back after breakfast, 'cause it's only," he squinted at the clock above the stove, "7:15."

"Thank you, Mr. Junior Executive. That's a good idea." She should let the answering machine do its job and return calls during official office hours. She should keep private time separate from job time, something she'd never done before. Wrapping the toast in foil, she set it on the counter. "We'll give that to the seagulls for lunch."

"Okay, but we have to take it way down by the ocean," he counseled, "so we don't get seagull poop on our deck. It's all gross and gunky." He tucked his thumbs in his armpits to create wings and flapped his elbows. "Seagulls sure poop a lot. Do they poop while they're flying?"

Chuckling, Kate put a fresh slice of bread in the toaster. "I don't know. Maybe you could watch them and take notes. Like a scientist."

He cocked his head, thumbs still in his armpits. "Cool. I want a notebook and a pen. No, a bunch of pens—all different colors."

"I didn't hear the magic word."

"Pleeeeeeeeease? And I need a telescope, too."

Kate thought of Dyson's fee. "I'll get a notebook and pens later today," she promised. "But let's wait before we buy a telescope. Try the binoculars first."

He clapped his hands together and held them as if in prayer. "But I can't see all that far with the binoculars. And a telescope would be good for watching the stars, too," he wheedled. "I already know the Big Dipper and the Little Dipper and Orion and I could learn lots more. It would be," he paused for a second as if to cloak the final word in an aura of importance, "educational."

Kate suppressed a smile as she spread peanut butter. Had he come up with this bit of persuasion by himself or picked it up from a friend? "Educational, huh? Well, let me think about it and we'll see."

His eyes clouded. "That's what Mom always says."

Dangerous ground. "Hmm." Kate turned to the refrigerator, stowed the peanut butter, and rearranged mustard, ketchup, and mayonnaise. If he was involved in projects, he'd be less focused

CAROLYN J. ROSE

on Amanda. Should she agree to the telescope? Or was it an emotional buy-off, an attempt to score points?

She closed the refrigerator and used the side of her hand to sweep toast crumbs along the counter to the sink. "And what happens after your mom says that?"

He scowled and rubbed his nose with his index finger. "Well, sometimes she thinks about it and says 'no.'" The frown vanished. "But sometimes she thinks about it some more and says 'yes.'"

"Ah." Kate nodded, hoping to indicate she knew that all along. "Then that's what we'll do. We'll research telescopes on the computer and learn about how much power we want and what they cost." She poured fresh coffee and added milk. "And then, if the seagull study goes well—if you keep good notes and make a logical conclusion—"

"We'll see," he said, sliding from his chair and carrying his plate and glass to the counter. "I'll do the dishes." He jerked her chair back from the table. "You sit down and finish your breakfast."

"Wow." Kate sat, smiling at him over her shoulder. "Thank you. What good manners you have."

"My mom taught me, remember?"

"And she did a wonderful job."

"I know." He collected the salt and pepper shakers and set them on top of the microwave, then wet a sponge at the sink and wiped his place at the table, leaving a mass of damp arcs and missing half the crumbs.

It's the thought that counts, Kate reminded herself. He's not even ten.

He moved his dishes to the sink, ran water, grasped the bottle of soap, and squirted it onto the sponge in a series of loops and swirls. Kate bit her tongue. He needed only a single small squeeze to get enough bubbles, but in a kid's world, more was almost always better.

Her parents, through discipline and indoctrination, had attempted to squelch that instinct in her. Each Thanksgiving they required her to cull her books, clothing, and toys—never many of those: a few board games, a tiny herd of stuffed animals, a long-legged doll with ballet slippers and a beret. She was allowed to keep half. The remainder went to charity. At the New Year, not on Christmas, she was rewarded with a new coat, a dress, two skirts, three blouses, a trip to the shoe store, a certificate in her mother's writing promising one new book each month, and ten dollars for her to spend as she wanted. Well before she was Way-Ray's age, the holiday season lost all surprise and wonder.

She swallowed the last of her coffee and Way-Ray squirted more soap on the sponge and sloshed her mug into a sink overflowing with bubbles. Kate made a mental note to rinse the dishes well before she used them again, rinse them when he was occupied elsewhere so he wouldn't be insulted.

Her parents would have halted her efforts and issued lengthy advice and instruction, turning a tedious task into sheer torture. They meant well, but she vowed she would do better. If Way-Ray was with her in December, there would be expectation and celebration, not sacrifice and obligation.

He seized the broom and, as if it were a golf club, swung wildly at grains of sand scattered on the linoleum. "I'm sweeping, too," he said, swelling his chest and tossing his head.

"So I see," was all she could manage without bursting into laughter. Escaping to the office, she checked for e-mail inquiries forwarded from the Wade in the Waves Motel site, then unlocked the door for guests searching for tide-table booklets, brochures for area attractions, or advice about restaurants.

Way-Ray soon abandoned his housekeeping duties, wandered into the office, and selected a video from the shelf of those offered for rent. "I'm going to my room so you can do the darn laundry. And I'll be real good and not come down until lunch time."

"Works for me." Kate patted his head as he passed, clipped the phone to the waistband of her jeans, locked the office again, and jogged up the outside stairs to collect damp towels and bath mats. She'd just finished giving the loaded washers a pep talk when Rhea appeared in the doorway, hair tethered with an assortment of bright plastic clips that made her head look like a refuge for exotic butterflies. "Hey. How's the kid? Did he settle down?"

"Yes. Thanks." Kate felt everything she hadn't told Rhea yawning like a chasm between them.

"His mother's probably taking advantage of her time off to have a vacation. I'd do that if somebody relieved me of my kids." Rhea pulled clean towels from shelves and stacked them on a work table. "Did he hire a detective?"

"Yes." Kate yanked the lint filter from a dryer and swept it clean with her fingers. "The guy rubs me the wrong way. He's a condescending know-it-all."

Rhea patted her apron pocket, then knotted her fingers together and stretched her arms, making her knuckles pop. "But can he do the job?"

"Maybe." Kate started on another lint filter. "But he—"

"I'll get to work on that hedge today," a gruff voice announced.

Kate turned to see Jackson slouching in the doorway. "Great," she said, wondering whether there was something that needed his attention more than a string of unruly bushes. She hadn't walked the grounds and made a to-do list. In fact, she hadn't finished the laundry room inventory. Time to get organized, compartmentalize her brain so concerns about Way-Ray and Amanda wouldn't paralyze her.

Rhea snorted. "You haven't clipped that hedge in about three years."

Jackson's eyes remained focused on the floor in front of Kate.

Rhea slammed a stack of bath mats onto the table. "Why the sudden burst of conscientious energy?"

Kate peered at her. Was she angry? Baiting him? Or was this how they related?

"Needs to be done," he muttered.

"What makes today so special?"

Hands fisted in his pockets, he turned on his good leg and limped across the parking lot toward the tool shed.

"Yep, he's definitely sweet on you," Rhea chuckled. "Nadine had to hold back his pay to get him to cut that hedge last time."

Kate turned and picked at the label on a bottle of bleach, fighting to keep a flush from her cheeks. "I didn't ask him to cut it."

"Nadine did. The neighbors have been bitching about it 'cause they put their place up for sale." Rhea chuckled. "He's sweet on you."

Kate yanked the last filter and scraped it into a cracked green plastic wastebasket with a gouge in one side about the same size as a man's shoe. "Thanks for pointing that out."

"Just thought you should know." Rhea transferred mats and towels to a cart. "Hey, I brought a diversion. For Way-Ray." She hooked her pinkies in the edges of her mouth and whistled.

Kate heard a scuffling clatter of gravel and two boys shot through the door trailed by a four-legged gleaming black cylinder of muscle with a tail. The boys ricocheted off the dryer and into the work table. The shorter one hurdled the dog and zipped back out the door, but the other got his legs tangled and sprawled across the wastebasket. It shattered, spewing wads of dryer dust.

"Arrgghhh." Rhea tore at her hair. Two plastic butterflies took flight, clattering against a washer.

The boy hauled himself to what Kate noted were two of the longest feet she'd seen off a professional basketball court. He stood as tall as Rhea and had her dense black hair and ironic eyes. He wore a sleeveless T-shirt and a pair of frayed jeans that stopped short of his ankles. "Sorry." He bent to gather shards of plastic.

"I'll get it." Rhea rolled her eyes. "This is my son, the one-man demolition team, also known as Kyle. Kyle, this is Kate Dalton."

"Pleased to meet you." Kyle stuck out a hand not much smaller than a baseball mitt.

Kate braced for a squeeze that would bruise her fingers. Instead, he exerted only a few ounces of pressure and released her as he might set free a captive bird. "I'm glad to meet you, too."

He brushed hair from his eyes. "Sorry about the wastebasket."

"Never mind. It was broken anyway."

As she spoke, the smaller boy jetted into the room with the dog at his heels. "And this is Sean," Rhea said.

"And Mutant the Mutt," Sean announced, bouncing on his toes. "Fastest dog on the planet. Watch this."

He flung a bright orange ball through the doorway. Mutant barked once and tore after it, tongue flapping, long ears flipped back, toenails scratching for traction. Kate heard the percussion of paws on gravel and Mutant returned the ball, shiny with spit, between his jaws.

"Take him outside if you're going to do that," Rhea ordered.

Sean seemed not to hear. He pried the ball from Mutant's mouth and flung it again.

"Sean Whitaker! You heard what I said. Don't you pretend you didn't." Rhea clamped a hand on his tie-dyed T-shirt. "Your brother's already done enough damage, thank you very much. Take that dog down to the beach."

"Yes ma'am." Sean shook himself from her grip, wispy blond hair settling like feathers across his bright blue eyes and over his ears. He must take after his father, Kate thought, or else he's a living example of the theory of recessive genes.

Mutant charged through the door once more, the ball flattened in the vise of his jaws, strings of slobber draped on either side of it. "Ugh," Rhea said. "If it was up to me, he'd go back to the pound where we got him."

"She doesn't mean that." Sean dropped to his knees and slapped his hands over the dog's ears. Mutant's whip-like tail whomped the dryer.

"She loves Mutant," Kyle assured Kate. "She's the one who rescued him."

"Well, it was obvious no one else would take him. A cross between a dachshund and a Labrador." Rhea shook her head, dislodging another plastic butterfly. "With jaws like a crocodile."

Kyle reached down and seized the part of the ball that protruded from Mutant's teeth. He worked his fingers between the jaws to get a better grip, and then lifted. Mutant grunted and his eyes flared, but he hung on as his front feet left the ground. Kyle continued to lift until Mutant was eyeball to eyeball with Kate. "Determined," Kate marveled.

"You'd have to cut off his head to get his jaws to unlock," Rhea said. "Now take him outside, Kyle, before he sheds all over the clean sheets. And don't annoy the guests."

Kyle trooped out, Mutant still dangling, Sean bringing up the rear. Rhea retrieved her butterflies and mashed them into her hair. "I thought Way-Ray could use some buddies." She stooped to help Kate collect shards of wastebasket. "Sean's barely nine and Kyle's almost thirteen. He's big enough to work, but too young to get a job—legally." She stood and unearthed a mangled broom and rusty dustpan from behind the door. "We pay him to keep an eye on Sean during the summer and he mows lawns and runs errands. But he's in a big hurry to get into his dad's painting business."

"Painting?" Kate opened a trash bag as Rhea corralled the debris. "Do you think he could do Way-Ray's room? I'll pay him."

"He'd like that." Rhea chased down a final ball of lint. "Jim has gallons of leftover stuff, and Kyle has a good eye for mixing colors, but the results might be pretty wild."

"The wilder the better." Kate tied off the bag. "Thanks."

"No problem." Rhea wedged a cigarette between her lips, stepped into the doorway, and flicked her lighter. "I'll tell Kyle to keep a close eye on Way-Ray and let you know if he takes a notion to run off." She lit up and strode off across the parking lot.

Kate stared after Rhea. It hadn't occurred to her that Way-Ray might do that. But Rhea had known. Rhea was a real mother.

As she started the washers, Kate felt inadequate, unprepared, and more than a little frightened.

# CHAPTER 17

The letter arrived on Monday.

At the rattle of mail in the box, Kate hurtled from the office. The thick, cream-colored envelope with Jacobson's return address was sandwiched between a flyer from a carpet cleaning company and an electric bill. With a glance over her shoulder, she crammed it into her back pocket.

Yesterday, Way-Ray had raced to her side every time the phone rang insisting, "In the movies, detectives call and make reports." At bedtime, he'd lingered by the phone, then tapped it with his forefinger and trudged upstairs to brush his teeth. "Maybe he's writing the report," he told her as she tucked him in. "Maybe it'll come in the mail tomorrow."

Kate's scalp prickled. If he spotted an envelope from an Oklahoma address, he'd open it. "Mr. Jacobson's secretary told me that TD doesn't have anyone to type his reports."

He jerked the sheet to his chin. "Then he'll write it with a pen or a pencil."

She nodded. "If he did, and he mailed it on Saturday, I don't think it would turn up here before, uh, before the end of the week."

"Nuh-uh. TD's the best. He'll send it extra-special-super-fast delivery."

"What if he doesn't have anything to report yet?" *Mistake!* Disparage the detective's abilities and Way-Ray would insist they return to Grassy Ridge and launch their own search. "Or maybe," she backpedaled, "he's following up a lead and can't stop to send a report."

Way-Ray considered that, his lower lip eclipsing the upper in a pout. "If he found out anything, then he's gotta call me. Right away." He kicked his feet for emphasis, pulling the sheet loose.

"You're exactly right." She squeezed his shoulder. "But maybe he's on the road." And maybe he's not a very good detective. She resolved to call TD when Way-Ray was asleep and inform him that part of what he was being paid for was providing reassurance. She would demand that he call every other day with a report that included something positive—even if he was only developing more leads.

"Maybe." Way-Ray chewed the inside of his left cheek. "He's a good detective. I know he is." He glared at her defiantly, and she guessed he was transferring his anger to her. After a moment, he burrowed under the sheet. "Good night."

Exhausted, she fell asleep without calling Dyson and woke up to find Way-Ray lugging the love seat cushions out to the mailbox to make himself comfortable. She was in a state of cold panic until Rhea arrived with Kyle, Sean, Mutant, and a load of stick-on stars.

Kate made certain Way-Ray knew the star project's success hinged on constant vigilance. "Otherwise," she warned, "Mutant might eat them."

"He eats everything," Way-Ray had agreed. "Yesterday he swallowed a whole hot dog. He didn't even chew."

"I saw that." Kate was amazed when Kyle tossed the hot dog and Mutant opened his long jaw and swallowed. For a second she saw a lump in his throat, then he coughed and the lump disappeared.

"Mutant's like a black hole," Way-Ray crowed. "Black holes are way out in space, you know. They suck up stars and all their light. If I had a telescope," he added with a sly smile, "maybe I could see a real black hole and learn a whole lot more."

Kate admired his gambit, but wouldn't commit herself. "We'll see."

"Rats," she heard him mutter as he climbed the stairs two at a time, just like Kyle.

Deciding she'd ask him to retrieve the mail later, she slid the remaining letters back into the box. In the meantime, she needed a private and secure place—not easy to come by at the Wade in the Waves Motel unless you went to the bathroom.

Perfect.

Casually, she walked through the office and slipped into the downstairs bathroom. Aging frosted glass in a window the size of a cereal box filtered out all but a smudge of bleary light and the listing fixture above the sink carried a warning to use nothing more powerful than forty watts. Thanks to a merciless scrubbing, the fixtures were again clean, but she had yet to replace the shower curtain. Brittle and yellowed, it hung on a set of rusting and mismatched hooks.

Kate closed the door behind her, making a mental note to buy and install a better knob—one with a lock that worked.

The envelope crackled as she drew it from her pocket, worked the flap loose with her nails, and pulled out the second envelope. Her name and Jacobson's address had been written with a skipping blue ballpoint pen. A few of the letters were missing segments and the "l" in "Dalton" was only an inkless indentation in the paper.

As Pearline told her, there was no return address. The postmark was faint and Kate squinted and held it close to the light. The two-letter state abbreviation seemed to start with an M.

Missouri? Mississippi? Montana? Kate racked her brain for the names of other states. Maine?

This envelope had stronger glue or had been licked with more intention; the flap refused yield so Kate wedged her thumbnail beneath an edge and tore along the crease. Sucking in a long breath, she pulled out the letter, shuffling through pages that appeared to have been torn from a spiral-bound notebook and written with the same faltering pen. Some characters were nothing more than scars, while others carried blobs of ink on their backs.

Kate stuffed the envelope in her pocket, leaned against the door, and tipped the pages to the light. They were dated more than a week ago.

"Dear Kate," the letter began. "I hope you and Way-Ray are well and that he isn't too much of a burden and brings you joy. He's a bright spirit and I miss him more than I ever dreamed. I guess by now you know you are his guardian, and I want you to adopt him even though Wayne's mother will fight it."

Kate winced. What would that fight involve? Did she have a chance of winning?

If Amanda had doubts, she didn't put them on the page. "I believe Mr. Jacobson can take care of Justine Maxwell in court, but the real problem is Wayne's half brother, Dwayne Vetter. If Justine wants Way-Ray, he won't care about the law or who's in his way. I thought he'd be locked up for another five years, but he's out. I saw him. In Grassy Ridge."

Kate shuddered.

"I expect Dwayne intends to finish what his brother started with me. Once he's done that, he'll come looking for Way-Ray. If—"

The door slammed into Kate's back. She clutched the shower curtain. With a harsh clatter, hooks ripped loose from the rod. Her head cracked against the shower stall and stars exploded around the dark silhouette filling the doorway.

# CHAPTER 18

Screaming, Kate slid to the bottom of the stall, clawing at the curtain. The looming figure advanced, something silvery in its grip. A gun? A knife?

Her scrabbling fingers found a shower hook. "Get back!" She flung it.

The figure raised long arms. Her fingers closed around another hook with a metal ball on one end. She heard yelping, barking, and pounding feet. "Kate! Kate!" Way-Ray's voice.

"No! Way-Ray, get away! Run!"

She clamped the hook between her fingers, pushed her heels against the corners of the shower stall, and struggled to rise, to escape the pulsing darkness that shadowed her eyes. "You can't have him. You'll have to kill me first." She braced herself, hook in her right hand, fingers of the left bent like talons.

"Mom, come quick!" Kyle's deep tones. "Kate's acting all weird and screaming at Jackson."

Jackson?

The hulking figure retreated. A smaller silhouette flung itself at her. "Kate! Are you okay?" Way-Ray wrapped his arms around her waist and they reeled against the wall, sliding on the shredded curtain.

"What the hell is going on?" Rhea's voice. "What did you do?"

"Nothing," a rusty voice insisted. "I came to replace the leaking faucet on that damn sink."

Jackson. Not Dwayne. The adrenaline left Kate's body in a rush. Her legs trembled. She dropped the hook and stroked Way-Ray's hair. "It's okay," she whispered. "I'm okay."

"You were yelling really loud at Jackson. It was scary." She blinked, her vision clearing. "He pushed the door and I fell into the shower."

"And bumped your head?" He twisted in her grasp and gazed up at her. "And didn't know where you were? Just like on TV."

"Just like on TV," she assured him, shivering, breathing in the boy scent of sweat, peanut butter, and bubble gum.

Rhea came through the door, speaking over her shoulder. "Go find something else to do."

"What about the faucet?" Jackson spoke in a resigned growl.

Rhea's voice sizzled. "If you mean the one that's been leaking for the past decade, there's no reason to inconvenience yourself today." She turned and peered into the shower stall. "Are you okay?"

"I'm fine. Just a little shook up." Kate released Way-Ray. "Go on upstairs and finish your stars."

"We're already finished," Sean squeaked from the doorway.

"Then find something else to do," Rhea ordered. "Take Mutant to the beach, fly a kite, go play on the highway."

"The highway? But you told us never to play on the highway!"

"Good. You remembered." She flicked her fingers. "All you kids get out from underfoot and let us get some work done!"

With a backward glance at Kate, Way-Ray flattened himself against the doorjamb, eased past Rhea, and darted off.

"What happened?" Rhea laid a hand on Kate's shoulder.

"I thought Jackson was—" No, she couldn't go there. She stepped from the shower stall. "I was right by the door. It doesn't lock. He pushed it open as I was . . ."

*The letter!* She spun toward the shower, kicked at the curtain. Not there.

"You sure you're okay?"

Kate spotted the pages between the vanity and the toilet. "Just a little disoriented. I went flying into the shower stall and hit my head."

Rhea frowned. "Maybe we'd better get you to the emergency room."

"No." She had to get back to that letter. "I saw stars." She prodded a growing knot above her left eye. "But I didn't black out."

"You sure?" Rhea patted her cigarette pocket and sucked her upper lip. "Jackson has the social skills of a wolverine, but this takes the cake. I'm gonna give him the lecture of his life."

"No." Kate caught her hand, felt swollen knuckles beneath rough skin. "No. I'll talk to him."

Rhea grinned. "In that case, it might have an impact. He's—"

"Don't start with the sweet-on-me crap."

"It's not crap." She glanced toward the office and Kate was aware of a mutter of voices. "If you won't let me beat up on Jackson, at least let me bullshit the guests." Rhea flung an arm around Kate's shoulders. "I've always been partial to the spider defense. No one asks any questions except, 'Did you kill it?' and 'Do you think there are any more?'" She dropped her voice. "Listen, I don't mean to butt in, but if you need to talk . . ."

Kate pulled back, wanting off this dangerous ground.

"Well, I got a yarn to spin." Rhea yanked her cigarettes from her pocket and strode off.

Kate dove for the letter, folded it, and slid it back into her pocket. She splashed water on her face, straightened her shirt, started through the office, caught a glimpse of a huddle of guests around Rhea, and went out the kitchen door.

143

The hedge rose in front of her like a green marble sculpture. Its sides had been trimmed as if with a straight razor. The top rose and curled like waves about to break. She blinked. "Wow."

Then astonishment gave way to embarrassment. If Jackson was trying to impress her for reasons other than a favorable review of his job performance, she'd set him straight.

She circled the building, spotted a toolbox on the sidewalk, and found Jackson in the laundry room, installing brackets on the listing shelves. Another chore put off for years. "We need to talk."

He turned his head, but his hands continued driving in a screw. His gaze was as intense as a raptor's, the gray of his irises so pale that the lenses seemed like pieces of onyx, polished and set into rings of beaten silver. "I'm sorry I frightened you."

The word sparked the usual flash of anger. Was he tossing out a knee-jerk, minimal apology and hoping she'd dismiss the incident without making him accept responsibility? She squared her shoulders. No chance. "Civilized people knock on closed bathroom doors."

The onyx centers in his eyes expanded. He continued twisting the screwdriver and offered a one-shoulder shrug. "People say I don't do 'civilized' well. And I thought you were in here."

"I wasn't," Kate fumed. "You flung me headfirst into the wall. I could have gotten a concussion."

He nodded, finished driving the screw, and started another. "Sorry."

"I hate that word." Anger Kate had been holding onto since the day she was fired erupted. "Sorry. Sorry. Sorry." She pounded her fist against the top of the nearest dryer and a hollow thunder swelled against the confining walls. "It's simplistic. It requires no thought. It's dangerous."

Jackson's gaze locked on hers. "It's all I got."

144

"It's not enough." Kate stared at him for a second, then looked away, disgusted with them both. Why make the effort? It was pointless to argue with a man who wouldn't hold up his end, who wouldn't invest in the possibility of losing. She wanted . . . she wanted to revel in her rightness. A burnt and bitter taste filled her mouth. She wanted to spit, to claw, to howl with rage.

He finished seating the screw. "Like I said, I don't do 'civilized' well."

There was nothing belittling in his tone, no sarcasm or swagger. She gulped air, choking down fury, pride, and a vinegar-brew of self-loathing at her loss of control. The edge of her hand ached and she massaged it with her fingertips.

She hadn't felt so stripped of options, so powerless, since her last year of college, since the day Andy told her he admired her but didn't love her. Later, she saw that she had no frame of reference for love. But then, enmeshed in the intensity of her passion, but determined to hold her emotions in check as she'd been disciplined to do, she felt the future drain away like water on desert sand.

Andy told her a quick break was best. He knew she'd agree because she was the most rational and logical woman he'd ever known. And then, before her numb lips could form words, he got into his dilapidated car and pulled away, aborting both her love and her anguish.

Clutching a bag of groceries on the sidewalk outside her apartment, she felt certain that everyone on earth pitied her, pitied this deluded woman who'd hadn't perceived the inevitable. Then her rage erupted. She dropped the sack of groceries, tore open a carton of eggs, and hurled one at his car. It splattered across the rear window. He looked back over his shoulder, eyes wide, jaw dropping.

Kate felt a jolt of jubilation. "Logical, huh?" she screamed. "Rational?"

She threw a second egg. It pelted the trunk. Andy accelerated. The third cracked against the rear bumper.

Long after he shot out of range, Kate kept throwing. Eggs arced into the air, shattering, spraying bits of shell and yellow-white guts across the pavement and parked cars.

Neighbors streamed from their homes, yelling at her to stop, but she didn't, couldn't. When the egg carton was empty, she threw lettuce, a slab of Swiss cheese, two cans of tuna, six onion bagels, and a jar of sweet pickles. When that didn't break, she kicked it against the curb until it broke with an eruption of sticky green juice.

A young police officer with sunglasses and razor burn arrived and ordered her to calm down and clean up the mess or he'd arrest her. She laughed and stomped pickle slices. Arrest would make her no more pitiful.

As the exasperated cop snapped open a set of handcuffs, a gray-haired woman in a floral-print dress, armed with a broom, a spray bottle, and a roll of paper towels, told him to run along and look for trouble elsewhere. Without a word of protest, he left. The woman shooed the neighbors, mopped egg from the cars, swept up broken glass, and led Kate into her apartment for a cup of tea.

"Was he what you wanted, or what your parents would have wanted?" she asked.

Kate, considering that for the first time, had no answer.

"Well, never mind. You'll get over it."

But now Kate wondered if she had. From that day on, she steered clear of those who met her parents' criteria and selected partners who couldn't or wouldn't evoke the least degree of fervor. And she was always the one who drove away.

She straightened, glaring at Jackson. How had he provoked this emotional flashback? He was nothing like Andy, nothing like a man she might allow herself to care for.

Jackson gave the screw a final twist, tested the strength of the bracket, and tucked the screwdriver in his rear pocket. "I'll get to that faucet now."

Kate flinched. She didn't want him in her apartment. "It can wait."

"Whatever you want." He scooped up cardboard and plastic casings and glanced around.

"Kyle broke the trash can. Toss that in a container outside." She made her tone crisp. Jackson worked for her.

He nodded, picked up a few more scraps, and spoke without looking at her. "There's no point in letting that faucet leak just to prove a point."

Unmasked, Kate crossed her arms over her chest. "Rhea says it's been leaking for years."

He wadded the scraps. "A few months."

"That's all?" Kate snapped her fingers. "And you didn't have a minute to spare until today."

He raised his head and she saw that his eyes had chilled and darkened. They glinted like the dense sapphire ice of a glacier's heart. "I didn't have the inclination before."

"What does that mean?" If he so much as hinted at Rhea's ridiculous theory, she'd slice his ego to shreds with scornful laughter.

"It means maintenance in that unit was Stan's job, but all he did was suck down beer and leer at female guests." Jackson's hands worked the scraps, molding them into a ball. "When he told me to do it, I refused. When he told me again, I took some time off."

"Time off with a bottle."

"Yes. I drink. Sometimes too much." He tossed the ball of scrap from hand to hand. "I'm sure Rhea told you all about it."

Kate felt shame, then anger. "She mentioned it."

His lips twitched. "And you probably *mentioned* it might be a good idea to fire me."

"I . . ." Why was she so defensive? She didn't want to close down bars and liquor stores. She enjoyed the bite of an icy beer on a broiling day and the way brandy flamed through her veins in winter. And it wasn't out of line to expect an employee to turn up for his job on a regular basis, and be sober when he did.

"Every new manager wants to fire me," he said with a faint smile. "Some even follow through."

Kate remembered what Rhea had told her. "But no one else wants the job, so they hire you back."

He tossed the ball of scrap into the air. "Not exactly."

"What does that mean?"

"This is a small town. People are . . . I guess you could say territorial. They look out for each other. Some think this is my place, my right." He glanced at his left leg. "They try to make sure the job is here for me."

"So I might as well let you do what you want, when you want, how you want?" she snarled.

He grinned. Kate was struck by how the simple flexing of muscles transfigured his features, realigned them, and made his eyes glow. "Or you could do the chores yourself. You're bright enough. I could train you in a week or so if you paid close attention."

She dug her nails into her palms, reminded herself that she could walk away from this ridiculous situation and this job. There were plenty of others. But they didn't come with rooms that looked out over the ocean and built-in friends for a lonely little boy.

"You're the one who needs to pay close attention." Her words sounded flimsy and trite, the kind of comeback a taunted child might use on a playground bully. "I'll expect you to fix that faucet tomorrow morning. At ten. Don't be late."

"Yes, ma'am." He grinned again, his sudden smile like a lure camouflaging a barbed hook.

"And when you're done, I want that hedge squared off the way a hedge should be."

"It's your call."

"Damn right it is."

She tapped the letter in her pocket, turned, and ran to the beach. She was stuck with Jackson Scovell. But right now, he was the least of her worries.

# CHAPTER 19

Kate jogged through whipping beach grass, cut across an abandoned volleyball court, and leaped to the beach from the wave-gouged rim of the dune. She landed in a drift of shredded kelp, broken shells, and splintered wood and careened against an enormous log. Stripped of bark, scoured by surf and sand, it was stained the color of whiskey and soda. She ran her hand along the silky wood. What a giant it must have been before a snarling saw took it down. How many years of fog and mist and rain had nurtured it? What forces had set it loose from the men who claimed it?

She leaned against it, dwarfed by its bulk. It felt immutable, enduring. And yet, gazing out at the foaming waves and, beyond them, rising swells spawned beyond the horizon, she knew that tonight a relentless tide could tug this log from the billion-grained grasp of the sand and ferry it away. How long before rock, wind, and water reduced it to a few sodden chips?

Her odyssey, like the journey of this log, had brought her to this spot on the earth. But there were forces as remorseless as the tide that could tear her loose again.

She turned her face toward the ocean, pulled the letter from her pocket and found her place.

"I expect Dwayne intends to finish what his brother started with me. Once he's done that, he'll come looking for Way-Ray.

He'll take him to his mother and they'll make him over in Wayne's image."

Wayne! A bloody image of him rose in Kate's mind, face contorted with brutal intent. She shivered and hunkered down against the log, stretching her legs on the warm sand. A seagull flew overhead, trailing its shadow across her feet. A bright yellow kite with a tail made of red bows soared and dipped behind a girl running at the water's edge. Her laughter, carved by the onshore wind, blew back to Kate in tatters. The gull, the girl, the kite—all that was so normal, so good. But there was much in the world that wasn't. She shivered again and read on.

"You might be thinking that I should go to the police and tell them about Dwayne, but I know from sorry experience it won't do much good. If Dwayne is willing to risk his freedom to kill me, he'll find a way. When I sent Way-Ray off with you, I was in a lot of pain. I'd allowed Wayne to turn me into nothing, and I believed I'd be better off dead. But now I have a reason to live—to protect my son and to pay my debt to you."

Kate shook her head. "There is no debt." But Amanda believed that. And Amanda was a stubborn woman.

"I know I could shoot Dwayne down in cold blood. I have it in me. Then we'd all be safe. But the stain on my soul would be too black and too deep to erase. If there are places we go to after, I want to be where my son will come when it's his turn. I want to see him again—if not in this life, then in the next. So I'll try to lead Dwayne far away. With luck I can find a way to send him back to prison or fix it so he sends himself to hell like you did with Wayne."

Kate gazed at the breaking waves. Until his specter rose to haunt her, she hadn't thought of Wayne as being anywhere—he was just gone. But if hell existed, it might not be a distant place.

"I'm not frightened, Kate. What will be, will be. I won't write again because it might be dangerous for us all, but I'll think of you two every minute. I'll imagine you laughing about those buzzard burgers and making up new jokes. You're what my boy needs now. My biggest hope is that he will be what you need, too. Love, Amanda."

Tears filled Kate's eyes and spilled onto her cheeks. She crumpled the letter against her chest, struggled to her knees, turned her back on the ocean, and laid her forehead against the log. Amanda would return. If there were any justice in this world, she would come back to Way-Ray.

Justice? A harsh laugh sliced Kate's lips. Justice! The past hadn't been notable for that. Why should the future be different?

She wiped her eyes, got to her feet, smoothed the letter, folded it into a small square, and slid into her back pocket. Should she destroy it so it never became an exhibit flaunted by Justine Maxwell's attorney? No. She'd find a safe place and someday, when Way-Ray was old enough to understand, she'd give it to him. She'd tell him about Amanda's bravery and sacrifices, paint her as certain and courageous, marching out to meet her fate.

As she trotted along the edge of the dune toward the steeply sloping trail, Kate wondered if Way-Ray had pictures of his mother. Had Amanda tucked a few into his suitcase, or had she wanted his memories to fade, to dissolve into images of a new life?

When she clawed her way through the sliding sand to the lip of the dune, the wind lifted her hair. A pair of gulls swooped low to inspect her. Faint shrieks of joy swept by on the wind. She shaded her eyes and watched the girl play out string, sending the bright diamond riding higher into an azure sky swept clean of clouds and mist.

This world was too beautiful to forfeit. She had to tell Dyson about Dwayne Vetter and Amanda's scheme. He had to find Amanda before Dwayne did. He had to protect her.

But could Dyson outhunt a predator?

# CHAPTER 20

Thanks to a spate of phone calls and a housekeeping crisis involving a clogged toilet, two hours passed before Kate could pry Way-Ray, Sean, and Kyle from the apartment by offering them five dollars to get some exercise. She proposed a walk up the beach to the center of town and a return by way of the ice cream and candy shops along the highway. "Walk slowly," she reminded Kyle in a whisper. "Way-Ray isn't as strong as he thinks he is."

Kyle stretched to full height and squared his shoulders. "I'll take care of him. You can count on me."

Watching Way-Ray disappear over the dune behind Kyle and Sean, Kate wondered if, as Amanda claimed, he was the spitting image of his father. When Kate was face-to-face with Wayne, his features were contorted by rage. Had Wayne's smile ever been as brilliant as Way-Ray's? Or was Way-Ray's luminescence due to the innocence and love his father had been robbed of?

Would Dwayne recognize his brother in his nephew if he passed Way-Ray on the street? More to the point, how would she recognize Dwayne?

"Don't weird yourself out." She stepped back into the office and closed the door. For all she knew, Amanda had led him to Nova Scotia by now and he'd given up on his crusade for revenge—if he was ever on such a mission. Perhaps he was still in prison. Amanda, suffering from delayed stress syndrome, could have conjured him from a mere wisp of apprehension.

"And if he is out, he'd have to violate his parole to follow Amanda." Her voice seemed thin and broken, as if her throat were filled with ice and the words had been chipped loose. She coughed and tried to blanket fear with logic. Dwayne Vetter would need money to trail Amanda. Where would that come from? Stolen goods he'd stashed before his arrest? From a friend? His mother?

Kate felt another icy jolt to her heart. What if Justine had enough money to fuel obsession for months, years?

She found the detective's number and punched in the digits. The phone rang three times, and then clicked over to an answering machine with a message she hadn't heard before. "Dyson Detecting. Cheating spouses, lost heirs, cold cases? We'll get the goods. Leave a message at the beep."

We'll get the goods? Kate waited through more than a dozen electronic blips, wondering about the origin of the expression and why Dyson had said "we." Hadn't Pearline said he worked alone? Kate rubbed her forehead. No, she said he didn't have a secretary.

The beep interrupted and she hauled in a breath. "This is Kate Dalton. In Oregon. I called you about Amanda Blake. I . . . we haven't heard from you for several . . . well, we haven't heard a word since we hired you and we're wondering . . . we need a report. I also need information on a man named Dwayne Vetter—and a picture if you can get it—he's been in prison—and whatever you can find out about his mother. Justine, um, Maxwell. I don't know where she lives." She paused and then added, "Call me right away. Today." She paused again and then tacked on her phone number. "Call me."

She remembered that Pearline said that Dyson filed sloppy reports, but returned calls promptly. Pearline! Maybe she'd heard from him. And maybe she knew more about Justine.

Flipping through her card file to Jacobson's number, she stabbed out the digits. The phone rang. And rang. And rang. "Philip Jacobson's office," Pearline answered with a fraying sigh. "Mr. Jacobson is in court. How may I help you?" She ran the words of that question together as if she hoped it would be impossible for a caller to understand and therefore take her up on the offer.

"Hi, Pearline. It's Kate Dalton."

"He's in court. Can I take a message?" Pearline's tone implied that the sheer effort of putting pen to memo pad would cause stress fractures of both hands.

"It's Kate Dalton," Kate repeated. "Out in Oregon. Remember?"

"Sure I remember, hon. I have a few years on me, but several of my brain cells still clock in. And, like I said, he's in court."

"That's okay. You can help me."

"Not with legal advice I can't, hon. Don't even ask. Just this morning his attorneyness pierced my ears but good because I let it slip about how some people write up their own wills to save money. I got reminded about who passed the bar exam and who was hired to type, file, and make coffee. Like I wouldn't be clear on that after fifteen glorious years."

"This doesn't—"

"So if it's a question about grinding your own beans or whether you want to go with dairy or non-dairy creamer, sugar or that no-calorie stuff, cups or mugs, why just ask ahead."

Kate abandoned hope of getting a word in. Venting had to run its course. And by listening she might forge a stronger bond with Pearline.

"Otherwise, I'll take a message for Philip Jacobson Esquire because right now he's over at the courthouse, practicing law. He's been *practicing* for twenty years, so I guess he doesn't have it right yet. Know what I mean, hon?"

Kate smiled. She'd wondered herself why some professions "practiced." Teachers taught. Gardeners gardened. Detectives detected. Why hadn't attorneys, notorious for their manipulation of the language, come up with a term that implied they'd achieved perfection?

"And while they're practicing, they're arguing," Pearline said. "Like a bunch of spoiled kids. Must drive the judges crazy. But this is your dime, hon, so whatya need?"

Startled by the conversational U-turn, Kate struggled for words. "I . . . uh . . . got the letter. It was from Amanda Blake, like you thought."

"I knew it. Where did she get off to?"

"I don't—"

"Wait, don't tell me. Just treat me like a mushroom. Keep me in the dark and feed me manure. Otherwise I'm liable to run off at the mouth and get myself in trouble all over again."

Kate rolled her eyes, understanding why Philip Jacobson had snapped, but remembering how he'd spoken of Pearline with respect. Perhaps, like a couple determined to make it to their golden anniversary, they marked their territory, and then sucked it up and got on with the job. For a fleeting second she wondered if she could have done the same with Emory McCoy. She shuddered. No. Definitely not. "Amanda didn't say where she was. That's the truth."

"Hmm. So what can I do for you, hon? Hop on the point before the dang phone rings again."

"Well, I was wondering about that woman who called."

"Which woman? Lots of females call here." Pearline chortled. "Especially since Mr. Jacobson got divorced."

For an instant, Kate wondered if Pearline's laughter screened a jealous heart. "The woman who claimed to be Amanda's mother-in-law," she prompted.

"The drunk? Talked to her again this morning as a matter of fact."

"This morning?"

"That's what I said. She was already half in the bag, not but a few hours after breakfast." Pearline's voice filled with sharp indignation. "Demanded that we bring her the boy. Said she had a right to see him and she'd hire a lawyer to get what was her due."

Could they force her to turn over Way-Ray? Kate's free hand clenched into a fist. She wouldn't do it. She'd take him to Canada. To Mexico.

"I told her to go ahead," Pearline said. "Lawyers are thick on the ground, and there's bound to be one so hard up he'd take an abusive drunk as a client. And that's *all* I told her."

Kate lungs emptied of a relieved sigh. "Do you know where she was calling from?"

"Nope. I'll bet it's in the file. Hold on and I'll dig it out."

While Kate waited, she peered through the office window at a slice of street, the underside of the deck, the wall of the opposite building, and an equally tiny sliver of parking lot. She'd spot Way-Ray only a few seconds before he bounced into the office. Killing time, she straightened a stack of brochures for a charter fishing operation, aligned the pen with the edge of the registration form, and then aligned both with the edge of the counter. A smudge on the window drew her attention. She fished a tissue from her pocket and scrubbed at it, then spotted a dead fly inside the cover of the fluorescent light over her head. Rhea would think she had fewer housekeeping skills than Belinda.

"Justine Maxwell," Pearline said. "Nice name. Doesn't suit her. The note says she lives near Tulsa, but there's a question mark after that." Pearline rustled paper. "Shouldn't be too hard to find her. Although why you'd want to is beyond me. She's poison."

Kate scribbled the information on a sticky note. If you knew enough about a poison, you might be able to find an antidote.

"Know your enemy," Pearline said, as if she'd read Kate's mind. "That's Mr. Jacobson's favorite motto. Know what you're up against, plan out your strategy, and get them before they get you."

Kate remembered the message on Dyson's answering machine and the words "we'll get the goods." "Pearline, I need to talk with Ted Dyson. Have you seen him lately?"

"TD? No, hon, I haven't." Kate heard a rapid clicking. Fingernails on a desktop? "And that's odd, come to think of it. His office isn't but half a block away and he generally stops by here every day unless he's out of town. Did you leave a message?"

"Yes."

"Then he'll call you. TD's real good about returning his calls. You just be patient, hon."

Patient. Like sorry, another word that could do more harm than good. Waiting could get you nowhere. But lack of patience could do damage, too. If she'd been more patient on the day Wayne Jessop came for Amanda, everything would be different now. Amanda might be dead. Way-Ray might be with—

"TD will get back to you," Pearline said once more.

"But if you see—"

"I'll tell him to call you. Cripes, there's that dang phone. Talk to you later, hon." Pearline broke the connection.

Kate replaced the receiver and, in a flurry of activity designed to scatter her dark thoughts, removed the fly, straightened videotapes, and lined brochures up with military precision. Dyson would call soon. If he didn't, she'd fire him and hire another detective.

# CHAPTER 21

Summoned by a muffled ringing, Kate surfaced from the depths of sleep and confronted the glowing numbers on the digital alarm clock. 5:20. Why had she set it for such an early hour? What had she intended to do at dawn? She groped for the alarm button and found it already depressed. Odd.

Pieces of memory dropped into place like images on the revolving drums of a slot machine. She'd waited up until eleven for Dyson to call, then turned off the ringer on the desk phone, reduced the volume on the cordless handset upstairs, and slid it beneath her pillow. She dug it out and put it to her ear. "Wade in the Waves Motel."

"Kate Dalton?" The voice rumbled like summer thunder.

"Dyson?"

"You bet," the voice boomed. "What time is it out there? You weren't asleep, were you?"

Kate sighed with both relief and annoyance as she noted dingy light oozing through the slats of the blinds. "It's 5:20 and yes, I was."

"Well, sorry to wake you, but I just now got your message. My machine's on the fritz and I'm on the road, so it's not likely to get fixed too quick."

A broken answering machine. And a cavalier attitude toward the problem. "We expected you to check in before now."

"Didn't have anything to report until just yesterday," he replied in a flat tone that she inferred meant that part of the discussion was over, he would accept no blame, and she would be a fool to try to place it. "And to tell the truth, my cell phone's broke and your phone number up and lost itself."

Up and lost itself? What kind of a detective couldn't hang onto a phone number? "But you have something to report?"

"Like I said, I've been on the road, tracking Miz Blake up through Missouri and across the Mississippi to Illinois."

Kate sat up, pressing the phone tight against her ear. The blurred postmark must have been Missouri. "Where is she? What's her number?" She jerked open the nightstand drawer, scrabbling for pen and paper.

"Hold on! You're jumping the gun there, lady. I never said I *found* her. I only said I've been *tracking* her."

Kate's hopes deflated as her anger spiked. Lady! She'd told him not to use that word. She opened her mouth to chastise him, but bit her tongue. Dyson was what he was. Change wasn't likely.

"I'm close, though," Dyson went on. "Maybe only a day behind. She's riding buses.

Kate imagined Amanda hoisting herself aboard a silver bus, one hand clutched to her chest, her eyes bleak but resolute.

"She'll get off here and there and then get on another. Ticket agents say she's jumpy, anxious, like she's running from someone."

"She is. Her husband's half brother."

Dyson grunted. "Thought you told me there was no family."

"None that Amanda wants her son to know about." Kate glanced toward Way-Ray's partially closed door and lowered her voice. "There's Dwayne Vetter and—"

"That's the name you left on my machine."

"Right. She believes he wants to avenge his brother's death."

He grunted again. "Is there a reason you didn't mention that?"

"I didn't know. She sent me a letter from somewhere in Missouri. Pearline forwarded it."

"Shit." Dyson breathed heavily. "Would have saved a bunch of time if she'd told me. Damn that woman. It's either talk, talk, talk, or a vow of silence."

"Pearline didn't know what was in the letter."

"Hmm." Kate sensed Dyson didn't believe that. "She got a restraining order? Miz Blake, I mean. Not that they're worth the paper they're written on as far as keeping dirtbags at a distance, but judges like to see that you connected the dots."

"She didn't say. But I doubt she had time before she ran."

"She go to the cops?"

"No. She said it wouldn't do any good."

"Maybe. Maybe not. Smart thing would be to stay in one spot, take precautions, go to the cops, the neighbors, the news, make yourself too visible a target for him to take a shot at."

The media? Kate imagined Amanda's plight dramatized on a true crime program or the basis for a tawdry reality survival show with a deadly twist. She shuddered, remembering the reporters and photographers who besieged her after Wayne's death, the insistent producer with his unprincipled battered babes concept. She remembered the lies she guarded Way-Ray from, lies the media would feast upon. "Amanda won't do that."

"She's a fool if she don't," Dyson said with distinct condescension.

"It's a complicated situation." Kate glanced toward the bedroom door. A nightlight burned on the landing. If Way-Ray got out of bed, the tiny spill of light would eclipse as he passed. She visualized him asleep, arms tight around his pillow, mouth slightly agape, a shimmering bubble of saliva on his lips.

"She got a gun? No jury would blame her if she shot him."

Amanda was unarmed when Wayne attacked her. Had she intended to leave no doubt that she was the victim in that equation? Or had she simply hoped the attack would never come? She'd said she was afraid that killing Dwayne would stain her soul. "I don't think she has a gun with her."

"Hmm. Well, I've got a couple of spares. I heard you took out the ex without one."

The gory specter of Wayne Jessop rose at the foot of the bed and pointed an accusing finger. Kate lifted her chin and glared. *You are not a martyr.* The apparition grinned with bloody lips. She clamped her eyes shut and waves of color washed across her mind. "He killed himself," she said. "He fell on his knife."

"Point is, she shoulda learned from that. She should go to the news."

"She doesn't want publicity. She . . ." Kate kneaded the back of her neck. She felt as if she'd carried this burden of truth for a century, as if her shoulders were about to break. And Dyson was far away. "Her son doesn't know that's how his father died. He thinks Wayne got sick and passed away eight years ago." The words came out in a rush.

"Hmm. Nice bit of fiction, but sooner or later the kid will learn the truth."

Kate gritted her teeth and opened her eyes. There was only darkness at the foot of the bed. She flexed her shoulders, loosening the muscles. "It's my job to see that doesn't happen until he's old enough to understand." If anyone could ever understand a creature like Wayne.

"I hope you manage that," Dyson said without sarcasm. "Now who's this Justine Maxwell?"

"The former mother-in-law. She's a drunk. She lives near Tulsa. She wants Way-Ray."

"Well, Phil Jacobson will put a stop to that nonsense. Unless he draws the wrong judge. I've seen some of them get all jacked up on that family values bullshit and not bother to check whether there's anything of value in a family." Dyson snorted. "So you're hiding the boy?"

"Not hiding." Not yet. "If someone knew Way-Ray went with me, he could find him."

"And Jacobson's stonewalling the drunk," Dyson mused. The man's a stonewalling genius. And I'll bet Miz Blake's leading the brother in the opposite direction. What do you know about him?"

Kate shivered and pulled the quilt around her shoulders. "Amanda says he's like Wayne. Only meaner."

"Meaner, huh?" Dyson was quiet for a moment. "Guess I'd better find her before he does."

\* \* \* \* \*

After she hung up, Kate hunched inside the quilt, watching milky light drizzle through the blinds. Her thoughts caromed like pool balls on the break, slamming into the edges of her mind, clacking off each other, spinning away, colliding with others. She hated depending on a stranger—a paid stranger. She hated the queasy, off-balance feeling that what would happen was not only out of her control, but might ricochet back and spin her life in another direction.

The only option was to tell Way-Ray the truth and go to the police. It would hurt, but then it would heal.

Or would it?

She slid from the bed and, quilt sweeping the carpet behind her, crept across the landing to Way-Ray's room. The glass doors to the tiny balcony faced south, blocking the summer rays, but the rising sun created a creamy, incandescent glow, the color of eggnog ladled into crystal cups by candlelight.

Way-Ray had kicked off his covers and slept scrunched up like an inchworm, face smashed into the pillow, rump in the air, toes curled and overlapping. His pajama top had slid up and a band of pale skin shone in the glimmering light. She stepped closer, stretched out her index finger, and touched a jutting knob of his spine. His skin seemed both hot and cold, the bone beneath it as fragile as a relic. He shivered and drew breath. She grasped the edges of the sheet and blanket, tugged them from beneath his feet, and laid them over him. He sighed and sprawled flat. One thumb slid between his lips.

The light shimmered to a golden yellow, the color of lemon pie, butter, custard, roses, sundresses, and hair ribbons. Normal things.

But normal was far behind them now. Halfway across the country, Amanda was leading a killer, prepared to make the ultimate sacrifice. If she survived, she would have to realize Way-Ray was too precious to give away. She'd send for him. And he'd go.

"And I'll be alone again," Kate whispered. Alone. With a dark and aching emptiness. There was no anodyne. Falling to her knees, she laid her head beside Way-Ray's. She hadn't meant to, she'd fought against it, but she'd bonded with this boy.

She drew in a shuddering breath and stood. She was strong. She'd weather the pain. She always had. In the meantime, she'd stay the course Amanda had set and protect Way-Ray. From his uncle and from the truth.

# CHAPTER 22

Rhea burst through the office door and plunked her purse on the counter with the force of a sixteen-pound bowling ball.

Kate winced.

"Gotta clean that out." Rhea checked beneath the purse. "No dents. Sorry I'm late."

Kate blinked at the clock. Five minutes past nine. She glanced at the shift schedule posted by her desk. Rhea was an hour early. "Late for what?"

Rhea rolled her eyes and mock smacked her forehead. "Duh. Late to fill in on your day off."

"Day off?" Kate peered toward the kitchen, saw Way-Ray beginning the ritual of pouring a precise amount of milk into the hollow he scooped into a bowl exactly half full of the sugar-coated cereal he selected from the boxes lined up alphabetically in the cabinet. Since he learned his mother had disappeared, he'd been cataloging and arranging his possessions in what Kate assumed was an attempt to exert control where he could. She'd wrestled with what to tell him about Dyson's call and decided on scant details and lies: Dyson was in Illinois, still following Amanda, and in such a hurry he hadn't wanted to wait for her to wake Way-Ray. She planned to pack a picnic lunch and take him to the hollow square of driftwood logs the boys called their fort and tell him there where he might have a sense of security to balance her words.

"You love this place so much you forgot? Tuesday and Wednesday you're off, free, outta here." Rhea pointed to the door. "Grab your stuff. Go."

Kate studied the rows of squares on the calendar. When Rhea had explained the time-off system, she assumed it didn't extend to tourist season, but now two of those spaces were hers. She and Way-Ray could buy bicycles, and then— What would she do with the forty-seven hours after that? Where would she go? What if Dyson called? Kate felt dizzy, off balance. "I'd rather stay here and—"

"Forget it. Nadine's on her way."

"Nadine?" An inspection tour?

"She's booked tonight and tomorrow." Rhea tapped the reservation book beside her purse. "She probably scheduled it months ago." Leaning across the counter, she patted Kate's shoulder. "Hey, don't worry. She might peek into your kitchen and living room, but she won't go any farther. If she spots anything Way-Ray's left laying around, I'll claim it belongs to Sean. Nadine pretends to like my kids because she's afraid I'll quit if she doesn't."

Kate nodded, her mind numb. She might dodge this bullet, but Nadine would turn up again, perhaps without notice. She'd discover Way-Ray and—

"Get going," Rhea said.

"Where?"

"Hell, I don't know. Take Way-Ray to a mall. Go whale watching." Rhea lifted the latch, pushed the swinging gate, and crowded into the narrow space beside Kate. "Or a museum or a baseball game. Peanuts, popcorn, and all that stuff." Rhea bumped her hip. "But get going. Fast. Nadine's an early riser. Right this minute she's probably gorging on a crab omelet just down the coast."

Kate gripped the counter. "But the guests aren't out of her unit yet."

"She'll prowl around, poking into other rooms, checking up on how we clean hers, measuring the length of the grass,

165

hunting down Jackson. Or trying to. He does quite the disappearing act when she's in town." Rhea laughed, a manic hooting like an owl high on meth and drew a heart in the air with her index fingers. "She'll be stunned speechless when she sees that hedge and finds out he's in love."

Kate's cheeks burned. "I told him to fix the hedge. And he's not—"

Rhea hooted again. "Don't argue. Go."

Kate pivoted toward the kitchen, then back toward Rhea. She felt like a cartoon character that had run off a cliff into thin air. "But I'm expecting a call."

"I'll take a message." Rhea pointed to the stairs. "Grab some shorts and T-shirts, buy a couple of sleeping bags, and go out to Evie's with my boys. She's got plenty of room at that old farm and she could use a few more hands."

Kate halted in mid pivot. "Who's Evie?"

"Evie Hopkins. She's my mom's cousin once removed, or something." Rhea poked a hairpin back into her topknot. "She runs a wildlife refuge and rehabilitation center a few miles north of here."

Kate heard her mother's voice saying it was impolite to drop in, especially on strangers, and the epitome of bad manners to expect to be put up overnight. "I can't impose on—"

"Trust me. Before ten minutes is up you'll realize Evie's the one who's imposing. I'll draw you a map." Rhea snatched a sheet of paper from the stack beside the printer and pushed Kate toward the kitchen. "Way-Ray will love it. I'll bet she's got a hundred birds out there, squawking and pooping and pecking at each other."

"Birds?" Way-Ray looked up from his cereal bowl. "What kind of birds?"

"I don't know," Rhea said. "Murres. Cormorants. Ducks."

"I want to see them." Way-Ray bounced in his chair. "Can we go see the birds, Kate?"

"Sure you can," Rhea answered. "Just as soon as Kate gets her sh . . . her shirts packed. Hurry up and finish your cereal."

"Cool." He dug into the bowl, sloshing milk onto the table. "Don't forget to pack my bird book and my binoculars and my notebook and my pen. Okay, Kate?" He shoveled cereal into his mouth and gulped it down. "The blue pen, not the black one."

Kate felt a flash of anger. She was stuck: either she took Way-Ray to the refuge, or she disappointed him.

"I'll call and tell her you're coming," Rhea said.

Way-Ray slurried milk and cereal down his throat. "Don't forget my sunglasses."

Kate's anger faded. He'd have his fill of disappointment far too soon. "Aye, aye, sir." She saluted and headed upstairs.

\* \* \* \* \*

Two hours later, with a bright blue bicycle, sleeping bags, towels, pillows, clothing, and several sacks of groceries crammed into the back of the SUV, Kate spotted the gravel road marked on Rhea's map. She crimped the wheel and lurched into a pair of deep ruts leading through a dense stand of evergreens.

Way-Ray poked the map, his finger smeared with the remains of the chocolate ice cream cone he'd conned her out of by claiming that he'd eat at least one piece of lettuce on his next tuna sandwich. "Now we go until we come to where it says 'fork'." He giggled. "I wonder if it's a big fork, like the ones by the barbecue grills."

"Maybe it's a little plastic fork," Kate speculated. "Keep your eyes peeled."

Way-Ray giggled again. "You can't peel with a fork. You need a knife. And why would you peel your eyes, anyway? That would hurt?"

Kate grinned. "It's an idiom."

"An idiot?"

She laughed. "Some idioms seem like they were created by idiots. They're figures of speech."

"Figures? Like one, two, three?" He wiggled fingers in front of her face.

Kate peered along the dim tunnel formed by overhanging branches. "I guess 'figure of speech' might be another idiom. It's an expression that doesn't make sense if you take it apart."

"Huh?"

She pinched the bridge of her nose. Did she understand the concept? "Like, um, twenty-three. If you take it apart, it's two and three. But that's five. So you don't take it apart."

Way-Ray frowned. "That's lame."

Her explanation? Or the concept? She sighed. "Just watch for the fork."

The road emerged from the trees and sloped into a hollow where gravel gave way to dirt and withered grass on a broad hump between deepening furrows. Kate threaded the SUV between massive clumps of blackberry bushes. Green berries pattered the roof like fat raindrops and gangly canes slapped the grill, scraped across the hood, and whipped the windshield. She rolled her window up to keep thorns from raking her arm. As she did, she remembered Amanda's cobbler, warm, fragrant. Would she live to make another?

"Ooohhh." Way-Ray squirmed sideways and thrust both hands out the window. "Slow down and I'll pick a whole bunch of berries."

"They're not ripe yet."

"I'll put them in the sun and they'll get ripe."

"They're too small to get ripe."

"Will so. Then you can make a cobbler just like my mom's and I can put lots of whipped up cream on it."

Kate felt herself sinking in the emotional quicksand that filled the gulf between his faith and her knowledge. She kept her foot on the accelerator as the road twisted, angled sharply upward, and emerged onto an overgrown pasture. "Evie's expecting us," she said in a tight voice. "How about we see the birds and come back later for the berries?"

"But I can—"

"Look!" Kate pointed to a barn with timbers the color of dust and moss-encrusted shingles on its sagging roof. It seemed bone-weary, about to collapse into the tangled grass. "Maybe the road forks there." She glanced at Way-Ray from the corners of her eyes. "Or maybe it will spoon instead."

He stared at her for a second and then crossed his eyes. "Roads don't spoon, Kate. And you're not even funny." His words were coated with disgust, but he drew in his arms, consulted Rhea's map, and leaned forward to peer at the ancient barn. "There." He pointed to the right. "That's the way we go."

Kate turned the wheel, noting that they could hardly have gone left. That road must once have led to the barn, but now it was little more than a faint track through hummocky yellowing grass. The ruts widened, narrowed, and widened again, making the SUV shimmy and rock. Way-Ray bounced in his seat. "Faster." He thumped the dashboard with his fists. "Go faster."

Kate gripped the wheel with aching knuckles as the wheels wallowed around copses of trees and more brambles. "This is fast enough."

He stuck out his tongue. "Aw, Kate, you're no fun. When I grow up I'm going to go as fast as the wind, as fast as a tornado. I'm not going to poke along like an old lady." Way-Ray bounced to the limit of his seat belt, snorting between giggles. "You drive like a snail, like a slow, slimy, sluggy snail."

"But the snail got us here." She pointed to a weathered two-story house hunkered in a grove of thick-trunked trees with spreading branches supporting massive dull green canopies. Beyond the house, scattered across a pasture, were a number of outbuildings, some long and low with curved roofs of what looked like netting stretched across bent pipes, some taller with three sides built of solid wood and the fourth constructed of chicken wire, and some little more than cubes of chain-link fencing.

The road widened into what, with a huge load of gravel and a day's bulldozing, could be called a parking area. The front wheels dropped into a massive pothole. Kate's teeth snapped together. The rear wheels followed, jolting her spine. Her teeth snapped again, catching her tongue and filling her mouth with the metallic taste of blood. She targeted a relatively flat space beside a primeval pickup truck languishing in the shade.

"Hey, there's Kyle and Sean." Way-Ray tossed the map to the floor and aimed a grubby finger at the boys jogging toward them with several prancing deer and two fawns in their wake. "We're gonna stay for two whole days," he yelled as he unbuckled his seat belt and scrabbled at the door latch.

"Wait until we stop."

"But I want to pet the deer." He yanked on the latch and the heavy door swung wide as the SUV rocked to a halt beside the pickup.

A flock of geese, wings outstretched and sinuous necks thrust forward, appeared from behind the house and charged, honking and hissing. Kate clutched his T-shirt. "I said wait!"

"You yelled at me." Way-Ray's eyes widened.

Kate loosened her grip. "I was afraid you'd get hurt. It's not safe to jump from a moving vehicle."

The geese circled the SUV creating a pulsing wall of sound. "But we were only hardly moving," he screamed over the cacophony.

"It's still dangerous," Kate shouted. "That door weighs more than you do. It could have slammed back and broken your arm."

"But it didn't," he bellowed, his face the color of new brick.

Kyle charged the geese, arms spread wide. "Get back to the pond!" The flock turned, the boys pursued, deer chased behind, noise eddied, diminished.

"It didn't slam back," Way-Ray repeated.

"That's not the point." This was about power: how much he would try to take, how much she would allow him. "Forget what didn't happen. It's important that you listen and do what I ask."

He cut his eyes toward the door and chewed his lower lip, apparently considering his next move. A sly smile twitched at his lips. "My mom never yelled at me."

Kate doubted that. But Amanda, because she wasn't here, was now the perfect mother.

Way-Ray seemed to sense his victory. "She never yelled at me. Never ever."

"I'm . . ." Kate caught herself. Not sorry. He could have been hurt. He—

"You're late," a voice rasped. "I was expecting you half an hour ago. I need a hand with a bobcat."

# CHAPTER 23

"A bobcat?" Way-Ray hurtled from the SUV. "Where? I wanna see."

"Not so fast, young man," the voice rasped in a tone that implied there would be no hesitation and no back talk, a tone part nanny and part boot-camp sergeant.

Kate shut down the engine and peered at Way-Ray and a woman Kate assumed must be Evie Hopkins. White hair shot from her head in tufts and her skin was tanned the color of hazelnut shells. She wore a red sweater honeycombed with holes and frayed jeans faded to the shade of a winter sky. She was perhaps six feet tall and without curves or angles. Like a broomstick. A ramrod.

"Later," Evie told Way-Ray. "Now find Kyle and Sean and tell them to get the towels out of the dryer and folded and put away. Then put the fish out to thaw."

Way-Ray gaped at her for a second and then raced off.

Evie pointed at Kate. "You come with me. Watch where you step." She pivoted on the heel of a knee-high rubber boot and headed down a weedy path. Kate followed past a domed enclosure in which a dozen rabbits huddled around a basin filled with greens. As she jigged around piles of dark pellets, she wished she hadn't worn shorts and sandals.

Evie moved toward a low trailer with the rolling gait of someone just ashore after a long ocean voyage "Can't bend like

I should. Threw my back out last week when I fell over a water trough getting out of the way of an eagle." She chuckled, a sound that reminded Kate of winter nights when her mother would mix up warm water and salt and have her gargle to ward off colds. "Didn't think that bird was ready to fly yet. Shows you what I know."

Kate blinked. Bobcats? Eagles? How large was a bobcat? Was it tranquilized? Or would this woman wrestle it into submission, further mutilating her tattered clothing?

Something cool and damp nudged the bare skin at the back of her thigh. She let out an involuntary squeak and spun to see a deer cock its head and fix cocoa-colored eyes on her. It was shorter and darker than eastern deer, stockier, too—a black-tailed deer? It lowered its head and licked her knee. Kate backed away, flipping her fingers. "Shoo."

"Smack her rump," Evie counseled. "Thinks she runs the place. A trooper found her in the ditch beside a dead doe. That's how I get most of my fawns."

Kate touched the deer's side. Its coat was coarse, but softer than she expected.

"I'm required to release them when they're ready, but the females refuse to leave. Then the bucks visit and I get more fawns." She sighed. "Eventually I'll have to relocate some but I hate to do it. They'll be in a stewpot before the year is out." She strode to the moss-encrusted trailer, stomped her boots on the remains of a bristly mat, stepped up on a pair of concrete blocks, and opened a gray aluminum door so mangled that it touched the frame in only a few places. "But all this yammering isn't helping that cat."

As she disappeared inside, Kate recalled another dilapidated trailer and the pins straggling along a sagging clothesline. Would Amanda return, or would they fall, one by one, to the assault of the wind?

"You going to stand out there all day?" Evie called. "The tranquilizer will wear off and you'll learn the hard way what 'fighting tooth and nail' means."

Consigning her dark thoughts to the back of her mind, Kate trudged up the steps and into a dim room stacked with cages lined with threadbare towels, furnished with water bowls, and filled with birds and small animals. A powerful mix of aging fish, disinfectant, and excrement stung her eyes and nose. Gagging, she groped for the door. It caught against the frame, metal grinding against metal.

"Don't run off. You won't even notice the smell after a bit."

Smell? This was a stench. Kate hung in the doorway, gagging and gulping at fresh air, grateful that her stomach was empty.

An aluminum window farther along the trailer slid open and Evie's head popped through. "Rhea didn't mention that you had such a sensitive disposition. Come on, girl, suck it up."

Suck it up? That was exactly what Kate didn't want to do. But neither did she want to be perceived as weak. She took three huge breaths and steeled herself to do battle with an odor meaty enough to be packaged. These creatures scuttling to the far reaches of their cages had to eat, had to eliminate. Passing through a low doorway, she entered a room lit by eight long fluorescent bulbs set in two hanging fixtures—the kind she'd seen in workshops and garages. The bulbs emitted a faint humming hiss and two flickered. Bright orange extension cord looped from the ceiling like streamers at a handyman's ball. Metal shelving held stacks of bandages, bottles of medications, rows of gleaming scissors, clamps, and scalpels. Evie wiped at a long metal table with paper towels and a bright green disinfectant spray that made Kate think of caterpillar guts. She gagged again and tried to conjure up a replacement image: shamrocks, limes, jelly beans.

"He's in that crate." Evie pointed the spray bottle toward a plastic dog kennel far smaller than Kate imagined a bobcat would need. Grateful to focus on something besides the neon green spray, she stooped and peered through the barred door. The cat sprawled on a pink and gray striped towel, mouth open, tongue lolling. Lines of dark speckles spattered the lighter fur of his belly, advancing and retreating with each breath like the dizzying special effects in old science fiction films.

"See the trap?"

Kate bent closer. One leg was grotesquely swollen. The flesh had puckered and split, releasing clotted blood and bile-green pus. Her stomach spasmed again and she gripped the edge of a shelf, rattling the tools it held. She hadn't blanched at the sight of Amanda's wounds or the blood spewing from Wayne's groin, but she'd been high on adrenaline then.

From the corner of her eye she saw Evie give the table a final wipe. "A hiker found him. I'm hoping I can drain off most of that infection." She balled the paper towels and spiked them into a black plastic wastebasket. "People who set those traps should be trapped themselves and skinned alive." She slammed the disinfectant bottle onto the counter. "I'm ready. Get him on the table."

"Uh, sure. The table." Kate thought of that inflamed leg, the oozing wound. "How do I do that?"

Evie's eyes, so dark brown they appeared almost black in the fluorescent glow, sparked like flint on stone. "Rhea said you were a fast learner."

Kate felt a rush of anger that cleared her mind. She gritted her teeth and bit off precise words. "I am. Tell me how you want me to do this and step aside."

Evie gargled another laugh and slapped the metal table with both hands. "We're going to get along just fine. Use that towel he's on to ease him out, then pick him up. Put on those gloves." She pointed with her chin toward a pile of crusty leather gloves stiffened into fists.

Kate wrinkled her nose. "Are there any others?"

Evie jerked a latex glove from a box beside the sink and snapped it on. "Just these. Won't help much if he rallies and claws at you.

"Then I'll do without." *And prove myself.*

175

Kate knelt beside the kennel, unlatched the door and, before she could hesitate, grasped the towel, pulled the cat to the front of the kennel, and slid her hands beneath him. His fur was thick, but there was little beneath it except bone and sinew. "You poor thing, you're starving," she whispered as she angled him out. "Hang on. We'll fix you up."

"Don't count on it." Evie's voice was flat. "Sometimes they get here too late."

"This one will make it." The trap clanked against the table as she laid him down. Harsh fluorescent light gave a blue wash to the white of his belly and revealed that the bands of speckles didn't end at his flanks, but spread along his legs, across his back. There were even lines of spots on his head and between his eyes. "He's beautiful."

"Hmm. This could gag a maggot. You might want to turn your back while I get the trap off."

"I'm okay." Kate held her breath and kept her eyes on the swollen leg.

Evie pried the trap loose, tossed it on the floor, and probed the wound with her fingers. "Not as bad as I thought. Didn't cut him too bad and he got to water, so he's not too dehydrated." She checked cat's paw. "Looks like he's got circulation to the foot. You ready to hand me my tools when I call for them."

"Yes."

"Good." Evie fixed Kate with her crackling gaze. "Believe it or not, I can't get many folks to volunteer out here. Word's out that I can be a little testy."

Kate couldn't, in good conscience, protest. She felt herself flush, her lips open and close.

"Ha!" Evie snorted and busied herself with the film. "I'm ornery as a hungry hawk if things don't go my way. My own son says so. Now let's get to work."

For the next half hour, Kate suppressed her gut reactions to the ripe stench of infection and followed Evie's clipped orders as the old woman's gnarled fingers performed the delicate work of paring away infected tissue, inserting a drain tube, suturing,

176

bandaging, and fitting a tapered collar around the cat's neck to keep it from chewing at the wound. Finally, she eased the bobcat back into the kennel and secured the door.

"How did you learn to do all that?"

"My husband and I had a dairy herd until he up and died on me. Cows always needed some doctoring." Evie worked her gloves off and tossed them into a wastebasket. "Time was when I'd shoot a bobcat and not think twice. Now I'm patching them up. Funny how the world turns around, isn't it?"

Kate nodded, thinking of how her own world had turned, wondering what drove Evie. Was it a version of that same mother/protector urge that sent Amanda out as a decoy? Was it triggered by the death of her husband? An incident with her son? Kate studied Evie's squared shoulders and decided she wouldn't ask. There was no veneer of convention and etiquette around this woman, but that didn't mean Evie would welcome an interrogation.

The black-tailed deer that had followed them stood chewing a mouthful of grass outside the trailer. Kate patted its back as they passed. The deer flipped its tail and stomped one rear hoof.

"I hope those boys remembered to put the fish out to thaw," Evie muttered, "otherwise we'll have some pissed off pelicans. You can come along when I feed them if you want, but stay back. They get nervous, they regurgitate."

Kate didn't allow herself to imagine *that* stench. "How many pelicans do you have?"

"Seven," Evie said. "Three eagles, a dozen gulls, a few owls, a couple of hawks, a falcon, two loons, dozens and dozens of murres, ducks, and surf scoters, geese, rabbits, deer, and another bobcat."

Kate blinked. "Wow."

Evie grunted as she climbed the steps to the porch. "Some folks argue that nature meant for these creatures to die." She spun to face Kate, jabbing a finger at her forehead. "But that's a bullshit excuse for ignoring man-made problems."

Kate stumbled, clutching at the splintered wood of the railing.

"It's not Mother Nature driving the cars that hit the deer or dumping the plastic that kills the seabirds."

Kate raised her hands. "Hey, I'm on your side."

Evie released a sigh that was half sob and shoved her fingers through her ragged hair. "Sometimes I wish I could harden my heart and walk away. Maybe I'm going crazy like my son says. But I'll keep on until the bitter end, until the developers shut this place down."

# CHAPTER 24

Way-Ray yanked the zipper of his stoplight-red sleeping bag up to his chin. "I never camped out before."

"I don't think it's 'camping out' if we're inside." Kate bent with a grunt that testified to her exhaustion and scooped up the T-shirt, shorts, and socks he'd shucked, used them to dust the windowsill, and tossed them into the paper sack she'd set on the warped seat of a primeval rocker. It and the narrow bed nearly filled this tiny room that had been used, abused, and neglected. Even the most optimistic Realtor would balk at describing the house as "needing a little TLC." Dark ceiling stains signaled the need for a new roof, and the floor in the upstairs bathroom was spongy. Decorating teams that slapped on paint and swapped furniture would rip out their moussed hair at the sight of Evie's furnishings.

But Way-Ray noticed none of that. He forgot about the absence of a TV when Kyle and Sean showed him the garter snakes in the cellar, and he was enchanted by this room tucked under the eaves with a steep-sloped ceiling he could bump his head on.

"Well, I have a brand new sleeping bag," he insisted, "and I've never ever had one before, so it's camping to me." He wiggled his flashlight, sending a beam through the bars of the tarnished brass bedstead onto gouged and tattered wallpaper. "Kinda like being out in a field."

"Kinda," Kate agreed. The top layer of paper, lacy ferns on a beige background, had fallen away in strips, revealing enormous sunflowers. Near the door, someone had excavated further and uncovered a fox-hunting scene. Kate smiled, thinking of Auntie Mame. She feathered Way-Ray's hair with her fingers. There were a hundred roads you could walk raising a child.

Way-Ray clicked the light on and off. "Besides, there aren't any screens, so all the bugs can get in and maybe even a bat Evie says, or a squirrel, and that's almost exactly like being in a tent."

Kate aligned his flip-flops so he could slip into them easily. The floor had long since shed its varnish and the bare path to the doorway bristled with slivers. "Except the deer can't walk right in."

"And the bunnies can't, either."

"Good thing, too." Kate touched his nose with her index finger. "Those bunnies like to be warm. They'd snuggle right up next to you and wiggle their noses and ears and tails."

"That would tickle." He giggled, ducking his head inside the sleeping bag and pulling the flashlight after him. The bag glowed like charcoal embers in the heart of a fire. "This is way cool. I wanna come back here all the time. Can we?"

Kate gazed through the window at the sky—a luminous purple tapestry sprinkled with glimmering stars hanging over the salt marsh at the western edge of land she learned had been in Evie's family for more than a century. She flexed her aching shoulders and thought about the long day behind her: cages cleaned, water dishes scrubbed and filled, dirty towels lugged and loaded into the washer. Striving to meet Evie's expectations was torture, and yet she felt a warm satisfaction from completing those tasks and more, and from earning a nod of approval when she surveyed the vast oak kitchen table littered with state and federal paperwork, told the boys to steer clear of it or else, and carried their hot dogs and beans outside. "We'll see."

Way-Ray peeped from the bag. "We'll see, yes? Or we'll see, no?"

Kate rubbed her eyes. Delivered by her parents, the expression had signified that study would be given and a decision made at an unspecified time. It also meant the discussion was closed and lobbying efforts, no matter how subtle, could cancel consideration. Had she ever attempted to decipher inflection, tone of voice, or volume? She had no memory of that, but suspected her parents had been inscrutable. Amanda, apparently, was more transparent.

Way-Ray kicked his feet and the sagging mattress jounced on reproachful springs. "I wanna come back here."

"We'll—" Kate halted. Repeating herself would show weakness and open the door to whining and teasing. She stood. "We have a lot to do tomorrow. Turn off that flashlight and get to sleep."

"Okay." He drew the word out into three lengthy syllables but didn't touch the flash. "Kate? How can I keep the 'velopers from hurting the deer and the eagle and the ducks?"

"Developers," she corrected.

"What you said." He flipped a hand.

"They won't hurt the birds and animals. They're not hunters."

He flipped his hand again, brushing away her words. "But there won't be room for animals if they build those crowdomimiums."

"Condominiums," Kate corrected, thinking she liked his take on it. Perhaps "crowdamaximums." "They won't build for a year or two. Maybe not at all if Evie gets the grant she applied for."

He puffed his lips, the flashlight tight beneath his chin, giving his skin a saffron cast. "Kyle says his mom says that Evie borrows from Peter to pay Paul. So how come Paul doesn't borrow it from Peter himself? Then Evie would have enough to pay her taxes?"

Kate chuckled. "That's another figure of speech. It means that Evie used the money she needed for her taxes and mortgage payments to build cages and ponds. Peter and Paul aren't real people."

"Nuh-uh." He shook his head. "You don't know anything, Kate. Paul is Evie's son. Only he's not a kid, he's a man, older even than you." He clicked the flashlight off and on. "Kyle says Paul's mad because Evie spends all her money fixing the birds and animals and buying medicine and fish and stuff. Kyle says his mom says Paul says Evie's going to spend up all of his inhabitants."

"Inheritance," Kate corrected automatically, her mind working out the chain of hearsay.

Way-Ray flicked the light again. "And Kyle says his mom says Paul says his father is rolling over in his grave." He erupted with a shout of laughter. "That's another figure of speech, huh? 'Cause my mom told me that when people are put in their graves, it means they're going up to the angels and in heaven they get brand new skin and wings and harps. So if they're up there," he pointed to the ceiling, "then they can't be rolling under the ground. Right?"

"So I've heard." Kate congratulated herself on coming up with such a noncommittal answer without a moment's hesitation. Back in Grassy Ridge, what seemed like years ago, she'd wondered how much Amanda had told Way-Ray about pain, death, and what came afterward. Unless Amanda survived and returned, Kate would have to piece together a belief system from his comments. How would that system account for where Wayne would spend eternity? Something else to think about later. "Time to go to sleep."

"Okay." He flicked off the light. "Kate?"

She paused, one foot in the hallway. "Yes?"

"My mom used to give me an allowance. Do . . . do you think you could, too? I'll do chores and stuff, and I'll give all the money to Evie and my mom will pay you back when TD finds her."

Kate winced, grateful that the only light in the hallway came from a fly-specked bulb in the bathroom. "I'd be happy to," she choked. "How about ten dollars a week?"

"Cool. Starting tomorrow?"

Kate sniffled. "Right after breakfast."

"Alllll right!"

"Now go to sleep."

"Okay." He flicked the flashlight on and targeted her face. "Hey, Kate, you know what?"

She put a hand up to shade her tearing eyes. "What?"

"I'm sorry I opened the door when you said to wait and I'll try real hard to do what you say from now on because Kyle says you were right and I coulda been hurt and I hope you're not mad but I guess you're not because you're going to give me an allowance." He clicked off the light. "Good night."

"Good night." Feeling absolved, Kate trudged along the hallway to the room Way-Ray had pronounced hers. It held a dresser missing its top drawer, a drop-leaf table with two claw feet chopped off at the first knuckle joints, an orange-and-white-flowered porcelain lamp with a baseball-sized hole in the yellowed shade, and a rug braided from what appeared to be support hose and bearing the distinct aroma of a territory-marking tomcat. A mattress slouched against the wall. Its ticking had ruptured in a dozen places and lumps of gray batting swelled from the wounds.

Kate took a deep breath, rolled up the rug, and stuffed it into the closet. Air quality improved immediately. She dragged the mattress beneath the open window and stomped across it a few times to soften it up. The remaining dresser drawers stuck, but she finally jiggled one loose, turned it upside down beside the mattress, and placed the lamp on it.

Her bedroom had no door, and the window had no shade or curtain, but she wasn't concerned about modesty: Kyle was outside watching for meteors and Sean was asleep on a mildewed sofa relegated to the back porch beneath a yellow bug light that seemed unaware of its job description. Evie had tossed a quilt over him. "He'll find his way to bed if he wakes up before morning."

Kate felt a frisson of fear. "You don't lock your doors?"

"Don't have a key," Evie laughed. "Can't remember if I ever did."

Kate shivered as shadows of flitting moths dappled Sean's face. No locks.

"What's the matter, girl? You look like you saw a ghost." Evie laid a hand on Kate's arm, eyes sparking.

For a few seconds, Kate felt as if Evie knew everything. Then she told herself that was ridiculous. The impression was simply a function of her longing to share the burden. But Evie carried enough burdens of her own. "I'm just tired," she answered, glancing away.

Evie shrugged. "Then go on inside and get your boy off my computer and into his bed." She yanked at the door which harbored only a few square inches of screen and two screw holes where a handle had once hung. "I sleep downstairs. The geese let me know if anyone comes around."

*And what will we do then?* Help would be slow in coming out here, Kate thought, slower than the day she fought Wayne.

"Everything will be fine," Evie had told her. "You'll see."

And maybe it will, Kate thought as she scrubbed her face and hands with a nubbin of soap and the thin trickle of water the sink begrudged her. She slipped out of her jeans, unhooked her bra, and worked it from beneath her T-shirt, spread her sleeping bag on the mattress, plumped up the pillow she brought from the Wade in the Waves Motel, and dug into her duffel bag. She found the book on the journey of Lewis and Clark and smiled. Her reading had slowed to the pace of the expedition's long portage. She stretched out and peered at the book, but the words blurred as her mind churned up questions: How much did Evie owe? Would the grants come through?

Closing her eyes, Kate reviewed her own finances. She'd paid off the credit card charges from the trip, but the balance was creeping up again—three hundred dollars just today for the bicycle, sleeping bag, gas, and groceries. Subtracting what she set aside for Way-Ray's surgery and adding in the coming paycheck, the number on the bottom line was puny.

From the age of five, Kate knew she would receive no inheritance. Her parents expected her to become self-reliant, to prepare for the vicissitudes of life. They told her their role was to nurture strengths, not encourage weakness with smothering attention and a financial cushion. She would succeed without help—as they had—or she would fail.

Sighing, she remembered how forsaken she felt when she signed over the deed to their house to an educational trust, wrote the checks to other charities that disposed of their meager savings, and watched the furniture go to auction. It took less than an hour to pack her grandmother's china and silver, her mother's simple emerald engagement ring, a few books, and the broken-spined albums stuffed with ancient photographs, borders cracking, colors rusting to a muddy brown like old bloodstains.

Prying a few pictures loose from their black triangular holders, she'd found names and dates written in a crabbed hand with a fine-pointed fountain pen and ink that had faded to the same brown. She spent an hour staring into the dim eyes of men named Clarence and Nelson, women called Ella and Ivy and Beulah. Because of them, she existed.

She clicked off the light and rolled onto her side. Amanda had attempted to mold Way-Ray's character by shielding him from his heritage and protecting his innocence. Kate pounded her pillow. But innocence was no barrier against evil. Innocence, in fact, could draw evil like a magnet.

# CHAPTER 25

From the corner of her eye, Kate saw Way-Ray bound into the office and shove through the gate. "Look!" He jostled her arm and her fingers slid across random letters on the keyboard. "Cool, huh?"

"Hang on." She backspaced and erased the gibberish. A prospective guest couldn't be expected to make sense of "hully rwuipprg kiyvhrnd." In fact, a prospective guest might think the motel manager tippled while she typed. "Let me change this to 'fully equipped kitchens,' okay?"

"I made this all by myself."

"Then it's wonderful." Kate added a line about rate reductions in the fall and another about salmon fishing, storm watching, nearby antique stores, and restaurants. Rhea had been too busy with cleaning and fielding phone calls to do more than glance through incoming e-mails for anything that needed immediate attention, and Kate found more than a dozen inquiries when she logged on after her morning chores. Nadine's fault. Rhea had called just as Kate was loading up at Evie's place. "Nadine's checked out, but she's got Jackson up on the dune building a driftwood bench. He's so happy he could cut his own throat. Anyway, I told her you're checking on a motel supply auction and running late."

Rhea hadn't given the "all clear" message until after five. Now Kate felt disoriented, rushed.

"You can't say it's good until you look," Way-Ray said.

"Okay." Kate hit "send" and turned to consider the object he thrust toward her. Once it had been a coffee can.

"Isn't it neat?" Way-Ray turned it to display pictures of birds clipped from magazines with an unsteady hand and secured to the can with shiny gobs of dried glue. Both rims were festooned with crinkly red and gold Christmas ribbon she suspected he'd scavenged from a sack of holiday decorations stashed in the dim recesses of the shed. She hoped Way-Ray hadn't disturbed Jackson's equipment. After two days in Nadine's clutches, the handyman must be on the verge of crawling back into a bottle—if he hadn't already. "It's unique," she temporized. "It's, um, eye-catching."

"And here's where people put the money." Way-Ray jammed on a plastic lid with a jagged slot hacked into the center. "I used a knife to make the hole, but I was real, real careful. And I cut it away from me like when you let me cut up carrots and celery for salad."

She smiled at the pride in his tone and decided to scrap a lecture about safety. The deed was done. "Careful is an important thing to be."

"Sean and I are going downtown," he told her. "At lunchtime. And we're going to get lots and lots of money."

Kate doubted that. Too many adults might assume their donations would finance colas, candy bars, and comics. She dug amidst the paper clips in the top desk drawer and found a quarter, two dimes, four nickels, and perhaps fifteen pennies. "Your first contribution."

He stuffed the coins through the lid and rattled the can. "I even put on old clothes so I wouldn't get glue and stuff on them." He plucked at a faded black T-shirt with a picture of a cartoon character Kate didn't recognize. Pop culture was blitzing past.

"That was good thinking, but now you should change. You don't want to look like a beggar when you're asking for money."

"Why not? If you're a beggar, you really need money, don't you?"

"Yes, you do, but . . ." Most people detoured around beggars as if lack of money was a communicable disease. Or they believe all beggars were scam artists collecting for fortified wine or cigarettes. How could she explain that to Way-Ray without sounding prejudiced or cruel? She rubbed her eyes. Her parents had never groped for platitudes. The truth, raw, unvarnished, cynical, that was their style. Shrugging that away, she touched his nose with her index finger. "Lots of people work hard for their money. Before they give to someone, they want to make sure that that person won't spend it on frivolous things."

He wiggled his nose. The summer sun had brought out a cluster of freckles. "What's friv . . . friv . . . what's that word mean?"

"Frivolous." Kate sounded it out. "It means not really necessary, maybe even kind of silly. Remember when we saw the yellow and white crocheted covers for rolls of toilet paper?"

"Yeah." He tugged at his ear. "So people don't give money to beggars because they might buy toilet paper covers?"

Kate fought back a laugh. "Well, no, but they might buy other stuff they don't really need. See, everybody has a different idea of what's necessary, and what's frivolous."

He rattled the collection can. "What do you think is frivolous?"

Kate glanced at the computer screen and the bold print of the e-mails she had yet to answer and marveled again how question led to question. "Electric windows in cars, jeweled collars for dogs, a hundred flavors of ice cream, or a television set in your bedroom."

"Nuh-uh," he pouted, "that's not friv . . . what you said." He pointed toward his room like a miniature attorney directing the jury to Exhibit A. "I need that TV so I can watch my stuff and not bother you when you're working. If I didn't have a TV in my room, you'd be all the time telling me to be quiet and, uh,

I'd get bored and maybe go down to the ocean by myself or get in Jackson's way."

Kate remembered Jackson's hands tightening the screw, his contained movements, his sparse words. "You haven't been bothering him, have you?"

"Nuh-uh." He shook his head, but his eyes rolled upward, left, then right. "You told me not to."

*I told you not to use a knife by yourself, too.* "Okay. Because you know that Jackson has a lot of work to do and he's—"

"Kinda weird. That's what Kyle says, anyway. Jackson was in a war before the tree fell on him. Kyle says fighting messed up his head so he gets mad when he's really sad and he doesn't know how to be happy and he drinks the stuff that pickles your brain cells."

Kate blinked at the wisdom of Kyle Whitaker, amateur psychologist.

"Kyle says Jackson's like the deer at Evie's," Way-Ray continued. "Not the tame ones, but the ones that come out of the woods to eat the grass. If you chase them, they run. But if you stand real still, they sometimes even eat apples out of your hand."

Kate's imagined Jackson, lips drawn back, chomping at an apple balanced in the center of her palm. She shook her head. What part of her brain spawned that? "Still, you shouldn't bother—"

"I'm not bothering him." Way-Ray stomped his foot. "He's glad I'm helping Evie. He's going to write letters. But I get to sign them."

Kate felt as if she'd missed not one step, but three. "Letters?"

"To people who make the rules in Washington. The DC place," he added.

Kate's fingers rolled into fists. Jackson should have consulted her before he hatched this scheme. "What will those letters say?"

He gave her a pitying look and rattled his can again. "Duh. That Evie needs lots of money for the birds and animals and everyone should help because . . . because they're orphans."

Orphans? Was his campaign more about allaying his own fears than helping Evie? If it was, then his anguish would double when he got evasive political answers: promises to study the problem, advice that his request had been forwarded to the appropriate agency. Kate forced a bright tone. "I think that's a great idea. When did you and Jackson cook this up?"

"This morning." He dug a toe into the carpet. "When you were doing that big pile of laundry Rhea said she was sorry she couldn't get to and she'll make it up to you after her days off."

Which will be Sunday morning. Kate recalled her intention to tell Rhea the whole story—or at least sound her out. Rhea might prefer to be blissfully ignorant. Glancing at the stack of mail on the counter, Kate realized Way-Ray hadn't searched through it when they'd returned.

Way-Ray flung his free arm around her shoulder and leaned his forehead against hers. "Don't you like Jackson, Kate?" His eyes peered into hers.

Trapped. Kate slipped her arms around his waist and drew him against her shoulder, ducking her head. A child couldn't understand the complexity of feelings Jackson aroused. She couldn't understand herself beyond feeling as if she'd written every thought and memory on index cards that he had shuffled through. "It's nice of him to help you," she said, evading the question. "You'd better get cleaned up. It's close to noon."

He broke the hug, cocked his head at the clock, and used his index finger to count off numbers. "I've got . . ." He chewed at his lower lip. "I've got twenty-two minutes. Right?"

"Right."

"No sweat." He clanged the can onto the corner of the desk. "Watch my money so no one steals it."

"Gotcha." Kate slid the can to a spot beside the computer monitor.

"And I'll get lots and lots more and save Evie's animal place." He touched Kate's nose. "And they'll all live happily ever after."

Kate kept a smile pasted to her face until he'd begun to climb the stairs. Happily ever after. An ironic phrase from the lips of a child whose crazed uncle was stalking his mother. But—for a few more days—what could be the harm in allowing him to believe that anything was possible?

# CHAPTER 26

When the phone clipped to the waistband of her jeans buzzed, Kate juggled an armload of dirty linen and snatched at it. "Wade in the Waves Motel," she said in the most cheerful tone she could muster on a Sunday when nine rooms had to be cleaned within three hours.

"We'll make it," Rhea had promised as she'd ground out a cigarette and shrugged into her smock. "We almost always do. Give them a twenty-dollar one-night discount if we don't."

Making the deadline would be easier if Nadine—who would fume about that discount—allocated money for more linens. On days like today, sheets were still warm from the dryer when they went back on the beds they'd been stripped from.

"How may I help you?" Kate prompted the silent caller.

"Well . . . ." The voice was male, low-pitched. "Is this a hotel?"

"Motel." Kate dumped her load onto the laundry room floor. If this clown had dialed a wrong number, she hoped he'd hang up and get on with his life. Yesterday a woman insisted Kate was mistaken and demanded she repeat the number three times. Fuming, Kate had. Saint Kate the Compelled. "Can I help you?"

"I'm not sure."

Kate longed to thump the phone against the washer, but instead hunched her shoulder to clamp the receiver against her ear and wrestled damp sheets into the dryer. She heard the tapping of high heels on the steps from the deck and canted her head to see a woman cradling a Pomeranian. She wore flowered slacks and a yellow silk blouse. The dog wore a scowl and a pink ribbon. The woman strolled past the plastic bag dispenser mounted on a stake beside the beach path. Kate bet she'd leave her pet's poop on the sand, expecting the ocean to clean up after her. Entitled. Imperious.

"If you want a room, we won't have any vacancies until August. Late August," she informed the caller. In just a few days she'd learned that indecisive guests could suck more time than demanding ones who at least knew what they wanted.

"Are you the manager?"

"Yes." Kate slammed the dryer door, rotated the dial and pushed the "start" button. The dryer shuddered and creaked into action. The manager of a motel with a sheet shortage. The high point of my career arc. "Can I help you?"

"Maybe. It's a long shot."

Kate rolled her eyes. He'd get to the point in his own time. Or he wouldn't. In either case, why waste more breath? She flipped open the washer's lid, rotated its dial, and pulled the knob. Steaming water gushed into the tub. She splashed in bleach and detergent. No time to measure. As the suds rose, she stuffed in dirty linens, banged the lid closed, popped the door on the second dryer, and fingered warm, damp sheets. The skin at the back of her neck prickled. Was this a potential guest, or . . . ? She straightened, gripped the plastic jug of bleach. "Who is this? Where are you calling from?"

The man on the phone cleared his throat.

Kate's heart thudded against her sternum. Where was Way-Ray? She hefted the jug. Five pounds? Not much of a weapon. All she had.

"My name is Pete Marlow. I'm calling from Ohio."

*Sure you are.* Kate struggled to keep her voice level. "As I said, we have no vacancies until late August. I can recommend several other motels."

"I'm not looking for a room."

*Of course you're not. You're looking for Way-Ray. You could be watching right now.* Kate stepped to the doorway, scanned the parking lot. "Then why did you call?"

Pete Marlow cleared his throat again. "I'm a homicide investigator." Marlow's plodding became almost a verbal sprint. He reeled off the name of a city and county and finished with, "I'm looking for some help with a case."

"At a motel in Oregon?" She jogged toward the office to find Way-Ray.

"I thought there might be a connection."

She opened the office door, heard the boys' laughter in the rooms above, stepped in and locked the door behind her. "A connection?"

"Yes. Listen, this isn't a hoax." His voice was laced with urgency. "I am who I say I am. Call back and talk to Chief Spencer if you want."

"At a number you'll provide?"

"No, damn it. Call information. Check the internet," he gulped air. "But please call, please."

Would Dwayne Vetter plead with her like this? Maybe. "Hang on."

Kate put him on hold, dropped into the chair behind her desk, brought up the site, and found Marlow's name. But anyone else could do the same and claim to be him. She called up the weather forecast for the Ohio town, then brought up a site with tourist information, took Marlow off hold, and grilled him about restaurants, nearby campgrounds, and whether he expected rain tomorrow. He passed the test. "Okay," she said, "Tell me about this case."

He sighed. "Thanks. Like I said, this is a long shot, but a man called this number five days ago. Early. He might have gotten you out of bed, Miss—?"

Kate shook her head. "My name's not important."

Marlow was silent for a moment. "All right. The call was made on the 19<sup>th</sup>. It was fairly long. I don't think it went to a machine."

Kate counted back on her fingers. The 19<sup>th</sup>? Dyson? "I got a call from Illinois that morning."

Marlow drew in a sharp breath. "Do you remember the name of the caller?"

Sweat beaded on Kate's forehead. She crossed the lobby, snapped the bolt, slipped through the door, and locked it behind her. If Way-Ray heard Dyson's name, he'd bolt to her side. A breeze fluttered pink and white petunia blossoms bursting from clay flowerpots hanging from the deck. She'd never planted flowers. Her parents thought them impractical. Now she longed to set some bright budding plants in soil, to sit and watch them bloom. She reached the laundry room and ducked inside. "Ted Dyson. But he was in Illinois, not Ohio."

"Ted Dyson," Marlow muttered. "D-y-s-o-n?"

"That's right." Kate imagined him filling in an official form.

"Why did he call?"

"Why does that matter? He was in Illinois."

Marlow made a soft click with his tongue. "I understand. We're trying to trace his movements and piece some things together."

The rolling surf of sound within the laundry room seemed to swell. Heat spiked. Her pulse throbbed in her forehead. "What happened? What happened to Ted Dyson?"

Marlow cleared his throat. "How well did you know him?"

Kate moaned. Did. Past tense. She sucked in scalding air. "I never met him. He's a private detective. From Oklahoma." He *was* from Oklahoma.

"Oklahoma," Marlow repeated. Kate imagined him drawing his own mental map, linking Oregon to Oklahoma to Ohio. Strange, those states all began with "O." Were there others? She tried to remember, trying to distract herself. "That's a long way from Oregon," Marlow said.

Kate stumbled to the doorway and sipped at the salty breeze the way a starving person must begin again to eat, letting it drift into her lungs in shallow breaths. "I hired him over the phone. He was searching for a woman who disappeared in Oklahoma."

Marlow jumped on her words. "A woman?"

"Amanda Blake. She—" The washer began the pulsing thump that signaled an unbalanced load. Kate darted to the machine and flung up the lid. When it shuddered to a halt, she thrust her hand into wads of sodden sheet. "She was a friend."

"Can you describe her?" Marlow's grated with rough urgency. "We have an unidentified female victim, too."

# CHAPTER 27

Black spots danced before Kate's eyes. Dyson. Amanda. Both dead. What would she tell Way-Ray? She thought of the dog's bark and the laughter she heard moments earlier. Soundtrack for the end of childhood. She heard a soft whimper, realized it came from her throat.

"Are you okay, Miss—?"

Kate blinked, released the sheets, and wiped her hand on her jeans. Her fingers seemed numb, disconnected; she couldn't feel the rough texture of the denim or the long muscle in her thigh.

"Dalton," she said. "Kate Dalton. And I prefer Ms."

"Ms. Dalton? Are you okay?"

What a stupid question. She felt like he'd put a stun gun against the back of her neck and shorted out her nerve endings. She lowered the washer lid. The machine groaned, shimmied, spun. Life went on. "I'm okay."

"Do you want to get a glass of water? Or something? I'll hold."

"No. I'm . . ." She keyed in on the sounds around her: the boom of the ocean, the sputter of a lawnmower, the roar of a vacuum cleaner in the room above. "Go on."

"Do you have a picture you could fax or e-mail to me?"

A picture? Way-Ray didn't have one. Had she asked Dyson to hunt for a photo in the trailer? She couldn't remember. She

197

rubbed her hand on her jeans until her fingers stung. "No, but I can describe her. She's maybe five-two or five-three, pale, and extremely thin."

She *was* pale and thin. She *had been* pale and thin. Past tense. Kate remembered how Amanda pressed her hand against her chest, remembered the black pain in her eyes. Amanda would always be that way now. Rays of sun would never brush color into her skin. She'd never gain an ounce. She'd never know if she saved Way-Ray.

"Hair color?" Marlow asked. "Eyes?"

"Her eyes were light gray and . . ." The ghost of Wayne Jessop seemed to rise through the concrete floor of the laundry room brandishing his knife. Kate turned her head from that grisly smile. "Her ex-husband tried to kill her in February. He stabbed her in the chest and hip. She sliced her hands trying to defend herself."

Marlow grunted and Kate knew he'd seen the scars. Had he wondered how a woman so small provoked such anger? Had he leaped to conclusions about drugs or prostitution? Kate felt tears scald her eyes. "Tell me what happened to her. To them."

"I . . . the policy is . . . oh hell. It'll be in the papers sooner or later." Marlow's voice thickened and he cleared his throat with a muffled cough. "A hiker found them dumped in a ravine in a state park a few miles from here. They'd been there a day or two."

In the silence that followed, Kate imagined two broken and bloated bodies sprawled beneath the dusty leaves of a summer forest. She rubbed her eyes, trying to expunge a horror she knew was indelible.

"They died hard," Marlow said.

Nothing in life had come easy for Amanda. Why should death have been an exception?

"Thank you for breaking the rules," Kate said, even as she thought how ridiculous it was to thank someone for conveying such ghastly information. "I had to know."

"I understand." Marlow's relief seemed almost tangible. "That's normal."

Normal. Such an odd word. As mutable as wind and weather. As elastic as a rubber band. It defied definition, and yet everyone seemed absolutely certain what normal was—and what it wasn't.

"This ex-husband you mentioned, you got his name?" Marlow's solemn voice had an eager edge.

"Wayne." The specter rose again. Kate slashed at it with the side of her hand and it dissolved into saturated air. *I've wasted too much time wondering if I should have fought harder to save your miserable life. If you had lived, you would have come for her again. And then for me.* "Wayne Jessop. He's dead."

"Shit." Marlow let the word hang for a moment. "Excuse me. When?"

"The same day he attacked Amanda. He, uh, fell on the knife during the struggle." Editing herself out of the story. "It's his half brother you want."

"Oh? A half brother?" Cautious.

Kate didn't fault him for that. "Dwayne Vetter. He just got out of prison. He was stalking Amanda."

"Hmm. Did she report that to the police in . . . Oklahoma? That's where you said she was from, right?"

Kate bit her lip. How much more she should tell him? Would he shield Way-Ray, or would he be a conduit to the media? Taking a deep breath, she walked to the pot of petunias, and turned her face into the wind, remembering the relief she felt when she'd told Dyson. Like a junkie, she longed to feel it again. "Amanda didn't have a lot of faith in the system. She was a martyr to it. You saw her scars."

Marlow grunted.

"More than anything, she wanted to protect her son."

"A kid?" His voice tightened. Did he think there was a body in that ravine they hadn't recovered?

She glanced toward the apartment. "He's with me."

She heard the clunk and rattle of a cleaning cart on the deck above. "You got those sheets yet?" Rhea called. "I could finish this room if I had them."

"Hold on," Kate told Marlow. She stepped into the parking lot, tipped her head, and shaded her eyes. Rhea leaned on the railing, a cigarette between her lips. "Five minutes," Kate said, thrusting her hand upward with fingers spread. Rhea blew smoke into the wind, and trundled the cart along.

Kate retreated beneath the deck. "Listen," she hissed, "for the past eight years, while Wayne was in prison, Amanda told her son he died of natural causes. She wanted to protect him until he was old enough to understand that none of what happened was his fault."

"I understand," Marlow said. "I have a boy of my own. He's five."

Kate gripped the phone with both hands. "Amanda's son is nine. She sent him with me while she, uh, recovered from the attack." Keep it simple. "I was about to send him home when she spotted Dwayne. She believed he'd come to kill her and take the boy to Wayne's mother."

Marlow inhaled, a sharp, sucking sound. "Does he know where you are?"

"I don't think so." Unless Dyson gave up her phone number. She wedged the phone against her shoulder and hugged herself. Dyson had been tough. But had he been tough enough to die with that in him?

"You got sheets for me yet?" Rhea called.

Kate put her hand over the mouthpiece. "In a second," she yelled toward the deck. "I've got to go," she told Marlow. "Please keep my name from the media. Don't help Dwayne Vetter find us."

"I won't." His voice carried conviction, but Kate suspected that might be beyond his control. "But hang on, I have more questions."

"I get paid while I'm waiting," Rhea bellowed. "I'll just have another smoke on Nadine's dime."

"I have to go," Kate told Marlow. "Call Philip Jacobson. He's a lawyer in Oklahoma. He can identify Ted Dyson." Jacobson wouldn't be at work on Sunday, but Marlow was a cop. He'd find him.

"I'll do that. And you go to the cops up there. Right now. They'll protect you."

Kate thought of that young officer, Curtis, barely old enough to vote. She shivered.

"I'll call you back in the morning," Marlow promised. "You be careful. Sounds like you're all that kid's got."

*And he's all I've got.* Kate took two steps toward the apartment, remembered Rhea, hooked the phone to her waistband, and hustled to the wheezing dryer. Yanking the door open, she thrust her hands among the twisted sheets. Damn. Not quite dry. She untangled them, pounded the start button, and spun toward the doorway.

A tall shadow fell across it.

Kate seized the back-up jug of bleach and raised it as a weapon.

# CHAPTER 28

Rhea gawked at Kate. "What the hell is up with you? You look like you just saw the ghost of your great-aunt Minnie and she was wearing thong underwear."

Kate set the bleach on the shelf and forced a smile. "I'm fine."

"If you're fine, I'm Cleopatra."

Kate thrust aside a fleeting image of Rhea on a barge on the Nile. "Really. I'm fine."

"Bullshit. Something's been eating at you for days. Even Evie noticed, and she doesn't notice much without fur or feathers." Rhea stepped close and peered into Kate's eyes. "As soon as we get these rooms set up, you're gonna spill your guts."

Kate held her breath, fighting the desire to turn away from Rhea's penetrating gaze and the scent of stale smoke on her breath and feeling an equally strong desire to comply with Rhea's order. Her secrets ate like acid at her brain.

"No arguments," Rhea said. "I'm your friend. And, who knows," she grinned, "there's always that snowball's chance in hell that I can help."

Friend. Help. The words twined together, swirling like the bright colors in the giant lollipops her parents said were full of empty calories, a waste of hard-earned money. "Okay," Kate breathed. She could almost taste peppermint. "Thanks."

* * * * *

It's like ripping off a bandage, Kate thought as words spilled from her lips. It stings like hell, but only for a minute. She hunched, cross-legged, on the weathered picnic table and kept her head turned toward the beach, her eyes on a neon green kite that spiraled into the sky and then dipped to skim the surf. She was afraid of what she'd see in Rhea's face: pity, disgust, fear. Twice Rhea had gasped, and Kate had closed her eyes with a wince, but hadn't turned. Before she began, she laid down the ground rules: Rhea wouldn't interrupt or make a judgment until Kate finished. Kate wouldn't read anything into Rhea's reactions.

She reached the part about the bodies in the ravine and forced her eyes away from the kite. It seemed profane to focus on something so innocent while Dyson and Amanda lay . . . where? In dark drawers in a medical examiner's cooler?

Kate shuddered. Where would Amanda be buried? Near her mother? Who would decide that?

She shuddered again, rubbed her arms, and studied storm clouds tumbled along the line between sky and water, colliding and compounding, rising toward the declining sun. She glanced at her watch. Nearly five. There would be rain soon. A fitful breeze brought a hint of damp, a tinge of chill.

Rhea held the silence for a moment, and then sucked in a breath. "And here I thought you were sweating something simple, like a maxed-out credit card." She gripped Kate's elbow. "No one's gonna fault you for holding a lid on this, but now we gotta go to the cops."

Kate felt a surge of gratitude for Rhea's use of the word "we."

"And we've got to tell Jackson."

Kate shook her head. Jackson might think . . . what? She stiffened. How did she dare worry about her precious little ego now?

"I'll do it." Rhea loosed her grip, slid from the picnic table, dug a cigarette from her pocket, and snapped a light to the end. "I'll call the police chief, too. Sam Lowell. Don't think you've met him yet."

"I haven't."

"He's an inch from retirement. He doesn't go looking for trouble but he does his job." Rhea checked her watch. "He'll be up on one of the rivers about now. He drops his wife at her mother's right after church and takes off." She glanced at the murky horizon. "Expect he'll be back soon, what with that mess cooking offshore." She took a deep pull. "How much are you going to tell Way-Ray?"

Kate chewed at her lip. An hour ago, collection can in hand, he'd headed for a huge motel on the north end of town with Kyle and Sean. Kate had been afraid to let him go, but more afraid of trying to explain why she wanted him to stay. "I don't know."

As she spoke, the green kite plummeted into the surf.

\* \* \* \* \*

Gnawing at her nails, Kate waited for Way-Ray, considering where to begin her story. Should she start with Amanda's death and see how he took that? Or should she begin with Wayne? She bit her thumbnail to the quick, drawing blood.

A crunch and clatter brought her to the window. Way-Ray, raindrops glistening in his hair, stood beside the SUV, kicking his new bicycle. It lay twisted in the gravel, front wheel spinning.

She felt her mouth press into a grim line, heard her mother's voice: "That is not acceptable behavior." Kate would have been sent to her room, after a supper of plain oatmeal, to write suggestions for further punishment.

As she started for the door, Way-Ray burst through and stomped to the counter, eyes narrowed, lips a thin slash. Kate saw what Amanda had feared—his father lived on in this boy.

She took a step back. He slammed his collection can on the counter and punched at the air with both fists. "I'm gonna kill them," he snarled.

Kate fixed Way-Ray with what she hoped was a frosty glare, and spoke at a near-whisper. "Way-Ray, this is a place of business. We don't raise our voices unless there's an emergency."

"I don't care." He mimicked her stance and raised his voice to a shout. "I'm mad and I'll yell if I want to."

"Then go up on the dune." Kate pointed toward the ocean, aware of the billowing pink windsock at the edge of the parking lot and the raindrops merging into rivulets on the window. "Come back when you've got it out of your system."

He stomped both feet. "No. I won't. You can't make me."

Kate could almost feel the gravitational pull of his father's ghost, almost see it in the corner. "Way-Ray, I don't want to 'make' you do anything. But you're throwing a tantrum. If you don't get control of yourself, lower your voice, and tell me what's wrong, then I'll—" Punish? Reason? Something else? "—carry you up to dune and yell back at you everything you yell at me."

"Nuh-uh." He pouted and stomped again. "I'm too big to carry."

"I'll drag you then."

Way-Ray sucked in a long breath and held it.

Kate glanced out the window, feigning nonchalance. "It's raining pretty hard."

Way-Ray's cheeks turned an ugly burgundy.

"Getting colder, too." She rubbed her hands together. "But it's your choice."

"I hate those guys," he hissed through gritted teeth. "I hate them!"

Kate blinked. "You hate Kyle and Sean?"

He sucked air and shook his head; hair swirled off his brow, releasing a glimmering mist. "No! I hate the guys at the government who didn't give Evie the money."

Kate felt Wayne's shadow recede. Way-Ray's anger wasn't twisted; it didn't originate in some warped, selfish, sick part of his mind. She laid a hand on his shoulder. "She didn't get the grant?"

"Now she can't pay her taxes and the 'velopers are going to take over!" Way-Ray charged through the gate, bumping the wastebasket. It fell with a clatter, spilling a flock of wadded-up envelopes and an empty juice bottle that rolled beneath the desk. He threw himself into the chair. "We heard it from the man at the newspaper." He knuckled his eyes. "Why didn't she tell me?"

Betrayal. Kate knew the bitter taste of that. During a September recess in the second grade when she overheard Brenda Finnegan telling two other girls, "Guess what? Katie only has one pair of school shoes and she has to wear them until her feet get too big." Kate stared dumbly at her brown oxfords, denouncing her parents' utilitarian natures while telling herself she didn't like shiny patent leather and hated penny loafers more than fried liver. But from that day on she stayed in and read a book at recess. And from that day on she'd been Kate.

Now she fished a tissue from a box beneath the counter and pressed it into Way-Ray's hand. "Maybe she was too upset."

"But she told him! And he's not even collecting money to help!"

But he's an adult, Kate thought. A journalist. Someone who's paid not to get involved. Had Evie chosen him to carry the message so she could dodge sympathy and commiseration? Or had she hoped for publicity and donations?

Way-Ray blew his nose, crumpled the tissue, and threw it on the floor. "What's gonna happen to the birds and the deer and the bobcat?"

Kate tried to force confidence she didn't feel. "I'm sure Evie will find homes for them." She stretched her hand toward his hair.

He swatted it away. "They're all gonna die!"

Kate bent to look into his eyes, but he lowered his chin. "They aren't going to die," she told the crown of his head. "There are other wildlife rehab centers. They'll take the ones Evie can't release."

"Nuh-uh. There's not enough room anywhere else. And what about the ones that get sick after?"

Kate felt a helpless certainty: many would die. But a boy about to find he'd lost everything needed to hope for something. She flicked a fingernail against his donation can. "Nothing will happen right away. Maybe we can raise enough—"

"I got seven dollars today," he sneered. "Seven dollars and four cents. Kyle says even if I collect that much every day for a year it won't be enough." He tipped his head back. His eyes glistened. "Do you have any money you could give her?"

Evie couldn't repay a loan unless she found a funding source. And unless that source provided more stability than a one-time hit of cash, she'd be in crisis again before another year passed. Her father's voice rumbled deep in her head, "Never loan money to a friend." He'd forbid this.

"I'll pay you back out of my allowance," Way-Ray pleaded. "Even if that takes me until I'm all grown up."

And it *would*. Kate bit her lip. She couldn't agree to this scheme. It was financial madness. But she couldn't turn him down flat either. She had to cushion the shock to come. Cold dread settled in the pit of her stomach. She wanted to run from this and never stop. Instead she gripped the edge of the counter and focused on the clock above her desk. 6:41. Chief Lowell would be here at 7:00. She had nineteen minutes. Eleven hundred and forty seconds.

"Look, I've got everything we need for grilled cheese and tomato sandwiches." She forced a smile so broad her lips felt like they'd split and bleed. "And chocolate chunk ice cream. Let's have dinner and then we'll see—"

"No!" Way-Ray kicked at her. His tennis shoe connected with the edge of her kneecap. Her leg buckled and she lurched against the counter. "You're not gonna help! I know you're not!"

He shot from the chair and through the gate, seized the knob, and ripped the door open. The cheerful bell rang in mocking counterpoint to his words. "You're mean. You don't care about Evie. You don't care about the birds!"

"That's not true. Way-Ray! Wait!" Knee throbbing, Kate limped after him. As she reached the doorway, she saw him wrestle his bicycle upright and swing a leg across it. She lunged, grasped at his rain-spattered T-shirt. The damp fabric slid through her fingers.

He stood on the pedals. The rear tire ground across a ridge of gravel, spraying stones against Kate's bare legs. ""My mother would give Evie all the money she had," he yelled over his shoulder. "I'm going to Grassy Ridge."

"Wait!" Kate screamed into the wind.

Way-Ray hunched over the handlebars, churned across the parking lot, and spun around the corner.

A horn blasted. Brakes squealed. Metal ground against metal.

Kate screamed again.

# CHAPTER 29

"He's okay, Kate," a deep voice shouted.

Jackson. Kate clawed at the gusting wind. "I'm coming!"

"Hey! Way-Ray! Where are you going?" Jackson's voice again.

"To find my mother."

"Catch him!" Kate reached the corner unit and caught a glimpse of two faces at the window: eyes wide, noses squashed against rain-streaked glass, mouths gaping. She spotted Jackson's mangy orange truck and Way-Ray's bike between its balding tires, one handlebar lodged against a corroded bumper sagging like the grin on a rotting jack-o'-lantern.

"He jumped off in time," Jackson grunted as he worked the bike loose. "Kid's got good reflexes."

"Where is he?" Kate panted. "Where did he go?" Her knee blazed and she rubbed at it with the heel of her hand.

Jackson pointed along the alley. Twin oblongs of white— the soles of Way-Ray's sneakers—flashed against a background of rain swirling in the wind like ash. He was half a block away, legs kicking out behind him, arms pumping, head butting the rain. He glanced over his shoulder, then veered through the gap between two houses.

"We've got to stop him." Kate pushed off with her good leg and hitched along after Way-Ray. Rain drenched her hair and ran into her eyes. Lightning sizzled somewhere above the dune.

An engine sputtered behind her, gears clashed. She passed a phalanx of black garbage bags shiny with rain, skirted a puddle, and sighted the weathered picket fence where Way-Ray had turned. She pivoted, her knee buckled, and she slewed sideways, grappling with a splintering post.

Something clattered ahead and to her right. "Way-Ray! Come back!"

"No." The word hovered in the sodden air and then was gone.

Brakes shrieked at her heels. "Get in."

Kate shook her head. "He went through this yard." She pointed south. "I heard him."

"We'll go around and catch him on the highway."

"*You* go around. I'll go this way." Sucking a ragged breath, she limped across slick grass toward a wash of sound: the highway.

Hinges grated. A hand gripped her arm. "Get in the truck."

She thrashed against his hold. "No."

He swung her around to face him and blocked her blows with his forearm. "I'm not on the clock. I won't take orders." His eyes were as gray as the rain and his voice rasped like a file on stone, but then dulled with patience and reason. "He'll go to the highway and head south."

Mr. Smug. She threw her weight against his grip. It didn't loosen, yet he seemed to exert no effort to hold her.

"He'll go the way he knows, the way you came." He nodded toward the highway, throwing a corona of raindrops from his ragged hair.

Kate recognized the logic. "You better be right."

Jackson released her, swung ahead, wrenched open the passenger door, and scraped a litter of crumpled food wrappers from the bench seat. Kate grasped the armrest and hoisted herself onto cracked vinyl patched with silver tape. The truck smelled of fried onions, mildew, and scorched oil. While Jackson slammed the door and scuttled around to the driver's side, she shoved aside a monkey wrench, a broken screwdriver, and a hammer with a single claw. She located the ends of a seat belt and snapped them together as Jackson heaved himself in and yanked the door shut. He slapped at a gearshift topped with a clear plastic globe that encased a scorpion. Kate grimaced. Totally high school.

The truck lurched backward and jolted to a stop, rattling her teeth and pitching her, despite the seat belt, against a fissured dashboard strewn with dead flies and ruptured ketchup packets. Disgusting. But cleaning this wheeled pigsty would detract from his drinking time.

Jackson smacked the gearshift again and fought the wheel around. The truck yawed through potholes and loose stones along the train tracks. Punching the gas, he sent them rumbling past the stop sign, heeling onto the asphalt in a blare of horns, a squeal of brakes, and a barrage of flashing headlights.

Shivering, she leaned to the limit of the belt and peered through the narrow arcs of windshield cleared by wipers trailing shreds of rubber. Was Jackson right, or was Way-Ray hiding on a porch, waiting out the storm? Damn. She should have followed him. "Go back. We'll go door-to-door."

Jackson tapped the defrost lever, but didn't brake. "If he saw you get in the truck, he's hiding, waiting for us to go by."

Kate moaned at the image of Way-Ray crouching in a ditch among broken bottles and crumpled beer cans. She wiped at the windshield, smearing the greasy fog that clung to it. "Slow down."

Jackson let off the gas and a horn blared behind them. "Get bent," he muttered, his voice barely audible over the rattle of rain on the hood and roof.

Kate focused on the penumbra at the edge of the headlights, searching for a smaller shadow within it. The defroster hissed but cleared only tiny half moons. She reached for the fan knob and noted it was already set on high. The vents were probably stuffed with calcified mustard and relish. Pathetic.

Turning to the side window, she swiped at pearly condensation with her sleeve. Water beaded and trickled, refracting light from on-coming cars. She pawed for the handle to roll the window down, found a hole and a protruding screw instead. Naturally.

"What set him off? Did you tell—?"

"Not yet." She slapped the window in frustration. "He's mad because Evie didn't get the grant." She squeegeed the window with the side of her hand. "He wants me to loan her the money."

Jackson grunted. "Losing proposition."

An echo of her father. *To hell with them both.* Right now she'd pay every penny she had just to wrap her arms around Way-Ray. She spotted a forty-mile-an-hour speed-limit sign and another for the jetty. "He couldn't have come this far."

Jackson tromped on the brake. The truck slid onto the muddy jetty road and a string of cars surged past, blasting horns and spraying rooster tails of oily water. "See if you can spot him on the way back." He nosed the truck onto the shoulder.

Kate looked north at a sooty sky sagging lower over Castaway Beach, squeezing out daylight. Vehicles whooshed past, speeding up as they left the city limits. Headlights illuminated taillights—white, red, white, red. She recalled that peppermint lollipop she'd been denied and now would never long for again. "We can't cross," she moaned. "No one will let us in."

"Then we'll make them." Jackson raced the engine. The truck shuddered. Ketchup packets skittered across the dash, the visor slapped against the windshield. "There's my guy." He pointed up the southbound lane. "See that green car?"

Kate squinted into the roiling mist. "No, I—"

Jackson floored it, challenging the on-coming car. Kate saw the driver's hands lock on the wheel, his head jerk back as if he intended to execute a reverse somersault. Stomping the brakes, Jackson spun the wheel, and slid the truck sideways across the northbound lane and into the parking lot of a defunct art gallery. The truck's engine sputtered and stalled.

"Are you crazy?" Kate shrieked.

"You wanted to get across, didn't you?" His voice was a sullen growl.

"Yes, but—"

"You're across." He turned the key and reached for the gearshift with a trembling hand.

He scared himself. Good. The truck juddered onto the highway and rolled north into the jaws of the storm. Rain washed across the windshield in waves that overran the wipers. The defroster wheezed and spit, but smog thickened on the inside of the glass. "We'll never see him. Open your window."

Jackson tugged at the handle. The window slid down two inches. He slipped his fingers into the gap and pressed. Another two inches. He went for the handle again. It popped off in his hand.

Kate pounded the seat, felt the monkey wrench bounce against her leg. She gripped it, wanting to batter the window until it shattered, then batter Jackson.

Jackson dropped the handle, released the wheel, and shoved with both hands. The window dropped with a scrape and a clunk. Rain slashed through the opening and carried the scent of him to her: wet wool, sweat, leather. She released her belt and twisted to her knees on the seat. Ignoring a burst of pain, she peered into the squall.

Haloed by mist, the headlights of southbound vehicles strobed the murk along the shoulder. She leaned an elbow against the dash and cocked her head, concentrating on the road slightly behind the truck. Was that a shadow within a shadow? She blinked. The next set of headlights illuminated Way-Ray, hair plastered to his head, thumb out.

"Back there."

Jackson glanced over his shoulder, trod on the brake, flipped the turn signal, and bent over the wheel. "Give me an opening," he muttered.

Kate jounced about and squinted through the dust-clotted rear window. White lights washed across Way-Ray's face, his image faded into the gloom, and then bloomed crimson in the taillights' glow. Crimson bleached to coral and then to white again. The white intensified. Had a driver flicked on his high beams? "Hurry," she moaned.

Jackson thrust his arm out the window and flashed his lights at the train of on-coming vehicles. "Come on, give me a break." Cars piled up behind them. A horn sounded.

Way-Ray lifted a hand and shaded his eyes. Was someone stopping? Kate rubbed at the window. Way-Ray's image seemed to dissolve into the rain.

She spit on the hem of her T-shirt and swabbed the window. A scarlet stain of taillights spread across the empty shoulder. Way-Ray was gone.

# Chapter 30

Kate hammered at the window. "Somebody picked him up!" She gripped the back of the seat, sick with loss and fear, furious at herself. She failed Amanda, failed Way-Ray. Saint Kate the Incompetent.

"Stay with me, Kate." Jackson's voice snapped her chain of thought. "Keep your mind clear. Way-Ray needs you."

He cranked the wheel and bulled the truck into the opposite lane. An RV, swaddled in aluminum lawn chairs, swerved and wallowed onto the shoulder. Kate braced her feet against the dash as Jackson launched them into the gap. The truck canted into the turn, righted itself with a scream of rubber and a shower of ketchup packets, and bore down on a yellow pickup. "Who got him? Was it that guy?"

"I don't think so." Kate had a vague impression of elongated taillights, a broad and boxy contour. "Maybe a van."

Jackson hit his high-beam switch, flooding the pickup's cab. Kate spotted the silhouette of the driver's head, long hair curling onto the shoulders. "Looks like a woman."

Jackson punched the gas and tapped the pickup's bumper. The driver glanced back, the whites of her eyes flashing. She twisted her shoulders and cornered onto the jetty road. Plumes of water spouted from her rear wheels.

"Not her." Jackson goosed the gas and they roared past. "Two roads coming up on the right. Let me know if you see anyone turn off or any taillights down along them."

Kate nodded and swiped again at the windshield. The roads flashed past. "No one." She mopped the side window again. Would it kill Jackson to do some maintenance on this beast?

A new set of taillights bloomed before her. The car was small and low, the color of late-summer grass. The license plate bore the outline of a truncated mountain. Washington State.

"Ragtop." Jackson closed in, but his headlights glazed the white vinyl roof instead of piercing the rear window. They leaned into a curve and swept past a speed limit sign. Fifty. Jackson grunted. "Straightaway coming up. Check this guy out when I go around. There's a flashlight on the floor."

Kate unhooked her seat belt, scooched forward, dropped into the well beneath the dash, and pawed through waxy food wrappers, smashed paper cups, bent plastic straws, loose nails, lengths of rope. Her frantic fingers touched a cylinder. "Got it." She scrambled to the seat and pressed the button. Nothing. "It doesn't work." Why had she expected it might?

"Shake it."

"It's dead," she snarled.

"Put your belt back on and shake it!"

She slammed it against the seat with a sense of righteousness and futility, heard the batteries shift and clunk. Not a glimmer of light.

"Top sounds loose." Jackson's voice was calm, toneless.

Wishing it were his neck, Kate gave the top a vicious twist. Light flared from the bulb. Seething, she aimed it at the side window. His tiny victory amplified her failures, deepened her guilt and frustration.

"Remember the plate." Jackson braked, backing off the convertible's bumper, and swinging into the northbound lane.

Kate repeated numbers and letters, playing the flashlight beam across the convertible as they drew alongside, picking out a jumble of bags and boxes, a bald head, and a hand with a brace of rings that glittered as the driver raised it to shield his eyes and flip the finger. She shifted the beam to the passenger seat. Empty. "Not him." She clicked the flashlight off.

Jackson outpaced the sports car, squeaked back into the right lane before they collided with an on-coming station wagon, and tunneled through gauzy darkness toward a receding red glimmer. Kate glimpsed white-capped water a few feet beyond the guardrail on her right and slope-shouldered firs marching up the steep hillside on her left. The ruddy glow separated into two sets of lights. "Van," Jackson grunted. The engine whined as he accelerated and the front end shimmied.

Kate crossed her fingers. Please don't let this heap fall apart.

"Get the license."

She squinted into the gloom, spotted only a sliver of white. "I can't. There's something on it. Mud maybe."

Jackson thumped the wheel with the heel of his hand and fed more gas.

Something cold coiled around her heart. Had the driver covered his plate on purpose? Who would do that? Why?

The icy serpent constricted. She knew who and she knew why. Pressing her arms against her side, she contained a shudder, then glanced at Jackson. At least she wasn't alone.

They closed the gap. Kate spotted thin strips of blue around the taillights. The rest of the van was a rusty brown.

"Not mud," Jackson said. "Paint."

Kate studied the back of the van, her eyes tracing the outline of the double doors, the shadow of what must be a handle, the rectangle of the license plate, and the curve of the bumper. As they closed in, she made out brush strokes and dribbles.

As the van plunged down a hill, Jackson flicked on his high beams. Light bounced back into their eyes. Kate raised both hands against it and Jackson cut the brights. "He's got the rear windows covered with foil. Get the flashlight ready. I'll get around."

She gripped the light as they careened through a turn. "Where? This road's a corkscrew."

"Except for a hundred yards . . . right . . . here." He wrenched the wheel and slid the truck into the left lane. Kate saw the van's brake lights flicker, and then a roiling black cloud belched from the exhaust pipe and it peeled away from them. "Damn it!" Jackson swung in ten feet off the bumper. The van rocked into a corner. Its brake lights flamed.

Jackson pumped the brakes. "Hang on."

Kate felt the balding tires shimmy and then the back end broke loose and slid like butter on a smoking griddle. The front bumper grazed the guardrail, grating off a shower of sparks. Jackson wrestled the wheel. The truck skidded into the oncoming lane. Headlights burst from the fog and Kate braced her hands on the dashboard, afraid to look but unable to close her eyes.

"I got it," Jackson said, without a trace of anxiety. He twitched the wheel. The truck angled to the right. The oncoming car did the same. They passed with inches between.

Kate's heart thudded between her collar bones. "Was he trying to kill us?"

Jackson shrugged. "Could be he's scared. Dark night, winding road, truck roars up on a double yellow." His voice was so calm he might have been talking about clearing a clog from a drain.

"No. He's got Way-Ray." She had never been more certain of anything. She wondered what Way-Ray was feeling. Was he afraid or was this as an adventure? Had he looked back and recognized Jackson's truck? Or had he been forbidden to? Unable to? Her stomach clenched and bile rose in her throat. "He's in that van. I know it."

Jackson nodded. Did he feel it too? She glanced at the speedometer. Sixty-seven. Too fast for this road, these conditions. Yet the van crept farther ahead. Jackson nodded again. "I'll force him over when he slows down at the next town."

Kate dug her nails into her palms until her arms trembled. "If he slows down."

"He'll have to. I see cars in front of him." He let off the gas and coasted into a long curve.

Kate spotted a speed-zone-ahead sign. The van's taillights flickered. "He's slowing."

"Memorize the configuration of his lights. Memorize everything so you can describe that van to the cops."

*You don't have to tell me.* Kate bit her lip. She had lost Way-Ray. Jackson had got them this far toward finding him again.

A speed limit sign appeared at the edge of her vision. Forty. Jackson kept his foot on the gas. The van's taillights bloomed. Another speed limit sign whipped by. Thirty. Jackson toed the brake. Twenty-five. Streetlights arched above the highway. Neon signs glowed red and blue. Tagging up to a line of vehicles, the van threaded its way past a gas station, bakery, restaurant, motel, and tavern. Jackson hung a length behind.

Clicking the flash on and off, Kate concentrated on the blobs and brush strokes on the rear doors. Another few blocks and the speed limit would jack up to fifty again. "What are you waiting for?"

# CHAPTER 31

Jackson thrust his chin toward a cluster of people huddled beneath umbrellas. "I don't have much to live for, but they might. If he's got a gun . . ."

A wave of despair washed over her. "We have to call the police."

"You got a cell phone?"

"No." Something else she hadn't done right. "Do you?"

"No." He pointed at a pay phone beside the tavern. "I could let you out."

"No." She clutched the armrest. She couldn't bear to be farther from Way-Ray.

A horn brayed twice. The umbrellas scattered before a rust-riddled mossy green truck with a cracked windshield and a hood secured with yellow rope. It bucketed across the potholed lot, fenders flapping. Jackson tapped his brakes. "Good old Bucky," he muttered, "right on time."

The van's brake lights flamed, its brakes squealed. The truck plunged into the gap ahead of it, fishtailed, and straightened, belching exhaust dark as squid's ink. The van dropped back. Hemmed in.

Kate pointed at the battered truck. "You know him?"

"We've leaned at the same bars on occasion. Bucky's what you might call a daylight drinker." Jackson's tone implied respect.

Kate watched the truck inch around a tight corner between a bed and breakfast and the train tracks. "Daylight drinker?"

"Controls it. Treats it like a job." More than respect, admiration, even awe. As if Bucky was a seasoned professional and Jackson a mere amateur. "Checks in at eleven, paces himself, leaves at seven."

Seven? Kate peered at her watch. Had it been just nineteen minutes since Way-Ray took off? Time had a way of telescoping during a crisis.

"He'll turn off up the river. Just a little bit out of town."

Kate waited a few seconds for Jackson to elaborate. He didn't. "How does that help us?" Her voice scorched the air.

A faint smile tweaked Jackson's lips. Bucky's truck bumped across a railroad crossing and trundled over a bridge. The van eased into the oncoming lane. Lights flashed. It swung back. Kate felt a sigh leak from her lips. Jackson braked to fifteen miles an hour. "Bucky gave me an idea. I'm thinking about a maneuver I used . . . well, in a place I can't talk about."

*Great! Classified information.*

Jackson rolled his lips together and the corner of his eye crinkled. "As you've probably noticed, Bucky's hell on wheels getting out of a parking lot. But then he dodders. He married a woman who never shuts up—even talks in her sleep." He aimed his chin at the narrowing road ahead. "So he's in no hurry to get home. He'll be going about ten when he hits the crossover on that S-curve before the river. That's when we'll get the van."

"On the curve?" The right shoulder was no wider than a shopping cart, and the guardrail leaned outward over the bay. If the van went into the water . . .

"The maneuver's based on the principles of physics."

"I don't care about physics," Kate snapped.

Jackson grinned. "Channel that energy, Kate."

*Mr. New Age Psychologist.* Kate pounded her fists on the seat.

"Get ready to jump out and get your boy."

221

Your boy. Her anger fell away, replaced by an image of Way-Ray running with the deer in Evie's pasture. Why had Jackson used that pronoun? Way-Ray wasn't hers. She gripped the monkey wrench. Way-Ray wasn't Dwayne Vetter's, either. Not as long as she had breath in her body. "Does your plan include the gun he might have?"

"A gun's always the wild card. But there are two of those in every deck." He glanced at her sidelong, eyes glinting. "Trust me."

What choice did she have?

A gust of wind buffeted the truck and hailstones, glowing like opals in the on-coming lights, peppered the windshield. The wipers jittered across the glass like fingernails on a blackboard. Bucky's truck joggled into the bottom of the S-curve, zigzagging between the double yellow and the white fog line. She glanced at the speedometer. Twelve miles an hour. Twisting, she peered through the rear window. Two cars trailed in their wake.

"Don't worry about them." Jackson rolled his shoulders. "Focus on the van." He flexed his fingers and feathered the brake. "Brace yourself. That seat belt's been known to lose tension."

Kate almost laughed. Of course it would. She grasped the wrench with her right hand and the seat belt clip with her left. Ahead of her, Bucky's truck tilted and straddled the center line. The van backed off. Jackson stayed a length from its bumper. Bucky's truck wobbled, drifted toward the shoulder as the road straightened in the crossover, and then tilted to the right.

"Hang on." Jackson fed gas, tapped the van's bumper, and, with a grinding shriek of metal, rode up over it. Brake lights flamed. Jackson downshifted and bulldozed the van across the northbound lane and down a slope. Branches clawed at the windows. Small trees appeared in the van's headlights and raked against the truck's undercarriage.

"Get ready." Jackson mashed the brake. The bumpers broke apart and the truck swung in an arc that brought Kate within a yard of the van's passenger door. She saw Way-Ray, nose pressed against the window, mouth open in a circle of surprise.

The truck shuddered to a stop. Kate released the belt and tore at the door latch, noting that Jackson was already out. Way-Ray shook his head, leaned away from the window, and bent over. Kate got the impression he was searching for a lever to lock the door. *No you don't.* She dug her thumb under the rain-slicked handle, flipped it up, and yanked. The door swung wide.

Way-Ray kicked at her grasping hand. "Get away. I hate you."

Over his shoulder Kate caught a glimpse of an orange T-shirt, beefy shoulders, shaggy blond hair. Dwayne Vetter? "What the hell are you doing?" The voice was deep, crackling like a smoker's.

Kate heard a pulpy crunch. The shoulders sagged. She saw Jackson's face, teeth bared, saw a flash of metal in his hand. "Putting you down." His voice was as cold as the hail pelting her back. The driver thudded to the ground. "Get Way-Ray, Kate." Jackson dropped from sight.

Way-Ray stopped kicking and squirmed to peer over his shoulder at the empty seat. "Is that Jackson? What's he doing?"

She heard another crunch and a moan.

"Get in the truck, Way-Ray."

Way-Ray swung toward her, gasped, and cowered to the limit of his seat belt. "Are you gonna hit me with that?"

Kate gawked at the wrench in her raised hand. "Of course not." But I'll club the man who took you.

As she tossed the wrench into the truck, Kate heard doors slam and voices call from the direction of the highway. Pivoting, she spotted two flashlight beams glinting on the rain-laced hail. "You okay down there? You need help?"

"Yeah!" The driver's rough voice. "Somebody call the c—"

"We're okay," Kate yelled, drowning out his demand. "We . . . we lost traction on the turn because of the hail." One more lie. "We're just a little shook up."

"Why'd you pick up the kid?" Jackson hissed. "Where were you taking him?"

The flashlight beams turned toward each other and Kate heard an indistinct exchange of voices. The man called again. "Can you get out okay? Do you need a tow truck?"

"No need. I've got four-wheel drive," Jackson yelled. "But thanks."

"The hail's stopping," Kate added. "It'll melt in a minute."

The lights bobbled again and moved away, gauzy in the rain.

"He was gonna take me to a truck stop so I could maybe get a ride to Grassy Ridge." Way-Ray unhooked his belt and clutched her hand. "Why is Jackson hurting him?"

Kate wrapped her arms around him and buried her face against his neck, breathing the scents of damp cloth, sweat, and fear. *I will hold you close forever.* "Because he was worried when you ran away. Because your . . ." She swept him off the seat and closed the door with her hip. "Because there are a lot of not-nice people in the world, Way-Ray. We were afraid this man might hurt you."

"Nuh-uh." Way-Ray called over his shoulder. "He didn't hurt me, Jackson. He gave me potato chips. He didn't hurt me."

"I didn't," the driver echoed, his voice clotted with what Kate suspected was his own blood. "He wanted to find his mother and help a woman and a bunch of birds. I was taking him to my place."

"Not to a police station?" Kate cried, stumbling around the van, across sodden hummocks of grass. She had to see this man. "You didn't wonder why a little boy was out on the road alone?"

"I'm not a little boy," Way-Ray howled. "I'm almost ten."

"He told me he was thirteen," the driver protested. He knelt beside the van, his hands behind his neck. His nose bled across his lips and through his beard, splattering his sopping T-shirt. Jackson stood behind him, a knee braced between the man's shoulder blades, a wide knife in his belt.

"You hurt him." Way-Ray wriggled in Kate's arms. His weight dragged at muscles twitching with the exhaustion that follows a surge of adrenaline.

"Put Way-Ray in the truck, Kate."

"No!" The boy wedged his hands against her shoulders. "You can't make me."

Jackson laughed. "Reminds me of you, Kate."

"I'll make a note to laugh at that later."

Way-Ray writhed from her arms and balled his fists. "Stop hurting him or I'll hurt you."

Jackson grinned, but released the driver's wrists. "Stay on your knees. Tell me your name."

"What the hell is wrong with you people?" The driver rubbed his shoulders. "You could have killed me."

"I might yet," Jackson muttered, fingering the hilt of the knife. "What's your name?"

"Mickey," Way-Ray said. "His name is Mickey." He wove his fingers with Kate's and she stifled a sob of joy at his touch.

"Mickey, huh?" Jackson seized a handful of hair, jerked him to his feet, ripped a nylon wallet from his rear pocket and flipped it open. "Hmm. Mickey Webster."

"I told you." Mickey scowled.

"Yeah. You get points for that." Jackson released his hair and tossed the wallet into the van. "Now you can explain why your plate is covered."

"I don't know." Mickey shrugged and studied his shoes. Rain pattered on his shoulders. Kate shivered. Way-Ray danced from foot to foot.

Jackson fingered the knife. "Kate, call the cops."

Kate opened her mouth to remind him they had no phone, then saw his right eye twitch. A bluff. "I'll get the cell."

"It's my brother's van," Mickey admitted in a rush. "His ex wants it because he hasn't made his child support payments. He painted it and told me to stash it in my garage." Mickey fingered his dripping nose. "I knew it was a stupid idea. Last time I do a favor for him." He nodded toward Way-Ray. "And the next time I see a kid hitching, I'll call the cops before mom runs me off the road."

"She's not my mom." Way-Ray spoke with force, but kept his fingers twined with Kate's. "She's my mom's friend. My mom is lost."

Lost forever. Kate's heart clenched. "Let's get in the truck, okay?"

He tipped his head to gaze at her. Rain, now little more than a drizzle, glistened on his cheeks. "Will you help Evie and the birds?"

Blackmail. A losing proposition. But she'd vowed to trade every penny for him. "I might not have enough."

"We can take my bicycle back to the store. And I can sell my books and videos. And . . . and my TV," he added with a note of regret.

She bent and hugged him. "That's very generous. But let's talk about it later." She flipped sopping hair from his forehead. "We'll order a pizza when we get back, okay?"

"How about we drop Kate off and go and get it?" Jackson offered. "She might have a lot to do at the office. People might be looking for her." She remembered the police chief and glanced at Way-Ray, so unaware of what was to come. Her knees trembled and her stomach roiled.

"Cool," Way-Ray crowed. "Can Mickey come have pizza, too?"

"Mickey's got to get on the road," Jackson said. "But he might want to get pizza later. And get his seat belt fixed." He drew four crumpled bills from his pocket and pressed them into Mickey's hand.

Twenties. Kate frowned. How could Jackson afford this gesture?

Mickey grunted and slid the bills into his pocket. "Sorry about the misunderstanding."

"Sorry about your nose."

Mickey fingered it. "Might get me some sympathy from the ladies."

"Could happen." Jackson nodded. "You need a push to get out?"

"Maybe." He climbed into the van. "I'd appreciate it if you make sure I get up that slope."

"Will do."

"Let's go." Way-Ray scrambled into the truck.

Kate watched the van wallow toward the highway. "That driver's license could be a fake," she whispered. "Are you sure he's not Dwayne Vetter?"

Jackson chuckled. "From what I've heard about Dwayne Vetter, I don't think he'd piss in his pants."

# CHAPTER 32

"Hmm," Chief Sam Lowell said when Kate finished. He wrote another line in a palm-sized notebook, squinting at it from beneath a pair of rogue eyebrows that twined like bindweed above black-rimmed half glasses he'd drawn from a holster on his belt.

Lowell set the notebook on the kitchen table, and drew his thumb and forefinger along his cheeks, rasping the nails against emerging whiskers. A thoughtful gesture? Or a sign of irritation at the way she'd handled everything.

She felt Rhea lean closer on the ratty loveseat, offering support. Stiffening her spine, Kate tilted her chin high and watched Lowell massage the knob of flesh at the point of his chin. "I'll let the county and state boys know about this first thing in the morning," he said. We'll coordinate with Ohio. Get the word out, see if maybe someone can stop this," he peered at his notebook, "Dwayne Vetter before he gets to be my problem."

The abhorrence in those final words reminded Kate of Emory McCoy. Her hands curled into fists. How long would it take to blot him from her mind? Rhea laid cool fingers on her forearm. "It's okay."

The chief tucked the notebook into the pocket of his khaki shirt and arched one of his brows. "I'll have Curtis swing by here regularly. He's green, but he could be a deterrent."

Or dead meat. If Curtis believed he could sideline a killer on his own.

"But the small-town factor works in our favor," Lowell mused. "Word gets around fast. We'll tape this Vetter's picture up in the market, the post office, restaurants. Locals will watch for him."

And then come by to gawk at the orphaned boy and the woman who killed his father. "No!" Kate catapulted from the loveseat. "You can't do that. Way-Ray will be a sideshow attraction!"

Lowell held his palms out. "No one has to know that part but us."

Kate recalled the persistence of journalists who hounded her after Wayne's death. "But reporters will—"

"They'll get nothing out of me," Lowell said, his left brow twitching. "Or Curtis."

"Thank you." Kate sank back onto the loveseat's apathetic cushions. Rhea patted her shoulder. "You can trust him," she whispered.

Lowell removed his glasses and popped them into their holster. His brows seemed poised to spurt across the gleaming dome of his forehead and put down roots among his thinning hair. "Rhea says Jackson will keep an eye out. He's the one I'd want watching my back."

Although awed by Jackson's strength and ability on the highway, Kate remained wary. How much protection could he provide if he took up a bottle?

Lowell fingered his chin. "As far as the boy, well, you might just let it ride a bit. As upset as you say he was this evening over Evie losing that grant . . ."

Kate shook her head. The albatross would hang around her neck until Way-Ray knew. She felt dread, cold and queasy, shift in the pit of her stomach and hugged herself, a futile gesture that brought no warmth.

Rhea touched her wrist. "Couldn't make things any worse to put it off another day."

Kate stared into Rhea's eyes, saw caring and empathy, not a shade of pity. "Is that what you'd do?"

Rhea shrugged. "I never came up against a situation like this. I'd probably run for the hills." She patted the cigarette pack in the pocket of her baggy black shorts as if touching a talisman, rubbing a worry stone. "I'd rather take out my own gall bladder."

"If anyone could manage that, it would be you." Lowell's face crinkled in a smile that faded as he turned to Kate. "I've had to tell four mothers their kids were dead on the highway, and I would rather have been scraped off that blacktop myself. It tore up my heart." He put a hand on his chest, then hitched his pants over the slight swell of his stomach and dug in his pocket for his keys. "I'll go let Curtis know what's up, tell him to keep it under his hat or he'll find he can't land a job walking a beat in Alaska."

Lowell raised his right hand and let it hang in the air for a moment—too high for a handshake and too low for a salute. "You call me if you need anything." He squinted at the hand as if seeing it for the first time, touched her shoulder with his forefinger the way a shopper might prod a tomato, and left.

"It doesn't matter what I'd do," Rhea said as she worked her cigarettes from her pocket, "but if you want my vote, I say wait until Tuesday."

A thirty-six-hour reprieve. Kate tried to find some significance in that number. "Tuesday?"

"Right. Your day off." Rhea's voice curdled with sarcasm. "It's followed by Wednesday. Your second day off." She tapped a cigarette from the pack and slid it between her lips. "I think the best thing would be for the four of us to—"

"Four?" Kate stood and paced the cramped room.

"You, me, Way-Ray, and Jackson."

"Jackson? No. This isn't his prob—"

"Way-Ray's tight with him. Go figure." Rhea removed the cigarette and twirled it between her fingers. "He'll listen to

Jackson when he won't listen to you or me. That's how it works with my kids. So, we'll all go out to Evie's—"

"Evie's?" Kate remembered she'd promised to see how much she could spare for the refuge.

Rhea stood and jabbed the cigarette at Kate's nose. "Do that parrot thing one more time and I'm lighting up right here." She slid the butt between her lips and fished out a red plastic lighter.

Kate stared at it, drawing up a mental list: check her bank balance, draw up a budget of monthly expenses, find out how much Evie owed. "Parrot?"

Rhea flicked the lighter and touched the flame to the tip of her cigarette. "I warned you." She inhaled with a deep sigh, blew smoke toward the ceiling, and pointed to the loveseat. "Let's take it from the top. Sit! You have the panicked look of the only canary at a cat show."

Panic? Kate watched the smoke swirl in the breeze from the kitchen window as she lowered herself to the loveseat. Her parents would have been appalled. It went against the grain of the independence and resolve they encouraged—no, enforced. She forked her fingers through her hair. By sharing her burden, was she handing those qualities off as if they were clothes that didn't suit her, shoes that never quite fit? She rubbed her eyes with the heels of her hands. "I'm not panicked."

"Didn't say you were, just that you're looking that way." Rhea took another drag, stubbed the butt out on the side of the sink, and tucked it back into the pack. "These things are getting so expensive they're worth more than my engagement ring," she said by way of explanation. "Okay, we'll take Way-Ray out to Evie's because he'll be surrounded by orphans—hundreds of them. We'll remind him of that." She winced and patted the cigarette pack. "It won't take the edge off of the pain, but it will help him get the message that we'll take care of him, he won't be out in the world by himself."

Why hadn't she thought of that? Kate hung her head. She wasn't worthy of raising Way-Ray. She didn't have the right tools, just the example of her parents. They would have sat her down on a ladder-back chair, explained the situation in clinical terms, and told her to get on with it. Not in those words—they felt slang was a pox upon the language—but with the same intent.

"What?" Rhea asked. "What's the matter?"

"Nothing." She wouldn't drag Rhea through the emotional minefield of her childhood.

The office bell chimed. Kate stood and peered toward the door. "We got the biggest pizza there is," Way-Ray called. "And we got all my favorite stuff on one side and I don't have to share." He came through the doorway, a steaming pizza box balanced on his head, a wide smile on his lips.

Was this the same boy who fought her two hours earlier? Kate marveled at his buoyancy, wondered how deep the next dive would be, and how long it might take him to surface. "Where's Jackson?"

"He said he had to check on the lawnmower. He said to give you this . . ." Way-Ray steadied the pizza box and dug a cell phone from his pocket. "It takes pictures and everything."

Kate closed her fingers around the slim silver phone warm from Way-Ray's body. Where had Jackson found money for this?

"And Jackson says to tell you . . ." Way-Ray cocked his head, and squinted. "Oh, yeah. He said he heard there's a big terrorist alert and you should lock the door."

"Terrorist alert?" Rhea reached for her cigarettes.

"Yeah. And spies and stuff, too." Way-Ray set the box on the table. "But Jackson says it won't be on the television or the radio or even in the papers." He lowered his voice to a whisper. "He says it's a secret alert and I could tell you, but nobody else because they'd get scared and act funny and then the terrorists might sneak away and the police won't catch them."

Clever. Jackson had made a game of it. Something else that hadn't occurred to her.

"I'll go lock the door," Rhea said.

Way-Ray flipped the box open. The aromas of garlic and onions and pepperoni filled the room. "Tomorrow we're gonna go to the police station and get a picture of one of the terrorists." He stood on tiptoe to slide a plate from the cabinet beside the sink. "So I know what he looks like."

Kate watched him pull a slice of pizza from the pie, wondering if he would recognize anything of himself in that photograph.

# CHAPTER 33

The phone woke Kate from a fitful sleep. She swung her legs from beneath the sheet, thrust her toes into her flip-flops, and then shivered, remembering Marlow had said he would call again, recalling yesterday's horrors. Seizing the phone, she slapped it against her ear. "Wade in the Waves Motel. How may I help you?"

"That you? Kate Dalton?"

The voice sounded thick and clotted. It made Kate think of cottage cheese, its lumpy texture and chalky taste. "Pearline?"

"One and the same, hon. I guess you know about old TD."

There was no hint of a question there and Kate guessed the texture of Pearline's voice meant she'd been crying. "Yes. Detective Marlow called me. I'm . . ." Kate sucked in a breath and studied the honeyed light drizzling through the blinds. What was the harm? Especially now, when it wasn't mere social convention, when she genuinely felt regret and sorrow—for the living as well as the dead. "I'm sorry." Her voice curdled around the word. Old habits die hard.

"Me, too," Pearline sniffed. "He was a pain in the butt most days—always bitching about the brand of coffee I bought and saying I should get the liquid creamer instead of the powder and telling me to wash out his cup, but he had a good heart. I expect he tried to protect Miz Blake long as he could."

"I'm sure he did. He was . . ." What could she say? Dyson was an old-school male chauvinist but, she realized, there were differing causes of chauvinism as well as degrees of manifestation. Emory McCoy's was founded on a belief that women were—or should be—lesser creatures, satisfied to receive orders from men instead of thinking for themselves, content with the pedestals that limited their movement. TD's version seemed to be of the courtly and caring variety, based on the concept that women should be shielded from a harsh world. The mindset evident in his use of the title "lady" may have bought Amanda a few more hours.

"And I'm sorry for you and that boy. It must have torn your heart out to tell him."

Kate clamped a hand to her chest, gathering the slack fabric of her baggy T-shirt between her fingers. "Actually, I—"

"But here I am boo-hooing all over the place and forgetting why I called. The boss would have a conniption. Always telling me to get to the point." Pearline blew her nose—at least that's what Kate assumed from a bubbling snort and soft crumple of paper. "Anyway, someone broke in here and went through our desks and cabinets. Left the place in an awful state."

Kate felt her breath freeze in her throat. *Don't say it. Don't tell me the rest.*

"I like to keeled over when I saw the broken glass in the door and the mess in my office," Pearline rattled on. "Looked like a tornado went through—twice. Took me the best part of three hours to get it back together and discover he'd looted the coffee fund, and made off with Miz Blake's file."

Kate's bedroom tilted and the walls shimmered. Until this moment she'd clung to a naïve belief that neither Amanda nor Dyson had given her up. But now Dwayne Vetter had her name.

A wave of anxiety, like black water, swept over her. The phone slipped from her fingers, clattered against the nightstand, and fell to the carpet. She put her head between her knees, gripped her ankles, and gulped at air with the consistency of putty.

Pearline's voice leaked from the receiver, distant, tinny. ". . . file drawer with all the others. I had it under my blotter to remind me we'll need to probate that will."

*The will!* Vetter would see his mother had been passed over as Way-Ray's guardian. He'd feed on Justine's fury. Kate straightened and groped for the phone. It thudded against the nightstand. "Are you there? Are you okay?" Pearline's tiny voice inquired.

"You okay, Kate?" Another voice. Jackson. He'd insisted on sleeping in the living room. No, not insisted, simply said he would. Way-Ray was delighted, and even more thrilled when Jackson continued the security game by sealing the sliding door to his balcony. Kate had held her breath, hoping Way-Ray wouldn't ask why foreign agents would target his room, but he'd been too excited about her decision to pay Evie's taxes to think of anything else.

"You okay?" Jackson called again, his voice tight. Feet pounded up the stairs, an uneven beat: thump, thud, thump, thud.

"Are you there?" Pearline repeated in a distant screech.

*You knew Vetter would come. You knew it from the moment you read Amanda's letter.* Kate managed a strangled breath. "I'm here."

Jackson thundered through the door, carrying a long-barreled revolver and wearing a pair of sagging gray gym shorts. His left leg was ridged with jagged burgundy welts that writhed like snakes when he moved.

Kate gasped, recoiled, inching toward the head of the bed. Tweaking a corner of the sheet, she covered her bare legs, feeling too exposed in her thin white shorts and the worn shirt with its sleeves ripped away.

Jackson winced and his eyes darkened. He slung his left foot to one side and used it to brace himself as he bent and snatched up the phone. "Who is this?" His voice was harsh. "What do you want?"

Kate stretched out a hand. "I'm okay. It's okay." An apology for the revulsion she hadn't masked?

He frowned, the planes of his face like ledges of stone in the slanting light, and thrust the phone toward her. "Pearline?"

"Amanda's lawyer's secretary. Vetter broke into her office. He took Amanda's file."

Jackson grunted. He handed off the phone, turned on one bare heel, and crossed the landing to Way-Ray's door, the revolver clamped against his right leg.

"Who was that?" Pearline's voice was no longer morose and viscous. It was bright, clear, interested.

"Jackson Scovell," Kate said. She studied his back as he peered into Way-Ray's room. She'd never noticed the hard ridges of muscle on either side of his spine, the bulk of his shoulders, the swell of his arms. He always wore shapeless clothing, and she assumed he was weak because he drank, because he worked a dead-end job. Assumptions had distorted her vision. "He's a friend." You respected a friend. You trusted a friend. A friend had your back. "A friend," she repeated.

"Sounds like a big man," Pearline fished. "Strong."

Kate watched Jackson turn from Way-Ray's door. The slouch was gone. With his shoulders thrown back, his chest appeared plated with armor. "He is," she said, hearing hesitant amazement in her voice.

"I hope he can protect you from the madman who got Miz Blake and TD."

"I hope so too." She nodded at Jackson who stationed himself in the doorway, watching through eyes like chips of ice.

"That poor motherless boy needs you. But anyway, back to the point." Pearline sniffed and leaned on the final word. "We figure he broke in last night, because I was by here on Saturday to finish up some dictation and the landlord had his son in Sunday to run the floor polisher in the hallways. Fred's not the brightest bulb in the pack—he's about a fifteen watt—but even he would have noticed broken glass."

Last night. Dwayne Vetter could be on a plane now. Kate's skin crawled, but then something tickled at the back of her brain, Pearline asking for her address in order to forward Amanda's letter. "Was my address in the file?"

"No. Just your name and phone number—without the area code. Figured I'd remember that."

A sigh leaked between Kate's lips. "That's all?"

"Right. Remember how I was worried that old drunk would worm something out of me? Well, I wrote the address on that envelope I sent on to you and that was it. I planned to call today and get it again so we could start probate. Why don't you give it to me now?"

Kate reeled it off, wondering if Dwayne Vetter would call. Would he pretend to be a tourist, book a room, and ask for directions?

Her hands grew numb. How could she tell which calls were real?

"That damn second line is ringing," Pearline said. "I gotta run. Call if you need a hand with the funeral arrangements. And take care of yourself, hon."

"I'll try," Kate told the dial tone.

Jackson closed his hand over the phone and transferred it to its cradle. "We've got another day," he said. "Maybe more."

"How do you know?" Kate tipped her head, and studied what she could see of his face: the outline of his jaw. The right side bulged, as if it had been broken and then patched by an amateur.

"He's driving." The jaw barely moved.

"Are you sure?"

"He needed a car to trail Amanda."

Even as she acknowledged the logic, Kate felt a buzz of annoyance at his certainty. Was some competitive, presumptive part of her galled because she hadn't reached that conclusion before him? Her fingers knotted in the sheet. "Maybe he decided to fly this time."

"That's possible." Jackson shrugged, giving no sign that he'd detected the sarcasm in her tone. "But he's got a gun. He'll want it with him."

Kate searched her mind. Marlow had never said that Amanda and Dyson had been shot, only that they'd died hard. "How do you know he has a gun?"

Jackson ran his left thumb along the length of his revolver. "I feel it."

"Wayne didn't have a gun when he came after Amanda."

The muscles in Jackson's jaw rippled. "Wayne's mission was vengeance. He had years to think about how he wanted her to die. He wanted to get close, make it last."

Lowering her eyes, Kate stared at the livid scars on his leg, and wondered what experience with revenge made him so certain of that. "Dwayne wants vengeance, too."

From the edges of her eyes, she saw Jackson stroke the gun again. "Not for himself. Probably not for Wayne, either. His mother's setting the agenda."

Kate clutched at faint hope. "Maybe he'll hide out for a few weeks. He has to know they're looking for him."

Jackson shook his head. "He knows, but it's a big country. Miles of back roads and only a handful of cops. He'll change cars—steal or borrow them."

Kate frowned. "Who would loan him a car?"

"Another ex-con." Kate heard no mocking in Jackson's tone, saw in his eyes no sense of superiority. "It's like a fraternity, right down to the initiations and hazing. Vetter's probably got a dozen 'brothers.' All happy to help with his hunt."

Kate remembered what Amanda said about the network of ex-cons who helped Wayne. "We need more time. We have to make plans."

"Plans can get in the way."

"You had a plan last night when you ran the van off the road."

"Did I?" He chuckled, a sound like water splashing over rounded stones. He walked to the bed and sat. She felt the mattress sag beneath his weight, canting her toward him. For a slice of a second, she hoped he'd put his arm around her—not because he was a man, but because he was a human being.

Her bare arm grazed his, the skin warm, the muscle beneath it taut. Kate felt a tightening in her stomach, unexpected, surprising. She fixed her eyes on the carpet, wondering if he had desires like other men. Or had pain and alcohol smothered his emotions? She recalled the force of his presence that day in the laundry room, the way it electrified the memory of Andy's rejection.

She leaned away, but the slant of the bed drew her back. Skin brushed skin, elbow to shoulder, tingling. She shivered. Why had he assumed this role of protector without question or negotiation? Was he using this in place of alcohol—getting high on her fear?

"Let the machine pick up," Jackson said. "In case he calls."

Kate nodded, noting the carpet nap worn nearly flat in the doorway. Jackson shifted. Skin rubbed on skin. She longed to stand and stride away, longed to lean closer. She held herself rigid, stared at the brightening window.

"But you already thought of that." His voice was calm, factual and she realized she hadn't needed to tell him she'd thought of that to prove her intelligence. That prideful need had boiled away, vaporized.

"It's easier to be the predator than the prey," Jackson said. "You want to grab Way-Ray and bolt. But if we're going to put an end to this soon, you've got to wait for him to come."

Like a goat staked out to entice the lion. "I know." Still, she couldn't help thinking she'd have a better chance if she ran.

Jackson leaned away and patted her back between the shoulder blades, his hand flat and stiff. Then he stood. "County offices should be open before long."

"Offices?"

"Evie's taxes." Jackson smiled and his eyes glowed like opals in the swelling light. "Way-Ray will want you to pay them first thing after breakfast."

"Or before."

"I'll get the coffee going. We'll get the taxes out of the way and then stay close." He moved toward the stairs, gun at his side. "In case I'm wrong about Vetter's timetable."

241

# CHAPTER 34

Way-Ray bolted through the heavy glass door ahead of Jackson and danced down a narrow corridor peering at signs on office doors. Kate smiled as he passed a blinking snack machine that would have captured his full attention any other day. "I'm gonna be the first one to find the door that says treasure on it, and I'm gonna give them the money," he called over his shoulder.

"Treasurer," Kate corrected. "And we're giving them a check, not money."

He turned, fists clenching. "You said we'd give them money. You promised."

"She will." Jackson intervened. "Checks are just like money."

"How about you write in the numbers, and then I'll put my name on the bottom line."

His lower lip thrust out like a shelf. "How come *I* can't put *my* name? It was my idea, remember?"

"I know it was." When this was over and Way-Ray had come to accept his losses, she'd establish rules, set limits, let him know that financial capitulation wouldn't continue. After she wrote this check, she'd be nearly broke. "But the name on the check has to match the name on the account."

He wrinkled his nose. "Can't you just tell them it's my 'count?"

Jackson snorted a laugh. Kate spun to face him, hissing, "If you find this interrogation so amusing, you field that question. And the next ones. They come in swarms like mosquitoes."

His eyes flashed silver like a shower of bright dimes. Lowering her gaze, she studied the misshapen plaid shirt that hung from his shoulders; its crisscrossed colors were indistinct, like old roads in the desert. She assumed his gun was beneath the worn fabric. His slouch had returned and he appeared as devoid of muscle tone as he had the day he asked for money to gas up the mower. Remembering his bare chest and shoulders and the way his arm felt against hers, she wondered if other women had seen him shirtless and strong.

Jackson winked as if he'd read her mind. She flushed and he pointed a finger at Way-Ray. "Banks need documents."

"What-you-mints?"

Jackson didn't falter. "Official papers." He bent to look into Way-Ray's eyes. "If you sign Kate's check, it's not official, so the bank won't hand over the money, Evie's taxes won't get paid, and you could be prosecuted."

Way-Ray frowned. "What's prosecuted?"

"Arrested. Taken to court. Maybe put in jail."

Way-Ray chewed a thumbnail. "Robin Hood went to jail, but he 'scaped."

Kate suppressed a giggle. Jackson glanced at her, eyes dancing. "Jails are stronger now."

Way-Ray balanced on one foot. "What if I write Kate's name?"

Kate's giggle morphed into a sardonic laugh.

Jackson smiled. "That's forgery. They'll send you to a big prison with barbed wire on top of the walls and no TV sets."

"No TV?" Way-Ray's eyes widened. He worried the nail and hopped to the other foot. "Okay. Then I'll write in the numbers—real big ones—and Kate can do the rest." He flung his arms out like wings and, with a strident "bzzzzzz," took off along the corridor, swooping from door to door, zipping around men and women who turned to gaze after him with indulgent smiles that spoke of memories of a time when the word "inhibition" was unknown.

"Nothing to it," Jackson said. "I didn't even break a sweat."

"Yeah," Kate snarled. "But this isn't a sprint, it's a marathon."

"I know," he said with another flash of silver. "But you've got endurance, Kate."

"Oooff!" Way-Ray collided with a man with a mop of brown hair.

"Careful, boy." The man gripped Way-Ray's arm.

Kate's heart thudded in her throat. Jackson shot forward like a striking snake, right hand beneath his shirt. "Let him go."

The man raised his hands. "No harm meant, Jackson. Just didn't want the boy to fall."

Jackson's hand slipped free, empty. "Hank? Didn't recognize you with all the hair."

Hank nodded and walked by, close against the wall. Kate let out a painful breath. What if that had been Dwayne Vetter?

"Stay close," Jackson told Way-Ray.

"Bzzzzz," he responded, spinning in a tight circle beside a water fountain.

"It's going to be impossible to keep him in today," Kate muttered. "And I've got a ton of laundry to do." She still hadn't worked out a system to spread that load among the housekeepers, hadn't looked into having the dryer repaired. One day left before Vetter reached Castaway Beach and she'd spend it wrestling with soggy towels.

She remembered a "live as if it were your last day" discussion in a college philosophy class, remembered arguing that it was little more than a way to give yourself permission to ignore consequences. Now, she longed to embrace that ideology. But she'd always met her obligations. Today would be no exception. Saint Kate the Reliable.

Way-Ray slurped water and then marched toward them with a gurgling giggle, index fingers dimpling puffed-out cheeks.

Jackson shook his head. "Spit that water at me or at Kate and I'll mop it up with your shirt—while you're still wearing it."

Way-Ray's jaw slackened. Water dribbled through his lips onto his bright blue T-shirt. He brushed at it, then clamped his lips, swallowed, and grinned up at Jackson. "Nuh-uh. You wouldn't do that." When Jackson didn't respond, the grin wavered and he slid his eyes toward Kate. "Would he?"

Kate shrugged, remembering how Jackson had handled Mickey Webster. He had so much to be angry about: pain and deformity, his status as the community's entitled drunk, the days he'd gone without drink on her behalf. She took a half step away. Could a teasing child light his fuse?

Jackson laughed, roughened his voice, and spaced out his words. "Do you want to get more water and find out?"

Way-Ray emitted a hollow bleat. "I've had enough water for now." He spread his arms, a plane again, buzzing toward the end of the corridor.

Jackson touched her arm. "You know I'd never hurt that boy, don't you?"

She shook off his fingers. "Sure." Did she?

He gripped her elbows and turned her to face him. "Look at me, Kate."

She raised her eyes, expecting to see his mouth grim, his eyes like flint. Instead she saw dark disappointment, deep enough to drown her. "I will never hurt him. Believe that."

She tried to pull away. Did the man making this pledge have control over the other man, the drunk? Would that man pass along pain to try to alleviate his own? Like Wayne Jessop had.

The disappointment in Jackson's eyes deepened and widened. He released her arms. "You'll see. I'll prove it."

"Come on," Way-Ray yelled. "I found the treasure place."

"Avast, matey, it's where the pirates wait to steal our gold." Jackson exaggerated his limp and swung off toward Way-Ray. "Step lively or they'll make you walk the plank. Arrr."

"Arrr," Way-Ray echoed, curling his lip as he swung the door wide. Kate crowded with them into a narrow space in front of a tall counter. Way-Ray bounced on his toes. "I can't see over it."

"Not much to see," Kate told him.

The office beyond was crammed with battered oak desks, humming computers, endless stacks of paper, and rows of industrial gray metal shelving stuffed with green-bound ledgers and topped with spider plants in red and blue ceramic pots. Someone had tried to make this more than a place where forty hours were traded for a paycheck.

A willowy woman in a jumpsuit the color of goldenrod appeared from beyond the shelves, her generous mouth curved into a smile, glossy red lipstick gleaming. She patted brunette curls with one hand and fingered a gold charm bracelet with the other. "Hello, Jackson," she said, her voice like buttery syrup.

"Arlene." Jackson acknowledged her with a scant nod. "How's Randy?"

"Back in Minnesota with his father. Remodeling their deer camp." She half closed eyes the color of milk chocolate and toyed with the lone ebony button that secured the fabric spanning her breasts. "I expected to see you at Billy's last night." The syrup simmered.

Kate knew the tavern, a concrete bunker sitting back from the highway behind an abandoned gallery. Every time she passed there were half a dozen cars nosed against it like piglets nursing on a sow. Did Jackson go there because of this woman? Kate edged away from him, feeling betrayed, telling herself she had no right to that emotion.

"I had other plans." Jackson's voice was curt as he stooped, caught Way-Ray under the arms, and lifted him to the counter. "This is Wayland Raymond Blake."

"Arrr," Way-Ray growled.

Arlene's narrowed eyes strafed Kate's hair and breasts. "And his mother?"

"Kate's my friend," Way-Ray corrected. "My mom's name is Amanda. She lives in Grassy Ridge, but she disappeared and we hired a detective. And I had to have an operation." He flipped up his T-shirt, and tugged at his pants, revealing the satiny pinkness of his scar. "And we live at the Wade in the Waves Motel."

Kate felt dirty and defiled to have this woman know so much.

Arlene arched an eyebrow at Jackson and curved her full lips as if they shared a risqué joke. Fighting a swell of resentment, Kate peered at Jackson from the edges of her eyes. He didn't return the smile. Kate shoved a hand across the counter. "Kate Dalton. Nice to meet you. I'd like to pay the taxes on Evie Hopkins' farm."

Both of Arlene's eyebrows ascended into her thick bangs and she made a show of straightening a pile of fliers. "Evie owes quite a sum."

"I'm aware of that." Kate withdrew her untouched hand and dug out her checkbook. "Could you give me the exact amount?"

Arlene's eyes strafed Kate once more and focused on Jackson. Cat's eyes. Calculating. "Paul's not going to be happy."

"Not my problem."

"Is that Paul who's Evie's son?" Way-Ray cocked his head. "'Cause if he's gonna be mad, maybe he shoulda paid the taxes himself and then Evie would be happy and maybe he could be happy, too."

Jackson choked on a laugh, threw his head back, and set it free. Kate felt it echo in her chest, like the peal of a bell. "Out of the mouths of babes." He tousled Way-Ray's hair. "It's not giving that makes Paul happy, it's receiving—especially blood money from developers."

"It's called a finder's fee," Arlene snapped.

"It's stabbing his mother in the back."

Kate's jealousy evaporated.

Arlene's eyes glittered. "Paul has a right to look out for his inherit—"

"Stop talking!" Way-Ray tugged at Jackson's sleeve. Give her the money so the birds and animals don't lose their home."

"What you said!" Jackson held up his palm. Way-Ray crowed with delight and hit him with a high-five.

Arlene's scarlet lips pinched. She spun to a computer, tapped keys, and spat a string of numbers. Kate copied the figure onto the checkbook calendar page, winced, tore off a check, and handed Way-Ray the pen. "Write that in the box by the dollar sign."

Way-Ray squinted at it. "All those numbers? I'll hafta write real small."

"Teeny tiny," Kate agreed. Where would she find the funds to bury Amanda?

His fingers whitened as he gripped the pen. "Where do I put the comma?"

"After the first two numbers on the left," Jackson said.

Way-Ray added the comma and shoved the check toward Kate. "Now you do the rest."

Kate filled in the remainder, signed it, and handed it to Arlene who grasped it between two carmine fingernails. "We can't credit this until it clears your bank." Her lips curved into that cat's smile. "That will be the end of the week, maybe later."

Kate frowned. Would the delay be crucial? "I could get a cashier's check."

"It would still be a few days before we credit it. It won't get to our bank until tomorrow. At the earliest."

Jackson snorted. "The bank's just down the block."

Arlene stared down her nose. "There are procedures we have to follow."

"Did you understand that big word?" Jackson asked Way-Ray. "Procedure is a bunch of time-consuming, nit-picking steps bureaucrats take to make their jobs look tough."

Way-Ray squinted over his shoulder at Arlene.

"Procedure can be very important, Way-Ray," Kate said. This woman could delay longer if she wanted. "We'll talk about it later, okay?" When he nodded, she turned to Arlene. "I'll need a receipt."

Arlene dropped the check on the counter, jerked open a drawer, drew out a pad of forms, and began to scribble.

Way-Ray tugged at Kate's arm. "This is boring. I want a soda."

"Then let's go get one." Jackson hoisted him from the counter.

"Can I get fries, too?" Way-Ray grinned up at Kate.

Nutrition didn't matter on the last day of childhood innocence. "Okay."

With a cry of delight, Way-Ray towed Jackson toward the door. "We'll wait for you in the hall, Kate," Jackson said. Not a word for Arlene.

Kate felt the vibrations of Arlene's wrath as she tore the form from the pad, tossed it on the counter, and stalked back among the shelves. How much of her anger sprang from Jackson's indifference and how much from the disruption of Paul Hopkins's plans?

"Thank you." With slow deliberation, Kate folded the form and tucked it into her purse.

Outside, Way-Ray again buzzed the corridor. Jackson leaned against the wall, his weight on his good leg. "Not that I think you care, but Arlene and I never had anything going. Randy's just not much of a husband."

Kate shrugged, concealing a mix of emotions. Way-Ray buzzed past, making tight circles on squeaking tennis shoes. Kate followed him toward the parking lot, Jackson falling in beside her. She wondered if Arlene was watching them walk off together, hated herself for hoping she was.

# CHAPTER 35

Shifting from foot to foot in the doorway to the living room, Kate bit at the ridge of tough skin beside her thumbnail and watched the red second hand nudge its black companion onto the seven-minute mark. The plan called for them to leave for Evie's before eight, but Dorrie Branscom, the housekeeper who agreed to cover the office, arrived late and confronted the simple reservation system as if it was military code. Rhea, who described Dorrie as a few doughnuts shy of a dozen, sighed and began a third explanation.

Kate switched thumbs and gnawed at skin already raw. Dorrie wasn't the only one holding up the parade. Way-Ray had dilly-dallied, searching for his blue orca shirt, quibbling about whether his hair could be washed without shampoo, and arguing for four spoons of sugar on his pre-sweetened cereal. Now he munched with his mouth open, providing a background beat for the soft shuffle of brochures Jackson rearranged in the rack on the lobby wall. Earlier, he sorted them alphabetically, but now, Kate noted, they were displayed by predominant colors and the positions of those colors in a rainbow, red at the top of the rack. She glanced at the dirty dishes on the counter. Washing them might provide an outlet for her frustration. If not, at least the chore would be done.

The second hand swept toward the top once more. Dorrie dithered over whether to put a period after a guest's name in the reservation book. Rhea, her voice tight, contended, "Sure. Put down two periods, three, four. Just write in pencil, okay?"

Dorrie worried her lower lip with teeth stained by orange lipstick. "Maybe we should use sticky notes instead."

"Great. Good idea. Sticky notes are terrific." Rhea's voice climbed toward a range audible only to dogs.

"What color sticky notes?" Dorrie asked.

"Yellow," Jackson boomed.

"Yellow," Rhea agreed. She snagged a pad from the desk drawer and slapped them onto the countertop. "These are the perfect color. The size is just right, too."

Dorrie studied them, her brown eyes sullied by confusion beneath a bloom of dandelion-colored hair. Kate touched the right rear pocket of her jeans and heard the crumple of the receipt Way-Ray intended to present to Evie. Yesterday he practiced the way he'd hold it, the exact words he'd use to deliver the news, and the precise way he'd smile when he was done. As he modeled an assortment of smiles ranging from serious to silly, Kate studied the mug shot of Dwayne Vetter they'd collected from Chief Lowell.

Amanda had described Dwayne as being meaner than his half-brother, and Kate imagined him with Wayne's angry eyes and predatory smirk. But this man had feathery blond hair, guileless violet eyes, a band of freckles across his cheeks and nose, and small, even teeth. His expression was earnest and open, as if he'd been posing for a high school yearbook portrait instead of against a grid that showed him to be slightly less than six feet tall. The profile view revealed a cowlick. He appeared likeable, trustworthy, even harmless. Yet he'd killed Amanda and Ted Dyson.

She'd shivered and Jackson took the photo from her and showed it to Way-Ray, telling him that this was a known terrorist, a man to watch out for, to hide from. Way-Ray held the picture close to his nose and stared into Dwayne's eyes. "He doesn't look like a terrorist. He's too happy."

"Terrorists can pretend to be happy. They're like actors. His hair could be longer or shorter, even a different color. He might shave it all off or wear a wig. He might put in contact lenses to make his eyes a different color."

Way-Ray frowned. "Then, how will I know it's him?"

"The shape of his eyes and nose and mouth will probably be the same. His ears, too."

Way-Ray traced the outline of Dwayne's ears and then his own. "His ears are different from mine," he announced, fingering a lobe. "Mine hang down more and kind of wobble."

"You've got a good eye," Jackson said. "Ears are all different. They're like fingerprints and handprints."

Way-Ray was intrigued by that and compared his hands to Kate's and Jackson's and later, when Rhea brought them over to keep him occupied, to Kyle and Sean's.

Way-Ray's spoon clattered against his bowl. Kate jumped, then turned to watch him set it in the sink, fill it with water, and hop across the kitchen on his left foot. "I'm ready. Let's go."

Kate gave her thumb a final nip, wishing she could put off the truth until he was a grown man—until time might allow him to forgive the messenger. "Okay. Go brush your teeth."

Way-Ray switched to his right foot and hopped on across the living room. "I don't need to."

"You do. You just ate."

"Only cereal," he argued. "And cereal doesn't stick in my—"

"It's your choice," Jackson growled. "But we're not leaving for Evie's until you brush."

Way-Ray hesitated for a second, then spun about and hopped to the stairs. Everyone was better at parenting, Kate thought. She should buy a how-to book or see about taking a class.

Jackson stuffed a handful of blue brochures into the bottom rack. "You about ready, Rhea?"

Rhea grimaced, rolled her eyes, and switched off the computer. "You know what? Just forget about the computer,

252

Dorrie. And forget about the reservation book, too. Take messages on the sticky notes and I'll return the calls when I get back."

Dorrie's hands fluttered toward the pack of notes. "Are you sure? I think I almost—"

"She's positive," Jackson said. "Rhea, call Curtis. Let's get ready to roll."

Rhea reached for the phone and Kate fretted again that a police escort would only call attention to them. But Jackson told her that was the idea. If Dwayne Vetter was watching, he might follow. Chief Lowell would be hidden at the turnoff, watching.

"He's on the way." Rhea returned the phone to its cradle. "He'll toot the horn when he's in the alley."

"I'll just get a few of these ready." Dorrie removed sheets from the tiny notepad and stuck them to the counter. Rhea mimed strangling herself and Kate turned away, gagging back a giggle.

"I'm done," Way-Ray shouted, bouncing down the stairs. "I want to ride with Jackson." He tugged at her hand, his fingers damp and his breath smelling of mint and vanilla. "Okay, Kate?"

Kate cut her eyes toward Jackson. Lowell's plan called for Way-Ray to ride with her. Way-Ray darted past, squeezed between Rhea and Dorrie, swept around the counter, and grasped a pocket of the splattered painters' pants Jackson wore beneath yet another fraying plaid flannel shirt. "Can I?"

Jackson disengaged Way-Ray's fingers. "You want to get there fast, don't you?"

Way-Ray smacked his forehead. "Duh, yeah."

"Then go with Kate. My truck's on empty. I have to stop for gas."

"All right. But I ride with you on the way back." Way-Ray tugged at the door knob.

Jackson's hand shot out and snagged his T-shirt. "What did you learn yesterday?"

Way-Ray peered over his shoulder at the hand that held him, poking his tongue into his cheek. "That I have to be careful because the terrorist guy could be hiding outside?"

"Right." Jackson released his grip.

"There's a terrorist outside?" Dorrie squawked.

"You never know." Rhea snatched the pad of sticky notes and tossed it into the desk drawer. "You stay in here where it's safe, take care of the guests as best you can, answer the phone, and write down messages."

"Okay," Dorrie replied, giving the word a dubious twist.

Rhea hefted her purse from a shelf beneath the counter. "Let's go before that damn phone rings. And before the boys drive Evie around the bend."

"Kyle and Sean are out at Evie's?" Way-Ray bounced onto his toes.

"Sure are. She got more sick birds in this week and she's counting on the three of you."

"And I'm gonna help all I can." Way-Ray nodded at Kate. "Just like I said. I'm not even gonna play with the deer or the bunnies."

Kate blinked back tears. Before she could speak, wheels crunched on gravel and a horn sounded in the alley: three short beeps and two long.

Jackson put his hand on the knob. "Remember, Way-Ray, no running ahead."

Way-Ray saluted. "Yes sir."

Jackson grinned. "At ease, soldier. But look alert."

Way-Ray curled his fingers and made pretend binoculars. Rhea strode through the door and along the sidewalk toward her battered blue car. Kate followed.

She passed the propane burners where guests boiled crabs, the hose and sloping concrete pad where they washed sand from their feet, the plastic tub filled with miniature shovels, pails, strainers, and rakes. She smelled salt on the breeze and the warm fragrance of petunias trailing from their pots. Hinges groaned as Rhea opened her car door. Kate felt the soft springiness of grass beneath her sandals and then the sucking grip of gravel. She heard Way-Ray behind her, hopping again. Gravel crunched. A white SUV rolled around the corner of the building. A woman leaned from the passenger window, shouting, "There she is! There's Kate Dalton. And that must be the boy!"

# CHAPTER 36

"Way-Ray, get behind me," Jackson commanded. "Kate, get him into the office."

"Who's that lady?" Way-Ray asked. "Is she a terrorist? Can ladies be terrorists?"

"Kate," Jackson roared. "Move."

Kate stumbled backward, searching with her heels for the strip of grass that bordered the sidewalk, thinking that if she turned her back, she'd be more vulnerable. Gravel lapped over the thin rubber soles of her sandals like a surging tide, slowing each step.

The SUV slid to a stop and the woman thrust the door open and slid out. She plunged toward them on shiny red high heels, a blue-black cylinder in her right hand.

Kate groped behind her for Way-Ray.

Rhea flung her car door wide, and hurled herself toward the woman, waving her arms. The driver was out now, and Kate caught a glimpse of blond hair as he balanced a dark canister on his shoulder, leveling it at her across the hood. A red light flashed. "We're hot," he yelled.

"Kate, get in the office." Jackson roared.

*Why didn't Jackson shoot?*

The woman raised her cylinder and pointed it. Kate braced for the bullet.

"Are you a terrorist?" Way-Ray's voice, excited, amazed. "Is that a terrorist gun?"

Time stretched like elastic. The driver trotted around the front of the SUV, sunlight glinting off the lens he sighted through. Rhea cocked her right arm, her heavy purse swinging from her fist. The woman smiled. "Marnie Phillips. I'm investigating the local connection to the murder of Amanda Blake. What can you tell us about her death?"

A roar swelled inside Kate's head, blocked out other sounds, then transformed itself into the absence of sound. Not Dwayne Vetter. Another type of horror.

She saw Rhea halt, her arm bent. A balding man emerged from a downstairs unit, a green bathrobe cinched beneath a keg of a stomach. A gull tilted, wheeled, and beat its wings twice. The silence shattered. "Amanda Blake is my mother's name," Way-Ray said, his voice hesitant, plaintive.

Kate spun to see him clinging to Jackson's hand, face crumpling.

"My mom's not dead." Way-Ray's voice dropped to a whisper. The tips of his fingers touched Kate's. Tiny. Cold.

"What's going on?" a woman's voice called.

"Nothing. Go back inside," Jackson answered.

Kate glanced at the second level of the motel and saw guests streaming onto the deck, rubbing sleep from their eyes, clutching coffee cups, toeing into flip-flops. She swallowed bile. How had this woman found them?

"We have nothing to say to ambush journalists." Jackson's voice constricted with rage. "Go inside, Way-Ray."

Way-Ray squeezed Kate's fingers and his eyes filmed with tears. "She's just lost, right Kate? My mom's just lost."

Kate swallowed a comforting lie that shredded her throat like barbed wire. "Let's go call Evie and tell her we'll be late." Her voice was a harsh croak, words jagged and indistinct.

Way-Ray released her fingers and gripped her arm at the elbow, pinching deep into the soft hollow between muscles and tendons. "And TD's looking for my mom. Right, Kate?"

From the edge of her eyes, Kate saw Marnie Phillips straighten the tight-fitting, gold-buttoned jacket of a crimson suit that matched her heels. "Get a two-shot," she instructed the photographer. "Would that TD be Ted Dyson? The man whose body was found beside Amanda Blake's in a ravine in Ohio?"

"Don't answer her," Jackson cautioned. "Don't say a word."

Way-Ray's fingers dug deeper. His eyes, clouded with confusion, darted from Kate to the reporter. "What's a ravine? Is my mom okay?"

His words pounded into Kate's heart like spikes. Her cowardice brought this on. "She's making things up. Go inside." Kate wheeled on the woman, Way-Ray holding firm. "How did you find us?"

"I don't reveal my sources," Marnie said.

With a flash of fury, Kate recalled Arlene, the woman scorned. Had she trolled the Internet, learned of Kate's role in Wayne's death, then linked Amanda's name to Ohio?

"This is private property." Rhea put her hip against the photographer. "Turn off your camera and get out."

He kept the lens pointed at Kate. "I'm not moving until Marnie tells me," he growled. "If you injure me or this camera, you'll be looking at a lawsuit."

"Lawsuit my ass." Rhea dropped her purse and raced toward the alley. "I'll get Curtis. We'll see who's got the law on their side."

"Yeah," Way-Ray chimed in. "Curtis has a badge and everything. And you're a liar and you're not allowed to be here."

Marnie's brow furrowed for a nanosecond, and then she snapped the smile back in place. "Now, let's be reasonable. There's no need to involve the police." She smoothed honey-colored hair behind doll-like ears studded with gold cubes.

"My mom's not dead," Way-Ray moaned. "You're lying. My mom's not dead." His grip on Kate's arm tightened until her hand throbbed. "Tell her to stop lying about my mom."

Marnie glanced from Way-Ray to Kate and her brow furrowed. "He doesn't know?"

"Turn off that camera and get the hell out of here." Jackson bore down on the photographer. He circled the SUV, aiming the lens at Kate and Way-Ray.

"What didn't you tell me?" Way-Ray pleaded with Kate. "What happened to my mom?" He bent his knees and butted her side.

"Let's go inside, Way-Ray." She grasped his shoulders, tried to turn him. "Come on inside and I'll tell you everything."

"Can you comment on your role in the death of the boy's father in February?" Marnie raised her voice over the hum of speculation from guests clustered at the railing.

Way-Ray broke from Kate's grip. "My dad got sick and died when I was a real little kid."

Marnie waggled one hand, brushing the fingers through the air, as if wiping his words away. "We've been unable to get the police to confirm that the boy's uncle is suspected of the murders and may be headed for Castaway Beach. Can you comment on that?"

Kate felt hollow, as if she might implode.

Jackson thrust himself between Kate and the reporter. "We don't know what you're talking about."

Way-Ray released Kate's arm and stood beside Jackson, fists clenched. "I don't have an uncle. I had a grandma but she went to be with the angels." His voice clotted with tears. "Now there's just me and my mom and TD's going to find her so we can live in Grassy Ridge again and I can get a dog."

Marnie's lips twitched. Kate wanted to strike her down, kick her.

"You people are trespassing." Curtis' voice rang out. He strode toward them, Rhea at his side. "If you're not paying guests here, get on your way."

"Yeah," Rhea echoed. "And don't worry about raising dust when you do."

"You're liars," Way-Ray shouted. "Go away."

"Get a shot of the baby cop," Marnie called to the photographer, "and then pack up. Maybe we'll have time for a real breakfast before the satellite truck rolls into town." She rotated on one gleaming heel and headed for the SUV. The photographer grunted and pointed the lens at Curtis.

Curtis puffed his chest and raised his chin before he spoke. "Turn that camera off and get off this property." His voice swelled with importance. "Or I'll arrest you for trespassing."

"We're going," Marnie called over her shoulder. "But there will be more of us before the day is over. Even the networks." She grasped the door handle and vaulted to the seat as the photographer stowed his gear. "You'd better tell the boy the truth."

"You wouldn't know the truth if it bit you in the ass," Rhea hollered.

The photographer gunned the vehicle into a wide turn, gravel spitting from the wheels.

"It was all a mistake," Rhea called to the guests on the deck and stairways. "Somebody sent those fools here instead of a place down the road."

Kate shook her head. Another lie. Another domino ready to fall.

Rhea made a shooing motion with her hands. "Go on. Don't forget to put your dirty towels outside before noon."

Muttering, mumbling, and nodding, guests retreated to their rooms. Curtis watched the news crew go with the expression of a kid who dropped his ice cream in the sand. Kate felt her anger transfer to him, building like an electrical charge. Jackson's hand settled on her shoulder. "This is my fault," he said, his voice solemn. "I pissed off Arlene."

Kate felt her anger dissipate, as if Jackson had taken the jolt and channeled off the current. She felt limp, empty. She longed to turn, rest her head against his chest, to say this was too much for her. Instead she bent her neck to the yoke of responsibility. "No. I shouldn't have tried to delay the inevitable." She touched his hand with her fingertips, felt his skin, thick and rough. "Let's get out to Evie's and see what we can salvage."

"I'll call the chief and tell him why we were held up." Curtis marched toward his car, chest still puffed. "And let him know about the other reporters coming."

Kate shuddered. It would be a feeding frenzy. "Come on Way-Ray. Let's go see how that bobcat is doing."

She got no response except the rusty caw of a passing crow.

"Way-Ray!" Rhea echoed Kate, turning in a circle. "Where did that boy get off to?"

Kate whipped around, rubbing at her arm. When had he let go of it? "Way-Ray!" she screamed, heedless of the guests. "Where are you?"

Without a word, Jackson swung toward the office.

Rhea rushed to Kate's side. "He was right behind Curtis a moment ago." She patted Kate's arm with her fingertips, a steady rhythm.

Jackson emerged from the office and headed along the side of the building at a faltering trot, his mouth a grim line.

"He's gone," Kate heard herself say.

"No, he's not. I'll bet he went around to Curtis's cruiser. Jackson will bring him back in a sec."

Kate shook her head. "He's run off again."

"There's no place to run to. You're all he's got."

Kate gazed into the empty sky above the dune. "He's in shock, Rhea." She felt a sob building in her chest, squeezing her lungs, strangling her. "All he knows for sure is that he can't trust me."

"Now don't go borrowing trouble. Jackson will find—"

Jackson rounded the far corner of the building in a lop-sided sprint. He shook his head.

Kate's knees buckled and the sky seemed to shatter.

# CHAPTER 37

Kate knelt in the gravel, struggling to draw breath. This is how it must feel to survive a tornado but lose everything and everyone to its fury, to be alive but to wish you weren't because there was no point in living.

"We're gonna find him." Rhea wrapped her in a hug. "Let's get you inside and then I'll help Jackson hunt him up."

"No." Kate broke from Rhea's grip, disgusted by her weakness, and by—in her mother's words—the spectacle she'd made of herself. "I'll go down the alley. We've got to find him before—"

"Don't say it. Don't say that name." Rhea seized Kate's hand. "I'll let Curtis know what's what, and then I'll round up as many others as I can." She bounded off calling, "We'll find your boy."

Your boy. Only thirty-six hours ago Jackson said that. Then it felt like a gift, now the juxtaposition of words was ludicrous, blasphemous. Kate blotted her eyes on the backs of her wrists and trudged south.

The blocky shadows of houses to the east stretched across narrow lawns to the ridge of weedy gravel that separated the potholed ruts of the alley. Kate shaded her eyes and searched for dark footprints in the dewy grass, but saw nothing. Two blocks farther on the alley widened to a rutted semi-circle at a littered vacant lot with gnarled rhododendrons, mounds of sprawling blackberry canes, and a weather-beaten For Sale sign.

Beyond the lot stood a wall of pines and beyond those, a stream Way-Ray could ford easily, a thicket of dense evergreens, and more homes. He'd leave a trail if he crossed the lot, but then his tracks would be lost on the mat of brown needles beneath the trees.

"Way-Ray! Way-Ray, come back. Let's go to Evie's."

Pointless. He wouldn't come to her. Why should he?

Far to her right, she heard Jackson shout. For a second, hope fluttered in her chest. He shouted again and the desperation in his voice resonated with hers. Then hope fluttered once more. Perhaps Way-Ray would come to Jackson. Or Rhea. He might believe they were also victims of Kate's duplicity.

She sighed. What a downward spiral of lies she'd ridden since the day she agreed to keep Amanda's secrets. "I'm sorry," she called. That once-despised word crossed her lips without hesitation. "Please come back so I can tell you the truth."

A woman with blued hair and a quilted pink housecoat stood on the screened-in porch of a house to the west. She crossed her arms across her bosom and stared at Kate with open curiosity.

"I'm looking for a little boy," Kate called. She drew a height mark in the air. "He has brown hair and he's wearing a blue shirt with an orca on it."

The woman cupped her ear with one hand. "A shirt with a what?"

"An orca. A black and white whale. Have you seen him?"

The woman folded her arms across her chest again. "He wander away? Or run off?"

"He ran off," Kate admitted, wondering what the woman imagined she'd done. She longed to explain, to say she hadn't abused Way-Ray. But her defense might be suspect and it would keep her from the search.

The woman nodded, chin settling into her fluffy collar. Kate felt the weight of that judgment settle on her shoulders like the framework of a pillory.

"Kids find sport in making you worry," the woman said. "Bake up a batch of chocolate chip cookies. That always brought my Jimmy back."

Cookies? She should bake cookies while Dwayne Vetter hunted them? This woman was drawing on experience gleaned in an age when life was simpler and most of a child's injuries could be salved with sugar and time taken to mix dough and tend an oven.

"Thanks," she called, and jogged along the alley to the vacant lot. Dewdrops glistened on spiky grass and in the pale throats of wild morning glories. Kate scouted the perimeter, but found no darker furrow where moisture had been whisked aside by the legs of a running boy.

"Kate! Hold up!"

Rhea strode toward her, a cigarette between her lips, her purse hanging from her shoulder like an anchor on a chain too short to reach bottom. Kate felt a burst of hope, as sweet and sharp as a lemon drop. "Did you find him?"

"Not yet."

Sweet lemon turned to chalk.

"But we will." She ground the cigarette beneath her heel. "Once he gets over his mad, he'll be back." She stretched out a tentative hand.

Kate twisted away from it. "So all I have to do is to wait and bake cookies, right?" Tears scalded her eyes and her voice rose to a screech. "Bake chocolate chip cookies and he'll come home and they'll capture Dwayne Vetter and all this horror will disappear."

Rhea blinked. "Cookies? What are you talking about?" She grasped Kate's arm, swung her about, and marched her up the alley. "Get yourself back together. Deep breaths."

Kate let herself be led. Why not? Everything she did on her own was wrong. They passed the blue-haired woman still on her porch. "It's too late for cookies," Kate screamed.

"Hush." Rhea dug her nails into Kate's arm and cast a wave. "Morning Miz Dillon. How you doing?" The woman didn't unfold her arms.

Rhea hustled Kate past the motel and along the short spur to the highway. "Chief Lowell told Curtis to get out on the road. He's alerting everyone in case Way-Ray tries to thumb a ride."

Kate felt cold, bleak despair settle in her gut. She should have gone to the highway first. What if he'd been picked up already? They might never find him.

"Don't think what you're thinking," Rhea told her as they crossed the train tracks. "My guess is that if Way-Ray sees patrol cars, he'll hole up. Nobody will find him. Not even . . ."

Kate imagined Way-Ray, hunkered in a shed or beside a log, sobbing.

"The search and rescue team's on alert. They'll be ready in an hour."

"An hour?" Kate pressed her hands against her gut. An eternity.

"My husband's coming with some guys from his job. I'll get the neighbors. Hell, I'll round up the guests, give them ten dollars off if they help us hunt."

Kate felt Rhea's wave of optimism sweeping in. If only she could catch it, ride it.

"Hey." Curtis swung out of the patrol car. His eyes, wide and bright, swept over Kate. She could almost taste his desire to turn his head as if breathing the same air would infect him with her despair. "Hey," he said again. "The chief says we need a picture of Way-Ray we can copy."

Kate thought of all the shots Way-Ray had taken of whale spouts and clouds and mountains and Disney characters—the photographs he intended to share with his mother. With a tight compression of her heart, she realized that she none of him. That would have signified attachment, provided a symbol for it.

"A head-on close-up would be best," Curtis said.

"I . . . I never . . . I didn't—"

"I took a few of him and my boys on the beach," Rhea said. "Camera's in my car."

"I'll let the chief know." Curtis folded himself into the cruiser, popped a cell phone open, and half closed the door. Kate could almost sense his relief at putting a hundred pounds of metal between them.

"You stay here with Curtis. Keep your eyes on the highway." Rhea slid her purse strap higher on her shoulder and took off for the parking lot. "I'll be back in a flash."

Kate nodded numbly, feeling her shoulders slump beneath the rough wood of that pillory. A real mother took pictures of her children. A real mother anticipated, prepared.

She scanned the highway with blurring eyes. If Way-Ray returned, the best thing would be to abandon the ridiculous idea that she could care for him. She'd find someone like Rhea. Perhaps even Rhea herself. Phillip Jacobson could arrange that. And then she'd find a better-paying job and pay for his food, clothing, school supplies, and a computer.

The highway shimmered as she made plans for his future. She'd set money aside from every paycheck for college. She'd visit at least twice a month and write letters or send e-mails in between. Maybe they could go on whale-watching excursions. He'd play baseball or soccer. She'd go to his games and his graduation, meet his girlfriends and—

Rhea's grasped her shoulders, and shattered the fantasy. "You haven't heard a word I said, Kate. You can't help your boy if you don't stop brooding on what you can't change."

The words rang in the voice of Kate's mother. "Brooding is not productive." She could see her mother, standing stiff-spined in the doorway. Kate had thrown herself across her bed, rolling into the goose-down comforter that her grandmother had brought from Germany, willing the world—and the girl who had snubbed her, the boy who hadn't noticed her, the teacher who hadn't understood what she'd meant—to go on without her. Never once had her mother inquired about the depth and breadth of her misery; she merely cited examples of people who focused on others and made the world a better place.

A question seared Kate's brain: had her mother been a *real* mother?

Rhea bounced onto tiptoes and peered into Kate's eyes. "Which planet are you on?"

"Earth. And I'm through brooding." She hugged Rhea to her. "Thanks for saying that. Thanks for being . . . real."

Rhea blinked, nodded.

"Where do you think that reporter went for breakfast?"

"Depends on whether she's on an expense account." Rhea glanced at Curtis who had his ear glued to his cell phone. "You're not thinking of ripping her into confetti, are you?"

Kate flexed her fingers and started for the SUV. "No, I'm going to ask her to interview me."

"Okaaaaay." Rhea dragged the word into five rising syllables.

Kate spun to see her rolling her eyes. "We need hundreds of people looking for Way-Ray. And for Dwayne Vetter, too. The more people who know about him, the less power he has."

"Yeah, but that witch is the reason Way-Ray ran." Rhea drew out her cigarettes. "I wouldn't ask her for a glass of water if my tongue was on fire."

"Can't be helped," Kate said in a curt voice that would have made her mother proud. She felt stronger and lighter. She was about to throw down her burden of lies.

Rhea hopped in beside her. "Hell, why not call a news conference? Get all the sharks in one pool?"

Kate paused, the key an inch from the ignition as Rhea wrestled her purse to the seat and slammed the door. "That's a great idea."

Rhea sucked on an unlit cigarette. "Too bad you can't shut Miss Marnie out."

"I think it will hurt more if she has to organize it."

# CHAPTER 38

"You're not the villain in this story," Rhea whispered. "Remember that."

Kate nodded and forced her focus across the lip of the dune to the glimmering line between sea and sky, away from the reporters and photographers gathered in front of television trucks with bright logos. Was it only a week ago that Dyson urged her to use the media as a shield?

"Reporters are like vampires," Rhea hissed. "A lust for fresh blood and immaculate grooming."

Kate rewarded her effort by twisting the corners of her lips into a tight smile, then grimaced. A smile could be misinterpreted.

Stomach churning, she glanced again at the scrawls on a napkin lifted from the café where they found Marnie dining on fruit and flakes while the photographer shoveled hash browns and gravy into his mouth. The notes, a chronological list of names and incidents, mapped ground she intended to go over only once. She flexed the knotted muscles in her shoulders. Strange that having time to prepare for a challenge could double or triple the stress level. When she stepped through the door of the shelter and took on Wayne Jessop, the clock was already running.

"Want me to give you some breathing room?" Rhea asked.

"If you desert me, I'll stomp your foot so hard you'll be in a cast until Christmas."

Rhea shrugged. "Any excuse to skip work is fine with me." She pointed to a corner market and launderette. "Here comes the chief."

Kate felt a surge of gratitude as Lowell, clutching three cans of cola, moved their way with the rolling gait of a man accustomed to balancing in a rocking boat on a snow-fed river. "Shouldn't have told you to put off telling the boy," he told her an hour ago. "Should have known reporters would be on this like vultures on roadkill. Not that they got it from my office. Although Curtis won't shun the spotlight now that it's beamed on."

He wrapped her in a clumsy hug, his brown canvas jumpsuit pungent with the scents of moldering leaves and damp earth. "We'll get your boy back." In a moment he released her, hustling away to "get into official garb" and "comb the burrs" from his hair.

"Chief Lowell's wonderful," Kate said. "So is your husband." Twenty minutes after Rhea introduced her to the stocky man with the springy hair, Jim had commandeered a computer, created a flier with pictures of Way-Ray and Dwayne Vetter, and persuaded a Realtor to loan his color printer.

"And Jackson," Rhea prompted. "He's wearing his shoes out walking the dunes."

"Yes." Kate imagined him searching hollows, hunting among tumbles of driftwood, and pressing fliers into the hands of beachcombers. Perhaps, even as she reached for the cola can, Jackson was shading his eyes and squinting at a flash of blue T-shirt in a sea of wind-winnowed beach grass.

Chief Lowell drank, Adam's apple bobbing. "Ahhhh. Ready to get this dog-and-pony show over with?"

Kate nodded and popped her can, the hiss of escaping air as sharp as a serpent's warning. Her fingers unfurled. Rhea snatched the icy can from the air, wrapped it in a napkin excavated from her purse, and slid it into Kate's hand once more. "Drink," she advised. "Then I'll hold it."

The chilled liquid numbed Kate's throat. Was Way-Ray thirsty? Did he know he shouldn't drink from the ocean? She'd never told him. Another failure.

She squeezed the can, heard the aluminum crumple, felt cold liquid on her knuckles. Rhea mopped at it and wiggled the can from her grip as the chief moved toward a podium jury-rigged from plastic storage crates. "When you get up there, don't look into their feral little eyes."

"I won't." Kate's voice was tight from the unleashed sob swollen beneath her sternum, roughened by tears sniffed back and swallowed.

"If you start to lose it, stomp on my foot," Rhea offered. "Once I start screaming like a banshee, you'll forget about falling to pieces."

Kate tapped Rhea's frayed running shoe with the edge of her sandal. "Thanks," she whispered. "I never . . ." She choked, coughed, and rushed to finish. "I never had real friend until you. I never—"

Rhea waved that off. "Me neither. But let's not make plans to sleep over and do each other's hair until this is done. If we get to boo-hooing, no one will hear the chief."

Kate sniffed, blinked, and watched Chief Lowell glower at the reporters from beneath his maverick brows, casting silence like a net. He straightened a listing microphone, cleared his throat, and spoke in a voice that boomed above the whisk of the gusting breeze and the rumble of passing traffic. "We're here this morning because of a tragedy. We're here because you and all your viewers and listeners," he nodded at a gray-haired man in a checked shirt, "and readers, have an opportunity to help put things right—to find a little boy and stop a killer."

He waited for a few seconds, glancing from face to face. "Now, some of you know me from that incident last fall—the mudslide that buried the Simmons family. Most of you were professionals, you did your job and let me do mine." He nodded to a woman in a blue pantsuit. "The rest of you . . . well, you didn't send flowers and I didn't write anything nice about you in my diary."

A sandy-haired reporter flushed and a brunette mouthed a two-syllable word.

"That being said," the chief continued, "let's make this get-together one we can all be proud of. Don't harass the search teams, don't block traffic with those satellite rigs, and don't tie up the phone lines pestering me for updates every hour."

Marnie fluttered a manicured hand. "My producers won't—"

Chief Lowell waved her off. The crate podium teetered and microphones bobbled. "Yeah, yeah. Your producers won't like that." A titter rippled through the pack. Lowell righted the podium and glowered. "But I'm warning you. Don't get in the way. If something breaks, I'll fill you in. If we make an arrest, I'll see you get your pictures."

He swiveled toward Kate and flashed a smile. "You ready?"

Kate swallowed air. It went down like lye. "Yes."

"I've got your back, kid." Chief Lowell turned to the microphones again. "I'm going to hand this over to Kate Dalton. You let her speak. If you interrupt, if you make this harder than it already is, I'll shut this news conference down."

"You can't do that!" Marnie protested.

"I can, and I will." He laid a hand on Kate's shoulder and drew her to the nest of microphones. "I'll be out amongst them passing fliers."

Kate nodded and wove her fingers through the holes in the plastic crate. Sharp edges dug into her skin and she tightened her grip, welcoming the pain. "In February, I took a risk. A woman lived, and the man who had come to kill her died. That's old news. I won't go over it again."

"That's not fair." Marnie fluttered her notebook. "We need—"

"First warning," Lowell's voice rumbled. Marnie snapped her arm down. The fresh-faced male reporter beside her snickered.

"The woman who survived, Amanda Blake, was tormented by the belief that she'd transform her son into another wife-battering monster. She asked me to take Way-Ray. She swore she'd give him up to foster care if I didn't."

"Was she serious?" a middle-aged reporter called. "Uh, sorry," she amended, ducking her head. The breeze lifted her long hair from her shoulders like bronze wings.

"I believed she was. I offered to take Way-Ray for two weeks. I thought Amanda would change her mind, but she made her will, named me his guardian, and disappeared. I hired Ted Dyson to find her."

A ripple of sound ran through the crowd. Two reporters flipped open cell phones. Marnie gave them a haughty smile, raising razor-thin brows. Kate clutched the crate, concentrating on pain, not anger. "Not long after, Amanda wrote that her ex-husband's half-brother, Dwayne Vetter, was stalking her. She believed he intended to kill her, find Way-Ray, and take custody of him."

*Take custody?* Why such a bland expression? Did she feel that if she gave Dwayne the benefit of the doubt, others might do the same for her? Kate focused on a pudgy woman with a ready smile and frizzled brown hair. She wore thick glasses, a pale green blouse, jeans, and red sneakers. A newspaper or radio reporter. One who didn't dress for a camera.

"Way-Ray didn't know how his father died—he thought he'd been dead for years. Amanda demanded that I uphold that lie, but when I learned she was dead, I knew I had to tell him the truth. Tell him everything." Kate speared Marnie with a glare. "Unfortunately, I waited a few moments too long. Way-Ray got the brutal facts from one of you. He was horrified. He was angry. And he ran."

Marnie shrugged, but Kate noted that she kept her gaze focused on her notebook, avoiding her colleagues' glances.

"Fault me for lying, for putting off a painful task, for making things worse. But don't fault me for loving a little boy who deserves a decent life. Help me find him before . . ."

Kate's voice gave out. Spinning from the unblinking scrutiny of the lenses and shouted questions, she clutched at Rhea, and leaned into her hug, inhaling the scent of stale cigarette smoke. She felt swollen with grief and despair, bloated by tears choked back.

"You don't owe them another syllable," Chief Lowell whispered. Then his voice boomed out to the crowd. "I'm gonna tell you about this Dwayne Vetter and his illustrious career as a thief, felon, and general all-around scumwad." He paused for a few beats. "Don't quote me on that scumwad part. I'd hate to be sued for defamation of what little character he has."

As the media mob laughed, Rhea steered Kate to the SUV on the street a block away. "You did the best you could for that boy."

Kate wrenched open the driver's door. "Everything I did was wrong." She threw herself in, slamming her elbow against the console. The jolting pain was a stroke of justice.

Rhea gripped the door. "I don't agree, but I won't argue a lost cause. You've earned your agony and you're entitled to wallow in it."

"You're right. I am." Kate tugged at the handle. She wanted to drive to a promontory and plow through the guardrail. She wanted, finally, to do something right—take herself out of Way-Ray's life. "Let go!"

"No." Rhea flung her weight against it. "You look like you're reading the signpost pointing to the land of lunacy."

Kate imagined surf-scoured rocks, broken waves rising, fingers of white foam grasping, the icy undertow pulling her down to oblivion. "Let go."

Rhea's brittle laugh fractured the air. "I know crazy when I see it. Slide over. I'm driving."

"No." Kate yanked at the door. A fingernail broke at the quick with a spike of pain. More justice.

"I'll have the chief put you in protective custody. Don't think I won't. That boy needs you alive." She laid a hand on Kate's arm.

The simple, soft touch melted Kate's cold resolve. Tears leaked from her eyes. A spasm ripped through her chest and she fell against Rhea's shoulder, sobbing, plummeting into a cauldron of white-hot emotion. When had she come to love Way-Ray so much? How had she become so vulnerable?

Rhea stroked her hair. "It will all work out. I feel it."

Kate clung to that as Way-Ray must have grasped the lies she'd told—with relief, gratitude, and hope. She raised the hem of her T-shirt and blotted her face.

"You've needed a good cry for a long time," Rhea said. "Now, go on back to the motel and have one. I'll give you . . ." She studied a watch fastened to its band with two red twist ties. ". . . half an hour."

Kate dropped against the back of the seat and blinked. "Then what?"

"If you're not back to what passes for normal, I give Jackson a picture I took of you wrestling a bag of garbage into the dumpster. Your blouse is gapping open." She shrugged. "I was saving that for a day when I needed a big favor."

A chuckle welled up from the pit of Kate's stomach. In her life before she came to the coast, she allowed herself what passed for friendships based on the qualities her parents valued. But she allowed those people no further than the vestibule of her life, left them standing, coats on, far from the hearth. But Rhea, like Way-Ray, had claimed a chair by the fire. "You're the best friend I've ever had."

"Yeah," Rhea said in gruff voice. "I know." She patted Kate's cheek with cool fingertips, then hustled around to the passenger door. "Let's get some lunch."

Kate slammed the door and gripped the wheel. I'm not hungry." Way-Ray might be starving. Eating would be a betrayal of faith.

"I wouldn't expect you to be," Rhea said as she climbed in. "But we have to keep our energy up and right now my stomach thinks my throat's been cut." She clicked her belt. "Way-Ray's likely feeling the same. Maybe he'll be making a sandwich in the kitchen when we get there."

Kate grasped that like a life preserver, but when she hurtled into the motel, she found only Dorrie, the phone clamped to her ear, fingers worrying a gold heart on a chain around her neck, tears glistening on her plump cheeks. "She's not here," she wailed. "I don't know where she is."

Kate's heart pounded. "Who is that?"

Dorrie's released the pendant and thrust the receiver at Kate. "It's for you."

Kate stared at the phone as if fangs might emerge from the holes in the earpiece. "Who is it?" she whispered.

Dorrie twisted her hair. "I don't know. Some woman."

Some woman? Justine Maxwell?

"She's been yelling at me for a long time because I didn't know when Rhea would be back."

Someone who asked for Rhea. Not Justine. Kate felt her muscles loosen. She grasped phone.

"I'm going down to the beach." Dorrie flapped her free hand in front of her face. "I need some air." She darted from behind the counter and scurried away, nearly colliding with Rhea.

Kate gripped plastic slick with Dorrie's sweat. "Kate Dalton. May I help you?"

"You never told me about that boy." A woman's voice boiled from the receiver. "You lied to me."

*I lied to everyone.* "Who is this?"

I could have you arrested," the woman raged.

"For what?"

"Don't play dumb with me. I have the TV on. I know your whole sick story. I want you out of that apartment and off our property."

# CHAPTER 39

Off *our* property? Nadine! Kate's gut cramped. "Mrs. Burgess, I can explain."

Rhea turned from her examination of the refrigerator and arched her eyebrows. Nadine's voice crackled down the line. "I know quite enough. You're fired."

Kate flushed and bent her head. Fired twice in two months. How humiliated her parents would have been. She raised her chin. Time to stop living within their proscribed limits. "Mrs. Burgess, I can't leave. This is the only home Way-Ray has to come back to."

Rhea closed the refrigerator and poked a thumb at the ceiling.

"And I sympathize, don't think I don't." Nadine's voice was as compassionate as a dental drill. "But that killer will come there, too. And this disastrous publicity will cost us a fortune."

Money! Kate had no defense against financial concerns. Emory McCoy taught her that hard lesson.

"Tell Rhea to call me," Nadine ordered. "She'll have to take over. I'll pay her an extra twenty-five cents an hour until we find a new manager."

"A quarter an hour extra," Kate repeated, pointing at Rhea.

Rhea shook her head. "No way," she mouthed.

277

"I'll give you until noon Sunday. That's generous," Nadine said with undisguised pride. "One minute longer and I'll have the police remove you."

Would Chief Lowell order Curtis to march her off the property? Kate smiled. How disastrous would *that* publicity be? "Sunday," she repeated.

"At noon." Nadine broke the connection.

Kate clicked the phone off and slammed it down. "I'm not leaving until Way-Ray comes back."

"Of course you're not." Rhea crossed the room and slung an arm around her shoulders. "And I'm not running this place for an extra quarter an hour. I'll go get Dorrie and then we'll have lunch and talk about it." She hustled off.

"I'm not leaving." Kate cocked her knee and kicked the wastebasket. It hit the counter with a gratifying crunch, spilling a flock of wadded paper balls.

"Let her call the cops!" She kicked the wastebasket again, sending it flying into the tiny living room, releasing a flurry of crinkly wrappers from free mints guests gobbled to get their money's worth. How many tantrums had she stifled? How many opportunities to vent her feelings had she forfeited because of the way she was raised? She dropped the registration book and booted it, pages fluttering, to the kitchen. "I won't go, even if they use tear gas."

"Tear gas?"

Kate spun to see Jackson, face glistening with sweat, shirt damp across his chest, a can of soda in one hand. Her gaze scoured the empty space around him.

"We'll find him, Kate." He moved toward her, swinging his bad leg, wincing. "What happened?"

"Nadine saw the news. She fired me."

Jackson's lips compressed. "Nadine's a fool."

"She gave me until Sunday at noon. But I can't leave. Way-Ray would—"

"I know," he grunted. "What's her number?"

"It's in there." Kate nodded toward the card file by the computer. "But it's about money. She says guests will cancel. It's pointless to—"

"I don't intend to argue." His eyes burned into hers. His voice was as soft as a baby's quilt, as sharp as obsidian.

Kate glanced away, her cheeks warm, as he punched in the number. "Nadine," he said after a moment. "This is Jackson Scovell. You can take this job and shove it up your skinny, wrinkled, bean-counting butt."

Kate gasped. "No. You can't quit." She grabbed at the phone.

He batted her hand aside. "Just so you know, I'm cold sober and I have a witness to prove it."

He dropped the phone, flexed his shoulders, and grinned. "Should have done that years ago."

"Jackson, you can't quit."

He poured the remains of the soda down his throat. "Why not?"

"Because . . ." She faltered, thinking of all the things she could say: because you're a drunk, everyone knows it, and you'll never find another job because you're crippled, because you've done things that messed up your mind, because if you're doing it for me I'll owe you. Saint Kate the Obligated.

"It's okay, Kate." He took her hand, his fingers chilled where he'd gripped the can. "This job let me pursue a . . . a certain activity that occupied too many hours. It's an activity I intend to give up."

Kate blinked, sorting through his words and the intention behind them, all too aware that she hadn't withdrawn her hand, that she would have shunned a man like him before she came to the coast. "Don't quit unless you're sure."

"Do you mean sure I want to quit the job? Or sure I want to quit drinking?"

Kate dropped her gaze, focusing on a paper ball that had stopped short of sanctuary beneath the desk. "I thought I understood you to say that those two things are connected." Her words were precise, prissy. Her mother's voice. She shuddered and drew her hand from his.

"I did make that point," he said with a chuckle. "So I'll answer both questions. Yes, I'm sure I want to give up the job. Yes, I'm sure I want to give up the bottle, too." He placed a finger beneath her chin. "Look at me, Kate."

She fought him for an instant, clamping her jaw, but then he smiled and she saw again how that rearranged the angles and planes of his face. What she'd thought of as homely, almost ugly, became spirited, remarkable.

"I drank to kill the pain," he said. The pain in my leg and in my head. But watching what you've gone through—seeing how much you care for that boy—made me appreciate pain and its purpose."

Kate almost laughed. How could you appreciate pain? She recalled an elderly neighbor calling to her as she walked home from school, warning her she'd suffer because her parents didn't attend church, telling her she'd pay for their pride. "Purpose?"

"Pain makes things real." Jackson dropped his hand to her shoulder. "It's made me realize what I want—who I want."

Kate ducked her head. This had gone too far, too deep. She'd lost control. Worse, she wasn't certain she wanted control. "I don't want . . . I don't want it to be because of me."

"I see." He dropped his hand, touched her wrist. "Well, you're part of the equation. But these are my decisions. You owe me nothing."

Kate studied his eyes, saw tenderness and torment. "Nothing?" Daltons always kept the balance sheet even.

"Well, how about a sandwich? Something quick, so I can get back out."

A guilty heat scorched her cheeks. He must be starving. She dug bread, meat, cheese, mayonnaise, mustard, pickles, and lettuce from the refrigerator and, without looking at him, placed them on the table with a plate and silverware. A sandwich alone seemed insignificant in the face of his efforts, so she rummaged in the cabinets for potato chips, pudding, applesauce, and olives.

Back at the refrigerator, she hauled out cartons of milk and orange juice and a can of cola. She spotted cold pizza in a plastic bag and slung it to the table.

Jackson laughed and crunched a potato chip. "I said I was hungry, not that I wanted to store fat to hibernate."

"I didn't know what you'd want." Hands quivering, she snatched a glass from the draining rack and tore two paper towels from the roll. She didn't trust herself to open the package of paper napkins without the flimsy squares exploding from the wrapping, hated herself for such self-indulgent awareness.

"You're shaking." Jackson laid four slices of rye on his plate. "Have you had anything to eat since breakfast?"

"No, but I had a soda." She folded the paper towels into quarters.

"You need something besides caffeine and sugar."

She shook her head, watching as he twirled off the top of the mayonnaise jar and used the spoon to scoop it out. "I'm saving the knife for the mustard. I hate it when condiments get cozy in each other's jars. Sit down before you fall down." He winced. "My father used to say that. I guess it's true: we become our parents."

"Not if I can help it," Kate muttered.

Jackson gave no sign that he heard. "Eat something before you collapse."

She watched him layer ham and cheese and pickles. "I'm not hungry."

"Doesn't matter. Eat." He unscrewed the mustard lid and plunged the knife into the jar. "That's one thing I learned in the military. Eat when it's there. Eat as much as you can."

Kate watched him spread mustard. Like Way-Ray, he covered even the brown rims of crust. She felt herself hurtling into the bottomless pit of loss and clutched the back of a chair. "I can't eat. Not while he's hungry."

"Hunger might bring him back." Jackson bit into a sandwich, chewed, and grunted.

Kate shook her head and slumped into the chair. "Rhea thought that, too. But he has his mother's determination and his father's temper. Hunger might just make him madder."

"Transferring the blame." Jackson opened his mouth, but then lowered the sandwich to the plate. "That's normal. He'll get past it, Kate."

Her mind flashed on an image of Wayne Jessop standing over Amanda, lips curled into a cruel smile, knife raised. "His father didn't."

Jackson's eyes slid away. In a moment he went back to the sandwiches, devoured every crumb, and drained a glass of milk. In a minute he'd leave. She'd be alone. "I'm going to help you hunt."

His eyes tightened. "You should be here. If you're gone—"

"He might think I abandoned him. I know. But I can't just sit here doing nothing."

He nodded, lips pursed, not saying what he must be thinking, that she drove Way-Ray off, that joining the search could drive him farther away.

"I'm going," she repeated. It was her right, even if it was wrong.

The bell above the office door chimed and a low-slung black streak shot into the kitchen and slammed into Jackson's chair. Mutant barked once and then bounced off of his front feet, periscoping up to view the table.

"I'm going to get one of Way-Ray's dirty shirts," Kyle shouted as he pounded up the stairs. "To give Mutant the scent."

"Mutant will follow Way-Ray's trail." Sean slid to a stop and seized the potato chip bag. His voice rang with contagious confidence and Kate felt a jolt of hope.

Jackson rolled his eyes. "I guess anything's worth a shot."

Kyle's feet thudded down the stairs. "Come on, Mutant!" The dog bounced again, whining and licking his chops.

"Let's go, Mutant," Sean mumbled through a mouthful of chips.

The dog twitched his ears, but didn't budge.

"Put the food away or he'll never leave." Jackson wrapped meat and cheese. Kate stowed milk and pickles.

"What the heck are you boys doing?" Rhea bellowed from the lobby.

"Mutant's going to find Way-Ray." Sean yelled.

"He just has to get the scent." Kyle burst back through the door waving a red pajama top studded with images of soccer balls and nets and caught the dog by the collar.

Mutant scrabbled at the linoleum and barked. "No, you're not getting anything." Kyle twisted his collar. Mutant flopped on his side, tongue lolling. Kate swallowed tears.

Jackson thrust the bag of chips at Kyle. "Take these as incentive."

Kyle snatched the bag and ran past his mother, Sean and the barking dog in his wake. Shaking her head, Rhea surveyed the remains on the table, opened a container of pudding, and found a spoon. "Dorrie quit."

"Quit?" Kate echoed.

Rhea shrugged. "Didn't like being yelled at and told she was stupid. If Nadine was any more short-sighted she'd be blind." She pointed the spoon at Kate. "I'm going to call and give her a piece of my mind." She scooped pudding into her mouth and aimed the spoon at Jackson. "You should, too."

He grinned. "Already did. I told her to shove my job up her butt."

Rhea gawked, coughed, and finally chuckled. "I guess if she shoved one job she can shove two."

Jackson raised his hand. Rhea slapped hers against it.

Kate felt as if she'd driven off the edge of a map into uncharted territory. Previous rules of life didn't apply. "You're quitting, too?"

"No, I'm quitting, three," Rhea chuckled. "When you leave, I'm outta here."

"Who'll run this place?"

"Who cares?" Rhea laughed and wrapped her arms around Kate. "I think it's great that you're so conscientious that you worry about people who don't give a damn about you. But right now you've got to put that impulse on hold and just tote your own load. Anyone who isn't with us is against us."

Kate remembered the Musketeers' pledge. All for one. One for all. But that was fiction. This was real. She couldn't flip to the final page to see how the story ended.

# CHAPTER 40

Kate awoke with her heart hammering. Wayne Jessop's malevolent spirit permeated the dim living room like a freezing fog. "Don't gloat yet," she muttered, stretching legs cramped tight against the arm of the loveseat.

Why had she allowed herself to sit? She'd vowed to listen for hesitating steps, the faint knock on the door. Guilt stabbed at her heart. She'd broken faith. If she truly loved Way-Ray, she wouldn't have sat, wouldn't have slept.

Standing, she stomped circulation into numb feet, driving back the ghost feasting on doubt and fear. She hobbled to the kitchen window and slid it open the inch the safety guard allowed. A moist, gusting breeze pushed through. She longed to gather up a blanket and hot chocolate, to go out into the night crying Way-Ray's name. But the wisest course was to stay put.

Trudging to the office, she spotted a paper on the floor beside the loveseat, a list of what she would do differently when he returned: be honest, take him to a psychologist, tell him she loved him, arrange a funeral service for Amanda, help him build a book of memories, buy the telescope he wanted. She didn't allow herself to consider what she would do if he never returned, or if he rejected her.

Shivering, she peered at the clock above the desk. 4:30, the cusp of that long hour before dawn. Too early to make breakfast and call Jackson in from his truck outside the door. He'd insisted on standing guard even though others were on patrol watching for Dwayne Vetter, even though public speculation held that the killer was a coward at heart, that publicity had sent him running for Mexico.

Kate trudged up the stairs, eyes on the carpet because the sight of Way-Ray's room would be impossibly painful. Edging into her own space, she flipped on the light and was astonished to see that the bed was made. She had no memory of completing that task yesterday morning. It was as if from the moment Way-Ray ran her life had been split by a yawning canyon. Everything on the other side was blurred, distant.

She shuffled to the closet, stared at clothing draped on blue and yellow plastic hangers: a few blouses, four pairs of jeans, white slacks, and a beige corduroy jacket. All seemed to belong to someone else.

She wandered to the dresser and ran her fingers across the pitted top, drifted to the bed and sat, head in hands. "Where are you, Way-Ray?" she moaned. "I'm so frightened for you."

Bolting to his room, she dropped to her knees, scrabbling beneath the spread for a pillow, inhaling his little-boy scent. "I miss you. I love you."

Clasping the pillow, she prowled to the sliding door, meeting her reflection at the glass and leaning forehead to forehead. The pane was cool, like a cold compress when she had fever. A single light flared from the horizon, glimmering along the dark water like a comet's tail. Could Way-Ray see it? She imagined them connected through that beacon bobbing at the curve of the earth. Her eyes felt sticky. She squeezed them shut.

The phone brought her awake to a sky and ocean gray as dust. She sprinted downstairs to the office and snatched it up. "Wade in the Waves Motel."

"I got a hurt critter," Evie said. "I need an extra pair of hands and I need them now."

Kate gripped the edge of the counter. "I have to stay here in case Way-Ray comes back. Isn't there a volunteer you can call?"

Evie snorted. "Not at this ungodly hour. I knew you'd be up and, besides, your boy would want you to help."

Blatant emotional string-pulling. But then, Evie was single-minded and pragmatic.

"You'll be back before you know it. Write a note and tell him you're out here. He'll understand."

Or think I abandoned him like a broken toy.

"This little feller's suffering." Evie's voice softened. "I need help fast."

Kate gritted her teeth and closed her eyes, trying to still her mind, sort her thoughts. If she went, at least she would help one wounded creature tonight. Jackson was outside. Given his anger at her, Way-Ray would probably prefer to be with the handyman. And Jackson had a way of calming him down. Maybe it would be better if she wasn't here when Way-Ray returned, if she was helping one of the animals he loved. "Okay. But I can only stay for a minute."

"Be as quiet as you can." Evie hung up without saying goodbye.

Kate splashed water on her face, shoved lank hair behind her ears, scrawled a note telling Way-Ray she loved him and would be right back, tucked her driver's license and cell phone in her pocket, snatched her keys, and went out through the office. Jackson's truck hulked not far from the door. His arms, folded across the steering wheel, pillowed his head, and his breathing was deep and punctuated by gasping snores.

Kate raised a hand to tap on the window, then drew it back. He was exhausted. Way-Ray would wake him if he returned. And she'd be back soon. There were others watching for Dwayne Vetter and maybe publicity had driven him off.

Drained by anxiety and fatigue, her brain seemed frozen, her thoughts rimed with ice. Nothing seemed clear except that Evie needed her to help an injured animal. Returning to the office, she scrawled another note, and taped it to the window where Jackson would see it. Then, keeping to the margins of grass, she walked to the head of the alley where she'd parked her car, opened the door just far enough to slide in, secured the seat belt, and started the engine. The crunch of gravel beneath the wheels sounded like machine-gun fire as she let out the clutch and rolled to the stop sign at the highway. An eighteen-wheeler rumbled by and then the road lay empty. She turned left, accelerating, slamming the door and popping on the headlights.

Driven both by fear and force of long habit, Kate checked the rearview mirror every few seconds. No headlights behind her. She watched the sky glow golden pink along the rims of the hills to the east, saw the highway turn the color of granite. Before she turned into Evie's road, she checked the rearview a last time. No lights.

Shreds of mist hung like Spanish moss from branches arching overhead. A deer appeared, its eyes glinting in the headlights. She hit the brake, slewing among the potholes as the deer bounded ahead, flung itself over a brush pile, and was gone.

Her heart fluttering in her throat, Kate accelerated again. Berry canes clawed at the bumpers and doors like fingernails. She shivered, flicked her gaze toward the dash, and groped for the knobs that controlled the heater and fan.

When she glanced up, a white-robed, hooded figure stood at the far reach of the headlights. Kate gasped and stomped the brake.

The figure loomed, raising an arm.

Kate hit the door lock and rammed the shift into reverse. Tires bit into the earth. The engine whined.

The figure waved both arms and pushed its hood back.

*Evie.*

Kate let out a trembling breath.

Evie stalked forward, the sheet fluttering around her legs.

Kate rolled down the window. "You scared the hell out of me."

"Wanted to make sure you saw me." Evie wadded the sheet under her arm revealing a gray sweatshirt and baggy black jeans. "Park it here so the noise doesn't scare him off."

Kate hesitated, trying to shake a prickling feeling that something wasn't right. "Where is it?"

"In the old barn." Evie turned and strode off through tatters of mist.

Kate unlocked the door and slid out. "What is it?"

Evie didn't answer and Kate felt another prickle of uncertainty. Was it a bear or a cougar? Was she worried Kate would be frightened, refuse to help? "I'm not afraid," Kate muttered, following into the mist. She stumbled over a rock and cursed under her breath, trying to remember what Evie had said about the creature: it was skittish and fragile.

"Hurry." Evie broke into a slow trot.

In a hundred yards the road emptied into the overgrown field and Kate spotted the barn, shingles bronzed by the rising sun. Its slouch seemed even more evident, as if today it would surrender to gravity. The hummocky grass around it was the color of ancient burlap and crackled under Kate's feet.

"Stay on the trail," Evie murmured. "Behind me." She slowed, picking her way along the faint track. Kate saw that two boards were pried loose from one door. They swung away from each other, creating a triangular opening. Evie stooped and peered through. "Still there," she breathed. "Have a look."

Kate bent to the notch and saw sunlight sifting between the shingles, spangling the far wall. A pyramid of moldering hay bales slumped in the center of the barn. Way-Ray lay midway up that pyramid.

# CHAPTER 41

Kate clawed at the rusted metal bolt that secured the doors. "Wait." Evie dug her fingers into Kate's shoulder. "He'll run again if we don't handle this right."

For a few seconds, Kate struggled against the old woman's grip. Then, scrubbing at her eyes, she allowed Evie to lead her a dozen steps back through the scraggly grass. "How did you find him?"

"Been thinking he was out of choices, he might turn up." She nodded toward the gap. "Those rusty nails have a way of complaining, and the barn's not far through the woods. The geese raised a ruckus."

Besieged by guilt, Kate stared at the notch Way-Ray had wiggled through. "What do I say?"

"Let's see how much of a mad he's hanging onto." Evie jutted her chin toward the barn. "Pick out a knothole—on the west side so you don't cast a shadow."

Without waiting for Kate to agree, she marched to the door and shoved the bolt with the heel of a hand. It rasped against its channel shedding flakes of rust and the door swung wide on creaking hinges. "Who's in my barn?" Evie shaded her eyes with one hand. "Declare yourself or I'll call the law!"

"It's only me," Way-Ray called.

His thin and trembling voice squeezed Kate's heart like a fist. She took two steps toward the door but Evie aimed a glare over her shoulder and whisked her fingers. Kate sighed and crept into the barn's shadow, grass rustling against her jeans. Patience. Patience.

"Who the heck is me?" Evie growled.

"Way-Ray." His voice sounded high and sharp, desperate. Kate squatted beside a knothole the size of her fist. The warm, moldy odor of hay filled her nostrils. A stack of bales blocked her view.

"Well, what are you doing in my barn, young man?"

"I ran away." His voice grew brittle, defiant.

Kate skirted a holly bush and spotted another knothole at chest level. Hunching, she pressed her cheek to the rough wood and spied Way-Ray in a checkerboard of sunlight, picking hay from his hair.

"Ran away, huh?" Evie's tone was as bland as if he'd told her he had a new T-shirt. "I ran away once myself. Went back pretty quick, though. Didn't want to miss out on the Sunday apple pie."

Way-Ray dug his fingers into the bale behind him. "I'm never going back. You can't make me."

"Wouldn't even try. I wait until a hurt critter is mended before I put it back where it belongs."

Way-Ray shook his head and chaff flew around him, glittering in the sunlight. "I don't belong with Kate. And I'm not hurt."

"Then why are you here?" Evie appeared, edging toward the east wall, leaving Kate's view clear.

"Thank you," Kate breathed.

"I like it here." Way-Ray raised his chin. "But I'm not hurt."

With a sharp grunt, Evie hoisted herself onto the lowest bale. "Maybe not hurt like that bobcat. But I'll bet you hurt somewhere."

"No." He scrambled to the bale above him and sat with his spine stiff.

Evie shrugged and put her chin in her hands.

Way-Ray gnawed at his lower lip and his shoulders drooped. "Kate lied to me. Lied and lied and lied. About my mother." He smacked the bale.

Kate jerked back, feeling as if he'd slapped her. Prickly holly leaves scratched at her arm.

"She said my mother was coming to get me, but she's dead. And TD is dead. And . . . and my father is dead." Squinting through the opening again, Kate watched him knuckle tears from his eyes. "She lied about him, too."

"That's a whole bunch of lying," Evie marveled. "Why do you think she did that?"

Way-Ray kicked at the hay, scattering more chaff. "Because she's a liar."

Evie scratched her head. "Why do you suppose liars lie?"

"So they don't get in trouble." Way-Ray's tone implied that Evie was three steps below too dumb to breathe without being reminded. "And to get their way."

"And what is Kate's way?" Evie didn't seem to offended, just curious. "What is it she wants?"

"She wants . . ." he gouged grooves with his heels. "I don't know. She's just a liar. I hate her!"

Kate doubled over, bile burning her throat. All Evie said in her defense was, "Hmm."

Kate swallowed, forced herself back to the knothole, and saw Way-Ray throw a clump of hay into the air, and bat it with his hand. It broke apart, showering Evie. "Hmm," she said again, brushing at her shoulders. "Do you see my gray hair?" She tugged at a tuft. "Do you know what it means?"

Way-Ray narrowed his eyes. "It means you're old."

"Yes, it means I've been around a lot of years. And I've learned that bad people sometimes do good things because they want to, and good people sometimes do bad things because they have to." She twisted to face him full on. "Do you understand that?"

"No." He glared. "It doesn't make any sense."

"Kate's a good person, right? She took care of you when you were sick, she bought you clothes and toys, and she paid my taxes."

"She's still a liar," he pouted.

"She lied because your mother asked her to."

He leaped to his feet, fists in front of his chest. "Nuh-uh. My mother wouldn't do that." He clambered down from the pyramid. Kate tensed, ready to pursue him. Evie remained motionless. He reached the row where she sat, hesitated, then dropped beside her. "You wouldn't lie to me, would you?"

"No, I wouldn't lie to you."

Kate shook her head. Pledging to be truthful was easy, but keeping that pledge . . .

Way-Ray grasped Evie's hand. "I'm an orphan now. So I can live here, right?"

"I expect you qualify."

"Then I'm gonna stay," he announced. "And never see Kate again."

Kate felt the cold, dizzying undertow of defeat and braced her hands against the barn.

Way-Ray shredded a handful of hay, squirmed, studied the rafters, then tucked his chin. "Evie, will you tell me what happened to my mother . . . and my father?"

"It's okay," Kate whispered.

"All right," Evie agreed, "but only if you listen with both ears, your mind, and your heart."

"How do I do that? It's only my ears that hear."

"But your mind decides what it will pay attention to, and your heart decides what's true."

"I guess." He cupped his hands behind his ears. "I'll try."

Evie pulled him to her, turning so they both faced Kate. "When your father was a little boy, his parents were mean and he got hurt deep inside, so he did a lot of bad things. The worst was that he hit your mother."

Way-Ray scowled. "Did he hurt her? A lot?"

293

"Yes. But she thought if she loved him enough, he'd stop. But then he tried to hit you. Your mother wasn't big enough to fight him like mother animals sometimes do, so she called the police and they took him to jail."

"Good." Way-Ray punched at the air, then knitted his fingers together. "Why didn't mom tell me?"

"She planned to. When you got older."

"I'm older now." His fingers squirmed against each other. "But how did my dad really die?"

Evie sighed. Kate did the same. She hadn't intended for Evie to carry her burden, but if she revealed herself now, it might make the situation worse.

"When he was in jail, he got even more angry—just like the bobcat is mad about being in a cage," Evie said. "So your mother went to a place for women who are scared. But your father found her and tried to hurt her." Evie's lips compressed for a moment. "Kate fought him—"

"And Kate won." Way-Ray's voice held a mix of triumph and dismay.

"When someone dies from violence, no one wins." Evie gripped his shoulders and turned him toward her. Her face was grim. "He fell on his knife, Way-Ray. Kate didn't want to hurt him, she just wanted him to leave your mother alone."

"But Mom said she got hurt at the store. So she told another lie."

Evie rocked him against her chest so that Kate could once again see his face. "Yes. She was afraid that you wouldn't love or trust her if you learned how your father died."

Love and trust. The core issues. Kate held her breath, ignoring a mosquito buzzing at her ear. Evie had brought Way-Ray to the edge of the chasm, but he'd have to leap it alone.

"But I would have." Way-Ray sniffed and swallowed.

"I know," Evie said. "And deep down your mother knew, too."

"Why did she send me with Kate?"

"She was sick. And she wanted you to have adventures, to see a whale." Evie stretched out a hand and Kate imagined she traced the orca on his T-shirt.

He held his spine stiff for a few moments, and then his head bobbed. Kate heard him sniffle. "But why did she run away?"

Kate longed to hurl herself into the barn, to hug him to her, to try to ease his pain—and her own.

Evie shook her head a fraction of an inch as if she'd read Kate's mind. "Your father had a brother. His name is Dwayne. He wanted to take you." Evie pressed her words tight against each other. "She did what mother birds and animals do to protect their babies, she led him far away."

"To Ohio," Way-Ray said with a painful blend of pride and pain.

Kate felt a jolt. How could he know that? Then she remembered Marnie's ambush, the words that must have etched themselves on Way-Ray's mind.

"But he caught her. And TD." Way-Ray's voice faltered.

Evie gathered him to her and tucked his head beneath her chin. "He was hurt when he was little, just like your father. He's sick. Like that fox that had rabies, the one I called Curtis to shoot."

Way-Ray jerked from her arms. "He's not going to hurt Kate, is he?" He struggled to his feet and leaped to the ground. "I gotta find her."

"I think that's a first-class idea." Evie stood with a grunt and brushed at the back of her jeans. "She and Jackson have been searching high and low for you."

"Really?" He gaped at her and toed a pile of chaff. "I thought she'd be all mad because I ran away again and she wouldn't want me to come back."

"Pffft." Evie blew air between her lips. "Of course she wants you back. She loves you. She loves you like crazy."

Way-Ray lifted his T-shirt to wipe his face. "I love her, too."

Kate stifled a whimper of happiness so powerful she felt as if she could move the world.

"Let's go." Way-Ray clasped his fingers around Evie's and pulled her to the door.

Kate straightened, smoothed her hair, practiced a smile.

"Quite the heartwarming scene," a malicious voice taunted. "Too bad I'll have to change the happy ending you had planned."

# CHAPTER 42

Dread, like sudden snow, chilled Kate to the marrow. Dwayne Vetter? The tone was his brother's: cocky, controlling. She bent a branch, spiky holly leaves pricking her fingers. Through the gap, she spied Evie, saw her shield Way-Ray, shade her eyes, and peer into the sun. "Who are you? What are you doing here?"

"Hunting." He laughed, a nasty eruption of sound. Kate shuddered and the stiff, waxy leaves rattled. "And who are you getting in my face?"

"I'm Eve Hopkins. This is private property." Evie's voice didn't tremble, but Kate sensed fear in the slow release of syllables. "Didn't you see the signs?"

"Signs don't mean a thing unless you give a damn about the law," the man said. "I don't."

Kate felt an icy lump in the pit of her stomach. This was her fault. He must have followed her. Her head felt empty, as if all thought had evaporated, but her fingers released the branch and clawed for the cell phone.

"Who are you?" Way-Ray's voice was tiny, a faint echo of an echo. "You look like the picture of the terrorist."

"I'm your flesh and blood, kid," the man snarled. "Your father's brother."

His voice was louder, closer, harsher. Kate flipped the phone open, dialed 9-1-1.

"You're a bad man," Way-Ray said. "You're sick like that fox."

The cell phone screen flickered.

"I thought you'd have the good sense to stay away." Evie's voice was layered with surprise, chagrin. "All the cops in the west are looking for you."

The screen flickered again. *Come on. Come on!*

"It won't help you to piss me off," he warned.

The words "no service," scrolled across the screen. Kate moaned, clapped a hand across her lips.

"I'm an old woman, hardly a challenge." Evie leaned on the last word.

A challenge? Was Evie sending her a signal? Kate weighed her options: reveal herself and fight—somehow—or get to Evie's house and call for help.

She flipped the phone shut, stuffed it in her pocket, and pawed at the holly. Before she did anything, she had to see this monster. Dry leaves crackled, releasing a cloying dust that tasted like moldy bread. The man confronting Evie wore jeans and a black shirt open over a V-neck undershirt as white as new snow. He swept blond hair from his forehead with the fingers of his left hand. It was a fastidious gesture, almost dainty, cancelled out by the gun in his right hand, the gun that glistened blue-black like a snake's skin and pointed at Evie's chest. "I came to get my nephew. Step aside."

"Forget it," Evie said without revealing a flicker of fear. She swung her arms back, penning Way-Ray.

"You killed my mother." Way-Ray gripped Evie's sleeve with one hand and pointed at Dwayne with the other. "You're a bad man like my father."

"Not true." Dwayne took three steps and halted, framed by the holly branches. Still life with handgun. In a flash of panic-bred clarity, Kate realized that if she could see him, Dwayne would spot her if she moved even a few inches from the well of shadow beside the holly. Her stomach roiled. Another mistake.

"You listened to Kate Dalton's lies so long you believe them," Dwayne said in a doleful voice. He lowered the gun and stroked his chin. "The truth is that when your father got out of prison—where your mother sent him after he argued with her about the way she spent up all his hard-earned money—he forgave her. He wanted to make a fresh start. But she and her friend Kate slaughtered him like a hog."

Way-Ray gasped and his face turned the color of paste. Kate yearned to claw out Dwayne's lying tongue, but her only chance was to wait for an opportunity to get to Evie's house or back to—

The SUV! He must have seen it. He must know she was close. One more mistake.

"That's not how it happened and you know it," Evie insisted.

"Shut your trap or I'll shut it for you." He flashed Way-Ray a smile that was all teeth, a barracuda's smirk. "Then your mother got sorry for what she'd done. She killed herself."

"She did not," Way-Ray shouted. "You killed her. And TD, too."

Dwayne gaped, widened his eyes, and scratched his head, a parody of innocence. "I don't know who that TD is. Kate must have told you another lie." He shrugged, but kept the gun trained on Evie. A gleam of sweat banded her forehead and her hands had knotted into fists, but she stood straight and still. "Who are you going to believe, boy, your blood kin, or a pack of lying women?"

He spat out the last word the way another person might say "vermin." Kate bore down on her lip, feeling the heat of blood in her mouth. She glanced behind her for a weapon, saw only tufts of grass and chunks of rotting wood.

"I believe Kate. And Evie," Way-Ray said. But his quavering voice, halting words, and the way he ducked his head told Kate he wasn't sure. Evie swiveled her shoulder, and patted his arm. She said something Kate couldn't hear.

"Shut up, old lady," Dwayne roared. He aimed the gun at her head. "Put the boy out in front so I can see his face, so I know he hears me."

"No!" Way-Ray flailed at Evie as she shepherded him into position. "I don't want to listen to him. He's a bad man."

"Do as he says, Way-Ray." Evie's voice was calm and firm. "Please."

Way-Ray nodded, but when she released him, he turned his back and crossed his arms, showing the recalcitrant blood in his veins. "He's a liar."

Dwayne made a clicking sound with his tongue. "Are you saying that because you're scared of Kate Dalton? Tell me the truth. I'll protect you."

"I am telling the truth." Way-Ray stamped his feet.

Dwayne scraped hair from his forehead again and raised his brows. "You're scared of her," he sneered. "You're a spineless crybaby."

Way-Ray spun away from Evie, his fists raised. "I am not!" He marched toward Dwayne. "I'll punch you if you say that again."

*Go back!* Kate felt pain radiate her chest and arms—the oppressive grip of impotent rage squeezed her heart as it had the day she watched Wayne attack Amanda—the day that made this one inevitable.

"Way-Ray, stop," Evie pleaded. "Stay by me."

"Go back," Kate whispered. "Go back to Evie."

Way-Ray hesitated, glanced over his shoulder.

"You're gonna listen to the old lady? You're not gonna punch me?" Dwayne taunted. "Your grandmother will be ashamed when I tell her."

"My grandmother's with the angels."

"Not the one back in Oklahoma."

Way-Ray dropped his fists. "I don't have another grandmother."

"Sure you do. Her name's Justine." Dwayne lowered the gun and half hid it behind his thigh. "Your mother kept you away from her."

"Why?" Way-Ray asked with genuine innocence. Kate saw Evie wince, reach toward Way-Ray, withdraw her hand as Dwayne twitched the gun. "Is my grandmother Justine not nice?"

*Bingo!* Consequences aside, Kate felt a perverse pride in Way-Ray's ability to reason.

Dwayne's jaw muscles bulged and his eyes tightened, but he flashed Way-Ray another counterfeit smile—too wide, too bright. "She's as nice as pie. I'll bet she's making cookies for you right now. You like cookies, don't you?"

Kate remembered the woman in the alley who said cookies would bring Way-Ray back. She felt the sting of bitter irony. Now they were bait for Dwayne's trap.

Way-Ray kicked at a clump of grass. "Yeah. I guess."

"Sure you do," Dwayne said, his voice hypnotic. "And your grandmother Justine makes the best." He swayed toward Way-Ray, a snake savoring the seconds before the strike. "She sent me to bring you to Oklahoma."

"Oklahoma," Way-Ray repeated. "Does she live near Grassy Ridge?"

"No, but she's got a house with a great big TV and a room just for you." Dwayne held out his hand. "You come along with me now."

Way-Ray lifted his hand a few inches, drew it back. "I gotta ask Kate."

Dwayne lunged, seized Way-Ray's arm. "You don't have to ask her shit."

"You said a bad word." Way-Ray squirmed loose. "I won't go until I ask Kate."

Dwayne struck him with the back of his hand, the sound sharp as a shot. Kate whimpered, willed herself to remain still. "I don't give a damn," Dwayne roared.

Evie leaped forward and shoved the tottering boy toward the trees. "Run. Get away from him."

"Shut up, bitch." Dwayne raised the gun, pointed it at Evie's chest.

"Run, Way-Ray," she screamed. "Run to the woods. Hide."

"I warned you."

Dwayne fired.

# CHAPTER 43

The explosion echoed off the barn, the reverberation holding them all in thrall as if they'd been turned to stone: Kate, knees bent to launch herself; Dwayne, lips curled into a smile; Way-Ray, arms stretched toward the shelter of the woods, eyes on the woman who'd tried to save him; Evie palms out, head cocked as if listening for the call of a distant bird.

Then Evie's arms dropped. She bent at the waist as if bowing to her fate and pitched forward into knee-high grass.

Kate slumped against the barn and clamped a hand over her mouth to hold back her sobs.

"Evie!" Way-Ray threw himself down. "Get up. Evie, get up."

Kate stood on tiptoe, peering through the holly, cursing the cruelty of her only logical choice. If she tried to cover the fifty feet between them and help Evie, Dwayne would shoot her. She had to remain hidden, wait for a chance to get help.

"She's not getting up, kid," Dwayne said in a voice like a January wind. He shoved the gun into his belt and grasped Way-Ray's arm. "Let's go."

"No. You hurt Evie." Way-Ray pulled away, made a fist with his free hand, and swung. "You killed her."

Dwayne thrust him aside before the blow connected, then snatched the back of his shirt, lifted him off his feet, and shook. Way-Ray's T-shirt tightened like a noose. "Try to hit me again,

you little bastard, and I'll make you sorry you were ever born."
He opened his hand. Way-Ray dropped and tottered a few steps.
"I warned her first." Dwayne shrugged. "She didn't listen."

Way-Ray rubbed his neck. "What if I don't listen? Are you
going to shoot me?" There was no challenge in his voice, just
weary innocence.

Kate's breath caught in her throat. Don't ask questions. Go
with him. We'll find you.

Dwayne's fingers strayed to his belt buckle. "No, but I'll
whale you with my belt, just like your daddy would if he was
still on this earth. Let's go."

"No." Way-Ray stumbled toward the woods. "I'm going to
find Kate."

Dwayne dove and slammed into him. They thudded to the
ground.

"My arm!" Way-Ray squealed. "You broke my arm. I want
Kate."

Dwayne got to his feet and rolled his hands into fists. "Kate
doesn't care about your arm," he jeered.

"She does so," Way-Ray sucked air with a wet hiss.

"Then why isn't she here protecting her little girlie-boy?"

Kate gripped the holly tighter. Points of pain burned, flared,
merged.

"She'll come." Way-Ray's voice was little more than a
whisper.

Dwayne bent and jerked him to his feet. "She's too damn
late. And I'm sick of your yowling." He raised a fist and
clubbed the boy's ear.

Way-Ray's piercing scream shot into the empty sky. Anger
burned like wildfire in Kate's chest. It blazed down her legs and
along her arms, it flamed in her fingers. Dwayne's next blow
might cripple Way-Ray. Or worse. She'd carry that burden the
rest of her life.

She leaped from the shadow and lunged toward them.
"Stop!"

"Kate!" Way-Ray howled. "Kate, he hurt me."

Dwayne's fingers unfurled from Way-Ray's shirt. "Sweet Christ." He drew his gun from his belt. "How many of you worthless women do I have to kill?"

Kate halted, stood in profile, narrowing his target.

"I knew you'd come." Way-Ray cradled his left arm against his stomach. Blood oozed from his ear and along the blade of his jaw. "I'm sorry I called you bad names. I'm sorry I ran away. I love you."

Kate's throat was so tight she could barely choke out the words. "I love you too, Way-Ray." If it all ended here, she had enough in her heart for eternity.

"Touching." Dwayne reached out with casual menace, snagged Way-Ray's tattered shirt, and threw him to the ground. "But he's coming with me. You have a funeral to attend—your own."

Kate shifted her eyes to the wicked opening at the end of the barrel. "Stay down, and be as quiet as you can, Way-Ray. Don't be scared. It will be okay." The last in a long series of lies. She studied Dwayne's eyes: the shade of a twilight sky and as calm as a lake on a windless day.

They didn't even flicker when he fired.

Way-Ray screamed. Kate felt a puff of air brush her lips and heard a sharp thwuck as the bullet bit into the barn. Her heart compressed and her skin prickled, but she kept her gaze locked on Dwayne. She had no choice, no plan, only fragile hopes: that his shots might be heard, that he might run out of ammunition, or that he might abandon his mother's mission and escape while he could. "Stay quiet, Way-Ray. It's okay."

Dwayne shoved his hair from his forehead, and fired again. The bullet hissed behind her.

Was he toying with her, or was the twenty-five feet between them enough to affect his aim? Could she make it harder to him to focus by giving him more to think about?

"Evie was right about the cops. They're everywhere. I can help you get away. To Mexico."

"Too hot." He leveled the gun.

"Somewhere else then. And I'll take the boy to your mother."

Way-Ray wailed. Kate kept her eyes on Dwayne. "You don't have to kill me."

"Don't have to. Want to." He grinned. "But go ahead and beg." He licked his lips. "I like a woman who begs."

*So did your brother.* "When you bring Way-Ray to her, will Justine finally love you?"

His eyes hardened.

Kate put an edge on her words. She beat Wayne because she hadn't bargained or begged. "I bet she won't even say 'thank you.' You're no more to her than a dog she told to fetch."

A haze clouded his eyes. He raised his free hand to steady the gun. "Shut up."

Kate needled at the nerve. "A junkyard dog she kicks whenever she wants."

He tossed his head as if the image were a hornet he could drive away. "That's not true."

Kate nodded toward Way-Ray. "How will you feel, dog, when she makes a fuss over this pup?"

"Shut up!" He squeezed off two shots.

They went wide, rustling the holly bush. Had she rattled him, or was he still toying with her. Four bullets gone. Five counting the slug in Evie. How many bullets were left? "I belt she'll be mad you damaged her merchandise."

Dwayne's eyes were as flat as if they were painted on clay. "I warned him. He didn't listen. It's his fault."

*Your mantra. That all-purpose excuse.* Kate shrugged. "She'll know different. She made you what you are."

"Don't talk about my mother that way!" His hand jerked. The shot went high.

Six.

"Don't talk about her at all." Dwayne's eyes narrowed and he rotated his right wrist, taking the weight of the gun into his palm, hefting it. He bent over Way-Ray, the fingers of his left hand digging at the boy's good arm. Way-Ray squeaked like a rubber toy. "Don't make another sound," Dwayne hissed. "Don't make me kill her."

"Whatever he does is not your fault, Way-Ray." Kate locked her gaze on his. "Whatever happens, be strong, remember that I love you."

A thought slithered down her spine and coiled in her gut, heavy as mercury. Had needling Dwayne been another mistake? Would he arrange for Way-Ray to have an "accident" on the way to Oklahoma? She forced quivering lips to smile. "I love you. Don't forget that. No matter what."

Way-Ray nodded. Dwayne hoisted him to his feet and locked his left forearm under the boy's chin. "Try to get away again and I'll hurt you bad." He backed down the road, the gun bobbling with each step. Way-Ray, canted at an awkward angle, jolted along on his heels, his right hand gripping his uncle's arm. His lips turned blue. His breath came in short huffs.

Kate willed him to stay on his feet. Her only chance was to run, but she followed them one slow step at a time, keeping less than ten yards between them. She couldn't let Way-Ray believe she'd abandoned him.

"Stay back," Dwayne growled. "Don't make me shoot you."

The warning. Shifting the blame.

Kate flicked her eyes toward Evie's crumpled body. It seemed smaller, thinner, impossibly old and frail. A dark red bloom of blood stained her sweatshirt and a fly, black, triangular, and as large as Kate's thumb, circled. Its whirr seemed as loud as a jet's engine. Kate longed to drop to her knees, cradle Evie's head, and shoo the fly away.

Useless. Already she heard the whine of another drawn by the sweet metallic scent of blood. Evie wouldn't be bothered by them. Or anything. Ever again.

Kate felt a curious sense of serenity and turned toward Way-Ray once more. He'd bitten his lip and a few drops of blood oozed onto Dwayne's arm. Woven through the drone of the approaching fly and the swish and crackle of grass were the wheezes and grunts of his labored breathing. His eyes, dark with pain, snared hers. She strained at a smile. As long as we're alive we have hope.

Way-Ray's feet caught on a hummock of grass and he toppled, sliding from Dwayne's grasp.

"Damn you." Dwayne wrenched him to his feet and clubbed him with the gun. Way-Ray's legs and arms twitched but this time he didn't scream.

"Stop!" Kate sprang toward them. "You're killing him."

"Take another step and I will."

Choking with fury, Kate halted ten feet away. Dwayne smirked, clubbed the boy again, and tossed him aside like a scrap of litter. He lay motionless. Kate heard no sound except the whine of that cursed fly.

"I warned him." Dwayne bent, grasped the waistband of Way-Ray's jeans and hoisted. The boy's head lolled like a sunflower on a broken stalk. His hands trailed through the grass as Dwayne shuffled sideways toward the forest.

The whine became a pinging rattle. Dwayne cocked his head. "What's that?"

Kate's heart swelled. An engine. Winding up on the slope through the blackberries.

"Damn you," Dwayne snarled. He raised the gun and fired.

Bright pain exploded behind Kate's eyes.

She fell.

# CHAPTER 44

Pain roared in Kate's ears, flamed across her skin, swirled tight, drilled into her right thigh. Her arms thrashed. Her spine arched. The fly. That horrible insect, circling in to bloat on Evie's blood. Now it would feast on her.

"Lie still," a voice hissed.

Evie's voice. But Evie was—

"I'll pull through," Evie said. "So will you if you play possum."

Pain flared across Kate's hip, sliced her leg. Her fingers strained toward the wound as if by touching she could diminish the torment.

"Don't move until he's in the woods. Help's coming."

Kate clamped her teeth and locked her fingers around clumps of rough grass. The ground seemed to tilt and vibrate, skidding her toward the lip of a void. Murky darkness lapped at her feet, her ankles, her knees, sucking her under.

And then there were hands on her thigh, hands working at the pain like modeling clay. Kate heard fabric rip and a gasp and whimper she knew must be hers. Her fingers tore at the grass, releasing a dry, sweet scent, and spraying grit across her lips. She spun on the axis of Evie's probing fingers.

"I won't lie to you. It's pretty bad."

Beneath the roar of an engine, Kate heard the rustle of cloth and a grunt. "I'll keep pressure on it. Scream if you need to."

Kate shook her head. Dwayne Vetter would surely hear. It would give him more pleasure, more power. She opened her eyes and saw Evie grit her teeth and remove her sweatshirt. Her skin was the color of old ivory and glistened with perspiration. A graying bra, lace frayed, a safety pin securing one strap, clung to her ribcage. A raw furrow plowed the skin below it. Blood welled in the furrow and dribbled onto her jeans.

Evie glanced at the wound. "Hardly a scratch," she boasted in a hollow voice. "Had worse from an osprey I didn't have a good hold of."

She slid her sweatshirt beneath Kate's leg, setting off a tidal wave of agony that darkened the sky. Kate grunted and rode the wave up to a squeal of brakes, and the stinging stench of scorched rubber. Evie tied the sweatshirt sleeves in a knot and pulled. Bright pain sizzled along Kate's leg, up her backbone, and into her brain. Evie tied a second knot. Pain beat like a bass drum, keeping time for pounding footsteps.

Jackson loomed over her, blotting out the sun. He knelt and laid a hand against her cheek. "Are you okay? Where's Way-Ray?"

"She needs a doctor bad," Evie snapped. "And that maniac took the boy."

"He hit him," Kate gasped.

"Knocked him cold." Evie pointed to the forest. "Dragged him off that way."

Jackson's eyes strafed the tree line. He stroked Kate's forehead. "I screwed up. I fell asleep."

Kate lifted her fingers and ran them across the prickly, graying stubble below his lips. "I didn't wake you. It's my fault."

"Oh, hell," Evie growled. "I wanted to surprise her. I'll take the damn blame for everything."

Jackson waved that aside. "Can you drive?"

Evie fingered her wound. "Bleeding's about stopped. I'll manage. But she can't sit."

"I'll get some hay." Jackson lunged to his feet and headed for the barn in a rocking lope. Surges of joy, fear, and despair buffeted Kate. Jackson would rescue Way-Ray. Dwayne would kill him and Jackson. Surgeons would repair her leg. She'd bleed to death before they reached the hospital.

Evie gripped her shoulders. "I'll take it slow, but it will be a rough ride to the highway. Then I'll lay on the horn, flag someone down to get help."

"Phone." Kate dug it from her pocket and pressed it into Evie's hands. "No service here."

Jackson slung bales into the idling truck, broke them apart, and scattered hay across the bed. Chaff rose in a glittering nebula, releasing a sweet, musty odor. Kate felt a burning tickle behind her eyes, sucked in a breath, and fought the sneeze she knew would unleash a whirlwind of pain.

Jackson dropped at her side, eyes like granite. "I'll bring your boy to you. I promise."

Kate tried to nod, but the ebb and flow of pain claimed her concentration. She felt chilled and yet her skin was slick with sweat. Shock? Could that create the sensation of drifting dizziness, the feeling of waves lapping, pulling?

"Put your arm around me."

Kate raised her hand and let her fingers graze the warm skin at the back of his neck.

"Hang on tight, Kate, I won't break." Jackson drew her against his chest and lifted. Pain shrieked along her nerve endings. She dug her nails into his shoulder and bit down on her tattered lip as Jackson and Evie slid her into the bed of the truck. Another chaff cloud billowed, another sneeze built behind her eyes. Then hinges squealed, and the tailgate clunked into place. Kate stared at the sky, concentrating on the end of a branch reaching for a single frothy cloud.

Evie squatted beside her, mounding hay around her leg. "Stay strong for Way-Ray when he gets back."

*If* he get back. If Dwayne doesn't kill the pup Justine would love better.

Evie clambered over the tailgate, laid a hand on Jackson's shoulder, and jumped to the ground. "Dwayne sliced the tires on Kate's rig," he told her. "You'll have to go into the brush to get around."

"Got it. Hurry. Find them."

"I will." His voice was confident, cold.

Kate shuddered. "Way-Ray needs us to be better than Dwayne."

Jackson's eyes narrowed and he raised a rifle. The barrel glinted in the sun. "That's up to Dwayne."

Gears clashed and the truck jolted into the rutted road, rocking like an inquisitor's cradle.

Rolling surf lapped at Kate's consciousness, drawing her under and tossing her up on a beach of sharp stones and broken glass. Brush clawed at the truck, sky and leaves flickered above. The dark tide carried her deeper into blankness, then flung her to the surface again. Gravel pelted the undercarriage.

The truck idled for a second, then lumbered onto the pavement. Tires whined. Wires stitched the sky. She heard a shot, clawed at the hay.

The truck hurtled on. The murky tide sucked at her once more.

She heard a second shot.

The tide bore her under.

# CHAPTER 45

"She's coming out of it for real this time. Her eyelids fluttered just then."

Kate heard concussions of sounds more than words, sounds alternately soft and drawn out like taffy, and then packed tight together, edges sharp and splintered. Kate heard that voice before. Where? When? She had no firm memories, no concrete sensations. She was adrift in a warm sea. The Dead Sea? Dead? Was she?

"Just like in the movies," another voice said. "Their eyelids always flutter in the movies. Romance novels, too."

Kate puzzled out the words. Her eyelids hadn't moved, no light had penetrated. Why, if she heard these people, couldn't she see them?

A rush of images swept past in stark relief against a rising wall of dark and pulsing pain: Evie crumpling, Way-Ray screaming, Dwayne aiming the gun, Jackson lifting her, the turbid tide swelling, gunshots. Muddier sensations followed: prodding fingers and needles, a mask and the hiss of cold nothing against her lip, Maureen telling her not to worry about the paperwork, the nurse with tight red curls tapping an IV line, a void opening beneath her like the trapdoor on a hangman's scaffold.

She dropped far past worry and pain. But now pain was back. The dark weight lay on her chest, sucking her breath like a demon cat.

Something brushed her cheek. "How about it, girlfriend?" the second voice asked. "Ready to get with reality?"

*Yes!*

*No!*

What fresh horror was waiting?

"Still doped to the gills," the first voice speculated.

"If she doesn't tune in soon, I'm going out for provisions. I need pizza and I need it now."

An image blossomed in Kate's brain. She knew pizza. It was round, bright with tomato sauce, and redolent of melted cheese, garlic, and herbs. Pizza was Way-Ray's favorite food.

Memory struck like an axe. Way-Ray beaten, stolen, maybe shot.

She tried again to open her eyes but the lashes were knotted. "Way-Ray?" It sounded like the croak of a distant raven.

"What'd she say?"

"I don't know. I couldn't make it out." A hand—she knew it was a hand—touched hers, stroking. Something cold slid between her lips. "Ice chip," the second voice said. Rhea's voice. "Let it melt on your tongue."

The ice was metallic, both cold and hot, searing her throat and soothing at the same time. "More," she whispered. The word sounded like "org."

"Huh?"

Kate tried again, frustration battering the inside of her skull.

"Let me get the bed up so you can swallow better."

Kate heard a hum. Her head and chest folded forward and her hips slid lower, detonating an explosion in her thigh. "Arrrrhhh." Flares burst in her brain, trailing red, orange, and yellow sparks.

"Too far," the second voice said. "You went too far."

The bed vibrated and reclined. Pain retreated, but stood at attention, ready to advance. She willed her eyes to open, felt as if the lashes were ripping from the lids, glimpsed gauzy light.

"Sorry about that," the dark blur that was Rhea said. "Here's another ice chip. Just enough to dampen your tongue."

"Don't want you spewing it back up on our watch," another blur informed her. "That nurse with the cast-iron corset will have our heads."

Evie's voice. Kate felt a rush of joy. She squeezed her eyes shut and tugged the lids apart. They scraped like emery boards, but brighter light laced through.

"Hold on," Rhea said, "and I'll wipe the sleep out."

Kate felt something wet and rough rub her cheeks and eyes. It smelled like sweet soap and alcohol. She blinked and wavering images appeared: the shapes of the two women; a spray of green, red, and white; a tumble of tubing; a needle that disappeared beneath a strip of white tape fastened to the back of her left hand.

"Yeah," Rhea added. "That nurse is scarier than a tax audit. I couldn't believe she wants Kate to get up this afternoon. Any fool can see she can't move with all those stitches and pins and what all."

"Way-Ray," Kate whispered. It sounded like "eh-eh."

"The inn?" Rhea asked. "Nadine overloaded one of the washers and it peeled itself away from the wall and flooded two downstairs units."

"Way-Ray," Kate whispered again.

"Surgery? I'll bet she's asking about her surgery."

Kate shook her head, setting loose an avalanche of agony, but Evie raised her voice and separated her syllables. "Six hours. Twice they thought they were gonna lose you. You've got so much donated blood you'll slosh—if you can walk, which I'm betting you can't no matter what that nurse says."

Kate shook her head again, aware of matted hair, the sour smell of sweat.

"And the anesthetic and meds will keep you off balance for a week," Rhea added.

Kate stretched her hand to touch her leg. Her fingers felt something tight beneath the sheet.

"You're bandaged up big time and they're got rubber tubing in there so all the gunk will drain out." Rhea slid another ice chip between Kate's lips. "You're gonna limp for a long time." She chuckled. "You and Jackson will be a matching pair."

Jackson! Jackson was alive. Kate crunched ice and wet the insides of her cheeks. "Way-Ray," she croaked. Her arms flopped against the sheets. Tubing clattered and tape pinched the skin on the back of her hand. "Way-Ray? Way-Ray!"

"Easy." Rhea cautioned. "Pull these dang tubes loose and that nurse will have my hide. Lie still. Way-Ray's . . ."

"Asleep," Evie said.

Rhea drew in a long breath. "Sound asleep."

Asleep. The ponderous weight lifted from Kate's chest. She smiled at the hovering women. Rhea's topknot tilted at an extreme angle and her forehead was creased like an accordion, her eyes streaked with red. A white T-shirt with the logo of a defunct ice cream parlor hung from the knobs of Evie's shoulders and her cheeks were caved in. "Jackson brought Way-Ray back," she said. "Like he promised."

"And sent that bastard down to the devil," Rhea spat.

Kate flinched. Evie gripped her wrist, flame at the back of her eyes. "Jackson didn't have a choice." Her fingers, bone and nail, stabbed Kate's skin. "Dwayne shot first. But Way-Ray—"

"—doesn't know. We haven't told him yet." Rhea patted the place where her smock pocket would have been had she been wearing it over her mottled green T-shirt and frayed jeans. "You want a few more ice chips?" She turned her back and Kate heard the rattle of ice in a cup, a sniff, and a sneeze.

"No. Why don't you go outside and have a cigarette? You're ready to jump out of your skin."

"Can't." Rhea pivoted, set the cup on the table, and prodded her topknot. "I'm going cold turkey."

Kate blinked. "You quit smoking?"

"When Way-Ray was missing I made a bargain with the big guy upstairs." Rhea coughed and patted the missing pocket. "Now I've gotta hold up my end."

"Yeah. A deal's a deal," Evie snorted. "Whether there's a big guy or not." She tugged at the sheet, pulling it tight across Kate's chest. "I need to get back and check on the critters. And you need another nap."

"I've been napping too long." Kate flicked the sheet aside. "I want to see Way-Ray." She rolled to the edge of the bed. Another set of explosions went off—bilious green and bug-splatter yellow. She fell back, taking short puffs of breath. Pain retreated, but halted closer this time.

Evie tweaked the sheet into place and tucked it tight "See? You're gonna fall flat on your face and tear your leg open."

Rhea plumped the pillow. "That hard-case nurse will be all over you like heat rash in a sauna."

"Then bring Way-Ray to me."

"He's asleep." Evie's eyes slid away from Kate's. Her chin quivered.

"The doctors don't want him disturbed." Rhea rattled the cup. "How about more ice?"

"I'll go ask if you can have a cola." Evie scuttled to the door and pawed at the knob. She glanced back, her eyes slick with dread.

Kate knotted the sheet in her fists. "What's wrong? What aren't you telling me?"

Rhea patted her imaginary pocket, a steady backbeat. "Don't get yourself all worked up. You're gonna be fine."

"I don't care about me," Kate howled. "What's wrong with Way-Ray?"

Rhea's eyes flicked toward the door. "He's just tired, that's all."

"Look at me." Kate peered up at Rhea's pinched eyes, saw spiking panic. "What's wrong?"

"Nothing." Rhea cut her eyes toward the window. "The doctors gave Way-Ray something so he'd sleep for a few days."

"Tell her the rest of it, Rhea."

Jackson stood in the doorway clutching a handful of drooping daisies. "Tell her the truth."

# CHAPTER 46

Kate felt the weight compress her chest once more. "The truth?"

Evie appeared behind him and Jackson thrust the flowers at her, crossed to the bed, and took Kate's hand. "We don't need another string of lies. That's what got us here."

"It's your call." Rhea glared at Jackson, but Kate heard gratitude in her voice. "They airlifted Way-Ray to a bigger hospital a hundred miles away."

"A hundred miles," Kate echoed. She gripped Jackson's callused fingers and frowned at her useless leg. It might as well be a thousand miles. A million.

"He didn't come around after that monster clubbed him." Evie slapped the daisies against the sheet, scattering grainy yellow pollen. She wiped it, spreading the stain like warm butter. "His brain's swollen."

A sob wound tight in Kate's chest like wire on a spool. She imagined Way-Ray, head shaved and splotched by electrodes, arms bristling with needles.

Jackson stroked her fingers. "He's in the best place he could be right now. The finest doctors in the state are working on him."

"But he's alone. He's all alone."

"He's not alone, Kate." Rhea's tone was placating. "He's in intensive care. The place is crawling with nurses day and night."

Kate felt a flash of rage. Rhea had two children. How could she not understand? "They're strangers. He'll think I abandoned him." She rolled to the edge of the bed through a glittering hail of pain.

Jackson clamped a hand on her shoulder and pressed her back. "Hurting yourself won't help. I was there this morning. I left a picture of you beside his bed and a note with this number." He nodded toward a squatty beige phone on a table by the bed.

A picture. A note. What good were those? Kate jerked her hand from Jackson's and punched at his arm, knuckles barely grazing the sleeve of a wrinkled cotton shirt as gray as her misery. She punched again, setting off a chain reaction of torment in her leg that left her gasping. "Why did you leave him?"

"Go find a nurse," Rhea told Evie. "She needs a shot of painkiller."

Evie dumped the daisies on the bed and turned for the door.

"No," Kate moaned. Painkiller would dull her senses, blunt her love, deaden her desire to care for Way-Ray in any way she could.

Jackson held up a hand. "Give me a minute." He bent close and Kate saw his face was crusted with whiskers and creased with exhaustion, his eyes rimmed in scarlet. She smelled coffee and cinnamon on his breath, but not a trace of alcohol. "I'm going right back," he said. "I left because Rhea called and said you were waking up. I wanted to . . . to know you were okay."

"But Way-Ray's all a—"

"Yes." He stroked her forehead. "But he doesn't know that. The doctors are keeping him asleep."

"Deep asleep," Evie echoed.

"So he'll stay still and heal," Rhea added.

Brain. Swollen. Evie's words came back in a rush. Kate dug her nails into Jackson's arm. "But he *will* wake up? Tell me he will!"

"He's a strong little boy. Tough." Jackson's lips stretched into a smile, but tears gleamed in his eyes. "He's a lot like you."

"And he wants to come back to us," Evie said. "Back to you. He knows you love him. You told him right before—" She blotted her eyes with the hem of her T-shirt revealing a long bandage on her side. "Kate, I'm so damn sorry about dragging you out there. If only I'd—"

"Let it go." Jackson straightened, drawing his arm from Kate's grasp, and faced Evie. "It's not about you."

Evie dropped the shirt and scowled, eyes glittering. "Don't you tell me—"

"He's got a point, Evie." Rhea held out her hands, palms up. "It's not helping Kate. Besides, it's not in your nature to harp on what's done and can't be changed."

Evie's scowl seemed to turn inward. She opened her mouth, then pursed her lips, and swallowed. "I'll get a vase. And the nurse." She scooped up the battered daisies and stomped out.

With a sense of awe Kate recalled Evie lying wounded in the grass playing dead. She ached for the older woman, longed to rush after her and apologize for all of them.

"She'll get over it," Rhea said without confidence. "Evie never holds a grudge."

Jackson shrugged as if that didn't matter and turned to Kate once more. "The doctors have a lot of faith in a combination of new drugs and diuretics to relieve pressure from the fluid on his brain."

"Then they won't have to cut open his—?" Kate imagined masked doctors with gleaming saws and scalpels.

Jackson winced. "Not unless the pressure builds too high."

Kate shuddered. Gloved hands, slicing, probing.

"That's the other reason I came back." Jackson released her hand and drew a folded paper from his back pocket. "They'd like you to sign this." He shook out the folds, the stiff paper rattling in the hollow way loose panes of glass do when a heavy truck rumbles past a sagging house.

Kate squinted at the paper. "What is it?"

"The standard cover-your-ass permission form to treat Way-Ray."

Kate gripped the paper. It was dense with close print. Words blurred, shifted, and overlapped. Her leg throbbed, sending seismic waves through her chest and into her head. She closed her eyes.

"She's exhausted," Rhea whispered. "And she won't listen to me. Maybe you could—"

Jackson snorted. "I'd rather wrestle a shark."

Rhea chuckled, and then the room was quiet except for faint sounds of breathing, the rustle of clothing, the slow shuffle of feet. Kate was conscious of their eyes on her, of a soft, fortunate feeling.

"If she's asleep, I think I'll head back to Way-Ray."

"What about the form?"

"Have her sign it when she wakes up and then fax it."

No matter how deep his sleep, Kate knew Way-Ray had to feel the emptiness of being alone.

"I hear you both." She opened her eyes. "And I want you to hear me. I'm going to Way-Ray."

"You're nuts." Rhea yanked at her topknot.

Kate reached for Jackson's hand, felt the elongated lump of scar tissue on his palm, cool and velvety beneath her fingers. "You know I have to be with him. No matter what."

He nodded. "I know."

"You'll help me?"

He nodded again.

"You're both crazy. The doctors won't let you out of here. No way." Rhea shook her head so hard strands of hair shimmied loose. "A hundred miles of jolting and jouncing will tear you up. What good will you be to Way-Ray if you're a crip—?" She glanced at Jackson, flushed, and dipped her head.

The throbbing in Kate's leg beat like a drum, echoing off the walls and ceiling.

"And the minute you go out that door, the media will be all over you like ants at a picnic," Rhea said. "That Marnie person is camped out in the parking lot in an RV the size of a school bus."

Marnie! Charging at them with her microphone. So eager for a story.

"An RV?" Jackson mused. "You could stretch out. We could cushion your leg with pillows."

Kate shook her head. "Rhea, get me a cup of coffee. A big one. Jackson, find that nurse Rhea's so scared of and tell her I want to get up."

Neither moved. Rhea blinked like an owl. "What are you going to do?"

"Give Marnie an exclusive."

"She blew up your life!" Rhea's fingers beat a tattoo on her missing pocket. "Are you crazy?"

"No. And I've got some fame coming. I cut my fifteen minutes short to spite Emory McCoy."

"Huh? Who's Emory McCoy?"

Kate flipped the fingers of her free hand. "A pompous jerk who helped change my life."

"Oooo-kaaay?" Rhea raised her eyebrows at Jackson. His face remained expressionless, placid.

"I'll deal with the devil," Kate said, "if that's what it takes to get to my boy."

# CHAPTER 47

"I could get used to this four-star treatment." Jackson maneuvered Kate's wheelchair into a chrome-walled elevator. "A corporate jet, free ambulance service from the airport, a private room in the hospital." He swung her around and pressed a button.

Kate winced and tamped down guilt. People gave for their own reasons: satisfaction, selflessness, penance, pity, the need to improve their images in the community, or the desire to use her publicity to generate some of their own. None of it meant a damn thing if Way-Ray didn't recover.

She attempted a joke as the doors swished closed. "Where's the red carpet?"

"Red's not right for your skin tone. You need teal blue or a celery color, like that T-shirt you wore the second time I saw you."

"Teal? Celery?" Kate gaped at his shabby gray shirt and frayed jeans, and then plucked at her washed-out blue scrubs. "You're kidding, right?"

"No." He shrugged. "Those colors intensify your sparkle."

Sparkle? Ducking her head, she studied her blunt fingernails. She was utilitarian coal, not a decorative diamond. She remembered a woman with twinkling eyes and cheerful words who worked at the grocery store where her parents shopped. "It's all a facade," Kate's mother claimed. Kate had looked up that word and then watched for signs of the true personality beneath the false front. After a year, she concluded the grocery clerk was purely good-natured. She kept the conclusion to herself.

Jackson stooped, tilted her chin, and looked into her eyes with the same intensity as that day in the laundry room when he unsealed the bitter memory of Andy's rejection. "It's okay to sparkle, Kate." His eyes glowed. "Way-Ray needs light to find the way back."

If only it were that simple. The elevator bell pinged. The doors stuttered open on a slab of worn but polished gray-green industrial linoleum. How could she sparkle without feeling phony, dishonest?

Jackson rolled her to a tall counter, conferred with a woman in pink scrubs, fitted them both with masks, and then wheeled her along another corridor and through a door. A high bed stood in the center of a barren room. It was flanked by blinking equipment and chrome stands hung with bags of fluid. A small table held a sheet of paper covered with blocky printing and a picture of her watering a basket of petunias.

"Got to write a new note." Jackson rolled her up beside the bed. "Tell Way-Ray you're close by."

Kate sucked in a breath and focused on the boy as pale as the sheet that covered him. She had imagined his expression would be serene and relaxed or vacant and slack-muscled. But his jaw was clenched, his cheeks bulged, and his eyes were squeezed shut as if he was trying to lift something.

Her heart lurched. He was so young, so small, carrying such a huge burden.

"He looks different." Jackson bent over the bed. "Like he's concentrating on something."

Kate leaned as close as the wheelchair would allow. "Is that a good sign?"

Jackson laid a hand on her shoulder. "I want to believe it is."

Kate recalled a baby at the shelter. She was certain the tiny girl was molding her lips to create words, but the infant's mother laughed and said her daughter was about to pass gas. Grimacing at her ignorance, Kate decided not to undermine Jackson's tentative optimism.

She touched the cast that encased Way-Ray's left arm from elbow to knuckles, then stroked his fingers. Chill skin lay across the bones like tissue paper, as if the blood vessels had emptied and cells had collapsed in on themselves. Kate squeezed. He didn't return pressure. His fingers were as nerveless as twigs. She glanced at the IV beside his bed and watched a pale yellow solution drip into the tube that led to his good arm. Another tube snaked from beneath the sheet, a thin stream of liquid drizzling out.

"Talk to him," Jackson urged, his hand warm on her shoulder.

She trembled. The doctor said there was seldom a sudden awakening, most patients emerged in stages, often by reacting to stimuli: contact, smells, sounds. Way-Ray hadn't responded to her touch, and she didn't see how the antiseptic scent of this room could spark memories of anything but his appendectomy. Could her voice send him deeper into the coma? "What should I say?"

"Whatever you feel." Jackson squeezed her shoulder and backed away. "Tell him what you'll do when you're both better. Show him the future. The way you want it to be."

Kate cleared her throat, thinking of beaches, whales, fried clams, video games, Kyle, Sean, and Mutant. And then she knew where to start. "When we get back home, we'll go out to Evie's and get the bobcat." She raised her voice a bit, pushing words through the mask, thinking of them as tiny prisms casting rainbows across his mind. "He'll be all better and he'll want to go back to the forest."

She peered over her shoulder at Jackson who raised a thumb and leaned against the wall. Kate stroked Way-Ray's fingers once more. "We'll put the cage in the back of Jackson's truck and we'll take him up into the mountains. Jackson will drive because he knows the way."

Kate closed her eyes, imagining a place fit for a cat. "There will be tall trees and ferns and moss and lots of streams so the bobcat can have a drink whenever he wants. And there will be caves so he can get out of the rain and meadows where he can hunt for . . ."

"Mice," Jackson supplied.

"Mice," Kate agreed, grateful to him for providing a more acceptable prey than chipmunks or rabbits. "And Jackson will put down the tailgate, but you'll climb up and open the cage all by yourself. And just when you do, the sun will come out."

A sob slashed at her throat. Way-Ray might never see the sun again. Some patients, the doctor told her when she demanded total honesty, remained locked down, locked in. "And the bobcat will creep to the door of the cage, and he'll sniff the air, and then he'll look right into your eyes, and . . ." Kate faltered, tears curdling her words.

"He'll wink," Jackson said. "That's how bobcats say 'thank you.' And then he'll leap across the tailgate and race into the woods." He nodded to Kate.

She sniffed back her tears. "And then we'll take the cage back to Evie and go out and get the biggest pizza there is. No, two of the biggest pizzas. One all for you because you're so strong and brave." She squeezed his fingers again, allowing herself a second of hope that he would respond.

But he was still. Despair and exhaustion swept over her and she bowed her head, but refused to beseech a power that allowed Dwayne Vetter to hurt this child. She wondered whether Jackson trusted in anything beyond himself and the forces of nature.

As if she'd asked, Jackson spoke. "Give it time, Kate. He's a long way off, but your message is in the wires." She felt the chair shift as he gripped the handles. "Let's get you to your room."

He didn't wait for her to agree, but spun the chair about. Kate peered over her shoulder at Way-Ray, tears distorting his image. Then they passed into the corridor and she could no longer see him.

# CHAPTER 48

Kate woke to the crackle of paper. Jackson stood by the room's only chair, pulling items from a white plastic bag: shampoo, conditioner, makeup, eye shadow, and mascara. "What's all that for?"

"You. You're going to be on TV a lot," he said. "You promised updates every afternoon."

She frowned. "I don't need makeup. This isn't about me. It's about Way-Ray."

"Right." He wrenched a black mascara tube from its cardboard backing. "But you're the one people will see."

She struggled to sit. "But I don't care what I—"

"I know." He snapped the seal on the eye shadow and opened the lid on a palette of blues and grays. "I respect and admire that. But you agreed to this media game and it has rules. Number one: 'a pretty face gets more attention.'"

Kate clenched her fists. To her parents, pretty had meant shallow. "I don't have a—"

"Discussion closed." Jackson turned his back and dumped out an enormous shopping bag, mounding clothing on the foot of the bed: khaki shorts, blouses and cotton sweaters in blues and greens.

Kate fingered the slick fabric of a short-sleeved shirt the color of a late afternoon sky. "That's silk." A luxury her mother would have scorned. "Take it back. Get T-shirts. They're more practical."

"When you shop for yourself you can be as practical as you want. But these are gifts." He grinned. "It would be rude to refuse them."

Kate felt her face burn. He'd noted her etiquette button and pushed it. "Take them all back."

Jackson shook his head. "Can't. Threw the sales slips away." He drew a jackknife from his pocket, sliced off tags, and tossed them into a trash can beside the bed. "Stop punishing yourself like a medieval penitent. There's no one here to say you can't wear silk."

Kate wrapped her arms across her chest. He was right. Her parents were dead, gone. Except from her mind.

He hung the blouses in the closet. "Thank me. Then let's move on."

"Thank you," she muttered.

"Wow, such sincerity." Tipping his head back, he released a roar of laughter. "Are you running for patron saint of gratitude?"

Kate flinched and stared at her knotted fists. Did he know about the self-image she'd created in jest and expiation? Was she that transparent? Biting her lip, she buttoned down the anger that would strip her further, and swore she wouldn't wear the clothing.

But the first news briefing loomed and the other choices were a striped hospital gown or the fatigued scrubs scavenged from the deadhead orderly who remembered Way-Ray and promised to burn some incense for him.

"By the smell of these scrubs you've been burning more than incense," Jackson told him.

"You picked the bottle. I picked the bong," the deadhead replied, tapping his fist against Jackson's. "Whatever it takes. Right, bro?"

Jackson hadn't protested that he was now sober. Was he afraid to jinx that, or was he certain he would lapse? She hadn't asked. She had no standing to disregard the privilege of privacy.

Feeling out-maneuvered, she sent Jackson from the room and shrugged into a turquoise blouse. The silk lay cool against her skin and whispered as if sharing a secret—more costume than clothing. And she had a part to play.

Jackson rolled her to the hospital lobby, parked her before a phalanx of reporters, and limped to a distant corner. A couple of photographers recorded his movements and Kate remembered with a jolt that he had a fame of his own—he was the man who killed Dwayne Vetter, barred from talking about what happened in the woods until the investigation was complete and a ruling made. Anxiety crimped her gut and she gripped the arms of the chair. They'd find he was justified. They had to.

Hauling in a deep breath, she tamped down the pain in her thigh, and got into the part. Pasting on a smile, she thanked everyone who had helped her get to Way-Ray's side, and responded to requests to describe his room and how he looked. When they asked how she felt she gave them what they wanted.

"I'm frightened," she said. "Frightened that he might never wake up."

She told them about Evie's wildlife rehabilitation center and how Way-Ray collected money in a coffee can. She listed his favorite foods, games, and movies. When questions came about the confrontation with Wayne, she didn't deflect them. When they led to other questions, she plunged on until she felt dry, drained, as if she'd sweated out a long fever and scrubbed with lye soap and a coarse cloth. "Aired your dirty laundry," her mother would have sniffed. But why not open the closet and set the skeletons free, set herself free?

\* \* \* \* \*

"They got Justine," Chief Sam Lowell told her on the phone late that evening. "Wearing a wig and trying to get on a flight to Mexico."

Kate punched a fist into the air. "They got her," she told Jackson. He looked up from a book and raised a thumb. "I bet she tries to put the blame on Dwayne."

"She can try," Lowell said. "But he had a letter in his car— she sent it general delivery to a post office in Idaho—and a money order inside for five hundred dollars. She said the money was to finish his work and bring the boy to her."

Work. As if killing was like mowing the lawn. "She'll say she didn't know he would kill anyone."

"Of course she will," Lowell agreed. "But she'll have a tough row to hoe. Now, how's that little boy doing?"

"Still the same. Kate struggled to keep desperate hope from her voice "But no worse."

"Well, you tell him to wake up and I'll give him a ride in a patrol car. Let him turn on the siren and lights." He paused and Kate had the impression he was wrestling with a decision. "Tell him I'll take him fishing the first Sunday he feels up to it."

Remembering what Rhea told her about the chief's love of solitude, Kate recognized the sacrifice. "Thank you. I'll tell him." She checked her watch. "In thirteen minutes."

"Call me if there's anything I can do. Otherwise I'll stay off the line. Sounds like you're on a tight schedule."

"I am." A schedule that helped her cling to sanity. She said good-bye, clicked the phone closed, and checked her watch again. Still thirteen minutes.

"You made the two-hour rule," Jackson said without looking up. "You can break it."

"No." She checked her watch again. Thirteen minutes.

Jackson stood and laid the book on the chair. "I'll walk slow."

Later, holding Way-Ray's limp hand and trying to blot out any glimmers of hope, she spun a tale in which he and the chief caught the biggest salmon ever seen around Castaway Beach and Way-Ray persuaded the chief to let the fish go so it could have babies.

"Salmon don't have babies," Jackson chuckled. "They spawn, lay eggs. Then they d—" He drew his head back like a turtle. "Then they're done."

Kate leaned closer to Way-Ray and made a joke of it. "Mr. Biology will explain the birds and the bees—and the fish—when you wake up."

Jackson shook his head and waved her off. "Don't let him weasel out of that, Way-Ray." Kate squeezed the boy's icy fingers and told the bobcat story again. It was her favorite, but she'd crafted others: one where Way-Ray went off to high school and became a star baseball player, one in which he became a marine biologist and the world's foremost whale expert, and a third where he made a fortune inventing new video games and bought more land for Evie.

The stories never included marriage or children. She wondered if she harbored fears that Way-Ray might not relinquish the family tradition of abuse.

\* \* \* \* \*

"It's unbelievable," Rhea said when she called the next morning. "Fifty thousand dollars for Evie's center already and more on the way. A lot if these e-mails are for real. And you have a job offer."

"A job?" Kate studied the bandage on her leg. A brown stain showed the wound was still seeping. "I can barely get to the bathroom without collapsing. What kind of a job could I do?"

"Run the Wade in the Waves Motel."

Kate yipped out a laugh. "We must have a bad connection." She tapped the phone on the edge of the bed. "I thought you said, 'Run the Wade in the Waves Motel.'"

Jackson glanced up from a thick book on Attila the Hun and cocked his head.

"I'm serious as the plague." Rhea crunched something. "Mint. Can't compare to a cigarette. Now that you're a celebrity-slash-tourist-attraction, Nadine wants you back. She'll pay a hundred more a month."

Kate snorted. "A hundred a month?"

"Maybe you could negotiate for new washers and dryers," Rhea hooted. "Or spare sheets and fresh gravel on the parking lot."

"Nadine wants me back," Kate told Jackson.

"Hold out for a new handyman." He grinned. "The one you had was a worthless drunk."

"I heard that," Rhea said. "Nadine wants *him* back, too."

"She wants you back, too."

"I'm busy." He turned a page. "Attila's horde is on the move."

"He's reading," Kate told Rhea.

"Reading?" Rhea gasped. "Like, a book?"

"A thick one." Kate heard pride in her voice, hoped Jackson didn't find it condescending. He may have read thousands of books. She knew so little about him.

Rhea crunched again. "I'll tell Nadine you've regained your senses and Jackson's now an intellectual. Hey, I saw you on TV. You looked darn good in that blue shirt."

"Jackson bought it." More pride.

"Intellectual and wardrobe consultant. Noted." Rhea's tone sharpened, probed. "How are you holding up?"

"I'm . . . I'm not thinking crazy thoughts, if that's what you want to know. But my leg hurts like hell and I'm petrified that Way-Ray won't wake up and I'm scared he'll hate me and I won't be any good at raising him."

Rhea laughed. "Any mother with a brain worries about that. You'll do fine."

Kate picked at the edge of the bandage. "Way-Ray needs stability. "Maybe I *should* go back to the motel. After all, Nadine gave me a chance, she—"

"—hired you because she was in a bind and in a hurry. And she fired you without a lick of sympathy. Anyway, I'm helping out until she finds someone, and you've got another offer on the table."

"Another job offer?"

Jackson canted his head and raised an eyebrow.

"Yeah." Rhea chortled. "The work is harder, the hours are longer, the boss is bossier, and the pay is even crappier."

Kate winced. Was this the shape of the future? Menial jobs? A life like Amanda's? Resentment swelled, then popped like a balloon. Amanda had the joy of Way-Ray.

"Evie wants you to work for her, stay with her. Way-Ray, too."

"At the refuge?"

Jackson nodded, raised a thumb, and turned a page. Kate fingered the edge of the bandage again. Way-Ray would love that, but he hadn't noticed splintered floors, leaking ceilings, mounds of disorganized paperwork, and the incessant demands of Evie's charges. Kate would be locked in an endless cycle of repetitive chores. But that didn't matter. Right now it was about what was best for Way-Ray, what would make him happy, and what, she admitted with a guilty flush, might help bind him to her.

"Evie's not much at organizing or socializing and she's never had time to look beyond the next empty gullet." Rhea sucked her mint. "You'll take over the paperwork, upkeep, planning, educational programs, and volunteers."

Not a serf, a partner. Kate smiled. "I could do that."

"Good. I told her you'd take it. I'm packing up your stuff right now. Evie's got three projects for you to get on right away."

Kate gripped the phone. This was moving too fast. "Rhea, I can't think about anything except—"

"Don't choke on your chewing gum. She knows it all hinges on Way-Ray. By the way, she wants you to bring Way-

Ray's mom to the Hopkins family plot—it's got a fine view of the ocean."

She could plant flowers on Amanda's grave, bright, fragrant blooms. "I . . . tell Evie I'm—"

"Already did. The next job is to find someone to fix a few hundred things out there."

"A handyman?"

"I'll work only long hours for lousy pay," Jackson said without glancing up. "That's not negotiable."

Another wounded creature longing to heal. "Tell her I've got one in mind."

"Thought so. Now the last job is to tell that little boy the deer and rabbits are waiting." Rhea sniffed and Kate heard her swallow hard. "We're *all* waiting for him to come home."

Home? Kate closed her eyes and conjured visions of a gull wheeling in the sky, surf breaking on the beach, a whale spouting among the swells, deer prancing across the meadow. She opened her eyes to see Jackson smiling. Yes, this was her home now—a warmer, more vital home than she'd ever had.

All that was missing was a boy's laughter.

# CHAPTER 49

In the few moments of hopefulness she allowed herself, Kate imagined Way-Ray would awaken while she held his hand and spun the tale of the bobcat. But it was a nurse checking his IV line in the heart of the night at whom he blinked. When she said, "Hi," he smiled, rubbed at his nose, and drifted off again.

"Cautiously optimistic," a young doctor with red-laced eyes told Kate an hour later. "We've changed his chemical cocktail in response. But each event is unique. He may have lost or blocked memory and there's still the chance of secondary damage."

Secondary damage. Kate turned the words over as she stroked Way-Ray's arm, touched his cheeks and eyelids. Secondary damage meant problems like pituitary gland dysfunction. Blinking that horror aside, she told him they would live at the refuge. "And you'll have the room under the eaves and take care of the bunnies."

"Better not put him in charge of rabbit wrangling," Jackson whispered. "Sometimes Evie tosses a rabbit in with a hawk or owl to keep their hunting skills sharp."

Kate nodded. She hoped Way-Ray's sympathy would always lie with the rabbit, that he would never take advantage of weakness to bully or humiliate.

She told the salmon story, embellishing it with details of the lunch Chief Lowell would pack: tuna sandwiches, cheese crackers, and berries with cream. Way-Ray's legs twitched.

Kate gasped.

Jackson catapulted from his chair and gripped her shoulder. Way-Ray's lids fluttered, revealing eyes dull and unfocused. His brow creased, he sighed, drew his knees up, rolled onto his side, and slid back into sleep.

She felt sick, bereft. "Come back," she moaned, leaning close, inhaling the air he breathed out.

Jackson's hand rubbed circles on her back. "I'll get the nurse." He bolted through the door, bad leg swinging, opposite arm flung out for balance.

Kate squeezed Way-Ray's hand and again told the story of the bobcat. When the cat winked, Way-Ray's eyelids fluttered again. She wove her fingers with his. "It's time to wake up, Way-Ray. Time for breakfast. We can't go to the refuge until you eat."

He sighed and flopped onto his back.

"I'll make peanut butter toast. And chocolate milk and—"

"Fried buzzard eggs," Way-Ray muttered.

Buzzard eggs? Tears scorched her eyes. He remembered.

"And buzzard hash," Way-Ray said, his syllables sticky. "A great big mound of buzzard hash with ketchup all over it."

His eyes opened, sharp and clear. "You're Kate," he mumbled. "You like buzzard burgers."

Kate smiled, sniffed back tears. "But we couldn't find any buzzard burgers, remember? So we ate crispy clam strips with tartar sauce."

"Tar tar sauce," he repeated. "Like the stuff on teeth, only not."

"That's right." Kate stroked his cheek, her heart thudding with relief. He recalled those tiny details. Surely that meant there was no permanent brain damage. She smoothed a clump of oily hair back from his forehead.

Way-Ray touched his stomach. "Is my appendix all out?"

Kate's heart constricted to an aching knot. "It's been out for three weeks, sweetie."

"Three weeks?" He frowned and poked at his stomach. "I was asleep for three weeks?"

"No, you—"

"Where's my mom?"

Kate breathed in, air like razor blades in her lungs. Where was the doctor? Where was Jackson? "She's not here, Way-Ray."

"Why not? You said it would only take her a few days to drive from Grassy Ridge." His voice rose to a petulant whine and he slapped his free hand on the bed. "I want my mom. I want her now!"

"I know you do." Kate reached for his hand, weighing the price of the truth.

"Don't touch me." He pulled away. "I want my mom!"

"What's this noise?" The young doctor strode to the foot of the bed. Kate sagged with relief, but this was postponement, not pardon. Jackson filled the doorway, raised an eyebrow. The doctor glowered at Way-Ray, a twinkle in his eye. "Who was yelling? Was it you?"

"Yes." Way-Ray glowered back and stuck his lower lip out. "And I'm not gonna stop, either."

"Hmm." The doctor took a stethoscope from his pocket. "Well, that's going to make it tough. See, I've got to take your temperature." He winked at Kate. "Usually I put a thermometer under a patient's tongue, but if you keep yelling I'll have to put it in your bottom."

Way-Ray clamped his knees together. "Nuh-uh."

"That's the rule." He poked his chin at Kate. "Would give us some privacy?"

Jackson jumped to wheel her into the hall, threaded her past two nurses and another doctor. "I heard him," a nurse said. "It's wonderful."

"Wonderful," Kate repeated, her voice dull, heavy.

Jackson wheeled her into an alcove with a narrow window, knelt, and peeled down her mask and his own. "What happened?"

"He doesn't remember anything after he had his appendix out. He wants his mother." Sobs fractured her sentences. "And now I have . . . unh . . . to tell him . . . hurt him again."

Jackson pulled her against his chest and she settled into his strength, wishing it could insulate her from the monstrous task ahead. She felt the soft pressure of his lips on her forehead, the whisper of his breath against her ear. "You can't lie to him again, Kate. You know that."

"Yes, damn it. I'm not stupid."

"That's the feisty Kate I know." He kissed her forehead again. "Use that energy."

"Ms. Dalton?"

Jackson relaxed his hold and stood. Kate twisted her neck and peered up at the young doctor.

"Ms. Dalton, Way-Ray is extremely agitated about his mother." He rubbed the sharp spine of his nose.

"Is he strong enough for the truth?" Jackson folded his arms across his chest. "All of it?"

Kate held her breath. The only way to the future was through the truth, there was no easier road.

The doctor spread his hands. "Physically, yes. But psychologically?" He shrugged. "We have experts on staff, but it will take some time to—"

"And he'll get more agitated." Kate blotted her face on a tissue Jackson thrust into her hand. "He needs to know now. And I need to tell him. But he should have someone to talk with. After."

"I'll arrange that."

The doctor hustled away. Jackson knelt again and Kate saw tears at the corners of his eyes. Surprised and frightened, she wiped them with her thumbs. "I'm sorry."

"For what?" He closed his hands around her wrists.

"For . . . everything." She brushed the razor stubble beside his earlobes.

"Let it go, Kate. Let the past go." He brought his mouth to hers. Kate felt the whiskers at the edge of his lips, felt teeth beneath skin, tasted coffee and vanilla. His kiss seemed strange and raw, but as familiar as sunlight. He drew away.

Kate breathed deep, holding the sensation. "Will you come with me? To Way-Ray?"

"I'll go anywhere with you. You couldn't drive me off with artillery fire." He lurched to his feet and turned the chair toward Way-Ray's room.

"Kate clutched his hand. "What should I say? Where should I begin?"

"I don't know." Jackson bent and kissed the top of her head. "But I believe that you will."

# CHAPTER 50

"Where's my mother?" Way-Ray screamed at Kate as Jackson rolled her through the doorway. He kicked at a pony-tailed nurse in olive green scrubs who kept a grim grip on the IV line. "Tell me! Tell me now!"

Kate saw Wayne Jessop's unquenchable rage spark in his son's eyes and sizzle in the air between them. She cringed, searching the corners for Wayne's mocking ghost, then caught herself and gripped the arms of the chair. *He's not yours!*

She levered herself to her feet and brought her voice up from the bottom of her diaphragm, invoking a spirit more powerful than the man who was a father by biology only. "Your mother raised you to respect others, Way-Ray. Your mother taught you good manners, to be polite and considerate. What would she say about the way you're acting?"

Way-Ray gaped for a moment, but then drummed his heels on the bed. "I don't care! Manners are stupid." He seized his pillow and flung it.

Jackson's hand snaked out and snatched it from the air before it struck Kate's chest. Way-Ray's eyes widened and his lips made a circle of surprise.

"Thank you," Kate said, her voice as casual as she could make it.

"You're welcome." Jackson placed the pillow on the foot of the bed. "Happy to help." The nurse gave a sharp nod of approval. The doctor grinned.

"Manners are stupid," Way-Ray repeated. "For sissies."

Kate invoked Amanda's spirit once more. "Your mother thought they were for strong people, smart people. She taught you to say please and thank you and think about others because she wanted you to be the strongest, smartest boy in the world."

The nurse nodded again and Kate felt Jackson's hand squeeze hers.

Way-Ray pouted. "That stuff's for babies."

Had Amanda martyred herself to a lost cause? "So are temper tantrums."

"Manners are for sissies," Way-Ray muttered, his eyes flickering.

His bright fury dwindled to smoldering resentment. Kate had to snuff that before it fueled another outburst. "Thank you for lowering your voice and respecting the sick people in this hospital."

Way-Ray pouted again.

Leg throbbing, Kate stepped closer. "Now, a boy with really excellent manners would apologize to the doctor and nurse—and to me and Jackson."

Way-Ray squinted. "Who's Jackson?"

"I'm Jackson." He offered the hand with the scar. "I live in Castaway Beach. I'm a friend of Kate's. I hope I'll be a friend of yours."

Way-Ray fingered the scar across Jackson's palm. "How did you get that?"

"It's a long story. I'll tell you later." Jackson drew his hand away. "Right now you have a job to do, apologies to make." He stepped back smartly and leaned against the wall, arms crossed.

Way-Ray drew in his lip and chewed at it for a moment. "I'm sorry, Jackson." He turned to the nurse. "I'm sorry I kicked you."

"Apology accepted," she smiled and tweaked the sheet over him. "Just don't do it again. And don't mess with that tube in your arm. It has to stay in for a little while."

His eyes traveled to the bag of liquid. "Okay."

"Good. I'm going to check on my other patients. Push the call button if you need me." She hustled out, the doctor trailing.

Way-Ray plucked at the sheet. "I'm sorry I yelled at you, Kate. But I really want to know where my mother is." His voice trembled with confusion and fear. "Why isn't she here?"

Kate fought back tears Way-Ray might perceive as phony, an attempt to win sympathy.

He frowned and pointed to the bandage on her leg. "How did you get hurt? Did they have to operate on you, too?"

"Yes, they did." She lowered herself into the wheelchair. "So if you don't mind, I'll sit down while we talk."

"Can I . . . *May* I see your scar some time?"

"Sure." Kate wheeled herself closer to the bed. "But I can't unwrap it for a few days. Why don't you lie back and I'll tell you everything?"

"Okay." His eyes slid toward Jackson and he flushed. "But I kinda lost my pillow."

Jackson chuckled, retrieved it, and slid it beneath Way-Ray's head. "There you go."

Way-Ray wiggled and pulled the sheet tight across his chest. "Now I'm ready."

*But I'm not. I never will be.* Kate glanced at Jackson. To her relief, he nodded and spoke. "Way-Ray, it's important that you listen hard to Kate and let her tell this story all the way through without interrupting. Can you do that?"

"I guess." His brow furrowed. "Do you know the story?"

"Yes." Jackson's splayed a hand across his chest. "I know it by heart."

"Then I want to know it by heart, too." Way-Ray slipped warm fingers between Kate's. "I'll be real quiet."

Kate swallowed a sob and began with the day his father tried to hurt him when he was just a toddler. She told him, as Evie had, that his father had been sick inside and done bad things because his own mother and father hadn't loved him, and that Amanda lied so Way-Ray wouldn't blame himself for the abuse. She told him how Wayne came to the shelter and what happened there.

Way-Ray's eyes hardened and his fingers straightened. "I'm glad he's dead. He was mean and he hurt my mom."

"Yes, he did." Kate's head pounded. This was a test. She must defend a man she loathed so that Way-Ray could see beyond black and white. "But don't forget that your father did a wonderful thing—he helped your mother make a smart, funny, loving boy."

Way-Ray wrinkled his nose. "Me?"

"Who else?"

He beamed and Kate told him how Amanda asked her to take him for a while and how she'd disappeared and he had to have his appendix out and Kate lied because he was been sick and scared and she thought the truth would hurt more. She apologized, promised she would never lie again, and praised him for being clever enough to hire TD to find his mother.

Way-Ray pulled his fingers from hers and Kate saw emotions clash in his eyes: anger, pain, confusion, pride. Something that could have been a glimmer of recent memory flashed, then vanished like a tiny fish in dark water.

Jackson brought her a can of cola and Kate swallowed half of it and told Way-Ray how they went to the refuge and he met Evie and the orphaned animals and how he started collecting money. She told him about Dwayne and how brave Amanda was when she led him away because she loved Way-Ray so much and wanted him to be safe.

"And TD found her." Kate closed her eyes and held her breath for a few seconds. Jackson gripped her shoulder. "But Dwayne found them. And . . ."

Way-Ray's face paled, stark as the sheet that covered him. "Did he kill my mother?"

"Yes. I'm sorry, Way-Ray. I'm so sorry." That word she once scorned, not worth the breath it took to say it.

He knuckled at his eyes. "And TD?"

Kate nodded. "He tried to save your mother. He did all he could."

Way-Ray clutched the sheet and whimpered. He seemed tiny, frail. Kate felt paralyzed. Should she try to hug him?

As if he read her thoughts, Way-Ray inched away. "Is that all the story?"

Kate shook her head. "No. Dwayne came looking for you because your grandmother wanted you to live with her." Her words collided with each other as she told him the rest. He cringed when Evie went down and put his hands over his eyes when Dwayne clubbed him, shot Kate, and dragged him into the forest. Kate paused, realizing she didn't know what had happened next or how Jackson would want it told. She laid her hand on his. "Could you . . . ?"

Jackson cleared his throat. "I used to be a soldier, Way-Ray. You probably know a lot about soldiers. You probably know that soldiers do what they have to do, what needs to be done."

Way-Ray nodded.

"Well, I promised Kate I would bring you back. So I followed your uncle into the forest and I did what I had to do."

Way-Ray nodded again. His eyes slid to the scar on Jackson's hand and then to the bandage on Kate's leg. He covered his eyes.

Kate laid her hand on his forehead. "Does your head hurt?"

"No!" He pulled away and rolled to the far side of the bed. "Don't touch me!"

Kate looked to Jackson and got only a shrug. "Do you want me to call the nurse?"

"No." He rolled back and faced her, his eyes hot. "What's gonna happen to me? Do I have to go to the orphan place?"

"No. No." Kate reached for him again. He scowled and she drew back. "You'll live at the refuge. Evie has a big house. And you and I will live upstairs."

He shook his head. "What if I don't want to be with you because you lied to me so much? What if I want to go someplace where you're not there, ever?"

Lost! Kate felt the same consuming pain she experienced when Dwayne shot her.

"That's your privilege, Way-Ray," Jackson said, his voice flat, toneless. "Kate loves you. Your mother knew that. That's why she wrote down that she wanted Kate to take care of you."

Jackson swung the chair about and Kate spotted a young woman with feathery red hair beside the door. The woman held a stack of boxed games and nodded in an encouraging way.

"Kate wants you to be happy more than anything else," Jackson said. "If you don't want to be with her, then we'll find someone you want to be with."

Kate bit back a scream of anguish.

Jackson rolled the chair toward the door. "No one will be mad if that's what you want. But we won't decide now. Kate's leg hurts. She needs rest and so do you."

"I do not," Way-Ray insisted. "I'm not tired."

"Then you can stay awake and talk with this nice lady who came to see you."

"I won't go to sleep," Way-Ray repeated. "You can't make me."

"No one's going to make you go to sleep," the woman said. "Maybe we can play a game."

The chair cleared the doorway and then they were in the elevator. Kate's words echoed from the chrome walls. "I've lost him."

"Give it time, Kate."

"There is no time. It's over."

"It's not over unless you quit."

How could he be so impassive? She pounded the arms of the chair, pain jolting her shoulders. "I let myself love him. And he hates me." She doubled over, clutching her gut. "It hurts so much!"

"That's what makes it real."

"I'm sick of real." She twisted in the chair and glared at him. "I don't want real."

The door swished open, but Jackson didn't move, didn't speak. His eyes were as bleak as a lunar landscape. Finally he shrugged. "It's your call."

# CHAPTER 51

Kate heard a whisper of sound and something grazed her cheek. A fly? She brushed her face with the edge of her hand.

It returned, tickling her upper lip.

She brushed at it again. Later she'd swat it. But now, she clung to the oblivion that pain pills delivered.

The fly returned, pressing against the tip of her nose. Heavy. Like the one she'd seen circling Evie. She shuddered. The fly pinched at her chin.

"She won't wake up." A faint voice.

Kate turned her head and burrowed into the pillow. She wouldn't abandon sleep. Anything was possible in dreams. Even love.

"Wake up, Kate." That voice again. Fragile. Something patted her cheek. "Kate, wake up."

She heard whispers and a giggle and then fingers twined with hers. "If you wake up, Jackson will get you a buzzard blizzard milkshake."

Kate's flopped to her side, rubbed at her eyes. Way-Ray stood beside the bed wearing a red T-shirt, creased jeans, and blindingly white sneakers. His hair shone and his eyes sparkled. Jackson lounged near the door wearing a shabby flannel shirt and a smug smile.

"It worked," Way-Ray crowed. "She woke up just like you said."

"The threat of a buzzard shake always works," Jackson said. "Especially when it's time to go home."

Home? Sepia-toned images swirled in Kate's brain: her mother's frown, her father's wintry smile. "Where's that?"

"The place with all the animals and the lady who makes them better. Evie." Way-Ray jounced and then, holding his cast to the side, scrambled to the bed beside her. He smelled of soap and mint toothpaste. A dab of that was crusted in one corner of his grin. "Guess what? Jackson says you and me are a lot alike."

"He does, huh?"

Jackson ducked his head and examined his fingernails.

"Yeah. He says that's a good thing almost all of the time. Except when we're too impatient."

"Really?" Kate noted a flush spreading across Jackson's cheeks. "Well, he's the expert. No one's ever tried my patience like he has." She chuckled. "And I'm sure the feeling is mutual. I guess that means we'll never get bored with each other."

Jackson lifted his head and smiled like the sunrise.

Way-Ray wrinkled his nose. "Um. . . " He worried the crust of toothpaste with the tip of his tongue. "Um . . . Kate, my mom went to be with the angels, so she's watching all of us all the time so we have to be real good and do what she said or she'll be sad. Right?"

Kate touched his hair, soft as dandelion down. "If you say so."

He slung an arm around her and squirmed closer. "Okay, so that means I have to stay with you like she said. And you have to take care of me. Until I'm old enough to take care of you."

Kate hugged him close and stretched a hand to Jackson. "I can't think of anything I want more."

# BIO

Carolyn J. Rose grew up in New York's Catskill Mountains, graduated from the University of Arizona, logged two years in Arkansas with Volunteers in Service to America, and spent 25 years as a television news researcher, writer, producer, and assignment editor in Arkansas, New Mexico, Oregon, and Washington. She lives in Vancouver, Washington, and founded the Vancouver Writers' Mixers. Her hobbies are reading, gardening, and not cooking. For more information, surf to www.deadlyduomysteries.com

Also by Carolyn J. Rose

*Hemlock Lake*

*Consulted to Death*

*Driven to Death*

*Dated to Death*


By Carolyn J. Rose and Mike Nettleton

*The Big Grabowski*

*Sometimes a Great Commotion*

*The Hard Karma Shuffle*

*The Crushed Velvet Miasma*

*The Hermit of Humbug Mountain*

351

www.ingramcontent.com/pod-product-compliance
Lightning Source LLC
Chambersburg PA
CBHW062009170626
46813CB00001B/94